# OSHENERTH

# OSHENERTH

#1 *NEW YORK TIMES* BESTSELLING AUTHOR
## ALAN DEAN FOSTER

**WordFire Press**
Colorado Springs, Colorado

**OSHENERTH**
Copyright © 2015 Alan Dean Foster

ISBN: 978-1-61475-380-3

Cover painting by Rob Caswell

Cover design by Janet McDonald

Art Director Kevin J. Anderson

Copy edited for WordFire Press by Bryan Thomas Schmidt

Book Design by RuneWright, LLC
www.RuneWright.com

Published by
WordFire Press, an imprint of
WordFire, Inc.
PO Box 1840
Monument CO 80132

Kevin J. Anderson & Rebecca Moesta, Publishers

WordFire Press Trade Paperback Edition December 2015
Printed in the USA
wordfirepress.com

# DEDICATION

*To Amos Nachoum, a real merson*

*"There is no science without fancy, and no art without facts."*

Vladimir Nabokov

# PREFACE

In the time when men first began to creep out upon the world, there were some who understood instinctively that they had come from the sea. Men and women who knew that the oceans were their place of origin and their true mother. So they spoke among themselves: "Why should we leave our birthplace and our mother?" And so saying, they shunned the dry land and began returning to the place of their origin. While the rest of the new race of men struggled to survive and to multiply and find themselves upon the land, these folk, who soon came to call themselves mersons, scattered themselves not upon the waters but beneath them.

There is more space in the oceans and more oceans in space than can be comprehended even by those who dream. In such a part and such a place so far from the land-dwelling that it became unknown to other men, the race of mersons fought and struggled and eventually raised up a fine and nurturing civilization beneath the mirrorsky. They came to breathe water like the fish, and like their ancestors to grow proper webbing between their fingers and toes, and fins upon their legs.

Others who had also found and populated these faraway seas benefited from the presence of mersons among them, in a time and place when mersons were not the only commanders of language and thought. Some of these gifted others had fins, some had tentacles, and some were of waterkind that no longer are. Sometimes they helped the people, and sometimes they fought with them, and on occasion they might even eat one another, but all benefited from the talking and the languages. While some were forever disgruntled, most were content with their lot.

While the men of other lands forgot the First Ways, and the great Dry Magic they had once possessed returned to the dust from whence it had arisen, those who dwelled beneath the mirrorsky did not forget. The ways of Wet Magic stayed with them, to be further delved and developed. There were great masters in those days, and enchantments you could taste and smell as well as experience.

Then one day, everything changed. In a backward and insignificant corner of the realworld that was Oshenerth, a demon appeared. One that was not already dead, like the isolated expressions whose bodies were seldom recovered, but one still just barely alive.

More confusing still, the demon was pretty....

As soon as he had the sleek, toothy slayer cornered, Chachel knew the shark was going to use magic. He was not worried. The heavy spear of pure white bone that he held had been shaped and carved by Fasalik Boneworker himself from the massive, scavenged lower jaw of a dead rorqual. You could slam it against rock and the shaft would not shatter. Furthermore, he had surprised the shark from below while it was busy patrolling the mirrorsky. Now it was trapped between the waterless void above and reef wall behind.

Cradling the spear under one arm and aiming it with the other, Chachel adjusted the strap that held the woven patch over the socket where his left eye had once resided and swam forward. The webbing on his left foot and the fin growing from the back of his calf fluttered in perfect synchrony with the artificial counterparts that occupied the space where his right leg was missing below the knee.

Above and in front of him, the blacktip's eyes darted nervously from side to side as it searched for an escape route. If the shark made a dash for it, Chachel was ready with the spear. If it began to spout time-honored shark sortilege, the hunter's well-honed vocabulary contained a clutch of stock counterwords. The gills of trapped shark and merson alike pulsed furiously, flushing water and extracting oxygen as they strained in expectation of the coming confrontation.

A powerful, yard-long tentacle slithered over Chachel's taut left shoulder.

"Watch for a combination of teeth and talk. It may try to attack and invoke at the same time."

Chachel nodded tersely. He knew that Glint was only trying to help. But it would have been better if the cuttlefish, who was as big as Chachel himself though not nearly as heavy, had stayed back out of the way. The last thing a hunter needed at killing time was to feel crowded.

Then the blacktip charged.

To anyone who has never seen a shark strike, it can be said that the great fish does not actually appear to move. One moment it is swimming lazily, and the next it is somewhere else, as if no water in-between has been transited. Some mersons called it wish-swimming: wish you are another place, and without a single kick or flick of a tail you find yourself therewith transported. After all, to catch something as fast as a fish, the shark must be faster still. Couple this intrinsic speed and ferocity with traditional shark magic, and surely an intended target has no chance to escape at all.

But Chachel was ready for the charge. Ready physically, because over the years he had pushed and worked his body to compensate for the loss of his left eye and right leg. Ready mentally, because he had laboriously learned the appropriate counterspells and protecttions. And ready emotionally, because he liked killing. He especially liked killing sharks because it was sharks who had taken his eye and the lower half of his right leg. It was sharks who had killed his father and mother in the same unanticipated pitched battle.

It was always sharks.

That this solitary blacktip had not been part of the murderous frenzy that had destroyed his family and crippled and half-blinded him did not in any way temper his fury. Exploding straight at him, it opened its mouth and conjured. Jaws suddenly gaped wide enough to swallow a grouper. Teeth expanded instantly to the size of the knives the villagers used to pry gastropods from their protective shells. On the surrounding, multihued reef, startled fish scattered for the nearest bolt-holes in the coral.

"*Uraxis!*" Chachel snarled as he kicked hard, driving himself toward the sandy bottom below.

Using his spear to shove off a huge nearby brain coral helped to drive his body downward. At the same time, his terse recitation countered the shark magic. The water between hunter and hunted blurred. Powerful jaws and formidable dentition returned once more to their actual size. The blacktip's teeth were still big and sharp enough to shred a merson's flesh, but with the countering of the shark magic, they no longer appeared so fearsomely intimidating.

Forcefully expelling a burst of water through his siphon, Glint blasted clear. His body color and pattern changed instantly from bright red stripes on white to a shifting, mottled blue-green that matched the surrounding water perfectly and made him almost impossible to see. A cloud of dark brown spurted from his ink sac. Writing in the open water like a pen on clear plastic, it formed several of the special words known to manyarms that were designed specifically to confuse an attacker. Most predatory fish would be sufficiently confused by the swirling sepia alone, but not a shark. The pores lining their snouts enabled them to detect prey by other means. Shot through with embedded sparks, the cuttlefish's inky conjuration was intended to blind the toothmaster's other sense as well as confuse its mind.

Unable to see, unable to locate its attacker by other means, the blacktip slowed as it passed through the far side of the ink cloud. As it reappeared, Chachel kicked hard with both his real leg and his artificial one. Gripping the spear tightly in both hands, he thrust it straight up and into the shark just behind the lower jaw. Then he let go, allowing the plaited line fastened to a hole in the blunt back end of the spear to run free.

The blacktip spasmed violently as it attempted to dislodge the length of polished bone that had pierced its skull straight through from bottom to top. A target with a more complex brain would have expired sooner, but the shark's simple nervous system kept it thrashing for long moments after it had been speared.

Knowing it was already as good as dead, Chachel busied himself scattering a masking spell. From the pouch secured at his waist he withdrew a stoppered bone container. Whipping it back and forth in the water, he muttered the appropriate complementary words as it dispersed a green, metal-based powder. Both powder and spell would adhere to the shark's spirit as well as to its body and act to mask the smell of blood. Without the talismanic cover-up, he and Glint would find themselves fighting off sniffing scavengers and curious sharks all the way home. Drifting next to the reef, he waited as the blacktip's violent side-to-side spasms lessened and finally ceased altogether.

Transparent lateral fins rippling hypnotically and normal color and stripes restored, Glint approached the blacktip's body and clasped it in six of his ten short tentacles. With his two longer, sucker-lined hunting arms, the cuttlefish leveled the corpse in the water. Pulling it close, he took a tentative bite. One S-shaped pupil swiveled toward Chachel.

"The kill has a good flavor, my friend. Tastes nothing of disease, and I cannot see or feel any parasites. Good for the larder."

"Good that it's dead," Chachel muttered upon concluding the cloaking spell. Swimming upward, he rejoined his friend. With Glint holding tight to the sleek carcass and using his siphon to maintain his position in the water, the merson hunter yanked and tugged in the other direction until the spear pulled free of the now lifeless body. "I can tow it," he added.

"No, let me." Pointing his tail to the east, the cuttlefish used all ten tentacles to secure his grip on the dead shark. Drawing in water and squirting it through his siphon, he accelerated backward, taking care to moderate his speed so that the much slower merson could keep pace.

Behind them, the finger of reef once again came to life with hydrodynamic splotches of color as wary fish and cautious crustaceans began to emerge from their hiding places. His dark fin cutting the boundary between void and mirrorsky, a solitary gray shark cruised lazily over the top of the reef. Thanks to Chachel's oft-employed and reasonably effective cloaking spell, she did not detect the recent kill—or the killers.

Fully occupied with the task of manipulating the dead body, Glint did not ask his companion if he intended, as was customary, to share the meat with the other manyarms and mersons who lived in Sandrift. He knew Chachel too well for that. Expecting nothing from anyone else (and usually receiving it), his "special" merson friend was not inclined to contribute so much as a sliver of his hard-won prey to the town's communal pantry.

Chachel's status as an outcast was self-imposed, he made no effort to alter it, and he was content with his existence on the fringe of the community. It did not bother him that one of his two faithful companions was a ten-tentacled, color-changing, ink-spewing manyarm given to the occasional display of rude body-patterns, and the other an enduring melancholy.

As befitted hunting partners, they took turns towing the kill. Once, a quartet of blue sharks swam within sight, but with the corpse cloaked to mask the smell of blood, they paid the travelers no heed. A cluster of caucusing prawns spewed the usual spralaker invective that crustaceans reserved for mersons. Busy hauling the blacktip, Chachel ignored them. When Glint diverted in their direction, they promptly vanished into a labyrinth of available holes in the reef. The cuttlefish could have winkled them out—manyarms loved the taste of hardshells just as much as hardshells loved the taste of manyarms—but Glint was concerned the prawn taunting might have been a diversion, an attempt to separate him from his friend and their catch. So he contented himself with mumbling a short, simple, transitory enchantment and squirting a shot of the resultant stink ink into the nearest coral cavity. The polyps would filter it out without suffering any harm, and his effort was rewarded with the sound of chitinous choking from the prawns hiding within the stony maroon warren.

Spralakers hated manyarms, and the feeling was mutual. Their relationship meant tentacle versus claw, and so it had been since before the time of Remembering. The fact that the manyarms had forged friendships diverse and frequent with the equally soft-bodied mersons had made the relationship that much worse. And while the spralakers had their own methodology of magic, its parameters tended to be flimsy, suitable only for fooling fish. Though there were known to be exceptions.

Exceptions that sometimes proved unexpectedly dangerous.

None of the hardshelled conjurers or warriors appeared on the reef to contest their passage, however. When they cut upcanyon through the coral into Yellecheg Lagoon, Glint allowed himself to relax a little. Despite the lagoon's considerable extent, few large predators came inside, preferring to patrol the outer reefs where they could not be challenged or cornered. It allowed him and Chachel to let down their guard.

Halfway across, a couple of massive drifting jellies posted the usual warning signs by flashing their bioluminescence in sequence. Jellies being even dumber than fish, Chachel and Glint had no trouble avoiding them. Merson and manyarm paused briefly to chat with some small squid. Then they were out again via a channel that cut through the reef on the opposite side of the lagoon. It being slack tide, there were no predators lying in wait.

It was while crossing the deep channel that separated Yellecheg and Singarol, with Sandrift less than an hour's swim away, that Chachel spotted the strange floating object. Frowning, he left Glint and their catch as he swam upward to inspect the curious intrusion.

At first glance it appeared to be a merson—but if so it was unlike any merson he had ever seen before. Though it seemed unlikely, there was always the possibility that it might be a clever spralaker trap designed to draw him away from his companion. So, as he would have with any unfamiliar manifestation, he approached it with caution. It was well that he did. On closer inspection, the true nature of the floating shape was revealed.

It was a dead demon.

At least, it appeared as if it was dead. You could usually tell with demons. To encounter one was exceedingly rare. In his life, Chachel had only seen one other. That demon had been brought into the village when he was still a child. He remembered his parents being among those who had marveled over it, noting the pale color, the lack of webbing between fingers and toes, and the absence of gills on the neck. To all outward appearances it had been drifting for a long time and had reached an advanced state of decomposition.

It had tasted bad, too.

This demon differed greatly from the one of his childhood memories. Its body was dark, very dark, though its webless hands were quite pale. On its feet it wore artificial fins not altogether unlike the one that was affixed to his own truncated right leg. Strange bulky objects hung from its back and the torso appeared to be bloated with some slick, black material. A few shiny objects whose purpose was unknown dangled from its chest. Remarkably, it floated in a vertical position, its body half beneath and half above the mirrorsky, so that he could not see its face or if it had gills.

"What a peculiar creature!" Still firmly gripping the dead shark, Glint had jetted up to rejoin his friend. "It looks like a demon."

"It is a demon, I'm sure of it." Hanging in the water, Chachel bobbed up and down in the slight swell that was rippling the mirrorsky. "But it is unlike any I have ever heard described. The color and the fins, they are entirely new to me."

"See how swollen its upper body is," Glint commented. "Could it be some unusual type of merson, from another sea?" A tentacle indicated the strapped-on fins. "Those are similar to the artificial one on your right leg."

Chachel shook his head in disagreement and found himself blinking. This near to the mirrorsky the light was intense and hurt his eye. In contrast, his vacant, patch-covered left socket was not affected.

"I don't think it can be another type of merson. The way it is floating, its head stays continually above water, so it must have drowned."

"Do demons drown?" Glint wondered. "Don't they dwell in the empty void?"

"Now you're confusing me." Chachel's expression tightened. "If it *is* a demon, it appears to be a dead one. We should take it back to the village so that Heranleck and the others can study it." Reaching up, he grabbed a dangling leg and tugged. The black skin was slick and taut, not unlike that of a shark. So unexpected was the texture that he almost let go. He tried a second time, grabbing onto the hanging leg and pulling with both hands while kicking backward. Still the dead demon refused to descend.

"Some kind of spell," he finally muttered, "is keeping it fixed to the void."

"Here, hold this a moment." Fins rippling, Glint passed the dead blacktip over to Chachel and gingerly approached the inert demonic shape. Sensitive appendage tips probed the bobbing body. Taking a deep breath, the cuttlefish shoved his head through the mirrorsky and out into the void. Chachel looked on uneasily.

Slipping back down, Glint inhaled strongly. "It's a demon, all right. It has no gills." Avoiding the metal cylinder fastened to the creature's back, tentacles tapped the bloated black shape that surrounded the rest of the upper body. "This material collapses inward when I push on it. Perhaps it is some kind of external swim bladder."

"There's one way to find out." Holding the shark by its tail, Chachel removed the razor-shell gutting knife from his pouch and pushed the sharp tip into the black sac that surrounded the demon.

He and Glint quickly drew back in alarm as a flower of bubbles burst from within. They dissipated in seconds. But the demon still drifted half in and half out of the realworld. Determined to give it one more try, Glint swam forward, and for a second time, wrapped his tentacles around the submerged waist of the creature. This time when he descended, the demon came with him.

Its face was mostly concealed behind some kind of hard, protective transparency. As soon as its head was pulled beneath the barrier of the mirrorsky, its eyes opened. The first thing they saw was Glint, staring back at them. They got very wide.

"It's not dead!" Letting the body of the hard-won shark drift free, Chachel hastily unslung his killing spear from his back. What hunter's spell-words would be useful against a void demon? He could not think of any. "Let go, let go of it!"

Moving fast, he maneuvered to get behind the creature so he could strike at it without endangering Glint. The cuttlefish, however, was in no hurry to release his grasp. As it flailed wildly at him with both unwebbed hands, the demon's actions indicated it was trying to claw its way back up to the barrier. It flashed no weapons and gave no indication it knew any magic whatsoever.

"Let it go," Chachel shouted again. "You're killing it!"

"How can I be killing it?" Glint wondered aloud. Then he remembered. Demons lived in the void. They could not survive in the realworld.

But this demon was different, and it proceeded to surprise them both.

Once it had broken back through the barrier, it paused there for a long moment. And then it stuck its head back down into the realworld. This time it had something clutched in its mouth; a small rounded dark object that was connected to the metal cylinder attached to its back by what looked like a piece of soft tube coral. Bubbles intermittently emerged from one side of the rounded object gripped between its lips. Reaching down with its right hand, it drew something from a sheath attached to its right leg. Chachel immediately recognized this as an object of great value: a knife made of metal.

Metal could be smelted only by magic or in the heat generated by the black smokers of the dark depths. Perhaps this strange demon knew more than it was letting on.

Now that the puffed-up black material that had surrounded its upper body had been collapsed, he was able to see that while the apparition might be lacking in webbing, it was possessed of something else. Unmistakably, the demon they were dealing with was female. That did not mean it was potentially any less dangerous. Since they were always found dead or dying, no one really knew what a healthy demon might be capable of doing. Chachel was not afraid of anything, not even the void. However, it was well known that the highest degree of bravery could be negated by an equal volume of stupidity. So he stayed cautious.

The fact that the void demon had drawn a knife instead of a spell suggested that it was not a very powerful demon. Perhaps its mastery of the arcane was as feeble as its swimming. Staring up at the blue eyes that peered back at him from behind the flat transparency, he wondered why it continued to remain half in and half out of the realm of void. Clearly, the strange mystical device that it held in its mouth was critical to its ability to breath in the realworld. Equipped with that capability, why then did it not descend to challenge merson and manyarm directly? Could it be that it wished to avoid confrontation?

Well, that was fine with Chachel. Pivoting in the water, he turned to leave. When they found out that one of their own had been given the chance to study a living demon, Telnarch and the other village elders would be aghast at his decision to depart. That realization did not weigh on Chachel. A good part of his life had been spent leaving others aghast.

Then a strange thing happened. One would have thought the demon would have been relieved by the imminent departure of a pair of potentially dangerous foes like Chachel and Glint. Instead, she began thrashing violently about, raising so much commotion that it commanded their attention. Together, merson and manyarm turned to gape.

"What can it want?" Glint spoke through arms once more clasped securely around the body of the dead blacktip. A free tentacle shooed away a curious remora, which departed muttering glumly. "Is it not enough that we are leaving it in peace?"

Chachel squinted upward out of his good eye. "See how it spreads its arms. Is the she-creature insisting on a fight?"

Turning to one side in order to see better, Glint's color changed from white with red stripes to a pale green spotted with brown that reflected both curiosity and confusion.

"I don't think so. It—she—is certainly gesturing, but in a fashion that I perceive to be non-hostile." Fins rippling, he looked over at his friend. "Maybe she is hurt, or hungry."

"She doesn't look injured," Chachel muttered. "Though on a merson, skin that black would indicate death. Perhaps it is normal coloration for this kind of demon." Kicking effortlessly with both his real leg and the prosthetic, he swam slowly up and forward toward the creature.

"Be careful!" Glint's body turned pure white, a sign of warning. "One should not trust a demon."

Glancing back over a shoulder, Chachel smiled thinly. "You know I don't trust *anyone*."

He stopped just out of arm's reach, hovering in the water. Male merson and female demon regarded one another. Swimming past at a safe distance, a silvery school of big-eyed trevally offered insulting remarks. Chachel ignored them. One did not waste time quarreling with food.

What *did* the demon want? Its gestures and its actions remained mystifying to him. Then it finally did something comprehensible. Slowly and deliberately, it slid the precious knife back into its sheath. He wanted to comprehend its very merson-like stare, but the hard transparency that covered its eyes and the device it held in its mouth combined to render any meaningful expression unfathomable. At least, he found it so.

What wouldn't elder Telnarch give for a chance to examine such a creature—alive? If he could bring it back to the village, Chachel would gain considerable standing among his peers. Alas for Telnarch, Heranleck, and the other elders, the hunter did not give a clam's damn for such "standing." Nor did he regard himself as having any peers. But doing something to satisfy his own curiosity— now that was another matter entirely. Would the creature come with him? Surely she must have demonic priorities of her own.

Swimming closer, still trying to interpret what lay behind those surprisingly normal-seeming demon eyes, he spoke to her.

"I don't know what you want or what you're thrashing about for, but if you like, I'll take you with me to Sandrift and you can parley there with the elders."

There was no reaction from the demon, unless one counted what might have been a look of some confusion. Again, with the objects in place over her face it was difficult to tell just from looking at her what she might be thinking. Was it possible that demons did not understand normal speech? She had not reacted to the impertinent comments from the passing trevally, either. Holding his position, he beckoned to his many-tentacled hunting companion.

"She reacts as if she doesn't understand. Actually, she's not really reacting at all. If not merson, perhaps she understands manyarm talk."

The demon's eyes cut sharply sideways as they took note of Glint's approach. They widened when the cuttlefish passed custody of the dead blacktip to Chachel. Her gaze focused on the manyarm's strong, sucker-lined tentacles; she held her space.

Glint began by flashing ripples of maroon and pink the length of his body; colors that designated a universal welcome among his kind. Cuttlefish or squid, octopus or nautilus, it would be recognized as a friendly blush. The demon looked on intently but did not respond with either words or a color change of her own. Chachel's friend tried darker colors like indigo, then offered up a rippling succession of stripes that ran the gamut from subdued yellow to a bold gold. He flaunted audacious stripes and irregular splotches, dark blue spots on gray, utilizing every trick in his epidermal chromatophoric arsenal of visual communication. He even formed words on his body in the merson language—a skill reserved for only the most educated manyarms. The demon reacted strongly to the display of script, but continued to offer no comprehensible response of her own.

Disgusted with the ongoing lack of comprehension, Chachel found himself wondering if perhaps they had stumbled across an especially moronic demon. Was she inherently incapable of any kind of civilized discourse? Very well then. If she could not be instructed, she would have to be shown. Reaching up, he grabbed her right ankle just above the artificial fin and started to pull her down.

Her other leg snapped forward and she kicked him. The blow was lighter than expected due to the pliable nature of the fin that struck his face. It had a strange, alien tactility to it. If anything, it reminded him of a dolphin fin. While its composition might be alien, the gesture was not.

"All right—have it your way." Pivoting fluidly, he turned to leave. When a webless hand reached out to restrain him, he whirled angrily.

"Make up your mind, demon! Stay or come, but I have no time for games!"

Glint slid forward. "Can you not see that the creature is conflicted? We are forcing it to choose between void and realworld, between nothingness and everythingness. Only Oxothyr might make sense of such a contradiction." Advancing slowly, he extended his two long hunting tentacles, wrapped the pads on the ends gently around the same ankle Chachel had grabbed, and exerted slight but unmistakable pressure.

The flow of bubbles from the object the demon held in its mouth slowed. It allowed Glint to drag it downward until it was once more fully in the realworld. Above, the mirrorsky rippled and flowed, defining the boundary between the void and reality. When Glint let go of the leg and drifted backward and down, beckoning as he did so, the demon slowly followed.

"See?" There was more than a slight note of satisfaction in his voice. "Even with demons one has to be patient."

"Then it is not surprising it resisted coming with me." Turning, Chachel headed toward the outer wall of the reef. "It is well known that I have no patience."

Since the preferred mode of manyarm travel was backward, Glint was able to lead the way while simultaneously keeping an eye on the trailing demon. "She swims awkwardly. We must have a care to watch our speed or we will leave her behind."

Chachel switched the tail of the dead shark he was towing from one hand to the other. "We can't go too slow. You know how blood-masking spells weaken with each repeated application."

Forcing water out his siphon, Glint flashed the color-pattern indicative of understanding. "We will reach Sandrift in plenty of time. You worry like a female with a clutch of unfertilized eggs."

He gestured with a tentacle. "Why do you suppose the creature keeps pointing to the strange bracelet on its right wrist? It is alive with markings that change continually and whose meaning is unknown to me."

Chachel glanced over. "Are you surprised to find demon markings incomprehensible? Perhaps Telnarch can decipher them. As village scribe it's his business to know script."

"Or Oxothyr might understand them." Glint sounded hopeful. "Even Oxothyr does not know everything Oxothyr knows."

No one troubled them as they descended to the bottom and headed out across the sand flats that marked the base of the reef. The occasional spralaker hiding in the sand cursed their passing, but whether crab or other kind of crustacean, each speaker was careful to keep to its hole. Both manyarms and mersons enjoyed the taste of fresh spralaker, just as the annoying hardshells themselves were happy to feast on any dead or injured they happened to come upon.

The remainder of the journey continued uneventful, except that with each passing moment the demon who had reluctantly chosen to follow them glanced with a frequency verging on agitation at the markings on her strange bracelet....

The demon's reaction to her first sight of Sandrift when the dissimilar trio topped the last reef rise was instructive. Eyes widening behind the solid transparency that covered much of her face, she stopped swimming and drew herself up straight in the water. One arm gestured violently at the village, as if she had never seen a simple reef community before. Despite his interest in the creature, her ignorance was beginning to grate on Chachel. Adjusting the patch that covered his left eye socket, he said as much to Glint. The cuttlefish replied dryly.

"Yes, truly you have little time to waste on such observations, given your busy schedule that awaits fulfillment."

An unsmiling Chachel thrust a hand in the cuttlefish's direction. The blow was easily avoided. Even a sick manyarm could dance circles around the fastest merson. The hunter was reduced to striking back verbally.

"You blow sour ink. Do you not realize that every moment in time spent is a moment in time never to be recovered?"

"You're a better hunter than you are a philosopher, my one-eyed friend." Clutching the body of the blacktip, Glint pulsed forward. Two tentacles gestured for the demon to follow, which she did. "See?" the cuttlefish told his hunting companion as he turned a pleased purple. "Even though she resembles you, she likes me better."

"You're welcome to her." Chachel grumbled as he finned forward, wondering as he did so why the prospect should bother him.

As shelf villages went, Sandrift was modest in execution and extent. The small subterranean canyon it flanked received seasonal slides of fresh sand from the void above. These periodic infusions of pulverized stone and silicate were the occasion for impromptu holidays. When the slides continued for several days, as they sometimes did, racing down them was held amid much merriment. Clinging to heavy chunks of flat rock, contestants would swim upslope, await the next slide, and speed downward on the avalanching sand while villagers on either side cheered them on.

Hewn out of solid coral, the individual dwellings and places of commerce were as colorful as the millions of tiny polyps that had built the reef. Windows screened with strands of seaweed, sea grass, or woven sea slug innards kept out all but the tiniest fish and invertebrate intruders. Doors fashioned of treated fish or whale skin were decorated with anemone appliqué whose living tentacles were arranged in patterns that identified the families or businesses that occupied the different premises.

Both East and West Sandrift were protected by a mesh of slender but strong coral that reached mirrorskyward to form a latticework half dome over each side of the canyon that gave the community its name. This was necessary since in the realworld an attack was as likely to come from above as from the side. No entrance to the community was possible from above. Heavy coralline gates mounted on lubricated slides admitted the villagers to each half of the community. These two halves faced each other across the canyon. An enemy attempting to force one gate would find itself under fire from the villagers on the opposite side, and vice versa.

In addition to homes and trades, the half domes of coral latticework protected small gardens from wandering schools of voracious herbivores. There, in shaded, cooler water, the populace raised all manner of crops, from sea lettuce to sea grapes to brightly tinted edible fungi and algae. Supplied by skilled foragers like Chachel, meat came from hunting. Except that Chachel did not share much of what he killed with the villagers, and they did not share much with him. Why should he share, since he chose to live outside not only the social order but the community itself?

Though they visited and interacted daily with the villagers, manyarms were as a rule too free roaming to live within the fixed boundaries of a house. This was the nature of squid and cuttlefish. The exception were the octopods, who like mersons were very much stay-at-homes and equally proud of their finely decorated dwellings. Even a demon, Chachel thought, should know this elementary fact. That the female who accompanied them was ignorant of it was evidenced by her constant staring and gesturing at the various biological cousins of Glint who came and went freely from the village. Unlike mersons only the very largest of them had to petition the gate guards for entry, since their boneless bodies allowed even someone Glint's size to easily squeeze through the existing holes and gaps in the overarching coral dome that protected the opposing halves of the town.

Manyarms and mersons alike paused in their daily routines to gawk at the demon accompanying the returning hunters. Children stopped and pointed or zoomed excitedly around their parents. A clutch of curious, forearm-sized squid offspring shot fearlessly toward the demon, only to jet away in puffs of ink and hyperactive squeals when a burst of bubbles emerged from the rounded object held in the creature's mouth. They were so startled they forgot to squirt the usual jibes at Chachel.

Merson and manyarm guided the demon across the canyon and fetched up in front of the gate to West Sandrift. Holding his bone spear perpendicular to the sand, his shark tooth-edged sword secured against his back, Seravach the Gatekeeper eyed the arrivals warily as he gestured at the demon.

"I don't know what that is or where you found it, but you can't bring that thing in here."

"It's a she-demon," Glint explained helpfully.

"Really? A demon?" Seravach's attention perked up, though he was still distrustful. "All the more reason then why it should not be admitted."

While he would have preferred to let Glint do all the talking, Chachel felt it was incumbent on him to speak up. "It's a harmless demon."

The Gatekeeper whirled to face him. "Truly? Harmless? Is he-who-sexes-alone suddenly an authority on demons? Not, I suppose, that such an expertise on your part should surprise me."

Swimming downslope, a school of a hundred long-finned banner fish fluttered past behind Chachel; their bright black, white, and yellow bodies catching the afternoon light. They were followed by a thousand iridescent purple and blue anthias. None voiced an opinion on the confrontation. In common with the majority of small, colorful reef fish, their conversation consisted almost entirely of inconsequential chatter focused largely on group gossip.

Under normal circumstances, Chachel would either have challenged Seravach to a fight or turned and left. But having come this far, he intended to see the episode through to its conclusion. And it would be have unfair to leave Glint to deal with the Gatekeeper by himself. Besides which, the cuttlefish presently had possession of the dead shark, and Chachel was getting hungry.

"I'll take responsibility." Moving forward, Glint displayed a liability pattern common to his kind—dark brown streaked with green. The Gatekeeper let out a grunt; the low, thumping sound carried clearly through water.

"I suppose it's okay." He studied the strange, black-skinned apparition. "It's not a very big demon. What kind of magic can it do?"

"So far, nothing," Glint assured him.

Snorting bubbles, Seravach set aside his spear and worked the simple mechanism that allowed one person to slide the heavy gate open just enough for the three of them to pass. As she finned through, the demon turned to look in his direction. Absently, he wondered what the creature's face looked like, concealed as it was behind some kind of reflective transparency. He supposed it must be classically grotesque. Regarding her peculiar attire, the Gate-keeper found its design and nature quite unfathomable.

As befitted his status and personal preferences, Oxothyr's home was built into a section of reef wall itself. A few staghorn corals flanked the entrance while the opening was shielded from the mirrorsky and its light by graceful plates of carefully nurtured shelf coral. When Chachel indicated to the demon that they were to go inside, she hesitated, shaking her head and pointing again at the bracelet with the strange markings. It was left to Glint to pass the blacktip to his friend and coax her forward, pushing and tugging gently with his tentacles while flashing his most reassuring pink and cerise patterns.

For a moment it looked as if she was going to panic and flee. Tilting back her head, she gazed upward at the mirrorsky, visible through the openings in the village wall overhead. Peering once more at her strange bracelet, she shook her head more slowly than before, let out a barely audible stream of bubbles, and finally allowed Glint to half pull, half push her forward.

The short tunnel opened into a large circular chamber in the rock. Lined with frail glistening tunicates and decorative soft corals of lavender hue, the space was almost devoid of current. Cemented to the curving walls, hundreds of shells of evicted mollusks and spralakers sparkled and shone in the light that filtered down the parlor's central shaft. Clusters of stiff black sea whips protruding from the rock offered the opportunity for precise backscratching. Utilizing colored ink rendered permanent by a fixing enchantment, several manyarm artists had decorated the remainder of the walls with designs both abstract and arcane.

While Glint jetted off in search of the habitat's owner, Chachel remained just out of the demon's reach. He hated surprises, and to be surprised by a suddenly hostile demon was a fate he would prefer to avoid.

This particular fiend, however, looked anything but threatening. As they waited, she hardly moved, apparently content to drift in center of the central, well-lit shaft that bored through the chamber from top to bottom. Her eyes were half closed, as if she was falling asleep.

When Glint reappeared with Oxothyr in tow, she woke up very fast.

Fully extended, the limbs of the manyarm mage were long enough to span the entire chamber from one side to the other. The fact that most of them remained coiled close to his body did nothing to reassure the startled demon. At the sight of Sandrift's shaman her head virtually disappeared in a sudden eruption of bubbles. Spinning around, she kicked wildly in an attempt to swim back in the direction they had come.

Sensing her distress, Oxothyr immediately changed hue from his normal relaxed beige-green to a pale turquoise streaked with pink—the most soothing color combination he knew. Since Glint had already informed him that the demon was incapable of civilized speech, the shaman did not try to reassure her with words. Instead, he compacted his body as best he could, twisted his eight arms around him, drew his eyes back into his head, and murmured a few choice reassuring words. Then, utilizing a combination of natural mimicry and a touch of wizardry, he changed shape.

Grabbing the fleeing demon by one leg, Chachel twisted hard and spun her around in the water. Forced to look backward, she saw—herself. Herself flaunting cephalopodan eyes and tinted turquoise, but unmistakably herself. The incongruity of it was enough to halt her frantic flight. Her arms and legs stopped thrashing.

All octopuses are natural mimics, able to alter not only their color but their shape to match their surroundings. These inherited skills the venerable and practiced Oxothyr had mastered long ago. Still, even sheened with magic, it required some of his most exquisite contortions to twist himself into a replica of the alien being currently hovering before him in the column of light shafting down from above. While far from a perfect facsimile, the resemblance was striking enough to unsettle not only the demon herself but Chachel and Glint as well.

When the wizard extended a thick tentacle in her direction, she bent at the waist and started to reach for her knife. As Chachel prepared to intervene, Oxothyr perceived his intent and with another limb waved him off. Lightly, the tip of his extended tentacle made contact with the demon's shoulder, ran down her side and leg. The extreme delicacy of touch must have reassured the creature. Straightening, her fingers slowly drew away from the weapon.

As Oxothyr examined her closely, she marveled at his coloration, size, and the bejeweled bracelets that decorated each of the shaman's eight sucker-lined arms. Scrunched up as near to his elastic body as possible, each armlet was fashioned of different gems, shells, and metals. For some reason she seemed to be particularly attracted to the circlet of hammered gold that encircled one tentacle. Watching her, Chachel just shook his head. Who could fathom the interests of a demon? Perhaps only Oxothyr—which was one reason they had brought her here.

"Are you going to kill it?"

"Are you going to eat it?"

The squeaky-voiced queries came from Sathi and Tythe, the shaman's sibling squid famuli. At their appearance, Glint flashed a disgusted pattern. Too often, the interests of the shaman's servants seemed focused on matters of feeding and reproduction to the exclusion of all else.

"Why would I do either to something that is plainly so frightened?" the shaman murmured reprovingly to his assistants.

Chachel frowned. "Frightened? The demon is afraid of *us*?"

"It is plainly afraid of something. Perhaps the same distant menace of which I have sometimes spoken lately. It suggests to me that whatever we have here is not a harbinger of that distantly perceived peril." Endowed as were all his kind with the ability to taste through his arms, Oxothyr reached out to drag a sensitive tip down the back of the creature's pale right hand. This time the she-demon did not jerk away. "Truly, the poor creature reeks of fear." He continued his inspection while Chachel used one hand to brush away the shaman's annoying servants, who were persistent in their efforts to snip off tasty pieces of the dead blacktip.

"A real demon," Oxothyr marveled. "I have heard and read tales of such, but never having seen one for myself I had come to believe that they were little more than legends. Now here is one alive and in the flesh, as it were." He moved forward again. "This is interesting…."

Using a pair of arms, he reached toward the neck of the demon. She tensed but did not try to swim away. As the tips of the arms grabbed hold and pulled downward, the black skin peeled away. Revealed beneath was another, partial layer of bright green skin and a good deal of pale flesh that was far more normal in appearance than what the mage was removing. From underneath the black "skin" that had covered its head, long hair spilled out. The strands were tinted a startling yellow-gold.

"How many skins does the creature have?" a bemused Glint wondered as he watched the operation.

Dragging the last of the limp black husk off over the artificial fins, Oxothyr cast it to one side. It drifted to the floor like a dead thing.

"Why are you surprised? Most spralakers shed their skin many times. True, this visitor far more nearly resembles a merson, but we must not suppose that superficial similarities necessarily hold true throughout the entirety of its demonic form." Extending an arm, he prepared to remove the second, shimmering green inner skin.

This time the demon resisted, strongly. Not wishing to force the issue, Oxothyr promptly withdrew the probing arm-tip. Setting aside for the moment the matter of skins within skins, he reached up and let the tentacle tip crawl across the transparency that covered the upper portion of the demon's face. It was hard and unyielding, like the clear crystals the mersons sometimes mined on another part of the sea shelf. Then there was the matter of the peculiar bubble-emitting construct that the demon continued to hold tightly in its mouth. Reaching up fast, he gently but firmly plucked it out.

It immediately began to discharge a free flow of bubbles, not unlike certain special places on the ocean floor. Clutching at it desperately, the demon took it and shoved it into her mouth. The continuous flow of bubbles ceased, to be replaced by periodic bursts from one side of the apparatus.

Waving an arm through the flow in order to sample its composition and consistency, an astonished Oxothyr pulled back. "Remarkable! Simply remarkable."

"Remarkable enough to eat?" wondered Sathi aloud.

"Remarkable enough to kill?" added a hopeful Tythe.

Ignoring them, the shaman turned toward the attentive hunters. He made no effort to hide his shock. "It seems impossible, yet there can be no doubt of it. The demon breathes void!"

Though he had more respect for the shaman Oxothyr than he did for any of his fellow mersons, Chachel was not quite ready to freely countenance such an outrageous claim.

"Wizened One, how can something breathe nothing?"

"I do not know." Oxothyr continued to hover directly in front of the motionless visitor. "Tales tell only of dead demons found. It is certain that the dead do not breathe at all. But I am convinced this wonderment before us is real."

Using his two padded hunting tentacles to keep the pair of hungry servants at arm's length and away from the tasty corpse of the blacktip, Glint exhibited as much curiosity as his merson companion. "How can you be sure, Master Oxothyr, that the demon is not a scout for the still unidentified danger of which you have previously spoken?"

"Admittedly, I cannot be certain of that because the nature of the peril is still unknown to me." Extending and spreading two arms wide, Oxothyr drew them slowly up and down the merson-like flanks of the creature. The gentleness of his touch seemed to calm her. "I can only say that for a demon, this she-thing behaves in a decidedly undemonic manner."

As if to deliberately give the lie to the shaman's charitable assessment, the creature raised her left arm, jabbed a finger at the crystalline face of its strange bracelet, and started to swim upward, using the light shaft that split the chamber for a guide as she kicked hard toward the surface. It took Chachel, Glint, Sathi, and Tythe's combined strength to hold her down. She struggled violently for a moment, trying to free herself. Then, as if resigned, she simply went limp in the water.

Leaning in close, Chachel peered at the transparency that covered the demon's face. "Its eyes are closed." He shook the figure. The feel of the bare arms was strange under his fingers, almost as if he was gripping a manyarm instead of a merson. In response to his shaking, the eyes behind the plate fluttered slightly but did not open more than halfway.

Coming nearer, Oxothyr brought one eye close to the peculiar bracelet. "This is a device of some strange manufacture."

Freed for the moment from the need to defend the shark from the darting depredations of the shaman's servants, Glint offered his own opinion. "Whatever its function, the demon is obsessed with it. During our journey home, she looked at it every other moment. Do you have any idea what it does, Wisearms?"

Oxothyr turned dark brown spotted with white, a sign of negativity. "The unobvious requires study." Reaching out with a tentacle tip, he felt of the apparatus that protruded from the creature's mouth. The irregular flow of bubbles it had been emitting had undergone a sudden and dramatic decline. With another arm he pushed at the body. It drifted backward in response as the creature made no effort to ward off the shove. Its eyes remained closed and its head lolled to one side.

"I think it is dying," he murmured. "The void it inhales to live is gone, or going. Something must be done, and quickly!"

"Why?" An indifferent Chachel had drifted backward. "It's a demon. Perhaps it is time to let it die."

Oxothyr favored the hunter with a reproving gaze. "I do not know why the other villagers take the time and trouble to insult you when you do such a commendable job of doing so yourself." Arms curling, he pushed away from the hovering body. "Consider that while this creature may not be a component of those disturbing rumors I have been perceiving, it may know something about them. In contrast, dead persons are notoriously uninformative." Extending his eight arms in all directions, the shaman made simultaneous contact with both sides of the chamber.

The chromatophores in their skin flashing excitement in rippling waves of silver and gold, the two famuli obediently released their respective grips on the hovering demon's legs and shot into the tunnel that led into the depths of the shaman's home.

"Magic be coming!" Sathi squealed excitedly.

"Coming is magic!" Tythe added redundantly.

Clutching the dead blacktip tightly, Glint started to back toward the entrance to the mage's lair. One eye fastened on the drifting Chachel. "You heard the squirts! Aren't you coming?"

"No." Chachel remained hovering where he was. "I want to watch."

"Those who linger too close to a shaman's magic sometimes find themselves caught up in it," the cuttlefish warned him.

"Go if you want. I'm staying. I might learn something."

"Like how to be turned into a limpet," Glint muttered nervously. But despite his apprehension, he stayed his flight to remain with his friend. It would not do to admit, even to himself, that a merson could be braver than a manyarm.

Before their eyes, Oxothyr began to spin. His extended arms churned the water until Chachel and Glint had to grab onto the surrounding rock to keep from being swept up in the strengthening maelstrom. As its velocity increased, the whirlpool the shaman was generating began to acquire color. The deepening of hue, the change from transparency to a fiery blue, suggested that everything in its vicinity had begun to descend. It had not. The shaman's home remained where it was, solid rock and coral affixed to the seabed. Only the light deepened.

Oxothyr's voice rose as he recited ancient axioms. Intoning the phraseology of the primordial depths, he summoned forth the deep water magic that was known to only the wisest of the wise. Within the roaring water outlines began to appear; streaks of light that seemed alive, flashes of mindful brightness, flares of shape-shifting scintillation that were the essence of ocean. Within the tunnel that led to the rest of the shaman's house, the two squid alternately gushed expressions of exhilaration and fear. Reflecting their heightened emotions, their slender bodies rippled with color.

Glint managed to maintain firmer control of his chromatophores, though he was still frightened. Never before had placid Oxothyr demonstrated this degree of power. This was intoxicating conjuring indeed. The water spun as the wizard spun; faster and faster, threatening to sweep up the sand below and drag down the plankton above, not to mention pull in his visitors and his servants alike.

But not the demon. It remained as it had been, hovering vertically in the water, eyes closed, head lolling to one side. Now not even small bubbles issued from the device held loosely in its mouth. Oxothyr reached toward it with an arm. How the shaman managed to do this while the rest of his body continued to spin like a vortex was a puzzlement sufficient to cause Glint to doubt the evidence of his own eyes.

The powerful suckers on the mage's extended arm pulled first one flexible fin and then the other off the demon's feet. They were instantly swallowed up by the howling maelstrom. Reaching forward again, the tip of the probing tentacle gently grasped the transparency covering the demon's face. Pulling it up and off, the mage cast it aside. Coiling its way around the creature's back, the powerful limb that somehow stuck straight out of the roaring whirlpool gripped the metal contraption lying against the demon's spine, pulled it free, and allowed it to be swept up in the screaming eddy that filled the chamber. As the cylinder was flung toward the mirrorsky, it trailed several lengths of black tubing. One such tube terminated in the no longer bubbling device that had been clamped between the demon's lips. Eyes closed, the demon continued to drift motionlessly.

Then, as Oxothyr's manipulating arms started to spin the demon in a dark blue vortex of her own, she began to change.

Between fingers and toes, proper webbing appeared, thickening and securing each digit to its neighbor. On the back of each calf, the first hint of fin burst through the skin to thrust upward and out. The flesh on either side of her throat began to ripple. Not from the movement of water against it, but from within. Distinct as grooves cut in rock, four lines appeared on each side of the demon's neck. Mere streaks at first, they quickly darkened in response to the mage's resonant drone. Soon eight flaps of skin, four to a side, were open and undulating. Open and breathing. Squinting hard while clinging to a rocky outcrop, Chachel was just able to make out a hint of redness behind each open flap.

Sucking in a sudden, sharp breath, the demon gasped, choking visibly. Its lungs cleared and its eyes opened. Eyes whose lenses had become thicker. The creature looked around wildly. Oxothyr slowed his spinning. Like a scallop caught in an eddy, the octopus drew his arms in toward his body. As they contracted, so did his voice. The ferocious swirling that had filled the chamber slowed, shrank to a tiny spiral, and vanished. The blue-black of the ominous deep was replaced by normal daylight falling from beyond the mirrorsky overhead. Behind the shaman, Tythe and Sathi slowly began to emerge from the tunnel. Their eyes were wide with astonishment. But then, Chachel mused, a squid's eyes are always wide, though not always with wonder.

Letting go of the outcropping, he finned curiously toward the floating demon. Emerging from where he had taken shelter in the entryway, Glint joined his friend. Chachel was pleased to see that the cuttlefish still held the body of the dead shark. Awe was all very well and good, but it did nothing to fill an empty belly.

Hovering in the water column, the demon blinked; first at Oxothyr, then at Glint, her gaze finally coming to rest on Chachel. Not knowing what else to do, he put his fingers over his mouth in a sign of friendship. Hesitantly, she raised a hand to imitate him. That was when she discovered, or realized, that the bubbling-emitting device was no longer clamped between her lips. Eyes widening, she thrashed frantically for a few seconds. When she finally calmed down, she drifted and gaped at the webbing that now linked her fingers. None of those present had any idea what she might be thinking.

Turning a slow circle, the transmogrified demon examined her surroundings. Absently, she reached up to scratch an arm, her chest, then her neck. When her newly webbed fingers reached her throat and encountered the first of her gills, they paused. Fingertips felt gently, then more urgently of the distinctive flaps. Two fingertips pushed inward. Understandably, she choked.

A changed demon perhaps, Chachel thought, but not necessarily a more enlightened one. This supposition was further confirmed when both her hands came up to feel more fully of the gills on either side of her neck, her mouth opened surprisingly wide, and she fainted....

rina Malakova loved the sea. Simply sitting in it, treading water, or lying on her back on the surface literally washed away all the weighty cares and concerns of everyday life. Her love had only deepened when she had learned how to scuba dive. It became her release, her vacation, and her therapy. Her passion for the hobby sometimes exasperated her friends and family, but she didn't care. Whenever she could find the time, she would go diving. Whenever she managed to scrape up enough money, she would book a trip to some faraway place with a strange-sounding name where the underwater scenery and its flora and fauna were new and exotic.

But not this new. Not this exotic. And certainly not this threatening.

The danger had initially manifested itself when, entranced by a patrolling moray free-swimming out of its customary hole in the reef, she had wandered away from her dive partner to follow the serpentine shape as it hunted along the rim of the steep coral drop-off. Her enchantment had only deepened when she had been lucky enough to see it actually catch and devour a brilliantly colored queen angelfish. Only then had she come back to reality long enough to realize two things: none of the other divers, including her partner, were in sight, and her tank was half-empty.

As she worked to retrace her route along the reef's edge, her usual quiet confidence in her diving abilities gradually gave way to increasing concern. Hadn't she come this way? Or had she first swam outward from that odd-shaped bommie? Despite the presence of deeper water below and the sky overhead, the reef seemed to take turns and twists she didn't remember. Once, the sky itself seemed to contort crazily, as if she was swimming at an angle instead of parallel to the light. She was starting to get hungry, and dehydrated. Still there was no sign of the other seven divers from the boat.

Something was wrong. The reef itself was all wrong. Though the coral looked familiar enough, and the creatures that crawled over it, and the fish that swam among it, somehow it did not feel right, did not feel natural. Had she been down longer than she thought? Or deeper, and having come up too fast, was now suffering from the hallucinations that could be caused by nitrogen narcosis? She glanced at her left wrist. Though her dive computer appeared to be functioning normally, there were worse things than a complete failure of the vital device. Defective instrumentation supplying faulty information could be more dangerous than one that had gone dead and displayed no information at all.

Of one thing she was now certain: it was time to terminate the dive. Once on the surface, even if she did not see the dive boat, she could utilize everything from the blare of her dive alert horn to a bright orange safety sausage to a dark emergency slick contained in the breakable tube in her buoyancy compensator pocket. Ascending slowly, careful to rise no faster than the bubbles from the regulator in her mouth, she paused at ten feet for a four-minute safety stop before kicking the rest of the way to the surface.

Once her head was clear of the water she let the regulator fall from her mouth, inflated the BC, and sucked in fresh air. Turning a slow circle, she scanned the sun-filled horizon for the friendly silhouette of the dive boat. There was no sign of it. Its absence was no immediate cause for panic. Searching for her, it might have gone first around the other side of the island where she and the other divers had been dropped off.

Except there was no island.

She blinked. Everything was far, far more wrong than she had initially thought. Uninhabited and fringed with coconut palms, the island had been there, several hundred meters of solid ground extending to north and south. As she stared, the sun blazed down, heating the synthetic material of her black and blue diveskin. She spun wildly in the water, looking frantically to left and right.

Where was the island? Where was the dive boat? In every direction, on every horizon, there was nothing to be seen but flat blue-green sea.

*Impossible*, she thought as a fearful panic began to take hold. It was impossible. How could she have drifted so far? She had kept the reef on her left or right at all times. Could she have swam, underwater, from the island where the dive had commenced to a shallow reef so far distant that the first could no longer be seen? If that was the case, how could she be sure of finding her way back? If she descended and tried to retrace her route along the submerged reef, how could she be certain it would lead her in the right direction? For the first time in hundreds of dives, she found herself wishing she had carried a compass. But who needed a compass when one always dove with a group?

Now almost directly overhead following the late morning dive, the sun was no help in determining direction. She tried to stay calm. Keep your BC inflated, she told herself firmly. Deploy your safety sausage, crack the emergency vial and spread the surface slick, and wait for someone to find you. Let off periodic blasts from your dive alert horn. Don't waste energy swimming to nowhere. Taking deliberate, deep breaths, she initiated the relevant emergency procedures. All the while, she fought not to think of sharks. As an avid diver, she loved being around sharks. But not like this. Not alone and trapped at the surface.

Of course, she wasn't trapped. She still had a fair amount of air in her tank. But going down would solve nothing. Assuming her absence had been noted on the boat and they were now looking for her, it was imperative that she remain on the surface where she could be seen.

Current, she told herself. Maybe she had been caught up in some kind of unusual and powerful inshore current and it had swept her far from where she and her fellow divers had entered the water. It was true that she had gone off a little ways on her own.

But she had felt no surge, experienced no dislocation. Could she have fallen asleep and then become caught up in a current, to finally awaken unaware of what had transpired? Such incidents had been documented, had been known to happen to exceptionally relaxed divers.

Surely she had been missed by now. Surely her dive partner or someone among the crew would have noted and reported her failure to return to the dive ladder at the stern of the boat. Surely.

She clung to that thought all the rest of the day and on into the night, until darkness and exhaustion overcame her. The gentle swell rocked her to sleep as ably as any consoling hand.

She knew no sharks had found her during the night because she was still intact when she awoke. A quick scan of her surroundings revealed the continuing and increasingly distressing absence of islands and boat. If an island, any island, had been close at hand, she could have swam for it. If nothing else, an island would have coconuts, which (if she could manage to open them) promised food and water.

Thinking of food and water while adrift on a landless sea was not conducive to her continued mental health.

The tropical sun, so often a welcome visitor on her vacations, had turned into an unresponsive, remorseless, soul-sucking antagonist. While the thin suit-integrated hood of her diveskin provided some protection from the direct unrelenting rays, the synthetic fabric's dark color also absorbed heat. By afternoon she was half-delirious.

At least, she thought crazily, I can always splash cool water on my face. It was her last conscious thought before she passed out for the night.

Her second morning adrift brought no relief. Pivoting in the water to keep her face pointed away from the rising sun, she slipped the regulator into her mouth and started kicking feebly toward a point of reef that rose to within a few feet of the surface. If she was not too weak, she could try standing on it for awhile. While it would not make her that much more visible to any searching boat, it would allow her to stimulate different muscles in her legs.

She stood thus, with only her upper body out of the water, for as long as she could maintain her balance. Despite the heat, she dared not slip out of the diveskin for fear of becoming sunburned. When her thigh muscles could stand it no longer, she slipped reluctantly back into the water, letting her inflated buoyancy compensator carry her wherever it might.

She had the regulator in her mouth when she passed out. It was still there when she felt herself being pulled under, though the sight of the big cuttlefish that was dragging her downward nearly caused her to spit it out as she screamed.

◊

Memory of her abandonment and desperate situation vanished as she contemplated her remarkably revised circumstances. Apparently, she no longer needed the regulator, nor the pressure hose attaching it to the aluminum air tank, nor the contents of the tank itself. Or her rubber fins, or any of the other accoutrements that were normally required to keep a human being alive and mobile while underwater. If the touch of her own fingers were to be believed, she had sprouted gills, along with webbing between her fingers and toes and fishy fins on the backs of her calves. Almost as amazing as her new gills were the altered lenses of her eyes. Though open wide, they did not burn, and she found herself able to see as clearly as if she was still wearing her mask.

She had been transformed. By the same process that had transformed the one-eyed spear-carrying male who was staring curiously at her? Her attention flicked back and forth between him and the shark-toting cuttlefish drifting nearby. Was it the same colorful cephalopod that had initially dragged her under? As if they were not enough to ponder, there was also the gentle giant of an octopus hovering nearby and the pair of two-foot long squid who kept darting in to cop exploratory feels of her emerald green swimsuit and its contents.

She realized with a start that she was no longer cold. She ought to be on the verge of hypothermia. The water surrounding her might be bathtub warm, but body heat would still migrate from ninety-eight point six degrees internal to dissipate in eighty-eight degree seawater. Everything about her body had been altered. No, not altered, she corrected herself. Adjusted. Fine-tuned. In the most literal sense of the term, she had undergone a sea change. The alternative having been a slow death from exposure or drowning, she was in no hurry to question the transformation.

His skin color darkening to a black-flecked beige, the octopus appeared to be consulting with the two squid. That was insane, of course. Almost as insane as her male counterpart swimming suddenly toward her, halting, and asking in clipped no-nonsense tones, "What happened to you, demon?"

She understood him. Clearly. Underwater. She was not sure which was more remarkable: the fact that she could now hear clearly at depth, that his words were comprehensible, or that she hardly reacted at all when he lifted up the patch that covered his left eye and began to use a finger to wipe out the empty socket. Was she capable of replying? Surely her words would not be understood. Shaping her lips around a response, she found that when she opened her mouth to speak she did not drown. This was reassuring.

"I—I'm not a demon."

Lateral fins rippling to propel it forward, the big cuttlefish let the dead blacktip it had been holding float free. Though its tentacles made it longer than she was, it weighed considerably less. Of course weight here, she reflected, did not have the same meaning as it did on land. Was it going to grab her again? And if so, should she resist?

Glint did not grab her. "If you're not a demon," he declared, "then what are you?"

She could understand cuttlefish chat. Why should she be surprised? Was this all a heat-induced dream from which she would shortly awaken, to find herself floating once more alone and abandoned on the surface of an apathetic sea? Until then, she decided, she might as well go literally with the flow.

"Yes." The male with the spear confronted her in a manner brusque enough to be considered threatening. "You must be a demon. You were found breathing void."

"Void?" She looked bewildered. "Oh, you mean *air*. Yes, that's what people breathe. Or rather, that's what I used to breathe." She looked over at Oxothyr. "That thing *did* something do me."

The shaman's boneless mantle bobbed slightly toward her—an octopodian bow. "The 'thing' respectfully acknowledges your thanks," he replied dryly. "Without my intervention you would have surely suffocated."

A talking octopus. A talking cuttlefish. I'm dreaming for sure, she told herself. If only she didn't feel so—so—overtly *wet*. Could she be sweating in her sleep, inside her restrictive diveskin?

"I'm a human being." A hint of desperation had crept into her voice. She turned to the spear-carrier. "A person, just like—well, maybe not just like you."

"A merson?" Chachel frowned. "It is true that you look like one now, but that is thanks to Oxothyr's miraculous intercession. Before, you looked like a demon. The dead of your kind are known to us, albeit they are found very rarely."

"Dead ...?" It was her turn to look confused. "Oh, you mean drowned. You call yourselves 'mersons'?"

"We do not 'call' ourselves anything." Be it demon or mage-inveigled changeling, he was finding this creature less and less to his liking. "Merson is what we *are*. Do you have a name, dem—do you have a name?"

"Irina." She did not see any point in giving her full name.

"I am Chachel." He gestured to his left. "This is my friend and hunting companion, Glint. You have been save-transformed by the esteemed shaman Oxothyr, whose skills are celebrated throughout the length and breadth of the Keleagh Plain and even unto the depths beyond. And you still have not explained what happened to you."

She nodded understandingly. Apparently the gesture meant the same in her dream as it did anywhere else. "I was diving—I am diving. I got separated from the rest of the group, I don't know how. We were diving around an island. I went off by myself, which I know I shouldn't have done, but I did it. When I surfaced there was no sign of the island, the dive boat, or my fellow divers. All I can think is that I fell asleep or otherwise lost consciousness for awhile, got caught in a strong current, and swept away. I'm not sure how long I spent drifting until now—a day, two days, a week. It was hot, and I think I lost my mind for awhile. I don't know. All I do know is that I'd really, really like to *wake up*."

"You are not asleep." The cuttlefish, she noted, seemed more sympathetic to her condition than did the human—the merson, she corrected herself.

*Why can't I wake up?*

She started to cry—only to discover that she couldn't. How do you cry underwater? She felt herself sobbing, but no tears oozed from the corners of her eyes. Or if they did, she could neither sense nor feel them. What did the body need with moistening, cleansing tears when one's eyes were permanently submerged?

The merson came even closer. He did not have to brandish the bone spear he was holding in order to intimidate her. It was enough that he held onto it.

"Do you think we are fools here? Sandrift is a small community but we are not provincial. Those of us who live in this corner of the plain are as aware of the wider world as those who dwell in the cities. Rumors of unpleasantness drift down to us from far to the north. Tales of ravaged societies and dead mersons, of unnatural alliances forged in the service of a threat implacable." The point of the spear suddenly dipped toward her. "You are a spy!"

Startled, she drew back. Her webbed feet and the narrow fins on the backs of her calves propelled her effortlessly, seemingly of their own accord. Always an excellent swimmer, her altered self had taken to their use without instruction.

"A—what?" The dream had turned unpleasant again. "A spy for who? I'm not a spy. I'm a dental assistant, I live in a condominium with one and a half baths, a single garage, two aquariums, and a partial bay view, I have more than one occasional boyfriend, I ..."

It was not necessary to see tears to realize that she was on the verge of a complete breakdown. Hands over her face, her crying emerged from her mouth in the form of sporadic disturbances to the water column. Chachel and Glint experienced her sobbing as periodic pulses against their skin.

Hovering nearby, Oxothyr had observed the exchange in silence. Now he glided forward, his body a uniform sienna from which thrust bobbing, sucker-lined arms held in loose coils. Behind him, Sathi and Tythe had discovered an errant blue-armed spralaker. Having successfully cornered the crab in a crevice in the rocks, they fought to see who would get to eat it. As they argued, the abject crustacean tried to fend them off with its comparatively useless claws while uttering, "Nonononono!" in a voice as pitiful as it was small.

A tentacle capable of tearing out her throat slid around Irina's neck. Its touch was at once rubbery and reassuring.

"Whatever this changeling is, wherever it is from," Oxothyr declared with sincerity, "she is no spy. Spies are calm, controlled creatures. This female is as confused in her apposite merson form as she was in the earlier one that breathed void."

Grumbling, Chachel returned his spear to vertical again and backed off. "Then if she is not a demon and not a spy, what is she?"

"Lost, I should think." Another arm came up and the tip touched Irina's lips. "Restrain yourself, female, or you will swallow more than you can breathe."

Choking back sobs (it was perfectly possible to cough underwater, she discovered), Irina fought to regain control of her emotions. There was something mesmerizing about the intelligent, cephalopodan eyes that peered back into her own. The dark, S-shaped pupils imparted a sense of serenity she had encountered only twice before; once in the approving gaze of a much-admired professor and later in the course of a romantic relationship that had lasted, alas, all too briefly. She ought to have found it completely alien, that octopodal stare. Allowing herself to be drawn in by it, she found only reassurance and encouragement. A backbone, it seemed, was not a prerequisite for compassion.

"That's better, my dear." Letting his comforting tentacles slide off her exposed skin, the sage drifted away from her so he could address them all.

"I think the female's supposition is correct. From what she has told us, I believe she was indeed caught up in a current. Not the predictable daily current that runs back and forth between Yellecheg and Singarol, nor even the powerful Jinakaloach that sometimes roars southward along the shelf, but one of those periodic mysterious currents that appears only when the flows of the entire realworld undergo a sudden shift."

As she listened to the sage's careful appreciation of what had happened to her, a captivated Irina ceased her crying.

"There are currents that run between homes," Oxothyr continued, "and currents that run between mountains. There are powerful water forces that groom the outer shelves and others that can sweep the unwary into the void itself when the mirrorsky is seriously disturbed. Flows can drag a swimmer into the deep or thrust them into caves from which they cannot escape. And then there are those currents that only but rarely catch and carry the unknowing not merely between seas but between worlds." Raising an arm, he gestured at the watching Irina.

"It is my opinion that this female void-breather, whom I have made into a whole merson, is one such unfortunate."

As the shaman's words began to sink in, Irina refused to accept them. "That's crazy. This is *all* crazy. I was diving in the ocean. It's the same ocean. You—you people are legends." Her gaze traveled from Oxothyr to Glint to the two arguing squid. "Maybe more than legends."

"No." Chachel had little sympathy for anyone who refused to accept reality, however harsh it might be. "You are the legend. Or were. Now you are normal." His spear point gestured in Oxothyr's direction. "You have yet to properly thank the shaman for saving your life."

"Perhaps," the kindly octopod murmured to Irina, "you are right, in some way that neither of us realizes. Oshenerth is a very large place indeed. The largest of all places. Currents that flow from your part to ours may also flow in the opposite direction."

She seized on it. "Then there's a chance—I could get home?"

"The universe does not operate according to chance," he corrected her authoritatively.

"Could—would—you help me?" She held up a webbed hand. "You changed me so I wouldn't die here. Thank—thank you. You would have to change me back or I would die when I returned to my own ocean. At least, I imagine I would."

Nearby, Glint shook his head sadly. "She *wants* to breathe void." He could not imagine what it might feel like to inhale nothing but nothingness, and did not want to.

"I regret that I am occupied with other matters." Eight arms formed a loose halo around the shaman. "Rumors and stories drift down to Sandrift from the far north, from the Dark Sea where the tarazok reside. They speak of unsettling changes, of migrations unnatural and forced. These concerns have been much on my mind of late." Sympathy for her situation dwelled in his voice as well as in those remarkable limpid cephalopodan eyes.

Observing the female, Chachel thought disgustedly to himself. *Tridacna's toes—the thing is going to start crying again.* But the changeling did not.

"I can't ask you to defer work that you think important just for me," Irina mumbled. "Maybe—maybe if I help you in it, you'll be able to find time to help me?"

Glint's body rippled with laughter: it was blue. Chachel almost smiled. The shaman's startling response killed both the cuttlefish's color and the merson's expression.

"I accept your offer, though I have no notion how you might help." The octopus flashed an appreciative pattern of stripes. "In a time when disturbing changes are in the water, an entirely different outlook on reality might be welcome. As I ponder them, I will try to find time to consider your unfortunate circumstances and see what might be done about them."

This time it was the visitor who swam toward the octopus. She proffered a hand. "Thank you! Right now, I guess all I have to offer is my thanks."

The mage studied the extended arm. "Am I supposed to do something with that?"

"It's how my kind seal an agreement. We shake hands."

"If I had one, I would comply." Oxothyr flashed mild amusement. "Fortunately, my grasp is not so limited as those of mersons." Reaching out with a tentacle, he wrapped the end of it around her fingers. She could feel the suction from its suckers. The sensation was not unpleasant.

The shaman withdrew his arm. "The question remains; what are we to do with you now? You cannot stay with me. As I mentioned, I am consumed with other worries. Nor do I have the proper company to offer you." One eye flicked to his right.

Sage he was not, but Chachel was immediately defiant. "No one stays with me, revered one. Not merson, not manyarm, and certainly not a changeling demon."

"Who would want to stay with you?" Glint whispered under his breath—and he was Chachel's best friend.

Oxothyr considered. One could tell he was deep in thought from the line of dark bands that ran in measured waves through his boneless body. As he mulled possibilities, Irina felt something tickle the small of her back.

Whirling in the water column, she found herself confronted by the shaman's multiarmed assistants. Tentacles waving, Sathi and Tythe hovered before her. Having been granted an unexpected reprieve, the spralaker they had cornered in a rock crevice hastened to flee via the nearest available crack in the surrounding coral wall.

"Looks like a merson now," Sathi observed thoughtfully, "but still talks funny."

"Say something funny," Tythe urged her.

"I wish I could." Irina managed a smile.

"So many teeth." Zooming in sharply, Sathi made her flinch. Tentacle-tips reached out to poke all around the rim of her mouth. It felt as if she was being probed by a clutch of educated worms. "Like all mersons."

"Beak is better," Tythe agreed. His skin flushed pink with orange dots.

"You know, you two are kind of cute." Reaching out, she began to caress the nearest squid, starting behind Tythe's head and stroking back along the mantle toward the tail. The manyarm responded by staying motionless in the water while alternating bands of dark blue and purple ran through his body, following the touch of her webbed fingers. Admiring the dramatic color changes the cephalopod accomplished without effort, she found herself thinking of the phenomenon as visual purring.

"I don't care what you do with me," she told Oxothyr. As she shifted her attention to Sathi, the two squid began pushing and shoving as each sought the caress of her soft but firm fingertips. "I'll do whatever you want. I'm just happy to be alive." Holding up her other hand, she marveled at the webbing that now connected its fingers. "Even if you had to change me into something—weird."

Oxothyr snapped out his contemplation. "I am sure we can find some kindly soul to take you in. In the meantime, I forget my manners. You must be famished."

"I am," she admitted readily. "It's been days since I had anything to eat or drink."

Glint flashed confusion. "What is 'drink'? Is it like an oyster?"

"No," she started to explain, "it's …" She stopped. In this world, none of her new acquaintances drank. If anything, their world drank them. Come to think of it, in the course of her dreamlike transformation her thirst had also vanished. Parting her lips, she sucked in a mouthful of salty water. There was no sensation of quenching. The utter absence of thirst, of any desire to drink, was unsettling—and not a little liberating. But she was still hungry.

"I have all manner of victuals," a gracious Oxothyr assured her. "Sathi! Tythe!" The two curious squid immediately snapped to attention; parallel to the mirrorsky, tentacles held out straight in front of them. "How would you like yours prepared?" Oxothyr asked her. "My kitchen is a simple one, but I myself am very fond of spices."

"I'm hungry enough to eat a whole mackerel raw!" she told him. Which, the sage's comment about spices notwithstanding, was quite possibly to be the case. It was self-evident that she was going to have to get used to eating uncooked food. A good thing, she mused, that she liked sushi. She turned to her rescuers, merson and cuttlefish.

"You'll stay and eat with me, won't you? There are so many questions I need to ask."

"Ask them of one whose business it is to dispense answers." His tone curt as ever, Chachel spun and finned back toward the entrance to the shaman's home. "I have wasted enough time here."

"Yes," murmured Glint, "you mustn't let courtesy and company, conversation or conviviality, keep you from an afternoon of solitary melancholic contemplation."

The merson stabbed his spear in the manyarm's direction, a half-hearted thrust the agile cuttlefish avoid easily. Then the gruff one-eyed merson was gone, swallowed up by the blackness of the tunnel. Altered among marvels, transformed in body and perception, a bewildered Irina still found time to wonder at the source of the merson's undeviating irritability.

"He doesn't like me," she muttered.

"He doesn't like anybody." Sidling up alongside her, Glint turned a reassuring maroon. "And nobody likes him. Except me."

She eyed the hovering cephalopod. "Why do you like him?"

"Haven't you heard?" Lateral fins rippling like strips of clear plastic held horizontal in a steady breeze, the cuttlefish moved forward to gaze after his departed companion. "I'm mad. Why else would I go on pair-hunts with an insufferable outcast like Chachel and risk the jeers of my peers?"

"You strike me as perfectly sane." Extending an arm, she used her fingers to stroke him the same way she had the shaman's assistants. His color and body pattern changed immediately in response to her touch.

"Ummm … a little lower and to the right. That's it," he hummed as he drifted closer to her. "Just behind my siphon."

Food soon appeared in plenty. While Irina devoured everything that was set before her and the two squid used their tentacles to wave off (and occasionally eat) the small fish and krill-like crustaceans who occupied the same ecological niche as terrestrial flies, she periodically interrupted her meal to ask questions of Glint. Having retired to his study to brood on the meaning of the disturbing rumors from the north, Oxothyr was no longer available to supply answers. Irina did not mind. She actually preferred to query the cuttlefish. Despite his unambiguous friendliness, the great bulk and penetrating gaze of the octopodal shaman was more than a little intimidating.

As she nibbled her way through the salty center of a decapitated butterfish (everything here was salty, she mused), she finally thought to ask Glint directly about what had been troubling her ever since their first meeting.

"What's wrong with your friend? With Chachel? Why is he so rude to everyone? And why is he, as you said, an 'insufferable outcast'?"

"He's not rude." Fragments of chitinous shell spiraled lazily downward from beneath the cuttlefish's mouth as he methodically demolished a crab. "He's brusque. He is an outcast because that's the life he's chosen for himself. The reason's the same, I think, for the 'insufferable' part."

"But why?" Sitting on a shelf of plate coral that grew outward from the inner wall of the greeting chamber, she found herself using her teeth to scrape the last bits of flesh from bone as naturally as a chef preparing the ingredients for a chowder. "He's more than unfriendly: he's openly hostile. Why? I never did him any harm."

Finishing the last of his crab, Glint turned toward her. As he spoke, he used his sensitive tentacles to clean the area around his beak. Indicative of his sudden seriousness, his body turned a dark yellow.

"It's not you," the cuttlefish explained in a tone turned suddenly somber. "It was a mob that made him what he is. It all happened many years ago."

So solemn was the cephalopod's manner that Irina felt compelled to set the remainder of her own meal aside. "A 'mob'?"

"That's what is called a school of sharks." Pivoting, Glint used both hunting tentacles to gesture back the way they had come. "In Chachel's case, they were mostly oceanic whitetips and makos, working together as a gang." Reflecting his feelings, his body turned white with unsightly black splotches. "It was ugly, it was bloody. I know: I was there."

Sitting cross-legged on the pale blue shelf, illuminated by the light that was still pouring in through the open top of the chamber, Irina stared at the cuttlefish. "You were there? But that's impossible. Your—you people—only live a couple of years or so, and Chachel is at least my age."

One eye regarded her intently. "What are you saying? My people live as long as yours."

"Maybe here they do." She considered thoughtfully. "That might explain why despite showing so much intelligence, cuttlefish like you, and octopods like Oxothyr, and squid where I come from, don't have any higher skills like communication. They don't live long enough to learn. I wonder—if you took an octopus from where I come from, from my ocean, and extended its lifespan by a factor of ten or twenty, how much knowledge would it be able to acquire? How smart could it become? As smart as its older counterparts here?"

"Ask Oxothyr. He is 'of an age.'" Pivoting, Glint gestured upward toward the open water and the mirrorsky above. "I will tell you how Chachel became the way he is...."

## – IV –

The crimson feather star was graceful, beautiful, and lost. Multiple downy bright-red arms propelled it slowly through the water. Though some of its kin favored the depths, that was not the case with the red wanderer. It had been carried away from the reef by a sudden surge of strong current. Now it found itself out in open water without a potential hiding place in sight. It could not avoid the hand that reached for it.

Tempting toxins, a youthful Chachel flicked his fingertips playfully at the ends of the feathery arms but did not quite make contact. The weak-swimming echinoderm bobbed in the water, unable to escape. It tried curling its fragile arms in upon its body, which was miniscule in comparison to the spray of furry limbs. Grinning, the young merson continued to toy inoffensively with the creature. In the open ocean, anything was a diversion.

Having commenced the long swim the previous morning, the clan group's destination was now in sight. Rising to within a couple of body lengths of the mirrorsky, the twin peaks of the seamount called Splitrock materialized out of the watery haze like some ghostly great gray spear. As the clutch of swimmers drew nearer, both its outlines and its rocky slopes acquired more and more detail.

The swift currents that flowed around and through the split-topped seamount made it difficult for corals, cnidarians, mollusks, or echinoderms to secure a grip on its precipitous flanks. A few who were hardy and determined managed a foothold. The rewards for those who succeeded were great, as the currents brought acre-feet of food swirling helplessly past waiting mouths and trolling tentacles.

Even fewer lifeforms succeeded in colonizing the crevice that split the seamount's double crown. Powerful currents kept it scoured almost bare. These drew rather than discouraged the vast schools of fish that congregated in its vicinity. Slamming up against the base of the mount, deep-sea currents were forced upward, carrying with them a torrent of nutrients that sustained whole communities of visiting and resident pelagics. As clan patriarch Jeralach had pledged, hunting promised to be spectacular. Reflecting their leader's optimism, the clan's hunters had brought along especially large carrynets with which to tow the hoped-for haul back to Sandrift.

The seamount was not generally hunted because to reach it required a two-day swim across open ocean from Sandrift's home reef system. Swimming for two days was easy enough. But spending nights out in the pitch darkness of open water, with no visible bottom, was sufficiently intimidating to dissuade all but the boldest hunters. Jeralach proudly counted himself among the latter. There was some debate as to whether it was safe enough to bring along eager young apprentices.

"Each of us will travel with tethered glowfish," Jeralach had explained. "They will provide enough light so that even if someone wanders away from the others, they will not pass from sight." He held up a tunicate that had been effusively enchanted. Showing a delicate mauve tint, the circular opening at the top of the otherwise transparent creature was pointed toward the northwest. "This was collected by me the last time I visited Splitrock. It has been imbued with meticulous charm by the subshaman Aseleaph so that no matter how it is held, its mouth faces always toward its home. It will be our good and reliable guide to the seamount."

The magicked ascidian Jeralach flaunted would eliminate the problem of finding Splitrock in the open ocean. That was the difficult part of the expedition. Young Chachel and the other apprentices knew that returning home following hunting would present no comparable difficulty. Marking the position of the light that moved across the mirrorsky, they need merely swim westward until they struck coral. From any location on the reef walls even a child could find its way back to Sandrift.

As finally constituted, the foraging expedition included fifteen experienced adult male and female hunters as well as an additional six apprentices and a trio of curious cuttlefish. Together with several of his best friends, Chachel was honored to be included among the select group of chosen youths. The fact that his parents comprised part of the hunting team only magnified the pride he felt in participating.

Leaving the aggravated feather star in peace to find its own way back to the reef, he kicked hard to catch up to the rest. The pair of fishing spears strapped to his back had come loose and the shafts were rubbing against his skin. He had not bothered to tighten the lashings because he expected that the weapons would soon be put to good use. Behind him, the feather star filled his wake with a litany of tiny curses that made Chachel smile. At fifteen, there was very little that failed to make him smile. Life beneath the mirrorsky was good, and he had no reason to think it would ever be anything but so.

Though Jeralach was the nominal leader of the expedition, having visited the seamount before, he was not in charge. The hunting expedition had no formal leader. As soon as they arrived, decisions were reached through consensus, with every veteran hunter having a vote. That left the apprentices free to explore the mount. While the adults conferenced, they chased one another around the stone tower that rose from the dark depths, taking care to pay attention to the time of day and any potentially dangerous shifts in the powerful currents. Sensing an as yet undefined threat but unwilling to abandon so fruitful a feeding ground, resident schools of fish kept wary eyes on the caucusing mersons while continuing to stuff themselves with the bounty provided by the cold upwellings that swirled around the seamount.

That was one thing about most fish, Chachel had already learned. It was always the *other* school that was going to bear the burden of any hunting.

His mother was as adept with a fishing spear as his father, and her reactions even faster. Rather than opt for the kind of one-on-one hunting that was common among the reefs around Sandrift, however, Jeralach had proposed a strategy that promised greater success with less effort.

Chachel could hardly wait.

◊

The following morning dawned the same as it always had for the abundant schools of trevally and snapper, jacks and mackerel who chose to feed in and around Splitrock. While busy snacking on smaller life, they remained constantly aware of the hunters' presence. So they were not taken by surprise when a number of the spear-armed clan rushed them. With the glare of the morning mirrorsky behind them and riding the strong north-flowing current, the hunters' intent was plain: trap the feeding schools against the rocky mass of the seamount and spear those too slow to swim around it. Except that the top of the seamount was divided in half, a distinctive geologic feature that gave it its name, and it was perfectly possible for even the dumbest school to shoot straight through the gap instead of trying to go all the way around the undersea mountain.

Driven forward by the shouting, gesticulating mersons, one shoal after another took the shortest, easiest path to escape. A school of a hundred big-eye trevally led the way—only to find the exit to the other side of the seamount blocked by the wide open, carefully positioned haulsacks of four mersons. As following schools began to rapidly bunch up behind them, the trevally fled upwards—straight into the waiting open haulsacks of another quartet of hunters. Assisted by the apprentices and harried by the excited, ink-squirting cuttlefish, filled sacks were drawn shut around wailing captives and tightly secured. It was only then that waiting spears and knives were brought into play.

As slaughters went, the one that took place at Splitrock that fine, clear morning was relatively serene. The fish nearest the outside of the haulsacks died first. Not all would be killed. A dead fish was only fit to eat for a few days before spoilage began to set in. While on site, the hunting party would kill only what could be eaten immediately or easily conserved.

The bloody work took most of the morning. When Jeralach finally called a halt to the methodical butchery, the haulsacks were gathered together and their contents prepared for transport. Diminished but not demolished, new schools promptly reformed around the seamount. These survivors returned to their own pursuit of feeding upon lives still smaller than themselves. That was the law of the realworld. That was the way of Oshenerth.

Every member of the hunting expedition, including Chachel's parents, was overjoyed with their success. They had harvested enough food to feed the entire village for many days. Jeralach had no doubt that upon their return, a general time of celebration would be declared. There would be feasting and games and music. Proud to have participated in the hunt and to have contributed in some small way to its success, Chachel felt more like an adult than he had at any time in his life. All that remained now was to tow the catch back to Sandrift and trumpet their accomplishment. Their achievement would not go unnoticed, their hard work would not pass unrecognized.

Unfortunately, such was already the case.

There was a reason why those who set out to search for food beyond the safety of their villages kept close to the reefs of Yellecheg and Hingarol, Sandrift and Colaroosek. There was a reason why the open ocean was for the most part avoided by hungry mersons and their manyarm friends. In addition to supplying food, the reefs of home also provided positions of strength from which to fight and defend. With rock and coral at their backs, both mersons and manyarms could defend themselves efficiently. Out in the liquid space of empty sea, others had the advantage. Others who were more maneuverable, swifter, and in many ways more deadly.

There must have been a hundred sharks, an alarmed Chachel saw. Mostly lightning-swift blues and makos, a couple of errant hammerheads along for the ride, and at the head of the mob—two great whites, possibly three. Not good odds, not good at all. As the clan bunched together, forming a school of mersons, the smaller of the great whites advanced toward them. The lazy side-to-side flicks of the immensely powerful tail hardly seemed to require an effort. At full thrust, Chachel knew, that tail could hurl its owner forward with enough force for the head to shatter rock.

For the moment the smaller of the two male whites seemed content just to swim a tight circle, flashing its frozen, bone-chilling grin. Spear at the ready, Jeralach swam out from the rest of the clan to confront it. Along with the rest of his friends and family and clan members, Chachel strained to hear what merson and shark would say to one another. Had he taken a moment to look behind him, he would have noted that every one of the thousands of fish that had previously been calmly circling the seamount had fled; vanished into the distance, into the depths, or into any and every available crevice in the rock. In the space of a moment, the seamount known as Splitrock had been transformed into an eerie, abandoned, underwater desert.

"Greetments, merson." The voice of the great white rumbled up from deep within as it cruised methodically back and forth, back and forth, in front of Jeralach.

"Good day to you and your fellow scavengers." Keeping a wary eye on the great white, Jeralach held his spear loosely in both hands—but not so loose that the point wavered in the current. "Out hunting for a change?"

"Indeed." If the massive shark noticed the merson's sarcasm, it took no offense. "A tiring and often futile proposition. This morning we are feeling lazy." The tip of his snout rose slightly. "We could not miss the smell of so much blood."

"True, some blood has been spilled." The leader of the hunters could hardly deny it. Not with his companions clustered around a dozen haulsacks full of fish both alive and dead.

"Indeed," observed the great white. "I see you have had good hunting. Myself, I am always admiring how you mersons, having such ridiculous poor teeth of your own, fashion killing substitutes from shell and stone, coral and bone."

"We make do with what we have." Jeralach gestured meaningfully with his spear. "It's true that our teeth are few. But they are sharp, and their reach is long."

"Long and efficient," the great white admitted. "As are the nets you make. I see that yours are full. Being so successful in your hunting, it would be polite of you to share with those who have had less luck and are also hungry."

A tense Jeralach studied the slowly swimming line of sharks. Led by a pair of makos, twenty or so blues were drifting off to the right, another dozen to the left, while the central body of the unusual school was working its way up or down. Not all nets were made of woven material, he mused worriedly. And the numbers were undeniably bad.

"We would be happy to share with our friends the sharptooths. There is enough for all. Freely will we split our catch with you."

The great white considered, flashing an occasional glance back toward the mob where his brother and the single female, larger as usual than either of the males, waited. Beneath him, his claspers twitched.

"We are very hungry."

"Sharks are always hungry," Jeralach countered with a combination of truth and a desperate attempt at humor. "Don't worry. There is plenty here to eat."

"That is truth," the great white agreed. "And we are ready to share in feeding. I think we should begin now—with you!"

Chachel thought he was prepared for what happened next. But he had never seen a great white attack—only inshelf gray reefs, blacktips, whitetips, and other much smaller sharks. The huge, perfectly hydrodynamic shape exploded through the water, heading straight for Jeralach. How the organizer of the hunting expedition managed to sideswim the attack while simultaneously stabbing with his spear Chachel did not know. The sharpened bone pierced the left flank of the great white. The merson had spilled first blood— but critically, had missed the gills.

Within seconds the area to the immediate west of Splitrock was boiling with activity. Closing ranks to form a schooling sphere, all weapons pointed outward, the hunting party faced their attackers. Haulsacks full of fish that had been the object of so much effort and coordination were abandoned. They were promptly shredded by the eager squadrons of blue sharks who tore through tough netting and dead fish with equal alacrity. The remaining members of the mob turned their attention to prey that was both larger and still alive.

Occasionally a shark would try a perceived weak spot in the hovering ball of mersons, only to be met by a spear thrust that would send it reeling backward, frustrated and bloodied. Hemmed in by adults on all sides, a frightened Chachel wielded his own hunting spear with all the skill and determination he could muster. Considered the strongest member of his peer group, he intended despite his fear to give a good account of himself.

His chance came when two blues charged straight at his side of the schooling formation. The adults on either side of him jabbed out immediately, instinctively. Remembering the teachings of his weapons master caused Chachel to hold back. The first two spear thrusts should be sufficient to dissuade the blues and—sure enough, coming up like lightning from below were a pair of ferocious makos. One of the adults beneath him and facing downward warded off the first shark, but the second slipped past. Even as he heard one of his parents' friends scream as the mako's jaws closed, Chachel was stabbing frantically downward. He was rewarded with the sight of the mortally wounded mako slinking off, the silver-blue streamlined body spasming violently as it fought to dislodge the spear that had pierced it completely through at the gills. Instantly surrounding their condemned comrade, a quartet of blues proceeded to tear him to pieces while he was still alive.

Though it raged for what seemed like days, the actual clash lasted less than an hour. Pierced by spears, one shark after another retreated with wounds some of which were survivable and others not. Meanwhile Chachel's hunting companions, adult and youth alike, suffered a steady and horrific attrition. Despite the constant current, there was so much blood in the water that it became more and more difficult to pick the fast-moving foe out of the increasingly red-stained gloom. Bits and pieces of torn flesh, still intact body parts, eviscerated organs, bone fragments that caught the overhead mirrorshine like flung handfuls of mother-of-pearl, all spun and spiraled and tumbled through the agitated water around him. Those bits that fell or were carried by the current out beyond spear-stabbing range were instantly snatched up by the ravenous horde of eager sharptooths.

What had begun as a relatively straightforward confrontation over food had rapidly evolved into a give no quarter and ask none battle to the death. By now subsumed in frenzy, the sharks would not retreat until all were sated or the last of them were dead. The increasingly desperate mersons were given no such choice. To the credit of his training as a fighter, Chachel did not vomit once, until he saw Aunt Selemoel come drifting past him. Spinning slowly in the current, tumbling end over end, the upper half of her body was like some grotesque sculpture of a memory of a merson and not a representation of the actual individual herself. The lower half of her body was nowhere to be seen. Entrails trailing behind the severed torso like a jellyfish's tendrils, the vacant-eyed half-body of his aunt was soon set upon and ripped apart by half a dozen blues. Gasping to clear his gills, Chachel found relief only when the lump of ragged flesh that had been his relative was no longer recognizable as the nightmare it had become.

Then he heard someone, perhaps it was his father Horaleth, shout, "Beware—the Bite comes!" Chachel knew he should have turned his back to the open sea. But he could only stare outward.

Facing the still-intact remnants of the spherical defensive formation of mersons and manyarms, the female great white, as big as a small whale and weighing as much as thirty mersons, had opened her mouth. Rolling her eyes back to black, what she spat was half shark and half magic. Inside the front of that gaping maw, as dark as the caves that riddled the reefs of Chachel's home, were multiple rows of teeth in various stages of maturity. Triangular in shape, serrated on two sides, precise of point, and sharp as any knife blade, some were large enough to cover his open palm. In response to the thaumaturgic urging of the shark sorceress, two hundred such porcelain daggers now shot from her jaws.

They shredded the merson globe.

Those teeth that did not find flesh flashed by in ivory arcs of varying efficiency and degree as they sought to slash vein and bone, artery and nerves. Trying to avoid them was worse than being caught up in a school of a thousand territorial triggerfish all biting and snapping at once. A tooth as long as his thumb sliced across the top of Chachel's left bicep, leaving a trail of blood to mark its passage. Despite his training, despite his resolve, he screamed. All around him, the defensive orb of mersons and spears was disintegrating, coming apart under the assault of hundreds of individually motivated triangular white razors. In shock from his injury, he saw one merson couple leave the school and make a break for the potential shelter of Splitrock. Should he follow, or should he stay and fight?

His mother made the decision for him. He choked when he saw that she was bleeding from half a dozen wounds of her own. But she was gesturing forcefully, indicating that he should try to swim for the safety of the rocky spires. He nodded his understanding and turned to kick hard in the designated direction.

Looking to him and not behind or beneath her, she did not see the approaching male white death. How something so massive and powerful could come right up to one in complete silence was one of the deadlier mysteries of the sea. Her lower limbs disappeared into its wide-open mouth. The great jaws did not close until they were halfway up her thighs. Then they snapped shut, and in one bite the shark neatly bit off both legs halfway to her hips.

Rendered as immobile by the sight as if the blood in his veins had suddenly ceased flowing, a paralyzed Chachel could only stare. So transfixed was he that he did not even feel the pain of individual white teeth slashing at his own undefended limbs and torso. His non-reaction was all that saved him. Perceiving him as unfeeling and therefore probably dead, the cursed triangular teeth sped elsewhere in search of more responsive targets.

Once the jaws of the great white locked tight, everything thereafter seemed to take place in slow motion. So massive was the trauma that shock kept his mother from screaming. Turning her gaze away from her offspring, she looked down at herself as the shark pulled away. Dark red liquid ribboned outward in all directions from the stumps of her legs. She stayed conscious for a surprisingly long time, until the reduced blood supply to her brain brought with it blissful unconsciousness. By then her drifting form had been swallowed up in an eddying boil of blood, entrails, fins, limbs, bone, and cartilage that mercifully shielded Chachel from the sight of last bites.

Something came down firmly on his shoulder. It snapped him out of his shock. Whirling, he brought his remaining spear up and around, halting the thrust in time to see that it was Glint, the youngest of the cuttlefish who had joined the hunting party. Behind him hovered Germael. A senior seeker, not as skilled as Jeralach but wise in the ways of hunting—and also of combat. Employing arms and tentacles in equal measure, merson and manyarm proceeded to half urge, half drag the wounded apprentice toward the dark towers of Splitrock.

All told, out of the entire hunting party seven of them made it to the wide fissure that split the stone spires. Three injured hunters, three traumatized apprentices, and the surviving juvenile cuttlefish who had helped to save Chachel. Under Germael's direction they hunkered down inside a cave at the base of the gap. Each of the mersons had managed to hold onto at least one spear; a couple still had both of theirs. They also retained their killing knives, and the cephalopod had his sharp beak.

"Not much to fight with." Tired and shaken, the senior hunter muttered disconsolately to himself as he took stock of the survivors' meager arsenal. The dearth of weaponry was hardly surprising. The hunting party had left Sandrift outfitted for foraging, not war. "It will have to do."

"What now?" The surviving female apprentice's name was Lillanech. She was trembling so badly that she could barely hold onto her spear.

"We wait." Germael's expression was grim as he turned to peer cautiously out of the cave mouth toward the canyon that separated the twin summits. "The mob may have enough to ea … may become sated. If not, we will have to fight again." Reaching up, he tapped the solid stone ceiling of the cave. "At least here we have something at our backs. A few spear points cannot defend the six directions at once, but here we need only guard this entrance. A big shark would have trouble getting in. Two or even three blues might manage entry in tandem, but that I think we have a chance of fending off."

"What if they're neither sated nor ready to challenge?" wondered one of the surviving hunters. That he had lost several fingers to a bite had not kept him from fighting his way to the cave.

Germael considered. "We'll wait them out. As far as food, we'll manage somehow. There are always shellfish affixed to the rocks."

All the rest of that awful day they huddled in the cave, but no sleek-finned shapes came to inspect the entrance. Night-time was the worst. The few bioluminescent lifeforms that visited the cave mouth emitted only enough illumination to light their own way. All of the expedition's tame tethered glowfish had been lost along with the rest of their supplies. Glint helped as much as he was able, but he could not illuminate more than a small portion of any one of them, or of their surroundings. In contrast to their ocular helplessness, Chachel knew that sharks could easily find a fish or a merson in complete darkness by utilizing the special sensory organs that lined their snouts. Mersons possessed no such extraordinary extra sense. In the blackness inside the cave they were blind. Sitting slightly off by himself, Chachel clung tightly to his spear and sorrowed silently for his dead parents.

On the positive side, while they could perceive things in the dark, sharks could not make weapons, he reminded himself. Magic, yes. Especially biting magic. That they could conjure. But not weapons.

Morning brought with it no sign of their attackers. Venturing partway out into the chasm, Germael scanned the open water to left, right, and overhead before reporting back to his fellow survivors. Swifter than any merson, brave young Glint extended the reconnoiter by jetting as far as the crest of the nearest summit.

"I see not one sharptooth," he reported back. "Not even a local patch reef claiming whitetip. The schools of fish we found when we first arrived have returned. They would not do so if sharks were still hunting here."

"But they might," pointed out one of the other hunters, "if there were sharptooths about who were just sleeping."

"Sleeping is almost as good as absent," Germael argued. "Especially," he added with obvious reluctance and an eye toward the trio of apprentices, "if they are doing so on full stomachs. If they are still in the vicinity but sleeping off a heavy feed, it would behoove us to depart before either their alertness or their appetite returns."

"I don't know." The hunter who had lost fingers was disinclined to agree. "It's dangerous."

"Staying *here* is dangerous," Germael shot back. "Going is dangerous. Everything uncertain and unknown is dangerous. This I know." His gaze flicked over everyone clustered in the cave. "I also know that starvation is a worse way to die than by fighting."

With his spear he gestured at the clear, mirrorlight water outside. "This may be our best chance to make a swim for it. This may be our *only* chance."

They emerged from the cave one by one; the hunters leading the way with the apprentices following. In spite of the danger, it felt good, Chachel decided, to be out in open water again. Caves were fine for sleeping, but in the mirrorlight a merson needed to be able to move about in a space that more than exceeded his own body length.

Led by Germael, they swam slowly to the northeast. Another hunter swam patrol slightly above the rest, watching the sky. Within the gorge they were open to attack from only three directions. Back out in open ocean, they would once more have to be alert to all six.

A single pair of eyes to keep watch in each direction, Chachel realized as he kicked steadily and slowly. At least they would not be taken by surprise.

They had not anticipated an ambush in waiting.

Whether the dozen or so blues had missed out on their fair share of the bloody feast of the previous day or were simply exercising the gluttony for which their kind was known did not matter. Rocketing out of the dark depths that had concealed them, they hit the little party of survivors simultaneously and from the same direction. The hunters were as ready as could be; the youngsters less so. As Glint shot a relatively futile burst of ink at a charging shark, Chachel had the satisfaction of seeing his spear go right down the throat of an over-eager blue attacker.

"Choke on this, gnawer of bones! Filth with fins!" Wrenching the shaft free, he slammed it forward again. Blood gushed from the shark's mouth as it struggled to free itself from the impalement. All around him, Chachel's friends and mentors were stabbing, thrusting, and kicking. The surprise had not been complete. One shark after another found itself impaled on a spear point. Wielding his filleting knife, the hunter who had been swimming above the others plunged downward to nearly cut one blue's head half off with a single powerful stroke.

Chachel felt something chewing on his right leg.

He hadn't seen the mako approach. There were three of them. Swiftest of all the sharptooths, they moved through the water so fast they made even the blues look as if they were standing still. The mako fastened to his leg was a big one. Viciously slinging its head and upper body from side to side, it tore most of Chachel's right calf muscle right off the bone. Left bleeding badly and unable to maneuver at speed, he still managed to fend off its bite at his face by ducking beneath the jaws and stabbing upward with his spear. He could feel himself weakening as he fought to remain conscious.

Then the mako came back and almost gently took the left side of his head in its mouth....

## – V –

As he finished the story, the last bits of crab shell fell from Glint's parrot-like beak. They spun and tumbled like baroque pearls toward the bottom of the chamber. Tracking their descent, Irina noticed that the floor was layered with a dull whitish deposit of hollowed out crab and lobster shells several feet thick.

"Now you know how Chachel lost the lower half of his right leg." His body pulsing with tints of black and gold, Glint faced the new merson. "It was Germael who killed the mako before it could kill him. But as it wrenched backward in its death throes, one of the sharptooth's teeth took Chachel's left eye." Tentacles splayed wide, the cephalopodan equivalent of a shrug. "The villagers think him mad, but I know that he sees more with one eye than the rest of them do with two. Except for Oxothyr, of course. But then the shaman looks at things with other than mere eyes."

Irina's gaze rose toward the tunnel that was both the way in and out of the mage's residence. "And he's been bitter ever since," she whispered.

"Bitter—yes." Lateral fins rippling, Glint came close. This time she did not flinch away from him. "Bitter and angry. He feels the senior hunters should have prepared better for such an eventuality. Especially Jeralach, whose idea the expedition was. He blames them for the deaths of his mother and father—insofar as one can blame the dead. It has been many years." The cuttlefish's cylindrical body bloated momentarily in a heavy sigh. "Chachel should be mated by now, with offspring of his own to chide."

"But the women—the female mersons—won't go near him?"

"Not so." One gold-flecked eye focused on her two. "He is the strongest hunter in the village, the best provider, and probably smarter than the other males as well. It is he who refuses to go near them. He will not even donate seed. He dwells outside the village proper and has as little contact with it and its inhabitants as possible. He lives in a cave. Not a proper merson home of carefully primed and groomed coral, but an actual cave. Myself, I think it reminds him of the cave at Splitrock. Of the last times he felt safe. Sometimes I keep company with him there outside of a hunt. But then, I am mad, remember." Ten tentacles fluttered in mock-threat at her face.

A beaked cuttlefish could no more smile than could a clam, but she swore she sensed the expression even if she could not see it.

A massive, rhythmically writhing shape emerged from the dark cavity that scarred the far side of the chamber. This time she was not afraid. She had come to realize that Oxothyr's bulk was exceeded only by his intelligence and compassion. The shaman's body sac was a reassuring sunny yellow in a place where the sun itself was known only as a burning blot that hung high above the mirrorsky. Kindly cephalopodan eyes danced from newly-made merson to cuttlefish and back again.

"You two have been talking."

"Not exactly." Irina smiled. By now she was used to the salt water that passed unhindered between her lips when she spoke; a saline stroke of her mouth and tongue she felt she had been missing all her life. "Glint has been talking. I've been listening."

The mage squirted a few bubbles from his siphon. "Our friend has short arms and a big mouth. I hope he did not bore you."

"On the contrary." Involuntarily, she looked back to the tunnel where Chachel had disappeared. "This is all new to me, and I'm learning a lot. That's how I mastered my own profession: by watching and listening."

"You would make a good famulus, I think." Behind him, Tythe and Sathi immediately turned an angry blue-black. "But I am already rewarded in that department." The mantle coloration of the squid pair faded to a more contented green with red splotches. "We will have to find something else for you to do."

"What I want to do," she responded tiredly, "is go home."

"Of course you do. We all want to go home." The shaman's tone was consciously soothing. "But until that can be managed, if it can be managed, we must find something for you to do and a place for you to dwell." Uncoiling like an awakening snake, one tapering tentacle gestured behind him. "You cannot stay here. Much as I might enjoy such unusual company as yours, I have much to do. Events are in motion that make no sense, and are discernible only through the contrary consequences they propound. Trying to understand what is happening so far from here demands my full attention. I cannot allow myself to be distracted by the fascinating conundrum your presence poses."

Feeling herself flattered and dismissed in the same breath, Irina barely protested. "I wouldn't be a distraction."

The octopus flashed hot pink. "Your saying that you would not be a distraction is itself a distraction." Two arms gestured commandingly at Glint. "Our unfortunate visitor will, I think, be happier in the company of a female merson."

The cuttlefish gestured his understanding. "I know one who might fill the need, and who is bold enough to be both willing and sympathetic."

Oxothyr's body bobbed approvingly. "Then present our guest to her, with my appeal, and explain that I will contribute to the upkeep."

With that the shaman whirled and disappeared back into his inner sanctum, a mass of arms trailed by his pair of beaming assistants.

Sandrift was not large, nor a tenth as impressive as a far southern city like Coreleatha, but it was strange and new and wonderful enough to take Irina's breath away. When the reflexive response caused her gill flaps to flare, it was a mark of her speedy adaptation to her new marine physicality that she did not even react to the fluttering of the skin slits on either side of her neck.

Sandrift's residences and commercial structures gazed out at one another across a broad and comparatively steep river of sand that started high up in the shallows and flowed downward to depth. Seeing it put Irina in mind of a dry, granular, yellow-white glacier. Except that unlike the tongue of a glacier, the sand river was in constant, if slow motion. A trickle would start and build to a tumble, a tumble to a spill, a spill to a rush that might last for seconds or minutes. Somewhere high above, she knew, there must be an enormous river that constantly deposited fresh material into the sand-filled canyon. Did anyone or anything live on the land here? What of the demons that had originally been spoken of? How deep was the connection of this world to her own?

She could not worry about that now. Glint was about to ask someone to provisionally take her in, and she needed to concentrate on making a good impression. Reaching up, she started to fiddle with her hair. If nothing else, the pointless activity turned out to be good for a quiet laugh. She had no comb, no gel, no spray, and it would not have mattered if she did. Here, underwater, her blonde tresses hovered around her head in an undisciplined aura, like so much golden seaweed. In this alien underwater realm, or for that matter in any underwater realm, terrestrial makeup was about as useful as a television.

She soon saw that the practice of personal adornment was not entirely absent from merson culture, however. Stylish jewelry was present in plenty. Bracelets, rings, necklaces, earrings—all were visible in abundance on the females she encountered as well as on many of the males. Some of the women wore strings of naturally radiant salps around their necks, blue and red being the most common biolumi-nescence hues. Others sported bracelets of complaisant comb jellies that flashed bands of rippling iridescence. One mature female had so many fastened around one ankle that as she swam she appeared to be dragging a strand of pulsating neon lights behind her. Each of the town's residents also carried one or two small woven or shell bags slung crosswise over their shoulders.

Some of Sandrift's manyarm inhabitants also sported individual ornamentation. In the case of several perambulating squid, their ability to change the color and patterns of their bodies combined with clusters of luminescent ctenophores attached to their mantles to produce blazes of tentacular glory that gave them the appearance of drifting pieces of an exploded casino.

Individual homes and businesses sported larger, if generally less elaborate decoration. While Oxothyr's enchantment had gifted Irina with the ability to breathe underwater, it had not enabled her to read the sweeping script she saw chiseled into tidy coralline walls, spelled out by transplanted anemones, or written in enchanted cephalopodan inks. Beyond their chromatic expressionist facade, signs that fluttered with the canyon current meant nothing to her. As she marveled at it all, Glint was happy to translate.

Both banks of the underwater sand river were lined with busy establishments selling everything from tools whose function Irina occasionally recognized, to distinctive foodstuffs she did not, to inventory whose purpose she found utterly unfamiliar. While the entrances to some shops were of normal size, shape, and location, others had their doorways in the roof. Nearly every window boasted a screen of fabric woven tightly enough to keep out all but the smallest intruders. Where human habitations suffered from infestations of insects and rodents, here problems consisted of tiny nibbling fish and curious crustaceans.

The dwelling Glint headed for was set on one of several parallel coral ridges that extended outward from the main reef into deeper water like so many questing rocky fingers. The entrance was located on the side of the structure. As for the residence itself, like its owner it was neither the smallest nor the most impressive they had encountered.

Poylee was truly beautiful. A lustrous blue-black, her hair was even longer than Irina's. Her eyes glistened green as peridots, her cheekbones were high and prominent, and her mouth inviting. Her skin was slightly darker than that of the average merson, though not exceptionally so. The outer edge of each of her eight gill slits had been pierced and sported individual loops of polished paua shell. Flashy paua also decorated the customary small bag she carried over one shoulder.

Irina realized immediately that merson and manyarm knew each other. When Glint extended his two longer hunting tentacles toward the female, she unhesitatingly reached out to entwine them with her fingers.

"Good day, tickle-tips." Her gaze shifted immediately to the drifting Irina. "Who's this odd-looking friend of yours? Hello—my name is Poylee. How do you make your hair the color of mirrorsky light?"

Irina stiffened slightly at what back home might have been construed as a veiled insult, and just as quickly realized the ridiculousness of her reaction. "I don't make it with anything. It's my natural color."

"Really-truly?" One short, sharp scissor kick of her webbed feet brought the woman practically into Irina's face. Openly fascinated, she examined the visitor's floating tresses. "I've never seen such a color on a merson's head."

"She's not a merson." Glint moved to join them. "Her name is Irina, and she is a morphed demon."

"For the last time," an exasperated Irina began, "I am not a ..."

Having backed off as quickly as she had approached, the intrepid Poylee cocked her head to one side as she studied the visitor. "Truly-really? A changeling?"

Having no neck, Glint could not nod. Instead, the cuttlefish bobbed expressively. "Oxothyr adjusted her. We think she used to breathe void."

"Astonishing-so?" Poylee continued to examine the new arrival closely. Feeling more and more like a laboratory exhibit, Irina finned backward, restoring the distance between them.

"Astonishing-true," Glint confirmed. "Oxothyr avows that she cannot stay with him, as he is presently absorbed in investigations of great importance, so he was wondering if perhaps ..."

"Why of course-sure!" Darting forward so quickly that this time Irina had no chance to dodge, the young merson wrapped both arms around her, spun the both of them thrice around in the water, and finally backed off. Her guest was left to stop the spinning on her own. "You *must* stay with me! How could anyone even *think* of you boarding with that squishy sac of soggy somberness Oxothyr! You can tell me all about the demon world ..."

"I am not a ...!" Irina tried to interpose, with no success.

"... and I will show you the craftshop where I work. The best quality adoration for the least amount of currentcy, and because I work there we can outfit you cheaply."

"'Currentcy'?" Turning away from her mildly overwhelming host, Irina eyed the studious Glint. The cuttlefish was presently beige with blue spots. Ever since the existence of 'shops' had been mentioned she had been wondering what the locals used for a medium of exchange. Some kind of pretty shells, no doubt. Perhaps cowries, like many ancient Amerindian tribes. "What is currentcy?"

"I don't have any of it," Glint told her. "Manyarms have little use for the artificialities of which mersons are so fond." Ascending slightly in the water, he shifted to face Poylee. "Can you show her?"

Swinging her shoulder bag around in front of her, the effervescent merson reached inside. "I don't have much with me." Pulling out a closed hand, she opened it toward Irina and flashed a fistful of pebbles. The recently morphed void-breathing demon caught her breath.

Some of the pebbles had been given a light polish but the rest were otherwise untreated. Either she was looking at a handful of sea-tumbled glass, or else Poylee was flaunting a handful of the biggest, brightest alluvial diamonds, rubies, sapphires, and other gemstones Irina had ever seen. It was an infinitesimal sampling of the riches of Oshenerth, utilized for a common everyday medium of exchange. Her mind whirled. If she got home ("when" she got home, she corrected herself hastily), she would have to try her utmost to make sure she did so with a pocketful of the local currentcy. First, of course, she would need a pocket. Or the local equivalent.

She gestured at Poylee's purse, or carrybag, or whatever it was called here. "Can I get one of those?"

"This?" Poylee's bag happened to be made of shell. "Nothing easier-simple. I will take you tomorrow. Only the best for a guest."

"You're all right with me staying with you?" Irina pressed. "You're sure it's okay? I don't want to be a burden on anyone."

"No, no!" The female merson's genuineness was exceeded only by her unreserved vivacity. "I insist-demand. I will show you off to all my friends." Finning forward, she put a comforting arm around Irina's bare shoulders. Her fingers felt of the material of the visitor's swimsuit. "What is this strange garment you wear that is so unlike ours in form and manufacture?"

Irina tried to formulate a reply that would make sense in light of the observation that mersons wore only the briefest of fabric strips to conceal their modesty. "It's called a one-piece. You wear it beneath your diveskin to …"

Pursing her lips, Poylee gestured down at herself. "I know what a dive is, and what skin is, but what is a 'diveskin'?"

This was going to take some time, Irina realized. But before she could continue, the effusive Poylee was already bombarding the patient Glint with additional questions, the last of them being, "How—where did Oxothyr come to seek-find such a charming creature?"

Though a fine fellow and boon companion, Glint was not without his faults, one of which was a sometimes disconcerting tendency to speak before thinking. "Oxothyr didn't find her. Chachel and I were out hunting when we saved her."

The change in their hostess's posture and expression was simultaneous and inescapable. Her voice fell and the smile that since their arrival had been as constant as the water temperature faded.

"'Saved her'? You and Chachel?"

Glint repeated the bobbing affirmation. "She was lost, drifting, confused. We didn't know what she was, except that she was plainly in trouble. We took her to Oxothyr, who performed on her a revision most profound. One that was necessary to ensure her survival. Now she is our guest until the shaman decides how further we can assist her. It's very good of you to help out, Poylee."

"Yes-sure." The small fins on the back of the merson's calves fluttered in a perpendicular parody of those that extended sideways from the cuttlefish's lateral line. "It is, isn't it?"

"Well then, I'll leave you two egg-makers to get better acquainted."

Glint did not turn to leave. He did not have to. All he had to do was stiffen his ventral siphon and shoot backwards out the open doorway, leaving in his wake rapidly dissipating eddies, a tiny arc of ink like an orphaned comma, and a gathering silence.

Her hostess's sudden hard stare making her increasingly uncomfortable, Irina turned away and pretended to admire the decorated dwelling. Shells intact and halved were everywhere, some crushed together with rock and water-smoothed crystal to form images of undersea vistas and lifeforms. There were shelves but no chairs. A single piece of scavenged, powder blue shelf coral still attached to its base served as a foot-high table. Storage cabinets had been fashioned of slabs of coral and rock held together by glue of an unknown nature. Restrained by netting, two groups of bioluminescent fish were affixed to the ceiling, their internal lights inactive while the dormant swimmers awaited the onset of night.

Irina did her best to ignore the distance that inexplicably seemed to have sprung up between them as Poylee took her on a cursory, almost brusque tour of the rest of the dwelling. There was a small food preparation area that in the absence of any appliances or cooking facilities could hardly be called a kitchen, a sleeping chamber, another boasting an ingenious integrated system for performing ablutions and related activities, and a smaller room that she was informed would be hers for the duration of her stay. Throughout it all Irina had marveled at the number and variety of adaptations to a permanent life underwater, all of which Poylee considered ordinary or boring.

*Truly*, the newly preoccupied merson thought, *the changeling knows nothing about the most basic aspects of daily life*. Perhaps she was after all no threat. While Poylee did not let her guard down and her initial effusiveness did not return, her attitude slowly shifted from one of active dismissal bordering on open hostility to a cool, collected courtesy. The hunter Chachel had been known to accomplish many things by simply adopting a position of studied indifference. Surely she could do the same.

They were in the food preparation area later when Irina, desirous of proving herself a worthy guest (and also because it was the right thing to do), offered to help in making dinner.

"Just watch-attend," Poylee told her. "Maybe you'll learn something."

Irina bristled. Back home she considered herself something of an amateur chef. But she was a guest here, in a place and time where her very survival depended on the good will of those around her. So she stayed quiet and watched.

In truth, she would have been hard-pressed to concoct anything edible given the tools and victuals available. Her hostess's tone notwithstanding, Poylee's easy skill with knives and skewers was instructive to behold. In less than an hour several dishes arrayed in the half-shells of giant oysters had been set out on the low coral table. Irina identified different oceanic plants prepared several ways along with chunks of treated meat that varied in color from white to gray. Utensils consisted of knives made from sharpened shell with handles of decorated bone, and skewers that were miniature versions of the bone weapons carried and used by hunters. A rack of tightly stoppered, calcareous tube-worm casings held liquid spices. Salt was not offered and, needless to say, unnecessary.

Sampling everything and finding that it varied from good to outright tasty, Irina did her best to lighten the mood as she and her hostess ate.

"Everything here is delicious, Poylee. I don't know how to thank you for your hospitality."

"Then don't." Almost angrily, her hostess stuck one end of a thin, sharpened bone in her mouth and used her lips to strip off the succulent mollusks it skewered.

The ensuing time on both sides of the table passed in uncomfortable silence before a determined Irina spoke up more forcefully. As she talked, hundreds of tiny bits of organic life drifted like flecks of powdered pearls through the light from the screened overhead opening.

"Look, you seemed fine with this arrangement when I got here. Then, all of a sudden and without any explanation you turned into a cold (she almost said fish) character. What happened? Did I do something? Did I say something?" Her heightened anxiety produced an odd itching sensation in her neck. It took her a moment to realize it was due to her gill flaps fluttering more rapidly in response to the need to draw in additional oxygen.

Poylee looked up suddenly, her gaze drawing even with that of her guest. "What did you think-consider of Chachel? The merson who saved you?"

*So that was it*, Irina realized with a start. Apparently not everything in this underwater realm was so radically different from conditions in her own world. She replied honestly.

"I thought he was brave, skillful, rude, and gruff."

Her evaluation seemed to lighten the mood again, though Poylee continued to remain more guarded than she had been when Glint and Irina had first arrived. "So—you didn't like him, then?"

"I owe him for helping me, but on a personal level I found him unpleasant and impolite. As far as convivial company goes, I'd rather spend time with Glint."

Poylee smiled. It was not the open, unfettered, bubbly expression that had first greeted Irina, but it was a vast improvement over what had just preceded it.

"Don't be too hard-heavy on him." Stretching herself out horizontal to the plate coral table and floating just above the floor, Poylee casually plucked something small and whitish from within a covered shell dish, popped the squirming tidbit in her mouth, and swallowed. Irina flinched. "He has a good heart, but he has had a difficult-troubled life."

"I don't care. He didn't have to be so rude. I didn't do anything to him." *And I never will*, she added quietly to herself.

Poylee was by now completely relaxed. Was her transparent interest in the one-eyed hunter typical of relationships here, Irina found herself wondering? There had not been a flicker of subtlety in the other woman's reaction. Not that it mattered. The idea that she, Irina, might have something to offer the merson who had saved her life anything other than a sincere thank-you was absurd.

Time passed swiftly with Poylee showing her guest through the remainder of her habitation as well as bringing out for inspection some smaller, more personal items of interest. Irina looked and listened and committed everything to memory until awareness began to fade. Her mounting fatigue was hardly a surprise, she told herself. It had been a day she could not have imagined even from one of her favorite books. Did they have books here, underwater? Paper and electronics were both apparent impossibilities. Though given the kind of conjuring ability demonstrated by Oxothyr, she supposed that through magic, anything might be possible. One thing she did know for certain. She would not need anything magical to help her sleep.

Following a dinner more elaborate and even tastier than the quick lunch Poylee had prepared earlier, her hostess showed her to the small spare room that was maintained for guests. It offered shelves Irina would not use and screened openings cut in the coral wall to hold the belongings she did not have. She would keep her dive knife and the few other small items she retained from her now superfluous scuba ensemble close at hand while she slept.

Her bed—the bed turned out to consist of dozens of healthy sponges. Maroon, purple, yellow, and numerous bright shades in between had been transplanted to the floor of the guest room and coaxed into existing there side by side. Sometimes round, often irregular in shape, they had been kept trimmed back so that all were precisely the same height.

"Good night-sleep, Irina." Standing in the doorway, Poylee offered a last smile that while not openly affectionate was at least tolerant. "Don't let the sea lice bite." Having delivered herself of that mildly ominous caution, she kicked once and disappeared down the hallway to the right.

Turning in the water, Irina contemplated her bed. Firmly affixed to the floor and walled off from all but the gentle flow-through current that kept the household clean, the riot of colorful living sponges beckoned. Sea lice, she knew, were tiny and dull colored. Even if present they were unlikely to bother her, though if disturbed they were as capable of any crab of delivering an irritating pinch. They were fond of concealing themselves in coral, on sea fans, and in sponges. Did some actually dwell in the bed?

By now she was too tired to care. Slipping out of her green swimsuit and hanging it from a projecting knob of branch coral, she kicked a couple of times until she was drifting above and parallel to the bed. Facing upward and letting herself turn horizontal to the floor, she sank downward until contact was made. While exceptionally welcoming, the tops of the sponges were also surprisingly stiff. Support *and* comfort, she thought sleepily. Such a sleeping platform wouldn't work back home, where her out-of-water weight would compress the delicate sponges as if they were made of wet cardboard. She found that she had no trouble remaining in one place on the bed. The flow-through house current was not strong enough to move her; only to occasionally rock her gently.

She had almost literally drifted off to sleep when a pair of strange new sounds caused her eyes to flutter open. Steady and recurring, the first originated not far from her room. Bubbles, she decided, as she recognized the submarine equivalent of a familiar problem. Her hostess was snoring in her sleep.

The other sound continued to rise progressively in intensity before achieving a specific volume and finally leveling off. It was the underwater equivalent of dozens of unseen crickets chirping in a creek bed on a summer night, or a kitchen full of fast-food fryers all crackling and bubbling away at the same time. In actuality, the clamor arose from millions of tiny shrimp and other miniscule crustaceans emerging from their hiding places within the reef to feed by the light of the unseen moon that smeared the mirrorsky with silver.

Between remembrances of her hostess's cheerful chatter and the continuous chitinous fizz that now filled the sea, her own thoughts and concerns fell by the wayside. Lying atop the bed of yielding sponges, lightly nudged by the current, she soon fell into what turned out to be the deepest, soundest sleep of her life....

◊

The water in the wide-mouthed cave that looked out over a lower ridge of reef was foul with blood and guts, drifting pieces of flesh, and indifferently cast-aside offal. The gory leftovers were sufficiently revolting to make Glint hesitate before finally entering. Not having a nose, he could not put a tentacle over one, and was reduced to perceiving the stink through his arms.

"Do you *want* to draw a frenzy?" he sputtered as he jetted into the opening, waving his ten arms to disperse the chum in front of him. "While you're out here beyond reach of help from the community?"

"I am not beyond help." Sitting on a flat, slanted rock that had been scraped clean of mollusks and other sedentary sea life, Chachel's knife flashed and sliced as he continued to fillet the carcass of the blacktip. "*You're* here."

Pivoting in the water, Glint looked back the way he had come. Unlike the majority of dwellings in Sandrift proper, the entrance to Chachel's cave was open and un-netted. There was nothing to protect against or even slow an attack from outside. Resident whitetips caused the cuttlefish no concern, but if all the diffusing blood, fish oil, and other bodily fluids should draw in a few big, hungry tiger sharks....

Observing that the cuttlefish had turned a nervous white dotted with black, a dour Chachel hastened to assure his friend. "Relax. Do you really think I'd engage in this kind of butchery without first taking precautions?" He gestured toward the large cave opening with the hand that was not holding the filleting knife. "See any scavengers?"

Glint looked. Outside the cave, the usual chortle of reef fish muttered past, occasionally pausing to fuss over a pocket of food lodged in the coral. Anemones sighed zen-like as they sieved the gentle current. A large squat lobster emerged from a hole, caught sight of the cuttlefish peering in his direction, and hastily scrambled back into darkness. Meanwhile, the current carried a steady flow of blood, guts, and grue out into the open ocean. Yet of sharkness there was no sign.

"Precautions?" Glint made no attempt to hide his uncertainty. "What precautions?"

Halfway through the process of removing the blacktip's valuable liver, Chachel waved the knife. "I've neutered the taste of the blood flow and the odor. It's a smellsmudge I've been working on."

Moving closer, Glint idly plucked a drifting strip of intestine before the current could carry it away and popped it in his beak. "You've been practicing more spells? Besides the usual minor hunting enchantments? Are you planning to displace Oxothyr? You're a hunter, one-eye—not a shaman."

"And I'll always be a hunter." Chachel reassured his friend as he returned to the bloody work at hand. "But as you know, I have a lot of time to myself." He shrugged. "Time to spend at things like reading and studying."

"Yes, the satisfactions of ornery self-imposed isolation." Like a wandering eel, another span of tasty gut drifted by. Glint eyed the awful offal for a moment, then let it go.

"Regardless," Chachel continued, "I have more time to meditate than most. I've been learning, asking questions." He looked up from the messy labor, his one blue eye flashing. "What is it to you?" he growled.

"Oh, I don't know," the cuttlefish murmured. "Maybe I'm afraid of losing your charming company." Spreading his tentacles, he sampled the surrounding water and was able to taste the minor spell. "Amazing! This could be a valuable protection for others, especially for other hunters. You could sell it."

Chachel did not look up from his work. "Let them figure out their own defensive spells. Or make a deal with Oxothyr."

Half of Glint's arms pressed together to wave a negative gesture. "Ah, that's how to endear yourself to your fellow mersons."

"I'm not interested in endearing myself to anybody. You know that." He held out a choice piece of pink-tinged steak. "Join me for dinner?"

Twin striking tentacles shot out to grab the proffered tasty before Chachel had finished speaking.

Later, as the rippling mirrorsky outside the cave began to darken and the reef's day shift began to give way to the night dwellers, merson and manyarm took their ease together on a coral-encrusted ledge above the rim of the cave. Off in the distance, the lights of Sandrift were beginning to come to life. Some of the radiance was sourced by spells propounded by Oxothyr and others of his profession while the rest were generated by bioluminescent growths and creatures who were held in check by netting or similar restraints. It was a time for mersons to keep close to their dwellings and not wander afar. Killing machines great and swift haunted the all-embracing dark of the sea. Manyarms could make them out and sometimes flee successfully, but not the slower mersons. Better for them to stay at home.

Chachel was one of the few bold enough to venture out at night, but he was not stupid. He would do so only in Glint's company, making use of the cuttlefish's excellent night vision, and then only for a good reason. Having at present no such reason, he relaxed on the projecting spine of coral and contemplated the onset of evening. On the reef nearby, a trio of coral-noshing wrasses, resplendent in purple, cerulean, and yellow, were spinning their individual sleeping robes of mucus, designed to camouflage their appearance and hide their odor as they slept. Watching them prepare, Chachel suddenly turned to his friend and posed an unexpected question.

"The changeling. How is she faring?"

Glint's golden eyes glittered in the fading light from above. "What? Why would you care?"

"I don't." Caught out of his characteristic indifference, Chachel looked away. "We found the demon-thing. We saved it. A mild curiosity, that's all."

"I—see. Oxothyr sent her to stay with Poylee. They were getting along extremely well when I left. Poylee will look after her until the shaman decides what to do with the poor creature."

Opening his jaws wide, Chachel allowed an attentive blue- and black-striped cleaner wrasse to enter, inspect, and clean his teeth and the inside of his mouth. When he felt the hygienic procedure was complete, he tightened his lips and shooed the obliging finger-length fish away.

"Poylee will be a good hostess. If she doesn't talk the visitor to death."

Reaching into the pouch hanging at his side, he pulled out a piece of freshly prepared blacktip. None of the fish swimming back and forth in front of the coral came for it. Though he was inordinately proud of the smellsmudge he had been able to place on the food, he would never brag about it, not even to the tolerant Glint. It was not his way. In any case, he felt he had little to brag about. Biting down on the tender flesh, he tore into it ferociously and swallowed half in a single bite.

To an outsider it might have looked as if he was revenging himself on his meal.

# – VI –

hile Glint drifted nearby in that half-awake, half-asleep state characteristic of manyarms, Chachel floated in fitful slumber near the rear of the cavern encased in the thin translucent film that mersons excreted through their pores. Not unlike the mucoidal sac that was exuded by parrotfish and other reef dwellers, it concealed his body odor and distorted his shape from the perceptors of any predators that might be in the vicinity. Had she not been deep in sleep herself, Irina would have been startled to see that her hostess Poylee lay cocooned in exactly same kind of glistening, diaphanous organic cloak. When retiring for the night, all mersons intuitively and spontaneously secreted such individual protective husks. When not reingested by their originators first thing the next morning, the extra source of protein was gladly consumed by any manyarms or fish that happened to find themselves in the vicinity.

As his beak sucked away the last of the gauzy material that had been excreted by his friend, Glint swam close enough to put one of his eyes close to those of his companion.

"Don't you think we should go and check on the changeling to see how she is doing?"

Chachel did not look up from where he was cleaning algae from the killing tip of a hunting spear. "No."

The cuttlefish persisted. "Aren't you the least bit curious to see how she fared yesterday and last night?"

A sharpened shell scraped clean the spear's pointed tip. "No."

Letting out a squirt from his siphon, the irritated manyarm jetted backward. "Well, I am. You claim to be a learner, half-leg, but Oxothyr would disapprove of your lack of curiosity."

This time Chachel did look up from his work. "Oxothyr disapproves of half of everything. I won't feel singled out."

Spitting a blob of ink, the cuttlefish manipulated it into a symbol for disgust before the dark fluid could disperse. "I perceive that your day is full. You clearly have a great many important matters to attend to. Like cleaning up the last of last night's garbage." He pivoted to face the high opening of the cave. "I will report back on what I learn. Or not." With that, he headed out toward open water and the reef edge that led toward the village, signaling his departure with a salute. For a creature equipped with ten arms it is possible to simultaneously convey much more than just one rude gesture.

Letting out a sigh, a resigned Chachel carefully put his work aside, allowed his arms to fall to his sides, and kicked hard in pursuit of his friend.

It was a bright and clear morning, the light that lit the mirrorsky shining overhead in full flare. Swimming just beneath the border that separated void and ocean, a school of silvery, nearly invisible needle fish advanced forward in fits and starts, breakfasting on tiny border dwellers unable to see them through the glare. A chorus of unique blue tangs ambled past, chirping *sui generis*.

Halfway to Sandrift, merson and manyarm were enveloped in a cloud of purple anthias, their thumb-length flanks dazzling in the morning shine like thousands of ambulatory amethysts. A green turtle munching a moaning moon jelly grunted a lazy hello that the always cheerful Glint was quick to return. Sequestered in quiet contemplation, Chachel offered no comment.

On a level plain outside Sandrift that had been cleared of coral, anemones, and other slow-moving but opportunistic invaders, villagers tended to crops of sea lettuce, shellfish, and other edibles. Side currents sliding away from the canyon that gave the village its name delivered organic material from beyond the mirrorsky while those that swept along the reef occasionally brought up nutrients from the depths. The combination made the carefully groomed terrain around Sandrift uncommonly productive.

On the rare occasions when Chachel deigned to appear in or near town, the workers in the fields usually ignored him. Not this morning. Wielding scrapers and diggers made of bone and rock, a small crowd of the particularly ill-tempered began to gather around him and his cephalopodan companion, casting insults and imprecations as they swam in parallel.

A trio of males appeared in front, blocking the route. When a silent Chachel tried to swim over them, they kicked upward to intercept his approach. Fresh arrivals began to form an enclosing sphere around the commuting manyarm and stoic merson. The hunter's lips tightened and he gripped a little tighter the spear he always carried.

"You want something?" Chachel would never say by way of greeting, "What can I do for you?"

One of the men blocking the way spoke up without hesitation. "There are all kinds of fish in the sea, Chachel one-eye. Big fish, small fish. Red fish, yellow fish. Fish that bite and fish that poison. One thing we don't need around Sandrift is another selfish. Why did you bring the demon into our village?"

Stockier and more muscular than the first speaker, the man next to him brandished a triple-pointed digging probe. "We don't need void magic here, hunter. We leave you alone. Why can't you leave us alone?"

A striped cleaner wrasse began picking at Chachel's left hand and he brushed it irritably aside. Indignant, it flipped its tail at him as it departed.

"I didn't bring her into the village. That was Oxothyr's idea. If you have a complaint, take it up with him." Lowering his spear, he started forward again.

Once more the three swam to block his path. "So say you," declared the third member of the blocking trio. "Don't try to shift responsibility onto the shaman."

"He needs to be taught a lesson in responsibility," muttered the group's erstwhile leader. "A message long overdue." Kicking hard, he struck out with the butt of the shovel he was carrying.

Backing water, Chachel brought up his spear to parry the blow. As the second member of the group tried to hit at his legs, the hunter brought the butt of his spear straight down. It made solid contact with his attacker's rising skull, sending the other man sinking to the bottom clutching at his head.

Dashing into the midst of an argument that threatened to dissolve into all-out combat, a frantic Glint waved every one of his arms for attention. "This isn't Chachel's fault! The demon is a harmless changeling that was dying. We saved it, and Oxothyr made it whole."

"Witch-bringers!" Ignoring the cuttlefish's entreaties, the third attacker nearly succeeded in slipping his probe into Chachel's side. The hunter did just manage to block the thrust. The probe's points slid harmlessly past his ribs without making contact. "I have seen the creature," the farmer declared. "It has hair the color of the gold flakes that collect in the hollows of Portelek shell reef, and the eyes of a barracuda. Unless we drive it away it will bring bad luck and ill fortune to all of us!"

The first assailant lashed out at Glint and the cuttlefish dodged the blow easily. "I don't know what it was originally," he insisted, "but thanks to Oxothyr it is only a merson now. Shame on you two-arms! You should leave the poor, disoriented thing be. It is far from home and very much alone."

The second combatant kicked in the cuttlefish's direction. "We do not take advice from noisy manyarms!" Reaching into the lightly weighted pouch bobbing at his side, he took something out and threw it at Chachel.

Sparks erupting from their projecting spines, the half dozen small, spellbound oysters threatened to strike Chachel with paralyzing force. Spiraling through the water, two of them made contact with each other and shorted themselves out. One glanced off Chachel's parrying spear. Two others missed. The last struck home. Fortunately, the hunter had raised both legs to assume a defensive posture. The electrified mollusk hit him on the sole of his left foot.

Shock spread up his leg and the limb immediately went numb, leaving him only the use of his right half-leg with which to maneuver. Circling the fight, a concerned Glint debated whether to squirt ink or even take a bite out of one of his friend's assailants. Meanwhile a small school of sweetlips and a couple of curious groupers had slowed to watch, drawn to the unusual sight of mersons hunting one another for a change. As the inquisitive fish looked on, they kept wary eyes on a gathering number of passersby from the community.

The newly arrived villagers observed the ongoing fight in silence. It was clear that the majority was not opposed to the assault. This implied condemnation of the hermetic Chachel was far from universal, however. Among those expressing their outrage at the unprovoked attack were a pair of females. Only one of them, however, elected to become personally involved.

As an enraged Poylee shot forward to provide what assistance she could to the hard-pressed Chachel, Irina was left behind. Her hostess had been showing her through and around the area surrounding Sandrift when they came upon the brawl. Now the subject and the reason for of the clash found herself the object of sometimes curious stares and occasional angry glares from the gathering of onlookers. She was only able to deal with the attention because she had been attracting similar looks ever since they had left Poylee's house earlier that morning.

She winced when she saw the blue flash that resulted as Chachel's foot was struck, even as she wondered what sort of technology or spell had been employed that would permit a humble oyster to deliver an electric shock. With his good leg partially paralyzed her merson savior was finding it increasingly difficult to fend off his assailants, who now pressed their attack with renewed vigor.

What should she do? Clearly, more than a few of the inhabitants of the village resented her presence. Were all strangers similarly shunned, or was it because she was an especially strange stranger? When queried about the matter, Poylee's response had been ambivalent.

"People always fear the new, especially something new they don't understand."

"But your own shaman changed me to be just like you," Irina had protested.

Her hostess had snorted bubbles. "The people are afraid-fearful of Oxothyr, too."

Poylee had thrown herself on the back of the smallest of the aggressors. Locked together, the two of them were spinning like seals as he fought to throw her off. Meanwhile the other pair continued to harry Chachel. One of them feinted and then struck sharply upward with his shovel. Trying to concentrate on both mersons at once, Chachel's deflection was late. Knocked from his fingers by the heavy impact, his hunting spear went spinning toward the coral below. Retreating at half speed, he dodged the swing of the other farmer's shovel, arched backward, and dove straight downward in a desperate attempt to retrieve his weapon. The first and biggest assailant charged after him.

He was intercepted by Irina.

Drifting aimlessly on the surface, seared by the sun, starving and dying of thirst, she had been rescued by Chachel and Glint. Transformed by an octopod mage, she had so far found herself largely shunned. If she was going to die here anyway, why not finish things in a quicker and more prosaic fashion while at the same time helping those who had helped her?

Maybe it was the blonde hair, floating free, that momentarily distracted Chachel's determined pursuer. Perhaps it was the knowledge that she survived among them only through the grace and skill of the shaman Oxothyr. Whatever the reason, the shovel-wielder hesitated. As he did so, she pulled her dive knife from the scabbard strapped to her calf. Sight of it brought forth an audible gasp from the growing crowd of onlookers. Come to think of it, she realized, while she had seen bits and pieces of metalwork in the course of her brief tour of Sandrift, the stuff certainly was far from common here. No doubt working metal underwater was fraught with all manner of inconvenience. In this environment, her titanium blade was probably priceless.

But while its appearance provided a reason for the resolute attacker to pause, it was also incentive for him to strike not at Chachel but at her. Holding the heavy farming implement in front of him, he kicked hard as he shot straight toward her.

And slammed into a wall.

Reversing course and ascending from below, the hunter had fashioned a barrier using the only material at his immediate command: water. As he rose he continued to gesture forcefully. Irina could feel the sudden pulse nudge her to one side. Something Chachel was doing with his hands was not moving the water between him and his foe; it was somehow making it stiff. But water was only water—wasn't it? Or could those who resided permanently in its depths induce that otherwise innocuous liquid to adopt other states? To perform feats her land-dwelling kind could not even imagine.

The reaction from the host of onlookers was enlightening. Eyes wide, expressions reflecting shock at the unexpected turn of events, they turned and fled in twos and threes. Equally instructive was the response of the watching fish. They vanished even faster than did the startled mersons. Nearby, Glint appeared to be struggling just to hold his position.

"Sorcery!" The assailant who had been pushed aside whirled and fled, not even bothering to see if his companions were following. It happened that they were, as fast as their finned feet would propel them.

Slowing their gestures, Chachel's hands drifted out in front of him as he watched his erstwhile assailants flee. To Irina those webbed fingers appeared unchanged. She moved toward him, wonderfully aware that the water between them had lost its momentarily inexplicable solidity.

"You firmed water," she murmured. "*Is* it sorcery?"

He spoke without turning to her. "No, of course not. A ruse I learned, that's all. If one has time to study and practice, one can do all manner of tricks with water." Now he finally did pivot to look at her. "I have lots of time."

Something swift and svelte zoomed in between them. Wrapping herself around Chachel and ignoring Irina, Poylee proceeded to plant a swift succession of kisses on as many exposed portions of the hunter's face as she could reach with her mouth.

"Chachel, are you all right! Are you hurt? I was so worried!"

Off to one side, Glint thrust half his arms toward the mirrorsky and the other five straight down in an unmistakable cephalopodan gesture of disgust. Though conscious of being snubbed, Irina simply drifted to one side and looked on. The mini-drama being played out in the water in front of her was none of her business.

Still, it was evident that despite Poylee's impassioned concern, Chachel had little more use for her dogged affection than he did for that of any of the other inhabitants of Sandrift. Pushing her away, he finned slowly over to where Irina was carefully replacing her knife in its scabbard.

"That's a fine piece of work." He gestured at her leg, added, "The knife, I mean. Demonic metallurgy, I suppose. What kind of metal is it?"

"I don't know how they're made. It's just something I bought in a store. It's titanium."

Chachel's one eye half closed in a speculative squint. "Titanew ... I've never heard of such a metal."

Hardly surprising, she thought. How metal of any kind came to be forged underwater was but one more mystery whose explanation eluded her. As she was trying to envision an underwater forge, he surprised her by kicking forward and taking her right hand in his.

"Thank you for helping me. It wasn't necessary." He squeezed her fingers. Submerged or not, his grip left them tingling slightly.

"I—you're welcome. I would have done the same for anyone."

"I know." Eye-patch and blue eye shimmered in the light from above the mirrorsky. "That's why I wanted to be sure to thank you."

"That's why I wanted be sure thank you!"

"That's why I wanted to sure thank!"

"Why I wanted be sure to thank you!"

The brilliant red and blue-spotted sextet of coral cod who swam past just below them echoed his words almost perfectly, each repeating the declaration of appreciation in a fashion slightly different from its swim-mate. Annoyed, Chachel took a kick at them with his good leg. Their evasion of his chiding, verbal as well as physical, was effortless. Meanwhile Poylee hovered off to one side, arms crossed and expression grim. Irina was left drifting in bewilderment.

The brief adrenaline rush she had experienced in hurrying to the hunter's aid was beginning to give way to mounting despair. Until now it had been held in check by the need subsequent to her rescue to deal with one captivating impossibility after another: humanoid folk fully adapted to living in the sea, conversational cephalopods and muttering fish, chittering crabs and a shamelessly shamanistic octopus, manyarms who boasted beaks and parrotfish that did not; all marvels suborned to the fact that she had somehow been swept up among them and co-opted to their environment. Even worse, there was nothing to indicate that anything remained of her own world. That increasingly distant reality was gone, all gone, swept away by currents marked on no map and measured in no meter.

What was she to do when the marvels grew mundane and the wonderment of it all turned sour? What skills and abilities did she have that might enable her to survive here? She could work no magic, spring no spells, tend no crops and hunt no fish—even if she could get past the unnerving fact that most of the prospective prey hereabouts was inclined to gossip. She had become a watery wastrel cast loose beneath the waves, with no way home and no prospect of finding one. Thus far she had made a number of acquaintances and no friends—least of all the capricious Poylee. Of everyone she had met, the most gracious by far had been a creature equipped with ten arms and a quick comeback. She was lost, lost, without anyone to share her peril or her pain.

What was to become of her? She didn't know where home was and she didn't know how she got here. She would have discussed her predicament with Chachel except that he was being swarmed afresh. Under the guise of tending to his very minor injuries, Poylee was trying her best to ingratiate herself with the hunter physically as well as emotionally.

Strong arms suddenly wrapped around Irina's left forearm as if the extended limb was being gently gift-wrapped in a series of sucker-lined scarves. His body flashing multiple color changes and patterns, a sympathetic Glint was trying his best to distract her from the funk into which she had fallen.

"You mourn for your lost homeland."

She mustered a smile, wondering at the same time why her eyes were not burning. Plainly, Oxothyr's changeling thaumaturgy had altered more than just her respiration.

"I can't help it. Wouldn't you react the same if you found yourself physically altered and torn away from your friends and family?"

"Not really." Proceeding to draw his tentacles in close to his body, collapse his mantle, and change his color to a lightly mottled dark brown, the cuttlefish assumed the exact shape and color of a floating rock. "As for being physically altered, I can do that any time I like. Concerning friends and family, I can meet the former anywhere and some of the latter would probably eat me if the opportunity presented itself. In a multitude of ways other than just appearance, manyarms are not like mersons."

*Neither am I*, she thought bitterly.

Unfolding himself, Glint turned a bright yellow. Green ripples flowed through his body from his tail toward his head; emerald rings of enthusiasm. "Be cheerful. Tonight is the festival of Colloth, when the night light above the mirrorsky is at its brightest. Tonight you will see things you have never imagined."

Sighing, she turned away from the sight of Poylee and an increasingly irritated Chachel. The female merson could not have wound herself tighter around the reluctant hunter had she been an eel. Not that any of it mattered to Irina.

"So the mersons have celebrations just as do my people."

Tentacles waved at her, one snapping out to just miss a passing ocellated cardinal fish. "They certainly do, but Colloth is not their festival: it is mine."

That disclosure was enough to engage her attention. "Cuttlefish have celebrations?"

"Not just my kind, but the squid participate as well." He proceeded to jet around in several tight circles, like a cylindrical dog chasing its tail. "You will see, Irina-changeling, you will see. Colloth is a wondrous time for all, including mersons. Including maybe even you." Though absent eyelids, she could almost have sworn that the cuttlefish winked at her.

What, exactly, was the significance of Colloth?

◊

A full moon. Of course, she told herself as Poylee escorted her out of the house and they swam together toward South Sandrift. Any proper nocturnal celebration anywhere calls for a full moon. She recognized it by the light it cast through the clear water.

As they passed through the wide-open gate in the coral mesh dome that covered the north side of the village she expected to be led across the sand-filled canyon that separated the two halves of the town. She saw immediately that was not to be the case. Something different from everything she had encountered thus far was afoot. Something new.

The sweeping cascade of fine sand and crushed shell that occupied the slope between the two halves of the community and gave it its name was alive with busy mersons, darting cuttlefish, and several species of squid. In contrast to their more sedate cousins the cuttlefish, the more mature squid dashed about like teenagers. The slippery, silvery rockets ranging in size from a foot in length to some individuals who stretched more than eight feet from tail to tentacle tip.

While the intense moonglow penetrating the water was sufficient to provide more than enough light for making out the coral buildings that flanked the sandy central slope, the surrounding rippling reef, and its increasingly energetic residents, it was far from the most striking type of illumination at hand.

Attenuated colonies of permanently affixed bioluminescent salps outlined the doors and windows of shops and homes like so many strands of elastic Christmas tree lights. Clusters of glowing jellyfish trailing ten-foot long luminescent tentacles that resembled strips of organic neon had been tethered to the tops of individual residences. The transparent bells of their fragile bodies pulsing steadily and softly, they cast light and shadow in every direction as they strove instinctively to go somewhere.

As a by now only erratically dutiful Poylee guided her toward the middle part of the canyon that separated the two halves of Sandrift, Irina paid attention as her increasingly preoccupied hostess waved at distant friends and spoke to passersby. Visibly distracted by the escalating celebration, even those who were wary of the newcomer paid the hesitant changeling little heed. Their attention was focused elsewhere, their hearts and minds concentrating on the light prevailing over the night.

In addition to the radiant salps and lustrous jellies, Irina's vision was assaulted by a profusion of bioluminescent fish she did not recognize. Having ascended the water column in order to join in the celebration, these flamboyant denizens of the neither regions supplied their own light. Blue, white, and red were the most common hues. All this organic illumination, however, paled beside the burst of new light that suddenly filled the canyon.

Ejected from hundreds, from thousands of participating cuttlefish and squid, ink charged with radiance spread like a luminescent blue-green cloud until it flooded much of the canyon. In the absence of current, the glowing ink lit the sandy slope with cold fire. Swirls of brighter luminescence were intense enough to occasionally force her to shield her eyes or turn away from the light. As more and more partying invertebrates arrived and added their own incandescent squirts to the accumulating mass of liquid luminosity, the slope became brighter than day.

In addition to the light they expelled, each visitor flaunted colors of their own via the chromatophores in their skin. To an awed Irina, it appeared as though the babbling streamlined shapes slicing through the water in all directions around her were engaged in a contest as chaotic as it was glorious to see who could blink the most intense hues and flash the most outrageous patterns. Utilizing their ink, some drew glowing phrases in the still water, employing an invertebrate script as alien to her as ancient Sanskrit. Others hovered in one place while turning their bodies into living approximations of nightclub strobe lights. Still others confronted one or more of their own kind to engage in exchanges of artfully patterned phosphorescence that were part dialogue, part competition, part cooperative hallucination. Coloration, pattern, writing, and verbalization carried out conversation on four levels at once. No human could have duplicated it—or made sense of it.

Neither, she surmised as she looked on, could the more limb-challenged residents of Sandrift. Though admiring of the lively exchange taking place among their cephalopodan friends, the community's contingent of mersons kept apart from it. Clad in jewelry fashioned of gems, shells, uncorroded gold, woven pearl, and wearing their finest bikini-like garb, they chattered among themselves while making their leisurely way through the spectacular living light show.

Marveling at the pulsating spectacle, dangerously close to sensory overload, an overwhelmed Irina thought to herself, *I am a butterfly, adrift in a sea of electric candy.*

The presence of so much light in one place attracted reef and ocean dwellers who were active at night. While allowing curious fish to pass through, joint patrols of manyarms and mersons kept avid packs of peevish sharks and other large nocturnal predators at bay. In addition to the spears and knives that were by now familiar implements to Irina, the patrols carried the first Oshenerth equivalents of terrestrial bows and arrows she had seen. Strips of scavenged baleen made for powerful bows, while arrows were fashioned from sharpened lengths of bone feathered with bits of sea fan and salvaged gill rakers. Even very hungry predators were wise enough to avoid such deadly weaponry, especially when a big skilled squid could handle, load, and fire three bows at once. Though merson archers, with their binocular vision, were more accurate than their soft-bodied allies.

She was aware that Poylee, having finished conversing with several friends, had taken her by the hand and was urging her forward through the water.

"Come, come this way, changeling Irina! The night nears midpoint and the all-consuming ecstasy beckons!"

Letting herself be drawn forward, Irina did not know what her vivacious hostess meant by those words. She comforted herself with the conviction that no matter how one chose to interpret them, they were anything but threatening.

Then she heard the music.

It came from a band—no, she corrected herself, from an orchestra—composed of dozens, perhaps as many as a hundred mersons and manyarms. In a serpentine procession, they streamed downslope to finally coalesce into a huge ring of sound near the very center of the rising celebration. As they puffed and pounded away on an extreme assortment of instruments even the smallest of which was new to Irina, shoals of squid and clusters of cuttlefish began converging from every direction, each trying to outdo the other in the intensity and variety of brilliant colors and shifting patterns their bodies were generating.

There were drums made of stretched skin and flutes carved from hollow bone; tooting panpipes of wrasse ribs and deep-voiced horns fashioned from coral tubes. Something like a crazed set of bagpipes gone amok employed a trio of hard-working puffer fish to power it. A xylophone-like instrument composed of a school of well-trained, well-tuned silver gars was being played by a merson wielding a pair of delicate gold-tipped hammers. Hand-held tom-toms were thumped by clusters of synchronized longtoms. Last and largest of all was a living organ comprised of trained fish of every shape and size, each of whom when their tail was flicked uttered a single, differently pitched note.

Mersons appeared to favor percussion while the participating manyarms, including the first octopods she had seen that night, gravitated toward anything that could be blown. With mouthpieces affixed to their siphons, they could generate greater volume and hold it longer than any of their merson counterparts. The fact that the performance was taking place entirely underwater only served to magnify the sound. Though the melodies and rhythms, not to mention the actual sounds, were all strange and new to Irina, she thought the performance magnificent. She told her hostess so.

Poylee looked back at her and laughed. "This is not the ecstasy, silly changeling! It is all part and parcel of Colloth, to be sure, but it is not the ecstasy." She waved a webbed hand at the storm of sound and color. "Splendid it is to see and hear, but it is not breathtaking. It does not hold your gills open to gasp. It is not all-consuming, like the ecstasy. Ah, there!" As she gestured toward the churning, thundering ring of musicians, her words were accompanied by a long, heartfelt sigh. "The nightglow is at its strongest and the ecstasy begins now."

As if by magic (and maybe it was by magic, Irina realized), the vast cloud of glowing cephalopodan ink began to dissipate and fade. Within the bounds of the canyon itself, soon only the general glow generated by the participating manyarms remained. Those individual lights began to swirl faster and faster, the patterns they formed to change more rapidly, more frantically—almost explosively, she thought.

It had grown dark around her. Not that far away but still in the distance she could make out the salp and jellyfish lights that lined the homes and shops of South Sandrift. Clearly the gathering darkness, the steady increase in the activity she was seeing, the strange aqueous music rising toward a barely perceived crescendo, all portended something of great significance. But what?

"Poylee, what does …?"

She spun around in the water, looking in every direction. There was no sign of her hostess. In fact, there was no sign of anyone she knew. Only the barely glimpsed silhouettes of merson shapes darting and swimming at the limits of her vision, visible only when they encountered groups of strobing manyarms rocketing to and fro through the reef's reassuring embrace.

A shape passed close by her, moving at a different kind of speed of light. Something unseen brushed her floating tresses and she flinched instinctively though no solid contact had been made. What if, say, a preoccupied hundred-pound squid traveling at full speed ran into her in the sparkle-lit shadows? How were injuries treated underwater, where omnipresent moisture would inhibit healing? Crossing her arms over her chest and drawing her legs up to her stomach, she struggled to espy a path out of the escalating pandemonium.

"Poylee. *Poylee!*" She found herself yelling, then screaming. It was fruitless. Her shouts could not be heard over the hiss of sleek bodies shooting through the water around her and the jubilant thunder of the musicians.

"Here, Irina!"

A familiar voice, though not a merson one. A shape materialized out of dark water rendered hallucinogenic by drifting constellations of phosphorescent ink. She exhaled gratefully, the bubbles momentarily blocking her vision.

"Glint! So glad to see you." She looked around. "Poylee abandoned me.

"Left you to participate, no doubt." Pulsing orange and cyan, the cuttlefish pivoted in the water. "I suspect she is searching hopefully for Chachel. I don't think she will find him, and it will do her no good if she does." He turned back to her. "But why are you not joining in? Colloth is a celebration for all."

"I'm not sure I'm ready for anything 'all-consuming.'" Surrounded by a detonating macrobiotic universe, she stayed close to the genuinely bemused cephalopod. "What is 'the ecstasy,' anyway?"

"You truthfully do not know?" The cuttlefish stared at her. "It is true; I see you do not. Come then with me, changeling, and I will show you—even though what you seek lies all around you."

Once again she felt herself being drawn forward, away from the comforting lights of North Sandrift, ever deeper into the raging confusion of light-emitting lifeforms that raced and tore through the ring of musicians. Enchanted, fairytale-like shapes zoomed around her; sometimes brushing her body, sometimes making firmer contact, but never bruising, never forcing.

"Let me hold your hands," Glint instructed her.

Extending her arms, she felt her fingers grasped as a single tentacle wrapped individually around each of her splayed fingers. That was when, for the first time, the numerical coincidence struck her: a human has ten fingers. A cuttlefish has ten tentacles. Gripping her firmly, his suckers holding fast but not painfully to her soft flesh, Glint bent his flexible siphon to one side and, pushing water, began to spin them. Slowly at first, then faster and faster, until she felt herself growing dizzy from all the light and sound and motion. In the real world, in her world, had someone spun her like that she might have lost her balance and fallen. But not here. It was impossible to fall here, coddled and cradled by the sustaining, supportive sea itself. Letting her head fall backward she started to laugh uncontrollably.

"Stop it! Glint, stop it, I can't see straight anymore. I can't …!"

A pair of cuttlefish whipped past her, their bodies locked tightly together, the light they were emitting incredibly vibrant and vivid. What took place in the realworld on the night of the occasional full moon, she found herself thinking wildly? As Glint spun her and she found herself growing ever more drunk with sight and sound and movement, she remembered. She knew. Not all things in Oshenerth differed utterly from those that took place in her own seas. The raison d'être simply had not occurred to her before because of the elaborate civility of her surroundings and the fact that cuttlefish and squid were not known to—celebrate—in such a fashion together. Certainly not accompanied by music.

Here however, mutual conviviality and intelligence counted for far more than mere species differences. It extended to manyarms including sociable mersons in their celebration. As Glint continued to whirl her helplessly and with increasing giddiness through watery space lit by visible expressions of cephalopodan ecstasy and underscored by all-enveloping otherworldly melodies, she finally understood the significance of Poylee's words. In the realworld, divers and scientists lucky enough to see and experience the massed festivity called it one thing. In Oshenerth they called it all-consuming. Here, on the reef, they called it the ecstasy.

Colloth was a celebration of, and a time for, mating.

# – VII –

For the first time since she had entered the village, a lightheaded Irina felt accepted. Resident mersons waved at her, or blew kisses, or ignoring her origins and setting aside their initial fears, extended invitations to visit. Could one blush underwater, she found herself wondering? She forgot her situation, forgot what had happened to her, forgot her displacement in time and reality as she let herself sink into the sheer shimmering splendor of the mass manyarm mating that was occurring all around her. Cuttlefish flashing every color of the rainbow locked and parted. Squid wrestled and writhed, the bands of color shooting through their bodies giving visible expression to their orgasmic release. Out of mutual delight and joy in sharing the celebration, mersons coupled nearby. She alternated between looking on in fascination and turning away awkwardly. The warm water that enveloped her was brimming with music and with moans.

What would it be like to make love underwater, she found herself wondering? To be locked in intimate embrace there among the bioluminescence and the warmth, drowning emotionally but not literally in a cosmic dispersion of liquid pheromones and an ocean of light? Without a hard surface to bruise one's body, drifting together effortlessly, plunging and swaying in perfect time with one's partner as if suspended in magic itself.

Then, without warning, as the tumult of music and flurry of activity and the frenzied discharge of bioluminescence blurred together in a maelstrom of orgiastic bliss, clouds of a different kind of phosphorescence began to illumine the sea in the space above the sand slope and below the mirrorsky.

Expelled almost simultaneously by several thousand female manyarms, a billion glistening eggs filled the water. Glowing pale blue and white, they pulsed with unnatural inner radiance. Within moments spawn, musicians, dancers, the exhausted cephalopodan birthing brood, and a dazed and dazzled Irina found themselves adrift together in swirls of dynamic milt that fluoresced a pale pink. Sunk in this sea of resplendent reproduction, a visitor from outside was presented with a choice of drifting in sticky enthrallment or vomiting. Though a lover of underwater life, Irina kept her mouth shut tight as she gazed in astonishment at the nova of luminous procreation now surrounding her. Gazed but did not gape. It was one thing to marvel at the miracle, quite another to inadvertently swallow some of it.

It struck her then that by taking her hands in his tentacles and the burden of her depression on his heart, Glint had sacrificed his time and opportunity to participate fully in the festivities—in other words, to reproduce. She would have shown her gratitude with a kiss, except that she was unsure how to work her way through the basket of sucker-lined arms that surrounded his face to find his beak. She settled instead for thanking him verbally.

He shrugged it off, the cuttlefish equivalent of a shrug being a slow ripple of gray down the length of his body. "I can reproduce anytime. There will be another Colloth next month. It's not every night I get to initiate a changeling." His ease turned to sudden concern as he looked at her. "What's wrong?"

Irina had begun brushing furiously at herself. "It's gooey—all of it, eggs *and* milt."

"Of course. What else would you expect? But there are other side effects. Look down at yourself."

Pausing in her futile brushing, she complied. Her eyes widened. Much of her body was covered with the combination of freshly laid manyarm eggs and fertilizing milt. From drifting strands of hair to the tips of her now webbed toes, she was glistening blue, white, and pink.

"You look beautiful," Glint told her unexpectedly.

She made a face. "Maybe to another manyarm. I sure don't *feel* beautiful. Not to give offense, Glint, but I feel—I admit that the phosphorescence is striking, but I'm afraid for someone like me there's an inescapable concurrent ick factor."

He gestured understanding. "Just relax and enjoy the rest of the celebration. Once the eggs have been fertilized, they'll drop off."

Arms spread wide, she gazed down at her shimmering self. "What about those that don't get fertilized, and the milt that doesn't manage to do any fertilizing?"

He moved toward her. "Don't worry. I'll eat them for you."

She hastily backed water. "That's okay. If you don't mind, I'll just keep brushing."

From the grotto he called home—or at least the place where he slept and stored his few possessions—Chachel could hear the music as it rose to a crescendo, signifying the cumulative reproductive vehemence that was Colloth. He could see the lights, too, enough concentrated in one place to send upward a glow sufficiently intense to light the underside of the mirrorsky itself. Drawn to the atypical brightness, all manner of nocturnal planktonic life danced and spun in a frenzy beneath the uncharacteristically illuminated ceiling of the world.

Sitting atop the flattened disc of dead shelf coral that marked the entrance to his abode, he watched as the ghostly shapes of half a dozen silky sharks swam silently past to disappear into the darkness downreef. They too had been drawn to the celebration, but they would find no sweet pickings in Sandrift tonight. Not with every one of the festival's non-participants drafted for patrol duty.

He ought to have been among those standing guard on behalf of the celebrants, he knew. But doing so would require voluntarily inserting himself into the social life of the community, something he declined to do. He would not stand guard for them. Conversely, should sharks or other dangers invade his own space, none would come to his aid no matter how loudly or desperately he called for it.

That was just fine with him. He already knew how he would handle such a potentially fatal situation. He would fight for himself and, should he lose, he would die. He was perfectly willing to accept either outcome. Except …

Except something had changed. As was true of most unforeseen changes, it was not one he had sought. Given a choice, he would have avoided it. But it had been forced on him by circumstance and accident and, like most accidents, could not be taken back.

In spite of himself, he found himself growing more and more curious about the changeling.

Don't think about her, he told himself angrily. Put her out of your mind. She's Oxothyr's problem if she is anyone's. Not your responsibility. In saving her you've already stepped beyond the bounds of noninterference you set for yourself. Concentrate on something else. On your inability to share, to participate in, to enjoy something as purely pleasurable as Colloth. Focus on your bitterness. Gnaw your own soul.

That was better, he told himself. He generated bile the way a mourner seeps grief. In his renewed melancholy he was once again content. What were the right words? Oh yes. Muttering under his breath, waving a hand, he numbed the water just outside his cave. It muted the thrum of joyful music emanating from town and dulled the distant effervescent light. Satisfied with this modest if idiosyncratic bit of amateur aqueous sorcery, he turned back toward the darkness of the inner cavern. A few forlorn shrimp and small-minded crabs muttered to themselves in its black back reaches. Each managed to emit a single unvarying and decidedly uncelebratory pinpoint of light. It was all the illumination Chachel desired.

It was all that he sought.

◊

The light and the music, the gaiety and celebration, did not reach into the depths of the reef where Oxothyr made his home and his magic. Lit by a single shaft of moonlight, the vaulted entryway where the visitor from the void had been transformed into a proper merson was all but empty. The soft argent glow from overhead made of swarming many-legged zooplankton a snowstorm of dancing gems.

Deep within thick coral that had accumulated over hundreds of thousands of years, acidic dissolution and natural erosion had hollowed out a maze of interlocking tunnels and chambers. At the center of this warren of wizardry Oxothyr held thaumaturgical court. Powerful yet sensitive tentacles drew special stones from their resting places on shelves that had been cut into the surrounding walls. From carefully tilted pots and jugs, oily spirals of liquids denser than seawater trickled into a waiting bowl fashioned from half a tridacna shell that had once been home to a now absent giant clam. Plucked from the transparent tunicate containers that contained them, select pinpoints of living light were carefully added to the expanding brew. Held in place by the shaman's spells, unable to escape, they infused it with an unearthly green glow.

As Oxothyr hovered above and to one side of the concoction within the clamshell, Tythe and Sathi darted hither and yon within the chamber, fetching ingredients and components for the increasingly concerned sage. The octopus's voice grew louder and more strained as the blend grew brighter and more potent. What it all portended the two famuli did not know. The intense olivine radiance was deviant and the faint moaning that was beginning to fill the chamber bore little relation to the music that underscored the delights of Colloth. Never before could they recall having seen their master so intense.

"Look at him," Sathi whispered in the near darkness. "His color stays dark brown and does not change."

"Not even a ripple," a troubled Tythe agreed. "What manner of magic it is that he works tonight I do not know—and do not want to know."

Sathi gestured with several arms. "Nor do I comprehend its import, save that it is of manifest significance. What spirits does the Master talk to, what demons does he invoke?"

An explosion of ruby light from the central concavity of the clamshell saw them simultaneously sink into silence. The green luminosity became edged with black, as if the magic the mage was so forcefully propagating had acquired a literal as well as metaphysical edge. The ominous emerald shadows cast on the walls reminded Sathi of a shallow cave he had once wandered into that turned out to be choked with noisome, poisonous algae. As he contemplated the resemblance, the unwholesome luminance seemed to prickle with tiny tendrils that sought to ingratiate themselves into the very walls of the chamber.

Even in the Master's moments of casting most serious, Tythe had never heard him speak in timbre so profound. Oxothyr sounded simultaneously worn and angry, frustrated and demanding. As he intoned, the two famuli clustered closer to one another. It felt as if the walls of the inner chamber were closing in around them as more and more of the green glow was overtaken by the expanding blackness.

Throughout it all Oxothyr continued to add to the insidious fusion that threatened to overflow the clamshell. Words cajoling and soul of periwinkle, threats implied and tincture of void. The calcium-white shell seethed with resonance. Green gave way entire to black, and then black to a discoloration that was not only new to the assistants but new to the realworld. This essence coiled and writhed upward from the shell, rising so strong and unforgiving that Oxothyr found it prudent to retreat slightly. Arms entwined, Sathi and Tythe looked on wide-eyed at this new phenomenon that had taken physical shape in the chamber before them. Their reaction was hardly surprising.

It was the first time either of them had ever seen cold.

Waving every one of his eight arms, Oxothyr uttered an incantation as commanding as any he had ever summoned forth. For a terrifying instant, nothing changed. Striking outward from the center of the gruesome conjecture that coiled snake-like above the clamshell, something touched Tythe. It was unlike anything he had ever experienced before. He screamed.

Then, just like that, it was gone. Reality returned to normal. Feeble though it was, the blue-green light that now returned to the chamber was soft and familiar. No more noisome green, no more oozing black, no more—cold. Sitting alone atop its supporting pillar, the tridacna bowl once more gleamed lustrous, white, and empty. Behind it—behind it Oxothyr floated; eyes shut, arms coiled in a ball around him, his boneless body a lightly-spotted drifting brown balloon.

"Master!" An alarmed Sathi rushed forward. Still trembling from his brief contact with what the mage had summoned, Tythe was slower to respond.

One eye opened. Tentacles unfurled. Sathi let out a sigh. The shaman was unhurt. Physically, anyway.

"What—what was it, Master?" the squid inquired hesitantly.

"Coldness." Oxothyr replied without hesitation. "Chill. Frigidity of a kind I have read about in the Old Tablets but never expected to encounter myself." He looked past the worried famulus. "Are you all right, Tythe?"

Trembling slightly, the other squid gestured in the affirmative. "I don't know exactly what you're talking about, Master, or even what I just saw. But I do know one thing about it. It bites."

Oxothyr indicated understanding. "Indeed it does. It will also kill."

"Why did you bring it here?" Sathi was not normally so forward with his master, but the experience had emboldened him. Given the gravity of the occurrence, Oxothyr took no offense.

"I did not bring it, little silver dart. I went looking for something else, and the coldness came in its stead. Something is using it. Something or someone is manipulating it. For what specific purpose or to what eventual end I do not know. Only that it cannot be good."

Tythe had recovered enough to ponder. "This something is a danger to Sandrift?"

The mage rotated toward him. "This is something that endangers the whole world as we know it."

The two assistants exchanged a glance before turning back to the shaman. "What is it then, Master?" Fear and wonder inflected Sathi's query.

Oxothyr let out a sigh so substantial it disturbed the volume of water within the chamber. "I wish I knew, Sathi. I wish I knew." He turned away. "I have been brooding on it much. I must brood on it a while longer still. Leave me now. Even serious contemplation must eventually surrender to fatigue, and fatigue to sleep."

Obediently, they gestured their goodnights and turned to depart. As they did so, Tythe looked back long enough make sure that the shaman was squeezing comfortably into his filament-lined sleeping hole.

"I can still feel the touch of this thing called 'cold.'" He shuddered. "And its appearance haunts my thoughts. Is the danger as serious as the Master says, do you think?"

"I don't know." Like his friend, Sathi traveled in reverse by pumping short, sharp spurts from his siphon. "But that is the first time in all the years I have apprenticed myself to him that he has called me by name."

Swimming together toward the sleeping chamber they shared near the main entrance to the shaman's lair, the two famuli continued to discuss what they had just seen and experienced. While their exchange was not especially reassuring to either of them, they knew it was better to talk about what they had just witnessed than to leave the foul memories alone, to fester and grow.

◊

The aftermath of the festival manifested itself in the village the following day in the form of dead silence. Nothing stirred. Every shop was closed, no school of children made its way to the schools in North and South Sandrift, no cuttlefish idled peacefully above their favored hunting promontories. The migratory squid who had come to town for one night of hyperactive merriment had departed. Those who had survived the frenzy of celebratory copulation had returned to the open ocean in search of the vast shoals of small fish on which they fed. The drifting bodies of other thousands, their life-force exhausted by the mating madness, had been gathered up the previous night by community patrols and suitably distributed among the survivors, both of their own kind and the resident mersons.

Local cuttlefish remained secluded in their homes within the labyrinth of coral. Currents had swept away the remainder who had given their lives in the service of reproduction. Schools of bemused reef fish wandered unchallenged through the community, free for a change to pick and nibble as they wished at local dwellings as they searched for morsels usually off-limits to their kind. Beneath the brightly lit mirrorsky, the village lay clean and calm.

Not all were asleep or dead, however. Not everyone had participated in the previous night's hysteria. Disinclined to work for another to earn his daily fillet and inherently unsuited to begging,

Chachel had to hunt if he wanted to eat. The morning after Colloth, or one of the many other fetes that were so popular among mersons and manyarms, was always a good time to be out on the westernmost reef line because he usually had the best hunting spots to himself.

He had settled in at one of his favorite locales—a point where the last thrust of high reef protruded out into the blue. The currents sweeping around the promontory were a magnet for flavorsome pelagics. This early in the morning plenty of potential dinner was out and swimming. Aware of the turbulent celebration that had taken place the previous night, open-ocean swimmers who normally stayed away from the reef and out in the safety of deep water felt confident hunting in close, unaware that they themselves were being watched by a pair of eager predators.

Well, by one, anyway. Drifting just above a nearby stand of staghorn coral, Glint was neither eager nor in predation mode. His lateral fins barely rippling, he was, in fact, sound asleep. More irritated than disgusted, Chachel was forced to turn his attention away from the outer reef in order to repeatedly nudge his friend awake.

"Hmm—what?" Cephalopodan eyes cleared. "Is it food yet?"

"I haven't speared anything," Chachel growled by way of reply, "and for someone who's supposed to be helping with the scouting you've been a non-presence."

"Sorry." Tentacles spread out in all directions, quivering as the cuttlefish stretched. "It was a good Colloth. A fine Colloth." One eye focused, albeit tentatively, on the merson who hovered stretched out above the last piece of land before the drop-off. "Your changeling friend is a good dancer. If encouraged, she can do multiple spins. It's wonderful to see that long hair stretched out behind her. Reminded me of the waltz of the golden garden eels, it did."

"She's not my friend." Chachel made no effort to hide his annoyance.

"Well, she's mine—I think," the cuttlefish shot back. "Even if she is a bone bag and out of her element." Advancing effortlessly, he halted just above and slightly behind his friend's left shoulder and joined him in gazing out into the limitless expanse of open ocean. "Anything?"

"Many things," an exasperated Chachel replied softly. "Whitetips, rays, big wrasses, some grouper. Enough so that I feel comfortable waiting for just the right meal and just the right moment."

Glint nodded. Since he had no neck, mimicking the merson gesture required him to rock the whole front of his body up and down. "Maybe this is the right one now." A tentacle gestured straight ahead. "I can't imagine an easier kill, since it's coming straight toward us."

Trailing through the water a wake saturated with color, the rainbow runner was indeed heading directly toward them. How very odd, Chachel found himself thinking. Rainbow runners were swift, streamlined, open ocean swimmers. They sometimes came in close to reef systems, but not onto them. At any moment, he expected this one to turn aside and head north or south parallel to the coral ridge. Instead, it just kept coming. In fact, he realized, if it didn't stop it was going to swim right into them. He was not particularly waiting for rainbow runner, but this one presented such an easy kill he could not justify passing it up. And their flesh was tasty. His fingers tensed on his spear.

"Get behind me, idiot!"

"What? Oh, right." Half-asleep again, Glint let himself sink back behind Chachel and out of sight.

A steel streak, the sleek silver-sided fish showed no sign of slowing down or changing its course. Even as he prepared to make the kill, Chachel found himself wondering if perhaps it was sick. They would have to gut it carefully. A bad meal could lead to much worse than indigestion depending on which toxins a free-swimming dinner might have ingested prior to its death.

Then he saw the sharks.

There were two of them. Silkies. Big, husky, powerful swimmers. Since they were never normally seen this close to the shallows, it followed that they had been pursuing the rainbow runner from deeper water. He found himself hesitating. Taking on one silky, even if he could rouse Glint to help, would be a challenge. Tackling two would be foolhardy, especially over a single fish when there was so much other food ambling about. Letting himself sink down below the ridge, he intended to let both prey and predators swim right over him—assuming, of course, that the silkies would continue to pursue their quarry into shallow reef territory.

"Help me! *For the love of your own, help me!*"

He could see the blood now, trailing from a nasty gash just behind the runner's left gill slit. It was also missing most of a ventral fin. No wonder the silkies continued to persist in the hunt. Strangely, the open wound looked more like a blade strike than a bite. In any case, he had no time to analyze it. The visitor had nearly reached the reef.

He hated it when circumstances gave him no time for contemplation.

Glint saved him the trouble. Ascending vertically, the cuttlefish was waving every one of his arms simultaneously, beckoning to the frantic fish. "Here, over here, color master!"

"Glint, don't ...!" Though only seconds had elapsed it was already too late. Trailing streamers of color, the desperate rainbow runner had already altered its course ever so slightly. Now it was definitely going to run into them.

He had no time to rebuke Glint. The frantic fish would duck down into their hiding place and the silkies would follow. Trapped in the slight depression in the reef, they would find themselves cornered together. Unless ...

His back up against the coral, he started counting to himself. One, two ... having observed the silkies swimming, he could estimate how fast they were traveling. Seeing their intended victim dip behind the slight rise of pale blue coral, they would be likely to put on an eager burst of speed. That would mean they ought to be ...

Kicking hard, he shot upward, spread his arms and legs wide, and bulged his eyes as he flailed madly at nothingness with the spear.

"ARRRAGHHAAA!"

His timing was nearly perfect. One moment the silkies had been preparing to dive down to pluck their prey from among the coral—and the next, something that might have been an insane merson or a reef spirit or who knew what magically materialized barely a tail length directly in front of them. It was as if Chachel had sprung from a twist in the water, had stepped whole and entire from the line of a particularly dense thermocline.

Startled and shaken, both sharks whirled instinctively and vanished back the way they had come as fast as their tails could propel them.

"Well done!" Chachel felt a tentacle on his left ankle.

Kicking it away, he looked down angrily. "Yes, they ran. They might just as easily have bitten me in half. What were you thinking, calling the runner right to us like that?"

Glint shrugged. "I saw someone in need."

"I saw dinner." Chachel swam downward. "I still may."

They found the trembling refugee backed up against a concealing, protective mass of yellow stinging coral. Longer than Chachel's arm and twice as thick, the normally confident swimmer was a mess. Blood continued to dribble from the ugly slash in its side. Able now to take a closer, more considered look at the wound, Chachel decided it definitely was not the result of a bite; not from a shark or any other predator. As for the missing ventral fin, it looked as if it had been cut rather than chewed off. What had caused such peculiar injuries?

Confronting the runner, he was his usual tactful self. "You came seeking help. Why should we not help you to dinner?"

Wide eyes flicked swiftly from merson to manyarm. "You are in danger. Both of you. All of you. Have me to eat if you will, but know that the normal order of things that permits such an understanding is itself at risk!"

Chachel frowned. He had never heard a fish talk like this. Especially not one fully aware that it was on the verge of becoming a meal. "What are you gibbering about? And what was that wild shout 'For the love of your own' about?"

Gasping for oxygen, the rainbow runner struggled to respond. Only after filling its gills was it able to wheeze a reply.

"Shakestone is destroyed! I—I have been sent from there to—warn you. To warn Sandrift and—any others I can reach."

"'Destroyed'?" Chachel took a closer look at the injured fish. Its attendant rainbow swirled behind its tail, a fitful swathe of trailing color. "You're not making any sense, visitor. Shakestone is much larger than Sandrift, and they have sturdy defense nets. How can it be 'destroyed'?"

Once more the rainbow runner struggled to breathe. Exhausted, clearly drained, he could only manage one word.

"Spralakers."

Merson and manyarm exchanged a look. Then Chachel, his attitude having undergone an instantaneous and dramatic shift at the mention of that word, extended a hand. Trying to draw back, the weakened runner found it no longer had the strength.

Pulling the erstwhile meal gently to him and cradling it firmly with his free arm, Chachel spoke grimly. "You'd best see Oxothyr." With a last glance backward to make sure the two silkies were nowhere to be seen, the three of them, hunters and refugee, started back toward Sandrift.

This was turning out, the stolid hunter reflected, to be an unusually busy week for the normally reclusive manyarm shaman. First the void demon found and then made into a changeling, and now this. Could two such singular events be somehow connected?

What, in the name of every snail track in the sands, was going on?

# – VIII –

A s they alternately carried and guided the badly injured rainbow runner, Chachel applied a thick salve from one of the many small containers he kept in his shoulder carryall. An extract derived from the internal organs of a particular sea cucumber, it was known for its ability to rapidly heal most wounds. It worked on the visitor's injury, though imperfectly. Almost as if, the hunter thought, the gash had been inflicted by something other than a familiar fang or weapon. At least the bleeding was slowed.

That did not permit them to lower their guard. A patrolling shark could detect one part of blood to ten million of water. Thankfully, the visitor continued to swim in a reasonably steady manner. Violent twitches or other unusual muscular exertions could also alert discriminating shark senses.

Chachel did not allow himself to relax until they crossed over the Galas reef line and were back in the shallows. Here, where multiple inner reefs formed a vast network of intersecting stony ramparts and stubby bommies that reached up to the mirrorsky itself, it would be exceedingly difficult for a big shark to maneuver.

That did not mean the area was devoid of potential predators.

The green moray that began to emerge from its hole in the reef was as big around as Chachel's thigh and three times the merson's length. Its bright white fangs were sharper than the bone spear he carried and they protruded from jaws powerful enough to snap a hunter in half. As it writhed toward the returning hunters, its slightly bulging, unblinking eyes were locked on the tempting shape of the injured rainbow runner.

Turning to face the olive-green killer, Chachel adopted the posture of false cheer and took time to wave. "Good day to you, Miss Longslayer."

Not two body-lengths away, the moray halted. As it sucked water, its massive jaws methodically opened and closed, opened and closed: death's own metronome. Thick folds and wrinkles along its lower jaw gave it the appearance of a being much older than it was.

"Is that you, Chachel Loner? Yes, it is you." Hungry eyes followed the wounded visitor as Glint continued to shepherd it onward and away from the moray's neighborhood. "You have made a catch, but it lives still. I can kill it for you."

"The guest is not for eating." Chachel held his spear loosely, careful to keep its lethal tip aimed unthreateningly skyward. "Shakestone is deaded, so it claims, and we take it to Oxothyr so the shaman can extract the truth."

"Rather would I extract its flesh." The massive moray hesitated. "When the flaccid mage is through with his cavalier questioning, I would share in any outcome that involves a rebuke. The head, for example."

"Should the visitor be found out a liar, I promise I will save the juiciest portion of him for you. Are we not friends?" He tensed slightly, tightening his grip on the spear. A glance showed that Glint and his injured charge were nearly out of sight, the only remaining hint of their presence being the weaving, fading rainbow that the visitor continued to trail behind him. The moray was lightning fast, but her kind preferred to dine in the immediate vicinity of their homes, and were not fond of extended pursuit through open water.

Still the giant dithered. Then she shrugged, a sharp sideways twist of her crushing jaws. "Always friends are Longslayer and Chachel Loner. Food is plentiful. Good talk is rare. Be healthy, my friend, and remember your promise."

"I have more time to do so than most," a relieved Chachel confessed.

Turning, the colossal eel slithered head-first back into her hole in the reef. It was remarkable to see such flexibility in a body so enormous. The hunter trusted the moray—he had known her a long time. But he still kept watch behind him as he hurried to catch up to Glint and the visitor. It was all right to leave a promise behind.

He did not want to leave a foot.

Slowing as he caught up to the others, he moved close to the injured visitor. "You had better be telling the truth, color-bearer. Already you have cost my companion and I a day of hunting, and an edgy exchange with a dangerous friend. It will be very annoying if you die before we reach our destination."

Displaying humor as well as spirit, the rainbow runner's reply was weak but clear. "I will do my best to comply."

As they drew near Sandrift, they began to encounter villagers. Some paused to stare at the improbable trio. Others continued about their business, secure in the knowledge that anything than involved the notorious and short-tempered recluse was unworthy of their notice.

A small but commanding voice stopped them outside the entry tunnel that led to the shaman's quarters.

"Halt or be anemonized!" Raising his two striking arms, Sathi confronted the arrivals with his usual brashness.

Glint advanced. Though the same length as the squid, he was more massive. "Drift aside, servant." Gesturing tentacles indicated the barely alive rainbow runner. "This herald carries grim news that begs the audience of Oxothyr, and cannot wait."

"What is all thi …?" Arriving alongside his counterpart, Tythe quickly appraised the confrontation. There was Chachel, the merson recluse; Glint, the half-mad manyarm troublemaker; and with them—a strange fish. It was the latter's all-too evident hemorrhaging that decided him. Though much reduced in flow thanks to Chachel's brief but effective ministrations, the rainbow runner's life-fluid continued to leak into the water. A bleeding visitor was never a good sign. The last thing the famulus wanted was for one, its importance unknown, to expire on his watch.

"Let them in." Several arms shoved Sathi to one side. As the trio started forward, Tythe welcomed them with a warning. "Be advised that Master Manyarms is tending to the changeling and may not take kindly to being interrupted."

"He will when he hears what our visitor has to tell him," Chachel assured the assistant.

Crossing through the entry tunnel and the open shaft beyond, they entered into the maze of chambers that honeycombed this part of the reef. While Chachel found himself immediately at a loss for direction, Glint's greater sensitivity led them straight to the wizard's study.

The curving walls of the roughly spherical cavity were pockmarked with smaller holes and niches. Many held stone or containers of volcanic glass in a myriad of shapes, sizes, and colors. Where their contents could be discerned, they frequently eluded identification. Among some that could be recognized, the visitors often wished they had remained obscure. Fastened to the walls, clusters of bioluminescent salps and carefully cultivated phosphorescent zooplankton filled the room with light that was subdued but sufficient.

Hovering in the center of the chamber, the changeling floated with arms outstretched and head tilted sharply back. In the virtual absence of current, her golden-hued hair haloed her head as it fanned out behind her. Her eyes were closed. A carryall hung loose from one shoulder and the remarkable demon knife was strapped to her left calf. A dim purplish radiance encased her like the mucus of a sleeping parrotfish.

The bulky, bulbous presence of the shaman Oxothyr hung just in front of her. His eyes were closed as well. Eight arms outstretched encircled her body, forming a supple, sucker-lined cocoon. Weaving slowly, they were manipulating the violet glow as effectively as a musician would draw forth music from an orchestra; strengthening it here, dispersing it elsewhere. Neither conjurer nor changeling reacted to the unplanned intrusion.

Chachel and Glint exchanged a glance. Dare they disrupt a session so profound? Mightn't there be consequences? It was left to their impatient visitor to settle the matter for them.

"Hurry," the rainbow runner gasped. His breathing had slowed visibly.

Reluctantly, Chachel finned forward. Usually, nothing intimidated him. After all, what was the worst that could happen to someone under the worst possible circumstances? One would die, that was all. But this....

He coughed lightly. "Oxothyr, Master, we come to you on a matter of ..."

There was a flash of light. For a second or two, nothing could be seen within the chamber save splinters of shattered indigo. As Chachel's shocked sight gradually returned, the mage and his patient once more came into focus. Only this time the shaman was no longer enveloping the changeling.

He was right up in Chachel's face.

When riled, Oxothyr could prove as domineering as any creature in the realworld. He was now so riled. Sparks of bioluminescent lightning flared from the tips of his tentacles.

"WHO DARES TO INTRUDE ON ...?" Recognizing his visitors, he broke off and lowered his voice. "Oh, it's you two. Again." Ropy arms that had been spread threateningly wide now coiled. "What is it this time?" Behind him, the changeling Irina had drawn her spread arms in to her sides. Blinking, she began to wake up.

Recovering his poise while striving to pretend he had not lost it, Chachel backed water. "Your sageness, we were hunting the outer reef when this refugee," he indicated the barely alive rainbow runner, "came fleeing in our direction, pursued by silkies. We saved him. What he told us in return seemed so hard to believe that we knew the only way to determine the truth of it was to bring him directly to you as quickly as possible." He finned further backward, putting more space between himself and the still irate shaman. "This we have done."

As he retreated, he found himself gazing not at Oxothyr but past him. Having recovered from the inert state of healing into which the wizard had placed her, Irina was coming to join them. When she met his gaze with a directness that Chachel found unexpectedly unsettling, he hurriedly looked away. Nor did he offer a formal greeting. She reacted to his indifference with a mix of irritation and coolness. That was fine with him. Their mutual distaste for one another was not the issue here.

"What's wrong with him? Or her." She nodded in the direction of the rainbow runner, whose wounds Oxothyr was actively inspecting.

"Shark attack," he explained tersely. Every time he met her she seemed less and less a threat. How could one fear a creature that could not even tell a male fish from female? "And if what he has told us on the way back is truth, also spralakers."

Her brow wrinkled up. "What's a spralaker?"

"You're likely to find out," Glint put in. "Or if you're lucky, you won't." The cuttlefish would have elaborated, but went silent when the wounded visitor started to speak.

Its words were soft and threatened to pass unheard through the water that surrounded him, but as there was so little ambient noise within the coral chamber even Irina could make them out.

"I am Zesqu the Fleet. My friends are dead, my school become food. Four others fled with me. Two had their skulls smashed by the spralakers who extinguished Shakestone. Two were caught and consumed by the opportunists who stood apart from the battle waiting to pick off any who tried to flee. Only I am left, and soon I will become one with the powdered coral that makes the sand." The silver-sided fish shuddered with the pain of his injuries and the agony of retelling.

"Shakestone is a strong village, well-populated and defended. How could mere spralakers raze it?" Reaching out with a tentacle tip, Oxothyr traced a line of dark blue along the rainbow runner's right flank. The visitor's pain appeared to subside momentarily. His voice grew stronger.

"These were spralakers, but they were not 'mere.' And they fought with a ferocity and a skill never seen before in their kind."

Glint edged close to the intent Irina. "Spralakers rarely fight together. When they try to do so, they invariably end up fighting among themselves. They would never dare to strike at an organized community unless they could gather overwhelming strength in numbers. Even allowing for that, what the herald says makes no sense. I cannot ever remember hearing tell of a spralaker attack on a village as robust and well-defended as Shakestone. Something's up. Spralakers are tough, but slow, and they can't really swim. That's why they're normally a danger only to wandering children or the solitary elderly."

"But not this time," she murmured.

"No," the cuttlefish bubbled. "Apparently not this time. Something has changed."

"They attacked during the night," the rainbow runner disclosed. "Shakestone is known as a safe haven. Few guards were out. The surprise was complete. Mersons asleep had their bones broken, resident manyarms had their eyes and their siphons torn out. I myself saw only a little of this, and I saw too much." For the pain the visitor was feeling now not even one as skilled as Oxothyr had a salve.

"I still fail to understand." The shaman's tone was gentle, compassionate. "You said they were not 'mere' spralakers."

A merson's eyes might have bulged. Those of a fish could not. "There were the familiar local spralakers you would know and recognize." His voice grew shakier as he explained, as he remembered. "But there were also spralakers of size and shape and kind never before encountered. Huge they were! Monstrous, overpowering, distorted as if they had been inspired by nightmare. Living, rampaging bad dreams! And they worked together, fought *together*. They had weaponry never seen before.

"The spears and arrows of the defenders could not penetrate such thick armor. Short swords and knives broke against them. They sliced manyarms in half as if they were starfish and broke the necks of those mersons who awoke to confront them. The rest of us who were not merson or manyarm hid deep within Shakestone's reef or swam for our lives. Most did not make it." His voice, briefly rejuvenated, now slowed once more. "Maybe I am the only one."

He stopped speaking. Tail and fins ceased their rippling. The colors that trailed from his tail faded away. Reaching out with two arms, Oxothyr shook the herald as firmly as he dared.

"Afterward, Zesqu. What happened afterward?"

Fins fluttered once more, albeit feebly. "I—I don't know, shaman of Sandrift. I and the others swam like we had never swam before. Cut down, cut down. I saw them die. Even now I can see the whiteness of their flesh flaking away from their bodies as the silkies shook them. They were not from my school, but even so ..." His voice drifted, then came back.

"Shakestone is no more. I am only a feeder and a schooler, not a thinker. But I can speak the truth of what I saw. From the beginning the attack never faltered, not even when the remaining defenders gathered in front of the village's main hall with their offspring huddled behind them. The last screams carried a long ways."

Oxothyr moved back. "I fear this will not stop with Shakestone. Something in the world is out of kilter. All spralakers are monstrous and distorted, but they do not form armies, they do not employ tactics. A spralaker's strategy consists of snapping at anything that comes within reach of its arms, and then eating or retreating as circumstances dictate. Some are large, but you would never call them huge." He turned back to the visitor. "You said they were overpowering. How overpowering? In what way other than size? You said they used new kinds of weapons. Can you describe them?"

Zesqu the rainbow runner did not answer. Not because he was pondering a reply. Because he was dead.

The ensuing silence that filled the spherical chamber was complete. Even the tiny shrimp who chattered and clicked away in the smaller niches and crevices had been frightened into silence. Eventually Oxothyr broke the stillness.

"Sathi, Tythe!"

Shooting into the study, the shaman's famuli caught sight of the dead rainbow runner floating in its center. "Master?" Tythe inquired uncertainly.

An octopod arm reluctantly indicated the dead herald. "As this selfless friend's work is done, so is he. Take him out and scatter him to the world, so that as many as possible may, should they wish, partake of his decency." One glistening eye focused hard on the two assistants. "See that you *share*. I'll know if you keep him for yourselves."

"Yes, Master," Sathi dutifully acknowledged. Coming forward, the two squid wrapped the dead body in their tentacles and retreated back the way they had come. As soon as they were gone the great octopus turned to the others. His body had turned a deep green and was now inscribed with an intricacy of dark brown symbols. With a start, Irina saw that they were unambiguous ideographs. By manipulating the chromatophores in his skin, the shaman was writing upon himself, utilizing his own body as a sketchpad. While she could not make sense of the cephalopodan script, Chachel and Glint were paying close attention to the shifting symbols.

"What are we to do now, Oxothyr?" A hovering Glint eyed the mage intently.

Looking up from reading the shaman's epidermis, Chachel squinted at his companion out of his good eye and said quietly but firmly. "What do you mean, 'we'?"

The mage chose to ignore the hunter's disclaimer. "For some time now, I have been troubled by auguries and portents the likes of which are worrisome in their lack of precedent." As he spoke, the ambulatory symbols on his body were being devoured by a slow darkening of his skin, as if a shadow was spreading over the words he had laboriously called into being. "I have alluded to them before and can catch only glimpses of what they might mean. Some are startling in their implications. Others merely terrifying. All are unsettling." As he looked up at his small audience the bioluminescence that illuminated the chamber seemed to shrink slightly in upon itself.

"I fear that this assault on innocent Shakestone is but part and parcel of something far greater and more evil than we can imagine."

Surprising everyone, Chachel suddenly spun in the water to point a finger at a startled Irina. "It has to do with *her*, doesn't it? The changeling is a harbinger of destruction."

"Why you greasy, self-centered, bad-mannered, arrogant fish-man!" an outraged Irina stammered. Another thus insulted might well have reached for her knife. Instead, she settled for cutting him with her eyes.

Oxothyr raised an arm for silence. His reaction was calm and reasoned. "Though it is true that the changeling's appearing among us is an event exceptional, I do not feel nor do I sense any correlation between her arrival and what has taken place at Shakestone." He turned to face her. "That may yet change, as may my opinion. Or it may not. But of one thing I am certain: change surely has come to this part of Oshenerth, and much of it unwelcome."

Trying to change the subject, Glint waved all of his arms for attention. "So what are we to do, inker of souls?"

Oxothyr's mantle pulsed. "For certain we cannot simply sit back, and weigh up, and hope that this will go away of its own accord. In order to learn and to know, I would journey to

Shakestone myself. But I fear more than that must be done. I am convinced by what the herald told us that if we do not respond aggressively and appropriately, then a response of a different kind will eventually find us here. It is always better to be proactive."

Chachel eyed the shaman askance. "I think I grasp your meaning, venerable Oxothyr. I hope I do not."

"Would that I could confirm your hopeful ignorance rather than your perception, hunter." Reaching out, the octopod draped an arm over the merson's left shoulder. Uncharacteristically, and reflecting the significance of the moment, Chachel did not shrug it off. "Regrettably, you see the truth. We have no choice. Either we confront these invading spralakers on our time and terms, or we will surely do so on theirs."

Glint rose skyward to execute a perfect somersault that just did clear the overhanging coral. "War!"

"Your rush to grandiosity does you no credit, manyarm." Oxothyr's tone was disapproving. "A punishing rejoinder may be in order, yes. In contrast, 'war' implies a generality for which we as yet have no grounds. It implies a specific enemy for which we have no name. 'Spralakers' is insufficient."

"So far," Chachel murmured softly. The shaman did not hear him.

"What are you going to do?" Feeling more than a little overwhelmed by the turn events had taken, a wide-eyed Irina hovered nearby.

"Do?" Oxothyr turned a great gold-flecked eye on the bewildered changeling. "Why, we are going to do what now must be done. Not only because it is necessary, but because it is right." As he settled himself down to rest on a rocky ledge that projected from one wall, his words were accentuated by gesticulations of his multiple arms.

Irina could not keep from thinking that watching one Oxothyr elaborating was the equivalent of watching four Italians arguing.

"Though the brave messenger died before he had time to go into detail, I believe that whatever foulness has befallen Shakestone will not be satisfied with its annihilation alone. Perpetrators of destruction are emboldened by conquest, not sated."

"Then you think these spralakers, if indeed that's what they are, will come here, to Sandrift?" Chachel was not so disinterested in the life of his fellow mersons as to neglect to look after his own interests, limited though they might be.

The shaman did not hesitate. "I do. Therefore, it is not only just that we confront these invaders as soon as possible, but prudent that we do so as far from home as we can."

Glint's arms twisted together to form a single tight coil, a thick fleshy cable, in front of him. It was, Irina would learn, a particularly vibrant gesture of cephalopodan emphasis. His body turned silver.

"If these spralakers choose to continue their depredations they are sooner or later likely to encounter citizens from Siriswirll."

Oxothyr's body bobbed gently in the water behind his head as both turned a responsive mauve. "For a persistent joker you show some grasp of stratagems, shot-arm. Yes, I fear that Siriswirll may be next to receive the attentions of these unknown marauders. Worse, those good people may be unaware of what has transpired at Shakestone. Unlike ourselves, they may not have had the benefit of hearing from one of that unfortunate community's remaining survivors."

"We have to warn them!" Blasting water from his siphon, Glint began swimming in tight, agitated circles.

"I suppose." Chachel made no attempt to conceal his disinclination.

"As the only community of size between Sandrift and Shakestone," Oxothyr continued, "Siriswirll presents an obvious target for these raiders, as well as our best chance of stopping them before they reach Sandrift." Brooding, he curled his arms into a ball around him. "And also perhaps of providing some clues to the nature of the greater concern that troubles my days and interrupts my sleep."

Glint finally stopped spinning. Maybe cuttlefish were immune to dizziness, but she was not, a queasy Irina realized. Just watching the multi-armed hunter's antics had left her feeling nauseous. To settle her stomach, she concentrated on something that was not moving at all: a cluster of bright pink lights that shone from the hindquarters of several speculated worms attached to one wall. A trick used to counter seasickness, it turned out to work equally well underwater.

"We are honor bound to do so!" Glint shouted his approval. Both long hunting tentacles snapped out to their full length, the fleshy pads on their ends quivering. "Onward to Siriswirll and to victory!"

"What victory?" Having carried out their master's order to efficiently and respectfully dispose of the body of the deceased rainbow runner, Sathi preceded his colleague Tythe back into the study.

Spinning, the energized cuttlefish reached out to the famulus. In a confusion of arms, the squid fought him off. "Master Oxothyr, has this fat flutterer gone mad?"

"He is merely excited." The shaman explained calmly. "Such demeanor will change when death is confronted. Combat is not like hunting," he informed the excited cuttlefish gravely. "It is nasty, methodical, unpleasant work. Your enthusiasm will flag though your efforts must not." Peering past the suitably abashed cephalopod, his gaze fastened on the silently staring Chachel. "You, hunter, will of course remain behind while your companion eagerly contributes to the defense of both communities."

Chachel refused to be baited. "Gladly will I do so. We each of us follow our own current."

"Truly." Oxothyr's tone betrayed no hint of condemnation. It did not have to.

That would have been the end of the gathering, if not for the fact that the opinion of one other present remained to be given. Drifting off to one side, Irina found herself more at a loss than ever. On top of everything else that had happened to her, it now appeared that she was about to be caught up in a fight that was not only none of her business, it did not even involve her species. Or for that matter, she told herself, her world.

Except that this was her world now, and for how long neither she nor anyone in it had any way of knowing. She could listen, observe, and ignore those aspects of it that did not directly demand her participation. Or, she could involve herself. Dare she? Everything of which Oxothyr had just spoken reeked of danger, even unto the risk of dying. What it was all about she did not know. She did not even know what a "spralaker" was. Why should she risk her life to participate in a fight against something she could not even identify?

It was with more than a little surprise, therefore, that she found herself paddling slightly forward and announcing, "I was going to drown. No, that's not right," she corrected herself. "I *was* drowning. I owe you all my life."

Arms crossed over his chest, Chachel grunted softly, not looking in her direction. "You don't owe me anything, changeling."

"All right then," she retorted curtly, "I owe Glint and Oxothyr my life. They're part of Sandrift, and Sandrift has taken me in when I most needed help." She turned to face the silently staring sack of colorful flesh, powerful suckers, and rarified intellect that was resting on the coral ledge. "I don't know what I can do, or even if I can do anything, but I'm ready to help in any way I can."

"You?" Chachel's tone was biting as he let his arms drop. "What can you, a changeling, possibly do to help? You're still learning how to breathe properly." His eyes raked her barely clad form. "You don't look like much of a fighter to me."

She drew herself up. "I'll have you know I hold a second-degree red belt in Tang Soo Do."

He blinked, uncertain. "What does that mean?"

*Not much underwater*, she thought, *but you don't know that.* "You'll see. At least I'm willing to fight." She glared back at him across the open space of the chamber.

Oxothyr might have been expected to ignore the offer from an outsider. Instead, the shaman eyed her shrewdly. "There is no knowing what unknown and unpredictable abilities might reside within a changeling. What alien skills and aptitudes." He thrust a tentacle in Chachel's direction. "Do not be so quick to judge, hunter." His attention remained focused on the drifting female. "Can you at least avail yourself of a spear?"

"Of course!" Irina spoke confidently despite having never handled a spear in her life. What could be so difficult? Surely manipulating a spear could not be any harder than learning a new computer OS? Compared to that, a spear was pretty low-tech. You aimed the pointy end at an opponent and shoved.

"Then your offer is most welcome." Oxothyr began to unfurl his arms as he slipped away from his perch. "I will call a meeting of the village council to explain what we have learned. We must gather our forces and move with all possible speed lest the invaders learn of our intent." He turned to his right. "Sathi! Notify the council members on my behalf."

"Yes, Master!" Pivoting, the famulus jetted toward the exit.

"Tythe!" The second assistant went rigid with attention. "Talk to the town couriers. Inform the swiftest of what we have discussed here today and entreat him or her to carry the news without delay to our neighbors in Siriswirll. If there is any hesitation invoke my name as executor."

"I vanish, Master!" And in seconds, the second squid proved as good as word.

"Now then." Fluttering forward, the shaman extended one cordial arm in Glint's direction while wrapping another, reassuring limb around Irina's waist. "There is much to do. Tythe and Sathi will do their best, but even they cannot be more than two places at once. As the first to learn of the danger with which we now find ourselves confronted, I intend to rely on both of you to …"

"Just a minute." Kicking hard, Chachel blocked the way out of the chamber. "What about me?"

Oxothyr stared at the troubled merson. "What about you, hunter?"

"Just because I'm not going off on some wild expedition doesn't mean I can't be of use."

Two of the shaman's remaining tentacles waved disinterestedly. "There is no need to involve yourself, Chachel. Your attitude is well known and your opinion has been noted. You need not trouble yourself further." Pushing water from his siphon, the mage used his bulk to edge the merson out of his path. "I'm sure you'll find ways of keeping yourself informed as to the eventual outcome of this solemn endeavor." Escorting both cuttlefish and changeling, he accelerated through the tunnel exit.

Chachel had to fin hard to catch up to them. "Alright then, all right!"

Oxothyr slowed. "What is 'all right'?" He inquired patiently, betraying no advance knowledge of possible responses.

Lowering his eyes and not quite sure why he was doing what he was doing, the hunter muttered sullenly, "I'll come too, I guess."

"I knew you would!" Jetting over to him, the ever-optimistic Glint tried to wrap half a dozen tentacles around his friend's face in order to give him a peck on the cheek. Swatting at the questing arms, Chachel fought off the embrace.

"That's very good of you." Oxothyr's voice was dignified as ever. Held loosely in one of his arms, Irina smiled at the hunter. Angry at himself and feeling that he had somehow been adroitly maneuvered against his will into helping his fellow citizens, Chachel turned and kicked hard for the exit.

"Someone has to come along to make sure the changeling doesn't endanger anyone else by doing something stupid!"

Already used to the merson's bad-tempered mind-set and constant carping a silent Irina watched him go. His persona was as unappealing, she decided, as his legs were good.

# – IX –

**H**overing in respectful silence within the meeting hall that had been carved from beneath a high arch of rock and coral, the Sandrift village council listened in silence to Oxothyr's presentation. When the shaman finished, he was peppered with questions from several of the representatives. These were more perfunctory than heartfelt, as the majority of those present were shocked and enraged by what had apparently befallen their neighbors to the north. At the conclusion of the emergency meeting, multiple shouts of "To arms!" and "Revenge!" resounded through the warm water.

Preparations for a response proceeded apace. They did not include Oxothyr, who together with his assistants had arrangements of his own to make. They did not involve Chachel, who hung back in the murky depths of his cave and brooded on the inexplicable decision that had resulted in his moment of uncharacteristic altruism. They did, however, engage the attention of a fascinated Irina.

As an outsider who had volunteered to participate in the expedition to aid Siriswirll, she was granted grudging acceptance even by those who remained suspicious of her presence and possible motives. As such, she was not challenged as she moved around both halves of the village observing the measures that were being taken. Though unable to contribute directly to the somber, disciplined preparations, she was allowed to swim freely anywhere she wished.

Having previously caught sight only of spears and knives, she was surprised to encounter several dozen archers loading their weapons into large carryalls. The latter had been fashioned from treated, flexible sea fans that had been fastened together. Fashioned from baleen that had been salvaged from the skeletons of dead whales, bows were sleek and extremely flexible. Bowstrings came from a variety of organic sources. Arrows of sharpened bone were common, as was a dizzying variety of tridents, halberds, and related long weapons. Some of these were tipped with vicious sea urchin spines or lined with embedded razor clams.

Though she looked for clubs, maces, knobkerries, and their ilk, she saw none. While not a fighter, much less someone with personal experience of such weapons, their absence did not surprise her. She might not know much about primitive weaponry, but she knew water. You could stab through it fairly effectively, whereas trying to swing an object of any mass would meet only increasing resistance the wider the arc it encompassed. Underwater a rapier would be far more effective than a broadsword. Not that she viewed the available arsenal with any proprietary interest. She had decided that if caught up in any confrontation she would stay back and rely on her knife for defense.

It was a small but impressive company that finally set out. Cheered along and waved farewell by those too young or too old to participate, the relief force consisted of more than two hundred male and female mersons. They were accompanied by half again as many manyarms. In addition to octopods and cuttlefish of varying size, there were species of squid larger than any she had yet seen. Some had bodies four feet long, as big around as her own, with arms that trailed behind them another twelve feet. Cylinders of pure muscle, they were given the task of hauling most of the expedition's supplies. Though they could sense direction quite well while traveling backward, while they were occupied in pulling the supply carryalls they often relied on others to assure them that they were indeed headed in the right direction.

Sweeping out of the canyon in a flat, winding column, the soldiers of Sandrift followed the lead of half a dozen scouts both merson and manyarm. With the mersons singing songs of defiance while the manyarms produced an accompanying lightshow by alternating colors and patterns in time to the music, Irina found herself dazzled by the martial display. She was not the only one. A familiar cuttlefish ascended directly in front of her.

"Isn't it grand, oh isn't it so grand!" Weaving up and down in the water, Glint generated small pressure waves in his wake as he stayed just ahead of her.

Irina could hardly deny it. Spectacle was spectacle, the last thing she wanted to do was rain on the cuttlefish's parade (though that could be done only in a figurative sense), and in any case, it would not have been polite. Still, she could not keep from adding somewhat circuitously, "Parades are what armed forces do best."

"'Armed forces'?" Glint eyed her with interest. "Is that what you call soldiers where you come from?" He spread his ten arms as wide as possible; a blossom with suckers. "I like it."

"It doesn't mean forces with lots of arms," she tried to explain, "it means—oh, never mind." As she swam behind him, quietly exulting in the extra propulsion Oxothyr's changeling spell had bestowed on her transformed limbs, she studied the procession surrounding her. Her present location was near the center and slightly to the rear. The biggest squid who were towing the largest carryalls full of weapons, supplies, and foodstuffs seemed to move through the water without any effort at all, their powerful siphons often ejecting hundreds of gallons of water in tandem. Such cephalopodan precision was wonderful to see.

Something bumped her hard from behind, throwing off her flutter kick. It took her a moment to regain her stroke. She was not entirely surprised to see Poylee swim up beside her.

"Sorry, Irina." Her erstwhile hostess smiled, an expression that conveyed mixed messages. "I need to look where I'm going. You're not hurt, are you?" Irina was unable to tell for certain from the merson's tone whether the query expressed concern or anticipation.

"It's all right, I'm fine. How are you?"

"Looking forward to a fight." A hand indicated the multiple bone spears that were strapped securely to her back. "I'm always ready for a good fight. As you'll see when the time comes."

Irina stared back evenly. "I'm sure when that time arrives I'll be prepared to defend myself. Where's Chachel? I thought he'd be with you."

The smile, sham or otherwise, disappeared. "He hovers around Telnarch, Kesreach, and the others, listening as they plot strategy. Sometimes they invite him to participate, but he always declines." Her expression brightened. "One day he will join fully in the life of the village. I know it. He just needs the right kind of encouragement."

"Oh, I don't know," Irina murmured by way of response. "I get the feeling he really enjoys his isolation. I've known men like that. Afraid to commit to anything. They live out their lives in isolation; sometimes happily, sometimes not."

Poylee's visage darkened again. "He just needs the proper encouragement," she repeated, more tersely this time. When she turned to swim away, her right foot came close to smacking the other woman in the ribs and Irina had to kick hard and fast to one side to avoid taking a nasty blow.

"She doesn't like me very much. I thought she did at first, but now she doesn't." She returned her gaze to the escorting manyarm. "Doesn't she realize I have no interest in Chachel?"

"It doesn't matter if you do or not," Glint replied. "All that matters is that she *thinks* you do. It would be much worse if my friend showed any interest in you."

"He doesn't—does he?" *What an odd thing to add*, she mused.

"Chachel is like a manyarm with its skin turned inside out. He has no interest in anyone—often not even himself." Glint proceeded to relate to her the lamentable details of his companion's personal history.

Afterwards Irina was quiet for a long time, swimming in silence behind the cuttlefish, feeling little but the occasional push of water against her face when he drifted close enough for her to sense the pulsing output of his siphon.

"That's terrible," she finally muttered. "It explains a lot." She looked up at the manyarm. "It doesn't bother Poylee?"

A flash of orange running from tail to head rippled through the body of the cuttlefish: a cephalopodan shrug. "She has made it her mission, I think, to rescue him from himself. Better odds to be had in recovering a turtle that has lost its shell. These relationships are so much easier for my kind. Once a month we go crazy, and the rest of the time we are sane."

Irina's thoughts wandered back to her world; a reality that seemed increasingly distant and strange. "I have friends like that. But with them it's more a mental imperative, not a physical one." She hesitated, suddenly desirous of changing the subject. "You know what I miss from my home?"

The most developed of all invertebrate eyes stared back at her. "Your friends and family?"

"Coffee," she told him.

Ten minutes of subsequent explication failed to enlighten the cuttlefish as to the nature and severity of that particular deprivation.

She had not thought to ask how far it was to Siriswirll or how long it would take to get there. Having built her spirits up to deal with whatever kind of violent confrontation might be forthcoming, she was therefore somewhat disappointed to learn that Oxothyr and the council had decided to stop at Shakestone first. Not only to ascertain the truth and the depth of the dead rainbow runner's account, but to see if a hasty examination of that village would yield any useful information about its assailants.

As soon as she set eyes on that town several days later, she forgot about everything else.

In the water in front of the column, the village slowly took on shape and form. Unlike canyon-clinging Sandrift, it had been built on the westward, seaward-facing side of a gently sloping reef. Customized coralline dwellings and other structures descended in terraces from near the top of the reef downward toward darker depths. Or at least, they once had done so.

If anything, the doomed herald Zesqu had understated the state of affairs when he had reported that Shakestone had been destroyed. Obliterated would have been a better description. After squads of mersons and manyarms had chased off the remaining sharks and other scavengers, a stunned Irina joined the rest of the expedition in fanning out to assess the totality of the devastation—and to see, unlikely as it seemed at first glance, if there were any survivors.

The inspiration for the name of the village had manifested itself early on. Eons ago a towering granitic monolith whose peak had reached nearly to the mirrorsky had been severely fractured by some unknown tectonic cataclysm. The collapsed pile of rubble that was the result of this violent geologic disturbance now stood mute sentry over the devastated town, a crumbled headstone that would forever serve as silent reminder of what had once been a thriving community of mersons and manyarms.

Though she had by now come to think of the continually gesticulating Glint as a good friend, she still had to remind herself that his kind had suffered here as severely as the population of more human-like mersons. It was a realization difficult to avoid, given the substantial number of brutally amputated sucker-lined arms that lay scattered throughout the ruins of the community. She did not have to hunt for them. All one had to do was look for a cluster of excited fish swarming to the attack. A dismembered cuttlefish arm, several of squid, another of octopus usually lay at the center of these morbidly enthusiastic piscine revels.

Less often, she came across reef fish picking bits of flesh from a piece of merson: a hand or arm, a leg or severed torso. She was able to cope with the appearance of a still largely intact dead squid. The two-foot long vacant-eyed body had been sliced open lengthwise as if by an enormous knife. Entrails drifted in the gentle current like deformed, attenuated balloons.

That encounter was not sufficient to prepare her for sight of a dead merson child. The six-year old's corpse was wedged in a crevice in the reef. It had been jammed there on purpose, or else the boy had tried to use it for a refuge. Proving that whoever had attacked Splitrock played no favorites, the small body had been opened up as neatly and efficiently as that of the squid. As with everything else she had seen thus far, this morbid tableaux proved educational. For example, she learned that it was perfectly natural and possible to throw up underwater.

As she struggled to recover from her nausea and the spontaneous evacuation of her insides, eager schools of three-inch long anthias and damsels, gobies and blennies, appeared as if out of nowhere to pick and choose from the rapidly dispersing upchuck. Acknowledgement of their unbridled enthusiasm for the undigested contents of her stomach threatened to resuscitate a tremulous urge to regurgitate. Despite her churning intestinal discomfort, she willed herself not to puke again and to swim away.

It had been a challenge to look directly at the bodies—or rather, at the fragments that remained. The dead boy was the most intact of any she encountered, perhaps because of his hiding place in the coral cleft. Elsewhere, teams of mersons and manyarms from Sandrift were recovering what they could. She wondered what would become of the salvaged tissue. Did the merson inhabitants of this world bury their dead, or their remains? She decided that was a question whose answer could wait for another, kinder time.

Not only were the inhabitants of Shakestone missing, so was a good deal of the village itself. In the course of her stay in Sandrift, she had seen enough of construction techniques and long-standing buildings to know that flattened dwellings and crumbling shop fronts were not representative of some new and eclectic architectural style, but rather a destructive force of unfamiliar power that had been ruthlessly applied.

As she swam through the natural passageways that had been cut in the coral by eons of tidal action she was unable to find a single intact structure. Strips of protective window and door netting clung like shredded rags to decoratively bred staghorn coral. Occasionally a loose piece would tumble past her like a sheet of newspaper caught in the wind. Roofs had been caved in, walls had been pulled down, and doorways smashed open wide. What sort of weapon or creature was capable of doing such damage to coral that had the consistency of solid rock?

"Spralakers" she had been told. She *still* did not know what a spralaker was. She was very much afraid that before too much more time passed she was likely to find out.

As it happened, the members of the Sandrift village council who had joined the expedition were at that same moment contemplating many of the same questions as their changeling visitor, and having as little luck in coming up with answers. Having positioned themselves outside the ruins of the town hall, the conversation of the ten venerable mersons and manyarms alternated between expressions of commiseration for the fate of the deceased, whose bodies had been so rudely treated, and sometimes heated argument over what to do once the last body part had been properly disposed of.

It was amid this emotional and tactical turmoil that Chachel arrived, accompanied by the ever easy-going Glint and escorted by the far more somber pair of armed squid who had been sent to fetch him. Detaching himself from the ongoing debate, counselor Telnarch swam over to greet the hunter.

"What's going on here?" Chachel nodded toward the discussion, the tenor of which was rising and falling with disarming irregularity. The shaman Oxothyr, he noted, was right in the middle of it all, verbally as well as physically.

"Having seen what has happened here and garnered some notion as to the gravity of the destruction," the counselor explained, "we are trying to decide how best to continue onward to the relief of Siriswirll. Or indeed, even if we should." Instead of the usual commanding tone, the senior representative's tenor verged on the apologetic.

Chachel nodded once, briskly. "What has that to do with me?"

Telnarch's voice shifted further down-volume, from the apologetic to the obsequious. "You have roamed farther than most who call Sandrift home, Chachel-hunter."

"I never call Sandrift ho ..."

"You have seen and encountered many things," the counselor continued quickly, cutting him off, "that the rest of us would find alien and strange."

*Like me*, Chachel thought, keeping the reaction to himself. "Go on." He could see that the counselor was increasingly uncomfortable with the line of conversation he had chosen. *Good*, the hunter thought. Let him twist in the current awhile longer.

"We—I—the council would appreciate your input. We must decide how to move to Siriswirll and what to do if we encounter any hostile force."

"So the council is seeking my counsel? How novel."

Telnarch swallowed. None of this was coming easily to him. He held the testy hermit in no more esteem than did any of his colleagues. With the possible exception of the village shaman, of course. But then, as befitted a mage it was to be expected that Oxothyr's tastes would occasionally run outside the mainstream.

"We would welcome any useful suggestions you might have," Telnarch finished stiffly. It required an effort for the counselor to articulate the request without scorn. Remembering the number of bodies of the innocent that he had encountered that morning helped him to moderate his tone.

Coming from a counselor as respected as Telnarch, the request qualified as barely a step above outright begging. Chachel therefore condescended to render a reply. Conversation ceased as counselors young and old turned to pay attention.

The hunter had barely opened his mouth to speak when Glint zoomed in front of him.

"It's a good thing you've decided to listen to us." The cuttlefish started in without waiting to be introduced. "Whatever attacked Shakestone are like no spralakers we have dealt with before." Waving tentacles gestured over the heads of the assembled. "See how the town hall was destroyed! Not just entered and wormed, but taken apart as if it was made of sponge."

A smaller, senior cousin of the daunting Oxothyr, Councilor Vararem let all eight of his arms drift in the indicated direction. "Tell us something we don't already know, idle-arms. We have seen the devastation for ourselves." One set of S-shaped cephalopodan eyes glared at another. "Hopefully your limb-challenged companion will not speak so eagerly of the painfully obvious."

Taken back but still defiant, Glint squirted a couple of sharp pulses from his siphon and backed up, once more relinquishing the water to Chachel.

"What Glint is trying to point out," the hunter clarified as he continued his friend's animated refrain, "is that this was no ordinary spralaker raid and that those who are responsible for it were interested in more than just pillage for the sake of spoils." When he gestured, it was to take in the entire scene of annihilation and not just the ruined village hall behind them.

"What makes you believe so?" Bigger than the shaman's assistants, the squid Golorn gestured with his two hunting tentacles as a deep blue flowed the length of his body.

Chachel was quick to respond. "Too many body parts left lying about." His gaze traveled around the assembly, meeting merson and manyarm stares with equal assurance. "Spralakers may be inconceivably ugly, they may be innately nasty, but one thing they are is efficient and deliberate. On the occasions when they do manage to carry out a successful raid, they don't leave anything edible behind."

"Then why commit such oversight here?" Merson counselor Serenda's hair was almost as long as that of the changeling, but black streaked with much gray.

"To frighten," Chachel explained. "To terrify. To discourage any pursuit or thought of revenge." Once more he indicated the carefully groomed and customized coral structures that surrounded them. "Why else expend the effort to destroy dwellings and storerooms, shops and schools?"

Oxothyr chose that moment to come forward. "I believe the hunter is right." Cable-like tentacles motioned. "This was more than a raid. This was an effort to exterminate and to intimidate."

"I don't follow you, shaman." Counselor Herremot rubbed at his short beard as he regarded the octopod.

Oxothyr looked past him, into the north. "Something is abroad in the world that has not been here before. It swims just beyond the edge of my vision. Every time I seek it and think I might be close to an understanding, it darts away quick-swift as a bluefin. I cannot get hold of an image of it. But this I do sense: it means to merson and manyarm alike no good, and it is spreading."

Anxious murmurs arose among the assembled counselors. Bony hands lightly made contact with soft mantles while tentacles of varying length stroked arms and torsos.

"What must we do, wise one?" The only cuttlefish present besides Glint, Abrelorn was young but eager.

"I can drift and dream in my abode in Sandrift," the shaman replied, "and hope explanation and answer come to me. Or," he added more forcefully, "we can do what we came for. Fight, and perhaps learn from one of those who carried out this atrocity what lies behind their motivation."

"Onward to Siriswirll!" Counselor Dyanbre thrust his spear toward the mirrorsky.

With varying degrees of enthusiasm the defiant cry was taken up by the rest of the assembled. Glint added his own exuberant screeching to the call as Sathi and Tythe chimed in with keen squeaks of their own. Only two among the gathering did not voice their zeal. Oxothyr refrained in order to maintain his dignity, and

Chachel never cheered for anything.

But as the meeting broke up, the counselors dispersing to inform their constituents of what had been decided, the hunter drifted over to confront the brooding mage.

"I listen to your voice, shaman," Chachel murmured quietly. "As your skin talks, I mark carefully the patterns and the colors. You speak of more than spralakers. You say you cannot see what is behind them or the uncommon ruination that has befallen this village, but I find myself wondering: do you have any thoughts on the matter that for whatever reason you choose not to voice to the majority of merson and manyarm?"

As his famuli hovered nearby, Oxothyr focused his attention on the hunter. "You are perceptive, Chachel. You would have to be, to survive and find food by yourself. Regrettably, I spoke the only truth I have. I see nothing." Reaching out, he rested the tip of one arm on the hunter's left shoulder. Chachel did not shake it off.

"The marks of the spralakers are all over the ruins of Shakestone. Evidence of their fury lies everywhere like a trail of slime. I only know that there has to be more to this than what appears. I can taste it!" Suckers gripped the merson's shoulder as the shaman's grip tightened. "But I cannot see it. Until I can, we must fight not only spralakers but our lack of knowledge." The arm withdrew. "Hunting solitaire, one learns how to fight. On my recommendation, the council will put you in charge of a squadron."

Chachel backed water. "Coming from you, revered conjurer, that's an honor. But I must decline. I take charge of no one but myself."

Little more than a soft sack of flesh, skin, and organs, the shaman's body shimmied in the current. "I understand. I am not pleased, but I understand." Obtruding his siphon, he jetted away, flanked by his assistants. Glint came forward to rejoin his friend.

Poylee had watched it all from a distance. Too far away to overhear and too uncertain to understand what had transpired solely from the gestures she had been able to observe, she knew only that Chachel's expertise had been called upon. Shunned until he was needed, she thought derisively. How typical of the council. At least they had eventually recognized what he had to contribute. She turned to rejoin the other volunteers from her neighborhood.

She, of course, had been touting the hunter's attributes for years.

The general queasiness that had invested Irina ever since the relief expedition's arrival at ravaged Shakestone continued to wax and wane. Convincing herself that it was not due to her system undergoing another sea change, she gathered up enough courage to start looking for possible remedies to her persistent nausea. Pills and potions failed to alleviate the fluctuating discomfort. When eventually she approached him for advice, Oxothyr told her that she was suffering from a sickness of the spirit: something only time and determination could cure.

Such counsel was of small comfort as she wandered among the busy mersons and manyarms. Everyone was working with a purpose. Everyone had something to do—except her. Having rediscovered a little of herself in the village, she now felt lost all over again. In a few days' time, it was possible that many of her newfound acquaintances were going to die. Every bit as aware of this as she was, none of them had time for small talk or was in the mood for idle chat.

In due course she came upon Chachel. Characteristically, the hunter had found a place off by himself in one of the ruined homes. Who it had belonged to originally he did not know and did not care. There was no sign of Glint. She swam down to greet him. Entering the abandoned dwelling was easy. The roof had been torn off by some unknown, powerful force.

Not roof, she told herself. Oshenerth structures did not have roofs in the manner of buildings in her world. There, a roof was intended to keep out sun and rain and wind. None of those threats were present here. Dwellings existed to provide privacy. Weather consisted only of currents of varying strength. In a sense, buildings served the same function as clothing, only on a larger scale.

When she found him he was busy sharpening one of the half dozen long bone spears he had brought with him. "Hello, Chachel." His acknowledgment of her arrival consisted of a curt grunt. She indicated the spears lying nearby. "You don't use a bow?"

"I can," he told her as he pushed the well-worn whetstone repeatedly along one side of the bone blade. "But I prefer the spear.

I believe it's more ethical to look into the eyes of the enemy you kill rather than to slaughter from a distance."

The ethics of slaughter not being a topic she'd had much occasion to discuss, she chose not to pursue that particular line of questioning. Then what to talk about? Hovering nearby, she watched him in silence until the rope that had been wound around her innards decided to knot once again.

Seeing her grimace and crook sharply forward, he paused in his honing. "You're feeling unwell?"

She tried to smile. The resulting expression was unflattering. "I don't know if it's something I ate, or just seeing all the death here. The decomposing body parts, the putrefying organs ..." She swallowed deliberately, hoping to hold off the worst of the symptoms.

He turned back to his work, indifferent. "People died. That's all. People die every day." He gestured at their surroundings. "The only difference here is that more met their end as part of a mass killing instead of as individuals. Ask one of the villagers working as a server to prepare some of the scraps for you. Maybe if you eat a little of those who were here...."

She threw up again. Not much this time, since by now her stomach was mostly empty. He looked on with interest. Apparently a changeling vomited no differently than did an ordinary merson. He remarked upon the similarity.

"You heartless bastard," she snapped when she could finally speak again. Then she began to sob, her eyes stinging in the absence of tears.

His tone softened—a little. "Why are you crying, Irina?"

"Why am I ...?" She fought to regain control of herself. "Oh, I don't know. My world is gone, my body's been transformed, nobody here likes me, I miss my home and my friends and my work, I'm stuck with people who eat everything and anything including each other." She eyed him pleadingly. "I don't want to be in somebody else's war. I don't want to be in *anybody's* war. I just want to go *home*."

"You think I want to be in this fight?"

She sniffed, sucked in ocean, and coughed, her gill slits flaring. "But I thought ..."

"What? That I like to kill? It's true I enjoy hunting." With a wave of his hand he indicated the center of the devastated village where the bulk of the expedition from Sandrift had set up temporary quarters. "Like many others, I hunt to live, to eat. Not, despite what you may have heard or may think, for the joy of killing. The realworld is a cruel and indifferent place, Irina. It doesn't care whether you live or die. You can fight to live, or you can become food for another whose will to exist is greater than your own. There are many out there, in the deep blue, who would be happy to relieve you of your anxieties. Life is a choice, not a right. Civilization is sustained by determination. It can't survive on its own indifference."

A little stunned, she blinked at him. "You—you sound like Oxothyr."

Picking up the spear he had been working on, he studied his handiwork out of his one eye. "He would not be flattered by the comparison. Because I choose to live apart from others does not mean I reject knowledge. Or wisdom, on those rare instances when it can be found."

Kicking lightly with her bare toes, she stirred sand and tiny mollusks underfoot. "I think there's more to you, hunter Chachel, than you like to let on."

"And I think you are a weak, nosy, irritating intruder whose return to her own place of being will certainly find both our worlds better off."

Queasiness and fear gave way to anger. "You—you think you're the only one who's suffered a loss in life? Glint told me your story. You think you're the only one capable of sorrow or deserving of sympathy? Just when I think there's a spark of humanity in you, you say something like that!"

He frowned at her. "What's 'humanity'?"

"Something that doesn't seem to exist here—or at least not in you." Kicking hard, she shot upward out of the ruined residence. Once clear of the walls, she angled toward the center of the village. The last he saw of her she was swimming full out in the direction of a small knot of females.

Glint arrived not long thereafter. He hovered in front of his friend, staring. "Something's the matter. Something has happened."

"Nothing's happened." Setting aside the now razor-sharp spear, the hunter selected another and began working on its business end with the whetstone.

Turning maroon, the cuttlefish moved closer. "Don't lie to me, Chachel. You've no one else to talk truth to, so don't lie to me."

He looked up. "It's nothing. The changeling was here, feeling sorry for herself. Either she ate something that upset her stomach, or else she doesn't have the stomach for this kind of work. She was seeking a remedy. Nothing more."

Cocking an eye sideways, Glint reached out with one tentacle to pluck a pair of passing copepods and thrust them into his open beak. "A remedy for upset guts, or for something else?"

The hunter's expression contorted. "What are you prattling about, finger-face?"

Swallowing the snack, the cuttlefish commenced a slow ascent. "You really have no idea, do you?"

"You know how I hate facile accusations that are made without any subject attached." Reaching up, Chachel took a half-hearted swipe at the rising manyarm. "Where are you going? You just got here."

"To find the changeling and see if I can help."

With a shrug, Chachel returned to his sharpening. "Why waste your time? Either she'll get over what's unsettling her or she won't. It has nothing to do with you."

Turning his tail end toward the center of ravaged Shakestone, the cuttlefish pushed water through his siphon and shot backward, leaving only a last observation in his wake.

"And they say that my kind are cold-blooded...."

There was a sameness to the terrain near Siriswirll that troubled her for reasons she could not pin down. The feeling of disquiet did not leave as she helped, insofar as she could, other members of the expedition to set up the rest of the camp. An explanation for her unease did not occur to her until that evening, when she realized the scenery and the sights that surrounded her at this new location were every bit as fascinating, absorbing, and colorful as those she had encountered at Sandrift or, its destruction notwithstanding, at Shakestone. Beauty was everywhere: in the outrageously colorful fish swarming the reef, in the striking pelagics who patrolled its outer limits, in the sand and the rock and the crevices in the coral.

That was the problem.

As an occasional visitor to the underwater realm of her own world, she had been endlessly enthralled by what she had encountered there. Living, existing in such an environment on a daily basis, was leading toward her already becoming jaded. That was why the "sameness" of Siriswirll had unsettled her.

As if responding to her newfound ennui, something entirely new and strange was about to present itself.

She was resting near several other merson females, listening to their discussion without joining in. They did not extend themselves to bring her into the conversation but neither did they shun her. Soon most of the tethered or englobed glowfish and coelenterates illuminating the camp would be shrouded for the night. Except for the light of the moon filtering down through the mirrorsky, darkness would descend upon the expedition.

Out at the extreme range of her underwater night vision a line of sapphires appeared, marching determinedly eastward.

Sitting up straight on the patch of white sand, she found herself staring hard into the distance. Her eyes were not deceiving her. The dots of incredibly intense blue light were wending a winding path upward toward the top of the circular reef that had been chosen by the counselors, for its location and defensibility, as a campsite. Risking censure, she broke into the ongoing chatter long enough to elicit an explanation.

"Oh, I forget," replied an older merson, "you're unfamiliar with the simplest things." She nodded in the direction of the cobalt column. "It's just a procession of hoobia."

"What are hoobia?"

The female shook her head slowly, pitying the changeling's ignorance. "Go and see for yourself if you want. Hoobia of all kinds are harmless. Messy sometimes, but harmless. But don't stray beyond the camp boundaries."

No worries about that, Irina knew as she finned off toward the line of intense blue. She had already lost her world. If at night in an unfamiliar ocean she lost sight of the camp, she might as well seal shut her gill slits and give up.

As soon as she drew close to what from a distance looked like a queen's unwound necklace, she understood what hoobia were. Nudibranchs, snails without shells or operculum, their backs were dotted with bioluminescent blue circlets that glowed in the darkness. Only, in the seas she was familiar with, there crawled nothing so brilliant, so beautiful, so utterly defining of the description *blue*. The organically-generated lights were almost electric, so intense was their radiance. Why the spectacular nudibranchs were marching in single file toward the shallowest part of the reef, where wavelets broke on its crest, she had no idea.

So she asked them. The last thing she expected was a reply. But in Oshenerth, it seemed, every creature large or small was capable of conversing to a greater or lesser extent. Where bioluminescent nudibranchs were concerned, it seemed that lesser was certainly the case.

Neither leader nor trailer, one azure crawler fluttered its feathery gills in her direction and explained in response to her inquiry, "We don't know. Some nights we go up the reef. Some nights we go down."

Hovering in the warm, dark water just above and to one side of the column of living jewels, she persisted. "But why go in line together? Where I come from, your kind always travel individually."

A second sapphire-laden snail spoke up. "They must be lonely."

And that was that. Turning, she kicked back toward camp. Behind her, the column of thrillingly luminous living blue continued to thread its shimmering cerulean path upward. As she swam, she felt improbably better about alien surroundings that could once again no longer be counted on to be wholly predictable.

Unrequited beauty will do that to a person.

◊

Preoccupied with her own thoughts and concerns, she had not seen the trio of scouts leave as darkness began to fall. While the rest of the expedition remained in temporary encampment, Chachel, the powerfully built Jorosab, and Glint struck out for Siriswirll on orders from the council members to reconnoiter the situation and report back as quickly as possible. Jorosab had been sent because of his fighting prowess and a professed indifference to whomever might accompany him. Chachel and Glint had been chosen because if they didn't make it back, the council presumed no one in Sandrift would miss or mourn them.

Guided by a negligible, pale red glow generated by Glint, they worked their way to the west, hugging the sea floor where the natural light from above the mirrorsky was least likely to reveal them to any patrolling spralakers. The occasional inquisitive night hunters they met hurriedly turned tail to avoid armed manyarm and mersons as soon as they were recognized. The one big shark they encountered out foraging was a ragged-tooth; impressive in size and fearsome of appearance but among the more inoffensive of its kind. It muttered a characteristically passive apology for getting in their way and slothfully moved off into the dark.

As morning began to seep through the water and the three scouts moved on, the constant clicking and chatter of nocturnal reef dwellers gave way to a distant and unmistakably unnatural clamor. Though still indistinct, its source lay directly ahead. Plainly, the commotion was coming from somewhere in the vicinity of Siriswirll. To the approaching mersons and manyarm it was at once alien yet familiar. All of them had heard screaming before; Chachel had heard more than most. But nothing like this. Never en masse, arising simultaneously from so many different kinds of throats.

"Slow and careful now," the hunter whispered. "If we are seen, we're lost."

"Don't tell me my business, hermit," Jorosab growled.

"Both of you shut up: all mersons talk too much." An annoyed Glint flashed a silently reproachful red-orange.

When the rising din had grown loud enough to all but vibrate the water around them, they surveyed the last barrier reef before Siriswirll itself in search of the highest possible overlook. Swimming and pulling their way up a steep coral slope, they paused at the very limit of breathability. Ascend any higher and they would find the mirrorsky itself breaking over them. Beyond it lay the Burning Void and all the horrors it held. A merson would suffocate there, if their flesh didn't burst into flame first. A manyarm like Glint would last no longer. Few creatures from the realworld could survive long in such hellish conditions. Among those who could, interestingly, were certain species of spralakers.

It was the perfect place to try and get a sense of what was happening at Siriswirll. No spralaker was likely to look for mersons or a manyarm this close to the mirrorsky, and at this time of day the Great Yellow Smoker that suffused the void with heat and light would be directly above them, making it impossible to single them out from below.

Finning to the edge of the overlook, Jorosab muttered an occasional curse as projecting coral nicked at his skin. A large patch of bright yellow fire coral forced them to detour to their right and descend more than Chachel would have liked. They were still high enough that they ought to be able to see everything, he assured himself. To his left, the much lighter Glint bobbed in the waves of the proximate mirrorsky. It was not rough today, but neither did it sit flat calm with the glassiness the hunter would have preferred.

Then he found himself peering over the rim. Chachel sucked in his breath. Beside him, Jorosab was equally transfixed, and as he took in the scene below even Glint's tentacles ceased their usually constant movement.

Siriswirll was built on the edge of a drop-off. Steep but not sheer, the cliff that marked the town's limits served as a conduit for an upwelling current so powerful that no permanent structures could be fashioned from or attached to the ragged, rough coral clinging doggedly to its edge. While the rear of the community was therefore devoid of the usual forest of anemones, cnidarians, sponges, and other immobile reef dwellers, it did attract swarms of hungry reef fish eager to dine on the rich deep-sea broth that came coursing upward.

The same current weakened and flattened out as it swept over the ridge where the community was situated. To leave the town all one had to do was rise from within a building or from behind a protective wall and let the surge from the west deep carry the body forward. Returning was much more of chore. The conditions also made the village difficult to assault, since any attacker would have to contend not only with the strong current blowing directly into their face but also with weapons that would gain an extra boost in velocity and striking power from the surge behind them.

That had not dissuaded a small army of spralakers from mounting a direct frontal attack.

None of the scouts from Sandrift's relief party had ever seen so many of the hardshell folk in one place. Usually they were to be found alone or in small groups. Cannibalism being a common and accepted feature of spralaker life, the rationale for large gatherings did not exist. It's hard to hold a dialogue with someone who is in the process of trying to make a meal of your legs.

Yet these spralakers seemed to have overcome their proclivity for fighting among themselves. Searching the field of battle far and wide, Chachel certainly saw no evidence of it. Driven by a single, unified purpose, the aggressors were focused on penetrating the town's defenses. Jorosab picked out places where vocal arguments had indeed broken out among the assailants, but nothing substantial enough to inhibit the attack. These spralakers were cooperating in a manner unprecedented.

Battling the current that blew in their faces as they marched forward, rank upon rank of heavily armed invaders advanced into a steady hail of arrows being unleashed by the towns' defenders. There must be hundreds of the hardshells, an unsettled Chachel decided. Despite the number of attackers, Siriswirll's defenders were giving a good account of themselves. Aided by the current behind them, one precisely placed arrow after another found weak spots in the enemy's armor.

A temporary low wall of rock and coral had been erected in haste on the sandy plain outside the village. No permanent bastions protected Siriswirll, and unlike Sandrift it was too large to be enclosed by a carefully propagated coral dome. Even an ingenuous stranger with no military experience would have seen the futility of erecting defensive walls in such a place. While many denizens of Oshenerth could simply swim over the top of such a barrier, spralakers could not. They were poor swimmers. But Chachel had yet to encounter one that could not ascend any wall, even one equipped with an overhang. A wall imposing enough to give an attacking spralaker pause would have to be higher than a town the size of Siriswirll could afford, and defended by more fighters than it could muster.

What the impermanent and hurriedly raised barrier of rubble *was* useful for was warding off incoming weapons. It was literally a line in the sand. The increasingly desperate defenders were fielding every strategy they could think of to keep their assailants from surmounting the wall and entering the town itself. Those hardshells who succeeded in reaching the temporary barricade flung themselves upon it with a directness and ferocity that was shocking to the three scouts looking on from above. Clearly, these were not ordinary spralakers. For one thing, most of them were at least merson-sized, and some were bigger. For another, they fought with a confidence atypical of their kind.

As for the sandy battlefield itself, it remained oddly unsoiled. Caught up by the remnants of the current that roared over the edge of the drop-off, bodies and body parts were swept away, to be cleaned up by wandering scavengers with no interest in the mêlée's eventual winner. Though he could not see them, not even if he'd had two good eyes, Chachel knew for a certainty that hundreds of sharks must be lingering far down current. Drawn by the dispersion of so much blood in the water, they would wait well away from the field of battle and when opportunity presented itself, swoop in to scoop up the debris. In a shark's ideal world, both sides would lose badly.

"This is madness, the world has gone mad!" Hugging the lip of coral, Jorosab edged forward for a wider view. "Spralakers never attack anything but food that is smaller than themselves. They are born defensive. They do not attack individual hunters, much less whole villages."

"The sight is indeed disarming." Glint straight away employed as strong a wording as he could muster. "Spralakers are meant to be food, not soldiers. I have never seen any so big."

"I have," Chachel put in, "but they were solitaires, like myself." He shook his head. "You are right, Jorosab. Something is very wrong here. The shaman hinted it might be such."

Jorosab started to fin forward, over the rim. Reaching out, Chachel grabbed his right leg to keep him from advancing. Looking back in anger, the other hunter tried to kick free.

"They need help down there! Can't you hear the shouts of the desperate and the dying? The current is stained with their screaming. Our brethren cry out for relief!"

"All the relief we can marshal," Chachel readily agreed. "We are three here." He nodded toward the battlefield. "Look at the weapons they are using, besides those they were born to. When did you last see a spralaker armed with a sea whip, or throwing something besides a rock? If we each kill a dozen, that would be helpful to the besieged, yes—but not as useful as reporting back what we have seen here and returning in strength."

Hovering a finger-length above Chachel's head, Glint added his own judgment. "I can regrow an arm. I can't regrow information." For emphasis he turned dark blue and flashed ripples of red.

The gill flaps at his neck spread wide, Jorosab looked from merson to manyarm, then spoke through clenched lips. "It is hard not to go to the aid of those whose shrieks fill my ears, but you speak the truth out of different mouths. We need to get back and tell the others." Rising from atop the brain coral where he had been lying, he turned to go—and nearly swam into the giant triton triggerfish that had appeared behind him.

Mounted on a simple woven saddle atop the triton was a single spralaker.

It was difficult to say who was more surprised: the enemy scout, or the trio who had been scouting the enemy. Of course, as far as their respective positions were concerned, from the startled spralaker's point of view the definitions were reversed. Recovering swiftly from the initial shock of their presence, the red and white spralaker nudged his mount and whirled to escape.

Jorosab's bow and arrows were still slung across his back. So were Chachel's spears. The hunter had to make an instant decision: he could draw and throw his knife, but it would have to be a perfect cast. Quick and powerful, too, before the intervening water slowed its momentum. Or he could throw …

Even flattened out, no cuttlefish had as hydrodynamic a shape as a squid. On the other hand, a manyarm in pursuit could change direction whereas a thrown weapon was committed to a single course. By throwing Glint instead of a spear, Chachel gave his companion just enough of a boost to let the cuttlefish overtake the fleeing spralaker. Extending his two hunting tentacles to their greatest extent, Glint plucked the enemy scout right off his mount.

Both adversaries were about the same size. In a one-on-one brawl Glint would have had the advantage of speed and agility, the spralaker those of strength and natural weaponry. But there was no chance and no need of such a fight. Chachel and Jorosab arrived almost immediately after Glint had neatly wrangled the armored soldier.

Well-trained and dedicated, the spralaker's mount uttered a Piscean curse and turned to charge the mersons. With triangular front teeth as long as a person's thumb and a thick, powerful body, the ferocious triggerfish was a formidable opponent capable of inflicting serious damage. Chachel's spear went right through the attacker's open mouth and past the saw-like teeth to emerge from its body near the right side of the tail fin. The impaled triggerfish fought and writhed on the hunter's weapon for quite awhile. Chachel ignored its death throes. The spralaker's mount was as good as dinner.

As for the scout itself, it found itself cornered and unable to flee. Raising both arms, it did its best to threaten its captors. "Kill me go ahead why don't you maybe you can't. Touch me and I open your veins!"

"I think not," murmured Chachel. "You're coming with us. There's a council and a shaman who'll want to ask you some questions."

Backed into a corner in the coral, the combative spralaker held his ground. "You'll suck my flesh anyway, so why should I tell any of you anything?"

"Because it doesn't matter." Chachel was careful to keep out of range of the spralaker's arms, weapons that were considerably more lethal than the triggerfish's teeth. "It's apparent your people are going to overrun Siriswirll anyway, and then probably kill me and my friends. So why not prolong your life? Maybe you'll find a chance to escape, or your superiors will work a prisoner exchange on your behalf."

Jorosab looked at him sharply. "Whose side are you on, hermit?"

Some of the tension went out of the spralaker. "Yes so, you speak correct. Why not then converse? It will be last time to see pulp faces of your kind twist and deform." He lowered his weapons. "I go with you freely then because I will enjoy final moments."

After tying its arms and legs, they put the spralaker in Jorosab's carryall, which when emptied of supplies was just capacious enough to accommodate the prisoner. Below, the battle for Siriswirll continued to rage. A last look back showed the inhabitants maintaining their position behind the temporary wall they had constructed. How much longer they could hold out against the relentless pressure none of the three scouts from Sandrift could tell. But at least for the moment, mersons and manyarms still had control of the battlefield.

Under normal conditions, Chachel mused as he and his companions swam in hard silence for the distant encampment, the spralakers should have given up by now, or fallen to chaos among themselves. But as the valiant rainbow runner Zesqu had intimated, these were no ordinary spralakers.

What was driving them? What power was guiding them and holding them together as a unified fighting force? Having succeeded in ravaging an entire town at Shakestone, an accomplishment beyond their wildest dreams, any sensible group of spralakers would have withdrawn to savor their victory and compose perverse ballads of triumph. Instead, they had moved immediately to attack a second, much larger community. It made no sense. Oxothyr was right for certain: forces were at work here that were as malevolent as they were abnormal.

He found his thoughts drifting again to the changeling. The demon changeling.

Hauling their valuable prisoner, the trio succeeded in making their way back along intervening reefs without being seen. No other hardshell scouts were encountered and the fish they met proved indifferent. Spralakers were possessed of many skills, but a loud voice was not among them. Their prisoner might cry out, but he was unlikely to be heard.

By the second day they were safely clear of the field of combat. Still, they did not slow their pace. Their observations had shown them that the citizens of Siriswirll were hard-pressed. Chachel, Glint, and Jorosab did not want to return in force to a scene like the one that had greeted them at Shakestone.

◊

By chance, Irina was listening to Oxothyr expound on a particular aspect of cephalopodan learning when their session was interrupted by the commotion caused by the scouts' return. When informed by a breathless Tythe that the trio had returned not only safe but with a prisoner, her interest was piqued even more.

"Can I come to the interrogation?" she asked the shaman. "I've never even seen a spralaker."

"A chance to further your education, then." Gathering his arms around him, the mage beckoned her to follow. Locking a few of his arms in her hair, Sathi allowed himself to be pulled along. His actions were both a game and an expression of low-key dominance. Irina didn't mind. Underwater, the squid weighed next to nothing and his streamlined shape contributed little drag.

Several counselors had already arrived at the semi-circle of bright green and blue coral marking the northern edge of the camp. Huge black sea fans growing on the coral wall arched outward to form a kind of crenellated half-roof. One merson was conversing with an elderly octopus whose pale pink color indicated his anticipation.

Of the three returned scouts, the two mersons sat patiently on the sand. Transparent lateral fins rippling like the edges of a debutante's silk gown, Glint hovered close by.

Catching sight of Chachel, Irina experienced a sudden and unaccountable urge to rush forward, throw her arms around the hunter, and congratulate him on his success in returning alive from the dangerous excursion. She focused on the impulse until it went away. What an odd whim. She told herself she would have felt the same sense of gratitude toward anyone who had risked his life on behalf of so many others. At the same time, she experienced no such urge to wrap herself gratefully around Glint. Or for that matter, the other merson who had accompanied them.

Very odd.

The counselors ceased talking among themselves when Oxothyr arrived. The shaman glanced briefly at the trio before summarily turning his attention to Jorosab. He did not waste time on greetings or congratulations.

"What news, then, of Siriswirll?"

The big merson drew himself up vertically in the water. "From what we could see, venerable mage, it lies under heavy and sustained attack. Hundreds, perhaps thousands of spralakers are trying to force their way into the town."

A concerned murmuring rose from the counselors. Attacks by spralakers were far from unknown, but a coordinated assault in such numbers on a community the size of Siriswirll was unparalleled. Jorosab's account supplied a perfect explanation of what had overwhelmed Shakestone, what now threatened to overcome Siriswirll—and if something was not done, was also likely to engulf their bucolic home of Sandrift.

"We must move quickly!" Waving all eight of his arms with as much strength as his elderly limbs could muster, counselor Vararem turned slowly from pale pink to an energized dark blue. "From what Jorosab tells us, not only is our beloved home in danger but every village from Sandrift to Soloss along the entire line of the western reefs!"

Oxothyr turned to his smaller counterpart. "Move we will— but with prudence and planning. A hysterical charge will do neither Sandrift nor the embattled citizens of Siriswirll any good." From the attentive Jorosab, he shifted his attention to the other members of the scouting party. Under that intense stare, an intimidated Glint retreated several body-lengths. Other than glancing up, Chachel did not stir.

A long sucker-lined arm indicated the large, opaque carryall lying on the white sand near the hunter's feet. "I sense that you have brought back evidence besides that of your eyes."

Leaning to his right, Chachel began to remove the clam clip that held the sack secured. "Company, even unwilling, can be informative." Pressing against a sensitive part of the mollusk with the fingers of one hand caused the bivalve to pop open. The top of the sack gaped free. The interior was quickly vacated.

Irina sucked in her breath, her gill flaps collapsing against the sides of her neck, as she realized she *had* seen spralakers before. Multiple times, on many occasions. But never one this big, this dangerous, or this intelligent. She had always thought of spralakers as entertainment, or food, or sometimes both. Never as a conscious enemy.

One look at the human-sized crab as it scuttled rapidly sideways across the sand, kicking up white grains in its wake, disabused her of any notions of cuteness.

A design engraved into the back of the crab's carapace graphically depicted its wearer disemboweling a merson. A second, smaller motif might have been a sign of rank. Because the hardshell had been deprived of manufactured weaponry did not mean it had been disarmed. The major claws had been sharpened to give them an unnatural edge capable of cutting through bone as well as flesh.

"So that's a spralaker." Her reaction was a mixture of recognition and disbelief. "That's the enemy that destroyed Shakestone and is attacking Siriswirll. Where I come from we eat them for supper."

"As do we here." Noting her reaction, Glint had hurried over to hover beside her. The cuttlefish had turned an unbroken gray. "The only difference being that we will consume them at any time of the day. They are a particular favorite of my kind and our close relations. That's why spralakers hate manyarms even more than they do mersons." He pointed to the prisoner, who continued racing in sideways circles searching for an escape route only to find himself confronted and blocked at every turn.

"The smallest species can barely mumble. Larger spralakers will make use of simple phrases. When they get this big, or bigger, they achieve a kind of rough civilization. There are no spralaker towns, no spralaker cities. They can raid and destroy, but they cannot really build. At least, that is what I have been told. Reality and stories often differ." Gold-framed, one black eye locked with hers. "A little intelligence can be more dangerous than a lot."

"From what I've been hearing," she commented, "they're smart enough to devise strategy."

"In its simplest form, yes. What is different here, it seems, is that in addition to attacking in unparalleled numbers they are employing tactics never before encountered. Almost as if they are being advised by a non-spralaker intelligence." He backed away slightly. "As to what is really happening, as to cause and effect, we will learn more, I am sure."

In front of them, Oxothyr had begun to do just that. Realizing there was no way out, the spralaker scout had squatted down in the sand. Sharpened claws raised high, he readied himself to strike at any captor who came too close. Oxothyr was not afraid, but neither was the shaman unnecessarily rash. He could query the prisoner just as effectively from a safe distance.

"Hardshell, if you cooperate, you might be spared. Our concern is not the killing of individuals. It would be in your interest to tell us how many are in your force, what weapons they are employing, and who among you leads and makes decisions."

The spralaker did not hesitate. "There are more of us than you can imagine and more coming to join with us every day," he declared, waving his arms. "We have weapons you cannot imagine, and those who lead us have prepared for this for some time." One claw swept wide to encompass the group of attentive counselors. "You are all become food. I am glad you have come to Siriswirll. It means more to die on behalf of the cold."

Oxothyr's confusion was evident. "The 'cold'? Coldness is a quality of being, not an adversary."

Swiveling on long stalks, both eyes turned back to the shaman. "You flaunt your ignorance, manyarm, the way a female does her eggs. Ours will hatch, while yours becomes sustenance only for memory." Claws clicked together, heavy razors backed by organic hydraulics. "Come close and let me partition you!"

"Why?" The constant, steady waving of Oxothyr's arms caused Irina to blink. Was he trying to hypnotize the spralaker? If so, it wasn't working. "Why the need for all this killing? If your kind has an unforeseen problem, can we not talk it out together, over a ball of fish?"

"There is nothing to talk about in this," the spralaker insisted, his contempt undisguised. "You will never understand until it is too late. The cold comes for all. Those who linger or fail to do its bidding will die. As you will die!" Kicking with all eight of his legs, he thrust himself upward off the sand directly toward Oxothyr.

As an attempt to inflict injury it was as bold as it was doomed. A quick squirt from his siphon sent the shaman skittering sideways and out of range of the spralaker's claws. Snapping only water, the defiant prisoner drifted helplessly back to the sand. Those spralakers—crabs—she knew of who could swim at all could do so only fitfully, Irina remembered.

Flashing impatience, Jorosab removed the knife from his waistband and started to swim forward. "Leave this to me, shaman. I can make him talk." He addressed the prisoner. "I will start with one eyestalk, hardshell, but leave the other so you can watch as I scrape your gill rakers."

"No need, merson." Before Jorosab could reach him, the prisoner reached back with one whetted claw, plunged it into his undershell, and in a single smooth motion tore out his own heart. Inhaling sharply, Irina swallowed enough water to drown herself— had she not been breathing the stuff. A couple of the assembled counselors uttered a startled word or two. It was Chachel who swam forward to wave away the swirls of life fluid that leaked from the dying body.

"Defiant words are nothing more than that: just words." He kicked at the multi-limbed corpse. "This is a foe fit for supper, nothing more. I myself look forward to dining on more of the same."

"The hunter is right." Oxothyr drifted over until he was directly above the body of the scout. "We have much to do and little time in which to do it. Return to your schools. Inform and explain. Command all to get a good night's rest. At first light we go to the relief of Siriswirll."

"Or to our deaths," Glint murmured from where he hovered close to Irina.

Taking the shaman's words to heart, the assembly dispersed in a swift and orderly manner. As Sathi and Tythe worked to dispose of the dead spralaker, Oxothyr was left to consult with the returned scouts.

Nearby, a resigned Irina looked over at Glint. "I'm going to have to fight tomorrow, it seems. I know how to fight a little with my hands and feet, but that's all."

"It's not hard to use a spear." Retracting his two hunting arms, Glint demonstrating by repeatedly thrusting them in her direction. "Keep your adversary in front of you, back up if necessary, don't let him get above or below you, and you'll be fine. Chachel and I will look out for you."

She nodded, not for the first time wondering if her altruistic instincts hadn't got the best of her. Had she not volunteered to participate in this expedition, she could be back in Sandrift helping to care for the elderly and look after the children. No one here would blame her for having stayed behind. Not only was she an outsider; as far as the inhabitants of Sandrift were concerned she had all but redefined the term.

Of course, if she had stayed behind, she would not just live: she would have to live with *herself.*

"I guess both you and Chachel are pretty good with a spear."

Glint's tentacles curled inward in disdain. "Oh no, we manyarms prefer the use of far more sophisticated weapons. Multiple knives, throwing shells, and bow and arrow. Myself, I can handle three of the latter at once."

She made herself envision a bow-wielding cuttlefish. It made sense. With its ten arms a cephalopod like Glint could fire off several arrows at once. Dozens of manyarms operating in concert would constitute a formidable force. She started to feel a little better about the battle to come. Clearly, mersons and manyarms brought complimentary capabilities to any skirmish. How could an army of cra—of spralakers, who could barely swim, hope to fend off an attack by agile mersons and swift manyarms who could strike at them from any direction?

She imagined that she would learn the answer to that troubling question as well as many others as soon as the sun once more rose above the mirrorsky.

ay came up softly, as it always seemed to on the reefs of Oshenerth. The light of morning percolated through the water is if a master bowl-maker was slowly blending glass with flecks of gold. Underwater, sunlight did not hit you, Irina had learned. You fused with it. The glow became a part of you. An invisible illumination changed the world, and everyone was inside it.

Little was said as the well-armed relief force broke camp. A few of the older volunteers remained behind to look after the expedition's supplies. Without supervision, the usual scavengers of the reef would help themselves.

One characteristic of underwater military movements struck her immediately. Traveling in three columns, the soldiers of Sandrift advanced in the absence of sound. Unlike on land, there was no tramping of feet to alert the enemy, no rumble of heavy equipment. Mersons and manyarms alike swam in silence. They also pressed forward, insofar as was possible, slowly and in single file to minimize the pressure wave their movement pushed out in front of them.

A perceptive shark might have detected their approach, the ampullae of Lorinzini along its snout picking up the presence in one place of multiple organically-generated electrical fields of a certain strength. It was a risk the counselors had no choice but to take. They could not hazard having their troops advance individually lest they be detected by any spralaker patrols.

Glint was explaining it all to Irina as Chachel swam ahead of them. "Hopefully we'll manage to surprise the hardshells. We didn't see evidence of any sharks working with them on the battlefield."

Clutching the spear she had been given as if it was a protective talisman, Irina concentrated on keeping her place in the formation as she listened to the manyarm. "But I thought sharks were a traditional enemy of your kind, and of the mersons?"

"So they are." Falling back beside her, Glint kept pace with periodic spurts from his siphon. "But that doesn't mean they're allied to the spralakers, either. A shark would just as soon enjoy a meal of hardshell as one of softbody. They are independent operators, are sharks. Some have access to special magicks of their own, others are nothing more than teeth with fins, and a very few will work together just long enough to facilitate a hunt. The two silkies who pursued the herald Zesqu all the way to Sandrift were an exception. They must have been very well paid." The cephalopod wiped at his left eye with the back of a tentacle.

"But sharks are not soldiers. They are the bandits of Oshenerth. One day they will work for reward and the next they will turn upon and eat one another. Not the kind of fighters, however skilled, around which one builds a stable army. Even the spralakers know that."

Irina considered. Off to the right a school of approaching trevally caught sight of the three columns, uttered a collective gasp of surprise, and quickly changed course. As the school was headed away from Siriswirll and posed no risk of giving the alarm, the soldiers from Sandrift saw no reason to pursue. Unsettled schoolish mutterings faded as the silvery mass vanished into the distance.

"I thought spralakers were also like that. Independent, I mean." She rubbed at her own eyes, wondering if she would ever get used to the fact that though she kept them wide open underwater they did not itch or burn.

Glint gestured with a couple of arms. "Normally that is so. But these are not normal times." He pointed sideways to a svelte mass that occupied the center of the middle column. "I have known Oxothyr a long time, and I've never seen him this worried."

She nodded perceptively. "About the spralakers."

"About the spralakers, yes." The cuttlefish flashed a querulous yellow strewn with black. "And about other things."

◊

The unseen sun was still low in the sky the following morning when, at a signal from the expedition's leaders, all three columns rose in unison toward the surface. As she followed Chachel and Glint upward, it struck Irina that she had not been this close to air since her transformation. Swimming along just beneath the barely perceptible wavelets, she found that she could see irregular shapes above, on the other side of the mirrorsky. Clouds. She hadn't seen a cloud in—how long had it been?

No one was looking in her direction. The pair of merson soldiers in line behind her were conversing among themselves. What would happen if she …?

Holding tight to the spear with her right hand, she thrust her left upward and broke through the surface tension.

For a moment there was nothing. Then she felt—heat. Not unbearable, not intolerable, but oddly foreign and unfamiliar. Her air-caressed skin began to prickle, as if that part of her arm was falling asleep. If she kept her hand out of the water, would it begin to burn? She didn't think so. If her skin had been rendered that sensitive, she would have begun to burn already. What would be the reaction of those around her be if they saw what she was doing? For all she knew, she might be violating some serious, unknown religious stricture.

This was neither the time nor the day to challenge local beliefs. She drew her arm back down and her hand underwater. Before she tried such a thing again she needed to discuss the possible physical and social ramifications with someone like Oxothyr. Anyway, there was no more time to experiment. The sun was behind her, and soon there was blood below.

Swimming over the last ridge of coral, they found chaos.

Screams, shrieks, and the sounds of fighting had been increasing for some time. Without intervening lines of solid reef to impede the din of battle, the volume now intensified many times over. She tried to take it in all at once.

Ahead, ranks of spralakers marched in unison toward the makeshift wall that stood between them and the village of Siriswirll. The town itself was something of a shock. It was much bigger than Sandrift or ruined Shakestone. Some of the structures, whose coral growth had been channeled and accelerated by merson architects and engineers, were four and five stories high. Fanciful spires and decorative protrusions erupted outward from the tallest buildings as the deftly nurtured polyps of which they were composed sought room to grow. The majority varied from a very pale pink to a deep purplish-red, though there were also edifices of bright blue, intense yellow, and in one spectacular instance, a sizeable domed structure of coral that was tinted a vivid violet.

There was no sign of either the community's senior or most youthful inhabitants. Either they had been rushed to a place of greater safety, she decided, or else they were huddled somewhere deep inside the town.

Where the advancing lines of spralakers had reached the wall, the water boiled with mayhem. She swallowed hard as she looked on. Every variety and species of hardshell imaginable, including many entirely alien to her, seemed to be taking part in the assault, from small blue snappers whose legs would barely have spanned her open palm to others who … that were …

Some of the attacking spralakers were as big as tanks.

She could hardly believe the evidence of her own eyes. What she was seeing was incredible. Even the largest relatives of the spralakers in her own world were no bigger than a human. Pressing the attack in front of and below her were gargantuan crustaceans whose dimensions had no precedent in her experience. Some boasted claws larger than her own body. They could easily snip a person in half. Repressing her gag reflex, she saw that at several points along the rubble wall they had already done so to some of the town's defenders.

Nor were the besiegers relying on their natural endowments alone. A few of the largest wielded double-headed axes whose ribbed blades were fashioned from the sharpened halves of tridacna shell. Others thrust and jabbed with spears no less lethal than those carried by mersons and manyarms. In lieu of the bows their powerful but inflexible limbs could not properly manipulate, they attacked from a distance by throwing chunks of coral and small boulders. Stones were hard to heave underwater, but once at the crest of their respective arcs, they gathered momentum as they descended. Many of the rocks had been shaped and given points that enabled them to move through the water with speed.

The gory sprawl of severed body parts and dismembered corpses would have crowded the battlefield enough to interfere with fighting if not for the powerful current that swept up from behind the town and carried much of the frightful detritus away. Somewhere off to the east, she knew, those same undisciplined and unmanageable sharks of whom Glint had spoken must be enjoying a feast of unprecedented dimensions.

An upsurge of spears and stones began to rise from below. While they fell short of their intended targets, it was a sign that the relief force had been spotted.

Sandrift's commanders wasted no time. The order was given and relayed the length of each line. One column peeled off to the right, the other to the left. Heart pounding, Irina gripped her spear so tight that her fingers turned almost as white as the bone shaft. Then, barely aware of what she was doing, she was diving downward, kicking hard as she strained not to lose sight of Chachel and Glint.

*What am I doing here?* she thought. Events left her no time to formulate a response. Soon she had leveled off and found herself joining several of Sandrift's fighters as they surrounded a spralaker the size of a luxury sedan. The raucous turmoil of battle that now enveloped her was deafening and she could hardly hear. Blood and body parts, including among the latter many soft shapes she did not recognize and did not want to, eddied around her position as she was caught up in a maelstrom of wide-ranging butchery.

Seafood, she told herself. It's all just seafood. Then the head of a merson came tumbling past, its body nowhere to be seen, the eyes open, vacant, staring, emphatically unfishlike, and the consoling analogy she had just invented for herself evaporated like spit in a steel foundry. She did not throw up only because she was too busy defending herself from snapping claws that could effortlessly rip her to shreds.

Sandrift's leaders had chosen the perfect time to attack. Shafting down through the warm water, the rising sun momentarily disoriented those spralakers who turned to fight back. Retracting eyestalks into protective shells shielded them from the light but sacrificed critical peripheral vision.

The relief force's surprise was nearly complete. Diving down among the rearward ranks of the attackers, the merson and manyarm soldiers of Sandrift proceeded to sow doubt, death, and destruction.

Rising above the tumult of battle, cries of excitement and renewed hope came from the vicinity of Siriswirll's defensive wall. In ones and twos, then small groups, and finally in a wave of spears and ink, the town's hard-pressed defenders came swarming out from behind their protective bulwark to confront their attackers. Beset from behind, in front, and from above by a reinvigorated defense, the methodical advance of the spralakers hesitated, stalled, and began to collapse.

In the midst of the ensuing vacillation and in an attempt to break once and for all the iron will of their assailants, the defenders of Siriswirll sent forth the shock force they had been holding back as a last reserve. Each individual steered and led by a single manyarm clinging to its back, the team of dark green bumphead parrotfish came swimming over the wall to hurl itself at the center of the spralaker line. There was no need for reins or other means of guidance. Equipped with multiple arms, the manyarm riders maintained effortless control of their mounts.

Boasting beaks powerful enough to crunch and consume solid coral, the bumpheads were able to bite through the tough protective shells of even the biggest spralakers as if they were made of paper. In lieu of human screams and manyarm squeals, dying spralakers emitted loud, discordant hissing noises. As the bumpheads wrought their havoc and the soldiers of Sandrift slashed and speared from behind and above, the battlefield became dominated by the horrid cacophony of collapsing crab-shapes.

Then, just as the spralaker force was on the verge of breaking and fleeing, they were rallied by a singular entity. There were larger crustaceans on the field, many who were swifter or stronger—but none so commanding. With his bright crimson shell inlaid with gold symbols and glyphs, the spralaker commandant cut a striking multi-limbed figure. Arms held aloft, claws clacking like castanets, he hissed out one directive after another.

Rejuvenated by the definitive commands and cool confidence that had appeared in their midst, uncertain spralakers rallied around their senior officer. Sharp-clawed fighters closed ranks. Instead of advancing in successive lines, they began to form concentric circles. Gradually the newly applied defensive maneuver drew the surviving spralaker soldiers into a series of larger and larger rings, each of which served to defend the one immediately in front of it as well as the one behind.

True, they were no longer assaulting the town or the improvised defensive wall, but in their new battlefield configuration neither could the attacking force be easily defeated. Soldiers of Sandrift and Siriswirll were forced to hold back. Attempting to spear a chosen target that was surrounded on every side by active, alert co-defenders was much harder than sticking a preoccupied attacker from behind.

Swimming well above the condensed spralaker throng, mersons and manyarms sheathed their spears and brought forth their bows and arrows. Occasionally a shaft would strike an unprotected spot and a spralaker would go down. But its place was immediately taken by one of its neighbors, and the defensive circle maintained.

Their confidence increasingly restored, the entire mass of shells, claws, and legs began to move slowly but relentlessly in the direction of Siriswirll. And this time no wall or line of defenders would be able to stop them.

Though no military tactician, even Irina could see what was happening. Finding Oxothyr flanked by his two agitated famuli, she expressed her alarm aloud.

"Use your magic, shaman! Can't you stop this?" Having retreated to a safe height, she gestured downward. "They've positioned themselves so that each one helps to shield the one next to it."

A reassuring arm snaked around her shoulders. "Patience, changeling. Watch and learn. There are things that in battle are even more effective than magic."

She didn't understand. "What could be more effective than magic?"

Both great eyes turned to her. "Pain, for one thing." Two arms gestured. "Having experienced a good deal of it himself, our reclusive hunter also knows how to convey it."

Irina looked to where the shaman was pointing. The first thing she saw was Chachel, diving downward. The other merson who had been with him on the scouting mission—Jorosab, his name was—flanked the hunter on his left. Somewhat disconcertingly, Poylee swam off to his right. Glint was there, also, together with a dozen or so other members of the Sandrift relief force. Each of the manyarms was wielding a single long-range bow of such size that every cuttlefish, squid, or octopus had to be pushed through the water by an accompanying biped. Serving now as mere conveyances, Chachel and his fellow mersons had sheathed their own spears. Freed of the need to propel themselves, manyarms were notching arrows to baleen bows that were being stretched to their limits.

How could a few oversized arrows make any difference, Irina found herself wondering as she looked on? They might make some kills, yet surely they could not halt the slow but methodical advance of the now rejuvenated and determined spralaker legion?

It struck her that there was something odd about the end of each arrow. Instead of the familiar bone or shell point the tips appeared bloated and globular. They looked too blunt to penetrate a sponge, far less the hard shell of a spralaker. She voiced her disquiet to Oxothyr.

"Your eyes work well, Irina-changeling." The shaman could not smile, but she received the impression of one. "Keep watching."

Reacting to the attack from above, a number of the advancing spralakers heaved rocks and long knives. All fell short of their intended target as the fighters from Sandrift unleashed their shafts. More than a dozen plunged downward to strike at the advancing horde. As Irina had predicted, the swollen, bulbous heads of the arrows did not penetrate a single hardshell. Instead, they burst on impact.

For several long moments it appeared as though nothing had changed. The concentric circles of spralaker soldiers maintained their steady advance. Then the center of the attacking multitude began to crumple. Shrieking and chittering, one spralaker after another fought to climb to imagined safety over the carapaces of its startled comrades. Others clawed frantically at themselves. Some went to the extreme of tearing off affected body parts that had begun screaming with pain.

The burst of frenzied activity served to spread the unexpected contagion to more and more of the unsuspecting foe. Curving around in a wide arc, this time the dozen or so manyarm archers and their grim-faced merson mounts dove on the front line of the spralaker swarm. Unleashing a second barrage, they sowed havoc in the center of the attackers' advance.

From above and behind, an uncomprehending Irina watched anarchy unfold like a black flower among the enemy. "I don't understand what's happening." She looked to Oxothyr, drifting contentedly beside her in a tangle of serpentine arms. "What are on the tips of the arrows our people are firing?"

"Spherical tunicates, Irina-changeling. Simple spherical tunicates. But not the harmless transparent creatures you may be familiar with. Each of these has had its body carefully stuffed with dozens and dozens of tiny jellyfish."

Jellyfish, she thought. "What kind of jellyfish, shaman?"

Oxothyr returned his attention to the continuing battle below. The entire spralaker force was on the verge of falling apart, the panic that had begun to spread among it doing more damage than actual contact with the contents of the manyarms' arrows.

"Very small creatures," he explained. "We call them Death Cubes. One who did not know them would be astonished at their toxicity and think it the result of some lethal magick. But the power of their stings is such that they require no thaumaturgical enhancement." He went on to describe shape and color and ...

*Cubes*, Irina thought intently. A cube was a small box. Box jellyfish—irukandji! Within its nematocysts, or stinging cells, was contained a poison that ranked among the most powerful known. Untreated, it could kill a swimmer in minutes—or in sufficient quantity, even the largest spralaker.

Venom, it appeared, retained its lethal characteristics across worlds.

If anything, the mounting chorus of inhuman shrieks from the seafloor below was intensifying. Not only was the sting of the irukandji deadly, it was also incredibly painful. Frantic spralakers were running in all directions now, scuttling desperately sideways on their multiple legs as the manyarm archers dove and struck for a third time. By now all thoughts of taking Siriswirll had evaporated in the attackers' desperate attempts to scramble or swim clear of the clusters of tiny jellyfish. Where a tentacle struck a fleeing enemy soldier, it left behind an angry welt on previously unscarred carapace. Where it made contact with a soft or sensitive body part, a spralaker died.

Everywhere Irina looked, spralakers were screaming, convulsing, and dying, helpless legs and powerful claws twitching and spasming uncontrollably as the frightful poison short-circuited their nervous systems. Yet despite the chaos and confusion being sown by Sandrift's bow-wielding cephalopods, the struggle for Siriswirll was not over. The spralakers had one more tactic, one more trick, hidden behind their eyestalks.

Sathi saw them first. Hovering above and to one side of his master, he pointed out the dark shape in the distance that was rapidly approaching the field of battle.

"Master, look! There to the north, where the reef line drops away to the deep. What can it be?"

Oxothyr pivoted upon himself as Irina turned less gracefully to gaze in the same direction. The shaman said nothing, staring at the oncoming darkness until it resolved itself into individual shapes.

"More trouble," he finally announced. "Tythe, Sathi—summon the silver squadron. The time for them to enter the fight nears." A pause, then, "What are you waiting for? Stop sucking on your own siphons and make haste!"

Turning tail, the two famuli immediately shot off in the direction of the rear lines, where the last and most significant reserves from Sandrift awaited orders to enter the battle.

Drifting nearer to a confused Irina, Oxothyr slid several arms protectively around her. "I think we will be safe here, changeling— but I cannot tell for how long."

"But why? What are …?"

The approaching dark mass resolved itself into multiple individual shapes, and she understood.

Some of the mantas in the fast-approaching school must have weighed more than half a ton. How the spralakers had inveigled, or forced, or persuaded them to take part in the fight Irina could not imagine. But it stood to reason that if the mersons could train or cajole fish to fight with them, as they had the bumpheads, then wily spralakers could do the same.

The rationale for the involvement of the big pelagics was immediately clear. Several armed spralakers rode atop each fast-swimming giant. In acquiring this single imposing ally the enemy had overcome the strategic liability posed by their inability to swim. As the school of mantas passed overhead, it began to rain spralakers. Spreading their legs wide and using their flattened bodies to slow their descent, the enemy for the first time was able to mount an attack from above. Short spears, rocks, scythe-like throwing shells and armfuls of poisonous urchins fell from the sky like lethal snowflakes.

Forced to dodge the shower of small weapons that could prove fatal to their soft bodies but that bounced or skid harmlessly off spralaker armor, the soldiers of Siriswirll and Sandrift found themselves exposed to renewed enemy strikes from below. Suddenly the tide of battle threatened to shift back in favor of the aggressors. Nor did the school of rays limit themselves to releasing weapons and soldiers onto the field of battle. Continuing onward to pass above Siriswirll itself, they began to drop dozens of spralaker troops directly onto the town.

While larger soldier's hardshells dealt with the villagers' handful of desperate internal defenders, smaller specialist spralakers who had arrived with them were removing containers from their backs. These contained a distinctive blend of acids. Heavier than the surrounding seawater, when poured out it dissolved holes in the coral rock of the town's buildings. In this fashion the spralaker invaders ate their way into structures intended to repel outsiders, where the community's young and elderly had congregated for safety.

Beyond the town boundaries and hovering above and behind the increasingly fractious and disorganized battle, Irina and the counselors from Sandrift observed the disarray with increasing dismay. Outwardly Oxothyr exhibited no anxiety, but it was clear as he stared off to the southwest that he was growing increasingly impatient.

"What's happened to those two idiots? If they've stopped to feed on anthias or cardinals, I'll turn them both into limpets!"

Floating beside him, Irina tried to ready herself mentally to rejoin the fight. It was evident that every hand was going to be needed or else the spralakers were going to take the town. She said as much to the shaman.

He regarded her out of sad, cephalopodan eyes. "You are not trained for this, changeling. But though there is much I would still like to learn from you about your world and your kind, I cannot in good conscience order you to stay back while others are dying. Go and kill, if you will. Watch out for the left claw of the spralaker: they usually feint first with their right."

She acknowledged the advice, lowered her head, threw her feet toward the sky and kicked downward. Her effort moved her only a couple of feet before a powerful tentacle wrapped around one ankle and held her back.

"Just possibly," the shaman explained by way of apology, "your exertions and possible sacrifice may not after all be required." As she straightened in the water, upside down and confused, she looked to where he was pointing. The other counselors were cheering. Sathi and Tythe had neither abandoned nor failed their instructions: they were just a little late.

The silver squadron of greater Sandrift shot past her, the speed and force of their passing knocking her off-balance and nearly causing her to drop her spear, and she found that she was cheering, too.

# – XII –

hough they shot through the water too fast for her to make an accurate count, Irina estimated there were between thirty and forty of the silver-sided attack squid. Slimmer and longer than any cephalopodan species she had yet seen, they moved like rockets. In its tentacles each fighter held half a dozen short, sickle-shaped knives.

They tore through the slowly descending rain of armed spralakers like a spray of shrapnel. Razor-sharp blades sliced cleanly through carapaces, eyestalks, and limbs. Clumsy while free-falling, the enemy tried fight back. The silver squid were far too fast and maneuverable for them. They would dart in, strike, and jet clear before even the most agile spralaker could land a counterblow.

Half the squadron went to the aid of the village. The others, having wrought sufficient havoc among the remaining descending foe, now sped downward. Zipping and zooming above the field of battle like so many multi-armed dive bombers, they unleashed the secret weapon with which Oxothyr had equipped them prior to the departure from Sandrift.

Overhead, Irina found herself frowning as she tried to make sense of what she was seeing. She glanced uncertainly at the shaman. "Trepang?"

When an octopus nods, his entire body bobs. "Through the application of a small spell I have enhanced the natural abilities of those that have been brought with us." His voice was thick with satisfaction. "Guts can be useful."

Irina let her gaze drop downward again. In addition to their half dozen of curved blades, each squid carried in its remaining arms a pair of the forearm-size, rubbery trepang. Known more evocatively in her world as beche-de-mer, when prodded or irritated trepang ejected not only their inner organs, which were easily regrown, but also white strands known as the tubules of Cuvier. On contact with water outside the body, expelled guts and tubules alike expanded and became—sticky. Very, very sticky. A threatened trepang could eject more than enough to entangle and distract most pursuing predators. As enchanted by Oxothyr, they now became veritable fountains of goo.

It was not pretty.

As the squid sped past above them, one spralaker soldier after another found itself entangled in the incredibly adhesive innards being forcefully ejected by the mindless conscripted trepang. Thanks to Oxothyr's literally gut-level enchantment, expulsion of the sticky insides of the prolific bottom-feeders did not stop. Instead, they continued to spew without pause.

One by one, individual spralaker fighters found themselves bound up in seemingly endless strands of repulsive slime. Legs were lashed together. Claws that could grind rock found themselves inextricably stuck to the tops and sides of hard-shelled armor. Eyestalks ended up adhering to mouths or undersides, ruining vision. Knives and throwing stones became glued to the very arms that were supposed to wield them. When one stumbling gut-trussed spralaker bumped into another, they ended up stuck together. Soon pairs, then trios, eventually dozens found themselves caught up in an ever-expanding gummy quagmire of gluey white strands.

The stymied masses of spralakers made easy targets for the revitalized soldiers of both towns, who converged on them with spears thrusting and blades a-butchering. Similar scenes of slaughter played out within Siriswirll itself. Emerging from their acid-attacked but still mostly intact homes and public buildings, tentative citizens found spralakers pinned to walls, glued to roofs, and dangling from towers. In place of the traditional weapons that had been commandeered by the town's soldiers, household utensils proved more than adequate for executing invaders unable to fight back.

Taken by surprise with this new weapon and unable to find a way to counter it, the remaining spralakers finally broke and fled. Led by their charismatic red-hued commander, many tried to escape by scuttling around behind the town. Clinging to the steep incline on its far side, they resolved they would be better positioned to defend themselves. Trouble was, they couldn't reach the slope. The same relentless upwelling that protected Siriswirll's rear from attack now forced any fleeing enemy seeking its perceived safety back to the field of battle. Many spralakers who had hoped to find refuge in the depths were swept off the rocks and flung into or over the town by the powerful surge. Feeble swimmers at best, they were quickly picked off by the much more agile mersons and manyarms.

Not all were slain. Some escaped the attentions of the defenders through sheer force of numbers. Yet even those who managed to flee the field of battle were not safe.

As she watched the disorganized retreat, Irina thought she could just make out a distant, furious buzzing. It rose and fell erratically. More than anything, it reminded her of the soft hum of the laser drill in the office where she worked. The shaman explained.

"Shark frenzy." Oxothyr's tone was one of quiet gratification. He nodded northward. "Even as we speak the largest of the sharptooths are finding satisfaction." An arm gestured down toward the rapidly calming battlefield. "Soon the smaller ones will risk coming here in search of still more food. There will be many and they will linger, as there is much to keep them occupied."

If anything, the mage's prediction turned out to be understated. In less than an hour the mersons and manyarms had abandoned the field to hundreds of small sharks. Whitetip, blacktip, lemon, leopard—arriving like a pack of stripped-down hyenas, they descended upon the carnage, ravenously consuming with equal relish not only fleshy body parts but bones and shells. Muttering their irritation, they nevertheless gave way whenever a live soldier happened by and momentarily interrupted their glorious feed. Of the customary hostility that existed between merson, manyarm, and shark, on this day there was none. In the presence of such an abundance of trouble-free fodder, traditional enmity was set aside.

On occasion disagreement did raise its scavenging head over possession of a body, mersons and manyarms being as fond of spralaker flesh as any shark. These isolated disputes were quickly and harmlessly resolved, with the grumbling sharks invariably conceding as they moved off to plunder another corpse.

Victory having left behind a real prize in the form of so much food, and a wealth of food being always an excuse for a celebration, the day's triumph was celebrated that night with a gala the likes of which the town had not experienced in quite some time. Siriswirll was suffused with so much music, dancing, song, and effusive expressions of unconstrained joy that even normally shy nocturnal reef dwellers were drawn to the lights and laughter. For one evening even the tastiest fish were not at risk of encountering net or knife, not even those colored silver or red. At any other time they would be candidates ripe for filleting. Tonight they swam freely with and enjoyed the company of those who would usually see them only as prey.

In contrast to the dionystic frenzy of Colloth, Irina observed, the victory celebration was more about amusement than reproduction. Merriment took the place of unbridled passion. It was just as exciting, but considerably less tiring.

Chachel viewed the exuberant festivities from a distance. Having finally succeeded in losing the persistent Poylee in the maze of buildings, he settled down to rest inside an empty passageway between two small towers. From there he could observe in solitude and with cool detachment the frenetic partying and over-imbibing of thick, heavy, intoxicating liquids. Such wastrelhood was not for him; none of it. To take pleasure in such revelry he would have to let himself go—and he never let himself go. There might be a shark lurking nearby, waiting to extract revenge for killings perpetrated last year. Or a wayward merson, jealous of his hunting ability. Or minions of the dark shadow that always seemed close at hand and ready to strike but forever just out of reach whenever he flailed at them from the depths of his oft-unsettled sleep.

Taking leave of the empty passageway with a desultory sniff, he turned and swam with steady strokes toward the west end of Siriswirll. The structures he passed were deserted and dark, lit only fitfully by the moonlight that filtered down through the mirrorsky.

Everyone had gathered in the town center to participate in, or at least to watch, the grand carnival. There could be found food, spice, entertainment, and the company of others. Who would seek deliberately to avoid that?

The one merson who chose to do so strained to kick more forcefully as he drew near the westernmost edge of the settlement. Here the windowless, westward-facing flanks of buildings sloped inward at an angle that allowed the powerful upwelling from the depths to rise up and over their roofs and disperse harmlessly above the rest of the town. He did not turn away as the irresistible power of the deep ocean current began to tug at his face and body. To the hunter, the steady pummeling was a form of rejuvenation, reminding him of who he was and what he had suffered. Subjecting oneself to such flagellation was an uncommon vice.

So he was more than a little startled to discover he was not alone.

Immersed in the full force of the upwelling, the instantly recognizable shape stuck out over the very edge of the precipice. Powerful arms, even eight of them, would not be sufficient to allow Oxothyr to hold such a position for very long, but the shaman had secured himself to the site with something more than mere muscle.

The body of even the least adept manyarm could generate striking changes of color and pattern. Only a master of exceptional chromatophoric skill (and not a little magic, Chachel reflected) could command light that clung.

From the pulsating red-green glow that enveloped the shaman like fog around a mountain, tiny tendrils of pure radiance extended outward in numerous directions. Like miniature luminescent tentacles, they gripped the surrounding rock. Nothing grew there. It was impossible for even the most determined mollusk or anemone to maintain a hold in the face of the relentless current that roared up and over the edge. But the glow-fingers of Oxothyr found places to grasp; holes in the weathered stone, projections of jagged rock, and long-dead coral.

Straining, kicking as hard as he could with both his whole leg and his prosthetic, a curious Chachel strove to reach the mage. The surge threatened to tear off everything from the strip of material that covered his loins to the patch over his left eye. Of the shaman's manyarm famuli there was no sign. Their master must have granted them permission to join in the revels—or ordered them to do so, Chachel decided as he fought against the current. Abruptly, he found himself swimming into a small area of unexpected calm. The powerful rip vanished and he found it easy to move forward. In the lee of the luminous haze cast by the meditating scholar, the current had absented itself.

Without having looked in the hunter's direction and continuing to stare out into the darkness of the deep ocean, the shaman murmured politely, "Good evening, Chachel. One solitary thinker finds another, I see. It is always so."

Chachel moved to hover alongside the mage. A finger-length too far to the left and he found himself once more subject to the full force of the upwelling. A finger-length closer to the pulpy, bulbous body brought him back into the shaman's aura of aqueous tranquility. The hunter did not question it. He was content to benefit from the marvel.

"I don't do very much thinking, venerable shaman. I find it slows my ability to react."

In the near darkness, with the jostle of unrestrained revelry forming a noisy backdrop, one great eye focused on the stolid merson. "Hunter, you think more than you think, I think. No matter." The eye turned away, to join its counterpart in gazing out at the unimaginable immensity that was the open ocean. "It is left to me to think for all. Sometimes," the brown mantle seemed to sag in upon itself slightly, "sometimes the burden grows heavy." A flicker of amusement played around the edge of his beak. "For one who is without bones, particularly heavy."

"You are the most knowledgeable of manyarms and wisest of the wise," Chachel reminded him gravely.

The sac-like body rippled, turning pale gold with black hieroglyphs. "What I know is scarcely a diatom more than nothing, hunter. My far-reaching ignorance drives me to study. It compels me to learn. It is a curse. The emptiness inside my mind rivals the one out there." Sweeping up and out in a wide arc, an arm indicated the vastness before them.

Merson and manyarm were silent for a while, until Chachel murmured, "I know why I am here, at this spot, now. Crowds of others make me uncomfortable. But what about you?"

Oxothyr did not hesitate. "Staring at nothing can sometimes be a most effective way of focusing one's thoughts. In the depth of night, landlords of the peculiar rise from the deeps. Occasionally the persistent can catch a glimpse of them. Out there away from the warm and well-lit reefs reside stranger things, reclusive hunter, than the mind of merson or manyarm can imagine."

Maintaining his position behind the shaman's shielding bulk, Chachel joined him in gazing out into the open obsidian ocean. It was not entirely black. Flickerings of light manifested themselves; pinpoints of color that twinkled and beckoned, tempting him to swim out, to follow, to identify. He knew better. He did not need the shaman to tell him that there were creatures who dwelt in the depths that could swallow a merson whole.

"What kind of things, Oxothyr?" Unlike the intimidated majority, Chachel felt no compunction about making familiar use of the shaman's name.

The glyphs on the mage's skin shifted and flowed, though there were none present to read them. "Beings that look like stone but are alive. Creatures of dream and nightmare. Teeth that seem to have no body behind them. Great beauty that can also kill." Once again the golden eye shifted around to peer at the attentive merson. "Looking at them, you feel as if your head is exploding."

"You have seen such phantasms?" Chachel asked uncertainly.

The shaman sighed. "Truth be told, mostly in my visions. That does not make them any less real. Just like the coldness I have been feeling." The one arm not holding onto the edge gestured backward, toward the rowdy celebration that filled the center of town. "I should be there, not here. I enjoy music and dancing, good food and entertainment, as much as the next manyarm. Instead I find myself in this lonely, current-swept place, contemplating the great emptiness, thinking too much, and occasionally shivering with a chill whose source I cannot fathom."

"I am sorry for you, Oxothyr." Showing none of the hesitation many of his acquaintances would have exhibited, Chachel reached out with his right arm and encircled part of the shaman's body. The soft skin and the flesh beneath was all but weightless in his palm, like a jellyfish that had donned clothing. Where he made contact, the skin changed from brown to indigo "I wish I could do something."

"Beware making offers you may have occasion to regret, hunter. The world shifts around us in ways I can sense but not yet understand. For the spralakers to attack established towns like Splitrock and Siriswirll is unprecedented. Something has driven them to do so. We must find out what, before every town on the western reef line finds itself under assault. Unfortunately, as we have recently seen, any of the foe taken prisoner finds ways, often inventive, to kill themselves before they can be questioned in depth. The result may be nutritious, but is decidedly uninformative."

Chachel considered. "You think these abnormal attacks by the spralakers are somehow related to this coldness that torments you?"

This time the shaman turned his entire body toward the hunter. "You see? You *do* think! Do not be so disparaging of the practice. It can be more useful than you believe. As to your question, I regret that at this stage any response I might give would not be definitive. I have a sense they are somehow connected, yes. As are all abnormal circumstances that occur simultaneously. But I cannot be certain. I have no proof, and all could be coincidence. One thing I do know: for the safety and sake of all, we *must* find out."

"When will you have an answer?" While not especially interested in the safety and sake of all, Chachel retained an abiding interest in his own well-being.

"I won't." One by one, tentacles of determined flesh and tendrils of ensorcelled light began to release their grip on the current-scoured rocky rim overlooking the deep. "Having striven mightily for some time now, I have sourced only puzzlement and confusion for my trouble. The resolution of this conundrum demands greater skill than I possess."

Chachel blinked. "There are those with shamanistic ability superior to Oxothyr?"

The octopus blushed amusement. "You have no idea, hunter. But you will, you will." He inhaled sharply, his body ballooning. "There is no alternative to it. We must consult the Deep Oracle."

Chachel paused but briefly. "Never heard of it."

"There is no reason why you should. The Deep Oracle is sought only by those whose wisdom has come to an end. As has mine in this matter." Releasing his last arm, the red-green filaments of light collapsing into his aura, he let the current take hold of his body and sweep him back toward Siriswirll. Caught up in the shaman's fading radiance and the indifferent upwelling, Chachel allowed himself to be carried along beside the mage.

"Where do you find this Deep Oracle?"

"Ah, that is the problem, hunter. It moves around." Oxothyr allowed the current to spin his body and the arms that trailed behind it in lazy circles as it carried both of them over fanciful edifices of coral and rock toward the center of Siriswirll. "All of Oshenerth is its home. It lives in the deep bare dark where few dare to swim, and is consequently exceedingly hard to find. But the Tornal might know. And the Tornal I *do* know how to find. Provided they are in residence and not traveling."

The shaman's thoughts were moving too fast for Chachel. His feelings of inferiority were misplaced. The shaman thought too fast for anyone.

"I don't know what the Tornal are, either," the hunter divulged uncomprehendingly, "much less where they might be found."

"As to what they are, you will see. Because you are coming with me, hunter-who-thinks-more-than-he-thinks-he-does." Before Chachel could protest, Oxothyr added, "As to their whereabouts, the last I knew of them, they were residing in Benthicalia."

*That* was a name familiar even to the cloistered Chachel. A powerful name. *Benthicalia.* A legend that leached charisma. And that was how most reef folk thought of it—as a legend. As a myth, a fable, not a real place. Yet Oxothyr talked casually of going there. Sometimes the shaman spoke in riddles, but there was nothing of the tease about him this time.

As they neared the festivities, the sights and sounds of general celebration began to make him uneasy. Yet feeling himself on the verge of some great discovery, he was loathe to leave the shaman's presence.

"I'm not coming with you," he yelled as he started to drift clear of the current's main thrust. "Not if it means traveling with others."

"Others are brothers," Oxothyr called back to him as they parted. "You will change your mind, you'll see."

"What should I do now?" Chachel had been swept almost out of hearing range. An attempt at a restraining spell failed, further delineating the erudition gulf that separated hunter and shaman.

"Convince yourself you're not going," the mage yelled back. "It will do you good to get it out of your system!"

A spire festooned with coils and curlicues of gardened barnacles slid between them and the master of magic was seen no more. Though Oxothyr could doubtless have made headway against it, by allowing the current to carry him into the midst of the rejoicing the shaman had deliberately cut himself off from Chachel. If so, why?

*To give me time to think*, Chachel realized. To force him to think. To compel him to cogitate. To oblige him to consider everything just discussed and imparted, whether he wanted to or not.

The shaman was not only intelligent. He was clever.

◊

*"Benthicalia!"*

Unable to restrain herself, an eager Poylee swam round and round in such tight circles that she generated a vortex beneath her feet strong enough to suck up sand, fragments of shell, and a whiskered goby that let her know in no uncertain terms what it thought of her before fighting its way back down into its disturbed burrow.

"I've never been to Benthicalia," she admitted when she finally stopped spinning. "In fact, I don't know anyone who's been to Benthicalia."

"That's because no one from Sandrift has ever gone there." Chachel's tone was dry and matter-of-fact as he pointed out the obvious. "Except for Oxothyr." He turned to the shaman, who was resting on the warm white sand of Siriswirll's broad village square, his eight arms splayed out around him like the petals of a brown flower. Everywhere villagers were going about their daily business, happy to revisit a normalcy that had so recently suffered from violent disruption. "You have been to *Benthicalia*, esteemed mage?"

The octopus paled to a reassuring beige spotted with green. "Several times, I am pleased to say. I only wish the journey before us was not haunted by so foreboding a purpose."

Nearby, Irina grabbed Glint's right fin and tugged to get the cuttlefish's attention. He went all over black for a moment until he located the cause of the feathery pinch.

"What's this 'Benthicalia'?" she asked him. "Another village?"

In the absence of either a neck or shoulders, Glint could not shake his head. Not physically. Cuttlefish conveyed the same response by flashing a particular shade of dark green accentuated by black bands.

"Hardly. Benthicalia is a true city. A great city. The greatest in all the lands encompassed by the southwestern reefs." Multiple arms gestured, taking in the village around them. "I have not been there myself, but I have heard the tales told by those who heard the tales told by those who listened to the tales told by experienced and knowledgeable travelers. They speak of wonders a simple hunter like myself can only imagine." He flushed cobalt. "To see it will be a life zenith, of sorts."

Reaching out, she nearly succeeded in snatching a preoccupied hawkfish. Realizing it had come too close, it hastily turned tail and shot off mirrorskyward. What would she have done had she caught it? Popped it into her mouth? She licked her lips distastefully. The longer she was here, the more she found her instincts and tastes changing to match those of her new friends. It was unsettling.

Busy conversing with Chachel and Poylee, Oxothyr did not appear to have heard anything of the exchange between cuttlefish and changeling. Irina knew that by now she ought to know better. The shaman missed nothing.

"You will come too, changeling?" he asked her. "There are colleagues of mine in the city who will find your presence and the story of how you came to be among us entertaining as well as instructive."

"Well, I don't know," she replied uncertainly. "I'm still not really sure of myself in these surroundings, in this altered body. I don't know if I'm ready to make a change again so soon. Everything's all still pretty new to me. I'm getting better at making adjustments, more comfortable at doing certain things, but I'm still ..."

"Afraid." Poylee's dismissive tone bordered on contemptuous.

Tensing, Irina glared at her. "On the other hand, the best chance I have of finding a way home is probably to consult with as many educated minds as possible." She nodded forcefully. "Yes, I'll come too, Oxothyr."

"Excellent. Your presence may bring you good and will certainly do me credit." The soft body turned. "And you, matchless hunter?"

Chachel kicked backward. "Not I, master flatterer. You can work magic on me, but not words. I thought about everything you said the other night, and I'm still going back to Sandrift with the others." His gaze shifted to his companion. "Go with them if you want to, Glint. I haven't been to Benthicalia, but I know the way is strange and dangerous."

Turning bright yellow, the cuttlefish darted up to him, his arms practically touching his friend's face. "You find those designations off-putting. I find them enticing."

Nose to tentacle, Chachel straightened in the water. "Go and be enticed, then. Or dismembered. Whatever tickles your cuttlebone." Snapping out a hand as efficiently as any manyarm, he snatched a passing leafy seahorse, popped it in his mouth, and chewed defiantly. Even at a distance, Irina could hear the crunch. She winced.

"As you will." The cuttlefish backed off. "I don't understand your lack of curiosity. We're all going to die someday anyway. It might as well be in the service of others and a search for novelty. How fortunate for you that you suffer from neither concern."

Chachel turned away, glancing back over a shoulder. "You should know by now, Glint, that you can hold me with suckers but not with words."

"Let him be." Drifting forward, Oxothyr wrapped an arm around the cuttlefish's tail and pulled him gently backward. "We'll do better without his constant complaining. Jorosab can come in his place."

Chachel paused and looked back. "A fine choice. He'll be a perfect complement to you, shaman. All muscle and no brain."

Oxothyr shrugged green. "We must make do with what we have, even though the future of every village and town and all who live in them is at stake. Come, my friends," he told the others. "We will draw additional volunteers for our escort. There are many who will be glad of the opportunity to serve—and to see the wonders of the great city."

"Who cares?" Chachel shouted after them. "I have my cave! I have peace of mind!"

Jetting backward in the usual fashion of his kind, Glint offered his friend a parting word. "Piece of mind, you mean. Don't worry. You'll still get to see Benthicalia—in word pictures, when I speak lavishly of it upon my return."

"Fools." Muttering to himself, Chachel turned and finned toward the temporary camp the members of the expedition from Sandrift had set up on the other side of the town square. "Fools preparing for a fool's errand. The shaman doesn't need a one of them. He just wants company on the long passage. Someone to talk to and pliant supplicants to venerate him." Swimming away, he noticed that Poylee was following him. He halted abruptly.

"What do you want? I thought you were going with the old bag?"

She looked and sounded uncertain. "I thought surely you were coming too, Chachel. If you're not, perhaps I should …"

"What?" he interrupted her curtly. "Stay behind? To look after me? I need no looking after, womb-with-fins. And you—you have your best friend to keep you company wherever you go. Your mirror."

Her mouth opened, her expression contorted, but she said nothing. Instead, she whirled and swam furiously to catch up with Oxothyr and the others. Chachel watched her go, relieved to be rid of her. He was sick and tired of her frequent attentions, the constant little touches she thought passed unnoticed, and hopeful insinuations. Better she disappear into the distance in the company of an aging sage, flighty manyarm, and incomprehensible changeling. As for himself, he had food to find, fish to fillet, and thoughts to ponder.

What thoughts? The saving of Sandrift, his own salvation, the color of the water or the changing sheen of the mirrorsky? How much time was needed for that? The rest of his life?

Benthicalia. Could he not do all those things as well there as here? Perhaps even better? If he didn't go, he would never know. Worst of all would be when Glint returned enhanced and enlightened. Chachel was sure he would never hear the end of it. He knew the cuttlefish. Not a hunt would proceed without the garrulous manyarm regaling him endlessly and at length with interminable anecdotes of his adventures. There was only way to prevent that inescapable harangue. Pre-empt it.

◊

The following morning when the small but skilled group Oxothyr had gathered around him assembled in the village square, a certain dismissive hunter was among them. Chachel was going along not to fulfill a desperate desire to set eyes on fabled Benthicalia, not out of any need to assist his fellow mersons, nor out of guilt or embarrassment.

He was going because despite everything he believed about himself, more than anything else he feared becoming an irrelevance.

# – XIII –

There was no coral, but there was algae. There were fish, but they had no color. Subdued of scale and anxious of eye, they swam mostly alone. In this place of gray gloom and dark shadows, schooling was not a wise defense mechanism. Better for one to be eaten than dozens.

The milieu through which they darted furtively had once been the throat of an old volcano. Like an actor shedding a toga, the softer exterior rock of the underwater mountain had eroded to expose hexagonal columns of cracked basalt where lava had rapidly cooled, as if a colony of giant morose bees had given themselves over to processing and regurgitating gray stone instead of wax.

Over millennia the raw minerals had been chipped and gnawed away, had been shaped and sculpted by generation after generation of spralaker masons until the core of the submerged volcano had been chiseled into a royal court whose majesty was matched only by its somberness. Here held sway the greatest of all spralaker rulers; monstrous and ugly, ruthless and powerful. Bioluminescent swimmers held captive in stringy cages hung from the walls and vaulted stone ceiling, illuminating their surroundings with a fitful, unwholesome gleam. Courtiers with decorated shells and claws scuttled to and fro in the tubular corridors. Here and there, slaves with scales and slaves with shells scurried about their tasks while doing their utmost to avoid the attention of their masters' spiteful claws. There was even a captured merson or two, or a lumbering, blubbery niracson. Tarazoks, cousins to mersons but far more fish-like in appearance, swam freely among the chambers.

Where the innermost core of the old volcano had once sent bloodrock gushing upward to pierce the mirrorsky, a sprawling circular chamber had been laboriously hewn from the solid basalt. When directly overhead, the sun shone straight down the ancient volcanic throat all the way to the bottom of the artificially enlarged cavity. This momentary appearance of vivid illumination was both worshiped and shunned as a harbinger of everything bright and vile that threatened the lives of spralakers, who naturally preferred the darkness of their burrows to the brighter world outside.

The terminus of the deep cylindrical shaft was marked by the bleak grandeur of the reception room. There could be found the ancient throne of the spralaker High Lords; a huge, flat slab of raw jadeite that had been polished to a glistening sheen. Even in the dim light of the chamber, its surface shone ever green. Intricate bas-reliefs depicting scenes from the glorious history of the hardshell peoples ran completely around the exterior. No soft pillows were piled high atop the perfectly flat slab. A harsh folk, spralakers preferred to take their ease on surfaces that offered protection and reassurance rather than comfort.

Kulakak was no different. With a merson-size body covered in stubby, irregular protuberances and legs that spanned the entire breadth of the jadeite throne, he was an intimidating presence even if not the largest of his kind. His eyestalks when fully extended were as long as a person's forearm. Sitting in front of him on the flat polished surface was a sea fan basket half full of live smelt. Periodically dipping a claw into the basket, he ate steadily. Flopping and writhing on top of one another, the terrified smelt did not swim away because all of their fins had been amputated before they had been served.

A dedicated personal guard of urchins clung to the circular walls and stone floor. Equipped with bristling black and violet spines, at a command they could instantly surround and impale any prospective assassin—or simply someone who happened to displease the spralaker ruler. A thick, strong shell would turn and defeat such weapons—except that they were present in such numbers on the walls that at least a few of the poisonous spines were sure to find a vulnerable place or two on any attacker.

The urchins did not have the walls to themselves. Dangling from the sculpted stone were the twisted skeletons of hollow-eyed mersons, the frayed and shrunken corpses of manyarms, and the occasional smartly engraved cuttlebone.

Relaxing within the throne room, Kulakak felt both secure and at home. As he systematically downed another squirming, helpless, softly screaming smelt, a new shape came sweeping into the room. Passing between the pair of massive sculptures of armed spralakers that flanked the vestibule, Advisor Gubujul's multiple legs propelled him toward the jadeite slab at a steady pace. Though ever wary, as Paramount Advisor to the throne the oversized stenopus shrimp knew protocol better than most. Otherwise he would long ago have joined in the royal food basket the unfortunates who had preceded him in his position.

Despite his confidence, he was not looking forward to the incipient presentation. With the Emperor, not all news went down as easily as did helpless fish.

Embedded jewels glittered on the Paramount Advisor's carapace. Gold dust glittered on his antennae forelegs where he'd had them shaped into a cosmetic bowl of glue-impregnated powdertuff. Looking more than anything like a handful of bejeweled candy canes, his pure white body highlighted by the natural crimson-red bands that striped his torso and limbs worked its self-important way across the stone floor. As he neared the throne, the half-dozen long, ivory-hued antennae that sprouted from his head dipped low and his voice segued smoothly into a well-practiced fawning.

"You look well this day, my Lord. Your shell gleams like the Whiteness that is Scraped, and your ..."

Spitting out small bones, Kulakak devoted one eye to his Advisor while keeping the other on his food. Gubujul did not take this as a sign of indifference. Nothing escaped the Great Lord's attention.

"Spare me your customary obsequiousness this morning."

Bending his forelegs beneath him, Gubujul bowed toward the throne. "As usual, my Lord wastes no time."

"And has my Paramount Advisor enjoyed his usual breakfast of sunrise refuse?" Another despondent definned fish vanished into the seemingly bottomless toothless maw.

"Gourmet refuse, my Lord," Gubujul replied unflinchingly. "I am blessed that others find my choice of cuisine unpalatable. It leaves that much more for me."

Kulakak belched memorably, sending forth a cloud of half-digested fish flesh, skin, and entrails. Tempted to snack on the spray of waste, Gubujul thought better of it, not wishing to appear the glutton before his master. It was difficult to resist, though, when one's sensitive antennae were enveloped in so much delectable emancipated garbage.

"Word has come from the southwest, my Lord. A messenger has arrived with intelligence." The Advisor's many legs fanned the water, keeping him upright.

That news drew the Great Lord's full attention. "Send him in."

That the him was a her did nothing to diminish the Great Lord's anticipation. With its red-speckled ivory-white body and white eyes, the porcelain crab was among the most beautiful of all spralaker-kind. But the one who scuttled in, claws held deferentially low to the ground, showed evidence of having been battered by time and distance. Kulakak was willing to overlook the messenger's unceremonious dishabille. It was a very long way indeed to the despised southwestern reefs, and she had clearly ridden long and hard to return as swiftly as possible to the ancestral home. That did not mean he was inclined to waste time waiting for her to catch her breath.

"How goes the cleansing?" he demanded to know before she could even give her name. To her credit, she did not waste time trying to interject it.

"Shakestone, the town that was selected for the first assault," she hissed wearily, "was easily taken: its habitat destroyed, its inhabitants killed or consumed. All went as intended. Our arrival was unexpected, our surprise complete, our victory total."

"I wish I could have been there." Off to one side Gubujul's long, delicate forearms stabbed through the water in bold martial gestures, the narrow pincers snapping at drifting fragments of latent organic debris.

"Yes," observed Kulakak dryly, "who among the mersons and manyarms would have been able to stand against your celebrated ferocity?" His attention remained focused on the messenger. "Pray continue." When she appeared to hesitate, Kulakak's massive body tilted slightly in her direction. "You falter. Why?"

"Next in line to be annihilated was the much larger community of Siriswirll. At first all went as planned." On hearing the words "At first," Kulakak's eyes seemed to darken. Having no choice, the miserable messenger plunged onward.

"Perhaps we were betrayed. Perhaps those assigned to prevent any word of our attack from passing beyond the vicinity of the besieged town failed in their duties. Whatever the cause or reason, an unexpected relief force arrived from another village: Sandrift." The messenger's voice sped up, as if she was anxious, even desperate, to conclude her report.

"Steps had been taken and the usual precautions put in place to deal with such a possibility. The relief force was not large, but its members fought much more skillfully than expected. They employed unanticipated tactics. Furthermore, they had a shaman with them and—a changeling."

"A what?" Gubujul blurted in surprise.

"Shut up." Kulakak's eyestalks barely moved. "Go on, messenger."

"We were unable to find out much about the changeling, but it quickly became clear that this shaman Oxothyr—his name and much of this information was gleaned from a prisoner—was much more than the simple dispenser of potions and parlor tricks usually to be found in such small merson communities. Potent sortilege was unleashed against us. Counterattacks were deployed with a military sophistication belying their rustic origin. Our leaders were outmaneuvered and—I must say it—out-thought."

The towering murk of the throne room was silent for long moments as its master contemplated what had been said. "What of Corolak, commander of the expeditionary force?"

The messenger swallowed as her eyestalks retracted fully into her shell. "Dead and dismembered, my Lord Kulakak. Like nearly all of our fighters. Only a few survived. More may yet trickle in," she added, trying to strike a hopeful note. "We scattered in hopes of surviving to fight again another day. I regret that I myself have not many who can confirm what I say. Only just enough."

Kulakak pondered aloud. "Corolak dead. I would not have believed it. He had the tenacity of a king and the claws of an executioner. Few survived, you say?" Reluctantly, the messenger waved her red-speckled left claw by way of confirmation.

So thick was the tension in the throne room that it seemed to freeze the tide itself. The urchins affixed to the walls trembled, the shivering of their spines seeming to set the entire chamber in motion.

Finally, Kulakak exhaled softly. "Well then, we will just have to assemble a new, greater army and attack again, won't we?"

At the Great Lord's matter-of-fact response, Gubujul relaxed—though not half so much as the apprehensive messenger. Sliding off the jadeite throne to advance on powerful chitinous legs, Kulakak put an arm across her scarred back, the pincers that tipped the massive claw at its end remaining closed.

"You have done a service to all spralakers by bringing us so promptly and thoroughly the news of this unfortunate happening," he declared as he half-guided, half-urged the smaller crustacean to one side of the throne room. "Had you fought and died in battle you would not have been able to deliver the information. I will consider what now must be done to deal with this disaster and how it must be gone about. But first there is another here who has listened to what you have said and who will doubtless be eager to express his own feelings."

Held out in front of him, Gubujul's red-banded forearms abruptly froze in position. Rising from the dark pavement, he began to tiptoe slowly backward, trying to displace as little water as possible as he retreated. His sudden desire for discretion was motivated not by courtesy, but by dread. He knew all too well of whom the Great Lord spoke.

"You should meet this individual," Kulakak was telling the young messenger solicitously. "He really is quite fascinating."

They had halted facing a blank wall. One roughly rectangular area was entirely devoid of the clinging, quivering, black and violet urchin guards. "I don't see anyone, my Lord."

"Look. Harder." As he spoke, Kulakak took a step back.

The messenger did not see the figure at first because it was masked by the same unbreakable spell keeping it imprisoned in the alcove in the wall. As the green-black opacity that she had thought was just another slab of stone began to clear, wisps of chain metal forged in the fires of the Great Deep came into view. They helped to bind, though by themselves they could not restrain, a most singular shape. She recognized it. She screamed.

Bound before her in metal and by the hauntingly enchanted talisman glowing softly celadon that was looped around both prominent eyestalks was the largest mantis shrimp she had ever seen. From the tail of its segmented abdomen to its eyestalks, it was nearly as big as a merson. The giant stomatopod was a blaze of color; its body emerald green shot through with red, the independently swiveling eyes mounted atop twin eyestalks a deep, dazzling violet. Those were the eyes that locked on her now, their matchless trinocular vision analyzing every aspect of the paralyzed messenger, seeing her in a hundred thousand hues from the ultraviolet to the infrared.

"Messenger," Kulakak intoned gravely, "you are privileged to meet Sajjabax. Commander of thaumaturgy, Master of the Arcane Arts, Orderer of Obscene Knowledge, Delver into the Depths of Otherness. Sajjabax the Shrewd. Sajjabax the Conjurer. Sajjabax the All-Knowing and Inscrutable. Sajjabax the Horrifically Beautiful. Sajjabax the Insane."

Few were the spralakers who had actually gazed upon the legendary stomatopod's countenance. The necromancer's name was well enough known, however. Parents employed it to frighten young spawn into ready compliance. Mere mention of it was known to panic the bravest fighters and most skilled hunters. Among others the name of Sajjabax remained nothing more than an especially fearsome rumor. But here, in the hoary throne room of the Spralakers of the Northern Realms, the myth arose clad in full flesh, chitin, and chains.

Bluish-purple eyes stared down at the unmoving ivory disc-shape of the petrified messenger. Having retreated to a recess near the entrance, Gubujul gazed upon the scene in expectant silence. Even though he knew what likely was coming, he knew also he would not see it. No one could, not even the exceptionally perceptive Kulakak. Perhaps another stomatopod might be able to do so. To find out one would have to ask. On this one matter the normally inquisitive Gubujul was quite content to dwell in ignorance. Certainly the messenger had no idea.

Leaning forward as much as his metal bonds and restraining talisman permitted, Sajjabax began to speak, vigorously and at length.

It was gibberish. All of it. Neither worldly commentary nor conjurer's code, the steady stream of forceful nonsense filled the water to disperse harmlessly.

Not so the trancer's thick cocked forearms. They flicked out once, faster than any eyes could see. Had the appropriate instrumentation been present, it would have measured the speed of the strike at eight milliseconds with a force of ten thousand gravities. The blow was accompanied by a barely discernible flash of sonoluminescence. Within the bubble of force created by the necromancer's double punch, cavitation generated an undetectable burst of heat in the range of several thousand Kelvin.

None of this was apparent to or sensed by either the Great Lord or his cowering Paramount Advisor. They perceived only the results.

The collapsing cavitation bubble generated by the all but invisible thrust of the insane incanter's forearms had simply exploded the messenger's hard-shelled body. Tiny fragments of shell and flesh, bits of organs and strips of gills, settled slowly to the floor; a shimmering silent shower that was the messenger's former physical self. No malicious spell could have done worse, no evil enchantment proven more lethal.

Stepping out from his provisional hiding place, Gubujul fluttered slowly back to where his liege was thoughtfully contemplating the utterly shattered remnants of the messenger who had been unlucky enough to be the one designated to deliver the bad news.

"She should have stayed and fought and died with her comrades." Looking up, Kulakak calmly regarded the talismaniacally restrained, monotonously babbling figure of the all-powerful crustacean conjurer. The Great Lord, Ruler of all Born with Shell, was careful to stay well back out of range of those incomprehensibly deadly forearms.

"But had she remained to fight, my Lord, as you yourself pointed out, she would not have been able to bring us the news of the tragedy."

"Also correct." Pivoting on his multiple legs, Kulakak turned to his much more fragile Paramount Advisor. "Of such contradictions are state decisions made." A sigh bubbled from his mouth. "It appears we have suffered a considerable defeat. One as thorough as it is unexpected. But it is a loss that can be sustained. We underestimate the inhabitants of the Southwestern Reefs. This is a mistake that will not happen again. A brief interruption in the inexorable surge of our eventual triumph. Our enemies will be exterminated and we will take the reefs for our own." Eyestalks inclined down toward the attentive Advisor.

"Even simple moves are rarely uneventful, craven manipulator of words. In the coming days I will need your full attention and your most incisive insight."

"You have it, my Lord! As always." All six of Gubujul's slender antennae dipped forward.

Three found themselves suddenly clamped in the Great Lord's right claw. Gubujul froze. The slightest increase in pressure from that massive grip would see them snipped off as easily as he would dismember a clutch of roe.

"See that it is so. I am afraid that for awhile you will have to forgo your usual pleasures and distractions. As will I. As will the members of the entire court." Almost indifferently, he released the pinned sensory organs. Gubujul allowed himself to swallow in relief. He was very subtle about it. The Paramount Advisor to the court was famous for his ability to retain his poise under the most trying conditions. It was one reason he was still alive when so many predecessors had been demoted to the status of a quick meal.

"Only one thing concerns me," Kulakak muttered. "This presence of a shaman who would seem to be a cut above the usual village idiot." In raising his eyes to the figure of the nightmare crustacean bound in the wall, he also raised his voice. "What do you think, prattler of perverse possibilities? Do the mersons have among them one capable of matching your flair for the foul? Gather your wits and speak!"

The spasming, shuddering body of the giant mantis shrimp suddenly stopped moving. It was if a cloud had momentarily been wiped from those disturbingly beautiful lilac eyes. Though they focused on the Great Lord, Gubujul knew they saw him equally as well. The eyes of a stomatopod were more efficient than those of any other living thing.

For a moment, then, the madness was mislaid. The feral gesticulations and sputtering inanities ceased. Sajjabax the Magnificent gazed back at the ruler of the North. In the throne chamber the conjurer's words resounded deep and thoughtful.

"I don't know this one of whom you speak. I cannot get a sense of his presence. It is a matter of clever dissemination, not distance. Almost casual is the cloaking, especially for a manyarm. A formidable opponent, I think, for all that he chooses to hide it." Thousands of ommatidia converged on the figure of Kulakak. "Watch your step as you move south, amputator of limbs, lest you forfeit a plateful of your own."

With that, the brief spark of sanity was extinguished. The violet eyes glazed over and the passionate incomprehensible babbling resumed. Disappointed, Kulakak waved a hand at the figure and murmured a string of words. The necromancer's head slumped forward, his mouth ceased spouting drooling drivel, and the greenish opacity that concealed him was revisited. The light from the inhibiting talisman that hung from his eyestalks faded but did not go out. If it ever did …

As Kulakak turned away, Gubujul made bold enough to ask a question that had intrigued him for some time. "My Lord, I have always wondered—and should you wish to decline to reply you need not tell me, of course—what is the origin of the amulet that imprisons the mad mage and allows you to control him? What thaumaturgic power anywhere is so much greater than that of the great Sajjabax himself that it could fashion such a thing?"

Kulakak waved a claw carelessly. "I don't mind telling you at all, Paramount Advisor. There is no spellcaster anywhere who exceeds in knowledge and skill our own mad Sajjabax. For you see, it was he himself who fashioned the talisman and presented it to me along with the appropriate words for controlling it."

Over time Gubujul had imagined many explanations, but this was not one that had been among them. "The wielder of such esoteric and unfathomable power gave you mastery over himself? But why? Why do such a thing?"

The Great Lord turned thoughtful, remembering. "Because he recognized his own madness, and in recognizing it, understood the damage it could do. Not only to me, to the court, to all his own kind—but to himself. So he took steps to see that he would be properly kept in check. There may be madness in that, but there is also great wisdom."

"Verily so," a surprised Gubujul readily agreed. "What then of his sickness? Will it always afflict him?"

"I hope so," the Great Lord murmured grimly, "because I fear what he might do if he were sane. I do fear it."

The Paramount Advisor considered, then remembered to inquire, "What of this changeling that was mentioned, my Lord?"

"What—oh, that. A diversion, nothing more. A curiosity we may examine at our leisure once it has been captured. The messenger spoke only of its existence, not of any strange powers it might hold. Were it possessed of such abilities, I am sure it would have been mentioned." Kulakak hastened as he moved toward the throne.

"What are we to do now, my Lord?" Gubujul waited anxiously for a response. He was always more comfortable carrying out an order than waiting for one to be promulgated.

"Why, we will gather a multitude that will make the force just lost look like little more than a scouting expedition. It will be the greatest army the North has ever seen. There will be no missteps this time. The southern reefs will be cleansed of mersons, manyarms, and any foolish enough to ally with them." He waved a claw. "It will not take long. When the call is spread, spralakers can assemble quickly."

"And the shaman of whom Sajjabax spoke?" Gubujul persisted.

Eyes dipped downward as the Great Lord scrambled back up onto the jadeite throne. "Send out the necessary word. Danger large or danger small, if he is worthy of Sajjabax's notice, then he is worthy of special attention. A castle in the current to whoever brings me this mage's beak. As I have said it, so let it be known."

"Yes, my Lord." Bowing obsequiously, antennae fluttering, Gubujul backed out of the room. Having had plenty of practice, he was able to do so swiftly and without having to look behind him.

Left brooding on the stark green slab that was his throne, Kulakak pondered how best to proceed. Only occasionally could

Sajjabax be relied upon to give cogent, worthwhile advice. When queried, the all-powerful and quite mad necromancer was as likely to spout the unfathomable as the efficacious. In the expansion of the war to come he could be a trump card—or a joke.

It mattered not. As sovereign of all the Northern spralakers, Kulakak knew he had no choice but to press forward with the attack and with the effort to take control of the Southwest Reeflands. There could be no delay, no turning back. That option had already molted. They would drive out or kill every merson and manyarm that resisted. It was a thing that had to be done, and as rapidly as possible.

Not even one as trusted as Gubujul knew what had become known to the Great Lord: that the People of the Shell themselves were running out of time.

◊

In addition to the village council, nearly all the surviving members of the expeditionary force from Sandrift and what seemed like the entire population of Siriswirll turned out to wave the small troupe of travelers farewell and swift current. Looking back as the little group that had been chosen to try to make it to Benthicalia started on its way, Irina noted that when any party of well-wishers could count among its number more than several hundred manyarms of various species, a great deal of waving was involved indeed.

Oxothyr did not consider it an ill omen the poor light that greeted them as they set out. As the day lengthened and Siriswirll fell behind them, it unexpectedly grew darker instead of brighter. Only when the mirrorsky itself started to dapple did Irina realize what was happening. She had been underwater for so long that the memory of surface phenomena had begun to slip from her awareness.

High above the world of Oshenerth, a strong storm had been unleashed. The stippling she was seeing arose from the impact of raindrops on the surface, and the darkening from congregated storm clouds. Yet again she found herself wondering what would happen if she swam just a little higher and stuck her head out into the open air. Thanks to Oxothyr's enchanting she had gills now. But while the mage had given her gills he had said nothing about removing her lungs. Was she then more amphibian than fish?

She decided against attempting the maneuver—at least while she was surrounded by her new friends. Though all were polite now and no longer said hurtful things, at least not in her presence, doubtless some of them still harbored suspicions about the strange changeling in their midst. Poylee in particular would seize on such an adventurous move to re-emphasize the visitor's difference from everyone else. If she was going to try such a stunt, Irina decided, better to do so when she was alone and unobserved. So she finned along quietly beside the others and contented herself with imagining what it would be like to once again feel fresh air on her face. In many ways, the remembrance and the imagining were enough.

After all, it was not as if she was going to get out of the water and wash off the salt.

Chachel insisted on leading the way. Not out of any sense of misplaced gallantry, but because it allowed him to keep as far away from the others as possible without being openly insulting. As usual, Glint accompanied him. Behind them and spread out in a tubular column came a dozen of the best fighters Sandrift and Siriswirll could provide, divided evenly between mersons and manyarms. In their midst swam the shaman Oxothyr and his two famuli. As the three manyarms jetted along effortlessly with their limbs trailing like vines behind them, Irina worked hard to keep up. It was a lot easier now than it would have been weeks ago. With every passing day she became more and more comfortable with the webbing that linked her fingers and her toes, and with the fins on the backs of her legs.

Despite this growing familiarity with her new surroundings she still would have jumped when her left calf received a sharp blow, except that it was impossible to jump underwater. Instead, she jerked and rolled—and found herself staring down at a smirking Poylee.

"What was that for?" She fought to contain her anger.

The female merson nodded at the changeling's legs. "You're about to lose your precious otherworldly knife."

Looking down, Irina bent her right knee and drew her leg upward. Sure enough, both of the plastic straps that secured the scabbard to her calf had come loose. Only a single buckle had kept her from losing the most valuable item she had managed to salvage from home. As she worked to refasten the straps she smiled gratefully at the other female.

"Thanks, Poylee. I would've hated to have lost it."

The merson's reply, like her expression, was hard to read. "I wouldn't have wanted it to slip free and cut you." With that she kicked hard to return to the forefront of the shaman's escort, leaving Irina as puzzled as ever. Was Poylee friend or foe, and would she ever find out? Clearly the female merson's concern had been for the weapon and not for its owner.

"Don't dwell on it."

"What?" She looked up and was startled to see how close Oxothyr had drifted. Underwater, it was easy to come right up to someone without making any noise whatsoever. Sharks did it every day.

Prior to her arrival in Oshenerth she would have found the presence of a giant octopus trailing twenty foot-long arms swimming along just above her more than slightly intimidating. By now, however, Oxothyr was a good and familiar acquaintance. Despite his suckered tentacles and goggling eyes, the sac-like body and serrated beak, in her mind's eye she saw him as a kindly old sage. Picture the trailing arms as the strands of a beard and the head-body as one wearing a soft crown and it was almost possible to see him as human. Glasses would have helped to complete the picture, but Oxothyr did not need glasses. Like the eyesight of even the lowliest manyarm, his was extremely sharp.

"Do not dwell on the encounter," he reiterated. "It is all part of an old and familiar ritual."

A blast of water struck her in the face as he shot ahead. Kicking hard, she managed to catch up. "What ritual?"

"You will find out. Or maybe you won't. Either way you'll learn something of importance," he concluded cryptically.

She decided to let the matter drop. There was too much else to concentrate on, too much to see, to spend time worrying about Poylee's motivations. Surely she still didn't think the visitor from the void had any sort of design on the hunter Chachel? Irina thought she had made that perfectly clear.

As a diver, she believed she had seen and experienced a fair sampling of what the underwater world had to offer. All of her experiences combined, however, could not equal what she saw in a single day's travel westward along the reef line. Where she recalled hardly being able to contain her excitement during a dive several years ago over an encounter with a cluster of several hundred yellow, black, and white bannerfish, the travelers swam through a school of twenty thousand. Later that day a hundred big dorado sped by heading in the opposite direction; their striking, mallet-headed green shapes shimmering with flecks of silver. As they swept past, each and every one of them proffered a resonant and rushed "hello!" like some traveling opera chorus cruising the open road.

A thousand spade-shaped black-and-silver batfish made an unhurried approach perpendicular to the travelers' route, yet not a single collision took place between merson, manyarm, and the flattened face-sized finners. Famously inquisitive, a dozen or so broke away from the main school to tag along for awhile, peppering Sathi and Tythe in particular with interminable questions about the travelers' direction and purpose that the two famuli were naturally prohibited from answering. The irritation lasted until a manyarm warrior from Siriswirll snatched up one of the most persistent questioners and began, unapologetically, to make of him a traveling snack. Along with the rest of their unanswered questions, the remaining batfish prudently made haste to rejoin their schoolmates.

In addition to species that she recognized, Irina found herself passing creatures that appeared to have been designed rather than evolved. One trio of angelfish, members of an always colorful family, boasted iridescent purple and yellow bodies propelled by brilliant golden fins, bright crimson eyespots near their tails, and jet-black eyes streaked with sapphire. A cluster of sea fans clinging to one coral cliff showed every color of the rainbow. Their section of reef looked as if it had suffered an attack by a contingent of crazed Crayolas. There were box triggerfish the size of trash cans, wrasses whose males boasted black stripes and the females black spots, giant snails with multiple shells that browsed the coral like miniature wandering churches, and graceful oversized nudibranchs whose flamboyantly colored unfurled bodies resembled a carton of Hawaiian dress shirts.

There was simply too much to take in, she told herself. Too much to absorb. Her senses were overwhelmed, her perception exhausted. For a while, a twenty-foot long tiger shark paced the party off to its left. The mersons and manyarms on that side closed ranks, forming a wall the shark could not penetrate in hopes of picking off a solitary swimmer. Irina could hear it mumbling as it tried to hypnotize first the female merson who was in front, then the squid who was bringing up the rear. Neither its unbroken stare nor its rudimentary shark magic worked. After an hour or so it gave up and swam away. As it departed, Irina was positive she heard it curse. It was a shark curse, of course, and therefore undecipherable, but there was no mistaking its tone or connotation.

It was late afternoon, the end of the week, and the atmosphere above the mirrorsky had cleared when Chachel and Glint returned from reconnoitering ahead. The merson was not smiling. Come to think of it, Irina realized with a start, she had never seen the hunter smile. His cuttlefish companion managed to display more good humor, and that without a mouth or teeth.

Slowing down as he entered the group, Chachel halted in front of Oxothyr. "Rays coming," he announced with his typical terseness.

The shaman continued forward, but adjusted his head-body so he could better see the hunter. "What kind and how many?"

"Hard to tell." Chachel glanced back the way he had come. "Will be easy to do so soon. Maybe forty, maybe more. Stingrays, eagle—many mantas."

"Mantas." Oxothyr considered. "Alone?"

"I'm afraid not." By way of emphasis and explanation, Chachel brought his spear around in front of him and gripped it firmly in both hands. It was a simple gesture, but more than enough.

Oxothyr let out a resigned sigh. "Pass the word. Get everyone into an appropriate defensive configuration. You two." Sathi and Tythe closed formation with their master. "Head off to left and right and stay outside. We'll need you to keep a sharp eye out for any other enemy that may have gone undetected."

"Yes, Master!" Tythe was one squirt ahead of his comrade in shooting off in the opposite direction.

"Why are rays an enemy of mersons and manyarms?" Irina gazed worriedly ahead, remembering the near crushing attack rays and their spralaker riders had delivered at Siriswirll. "They're not spralaker-kind."

"No indeed." Changing from a benign beige to a bright orange laced with red, the shaman's color shift revealed his own mental and emotional preparations for combat. "They are easily engaged, however, by whosoever will promise them food. Remember that they are cousin to the shark, and therefore not to be trusted." The shaman was clearly troubled. "Still, it is curious that we should find ourselves dealing with them here and now, so soon after many of their kind were slain at Siriswirll. I fear my studies and my presence may have become known to malevolent elements, and thereby drawn unwelcome attention to the rest of you."

She hesitated, then reached over to draw a hand down the upper length of one of the mage's eight limbs. "Anything that threatens you threatens all of us, Oxothyr."

Both eyes peered back at her. "You show hidden wisdom, changeling." Suddenly a pair of tentacles gestured ahead, past the mersons in the lead. "Ready yourself—here they come...."

# – XIV –

Swift they were, the different kinds of rays. The expanding cloud of rapidly approaching, flapping wings made it look as if the waves that disturbed the mirrorsky had taken on color and form and somehow managed to descend to deeper depths. Eyeing the flock of oncoming aggressors, Irina thought she could make out four distinct species. One that boasted of four wings instead of two was plainly an inhabitant only of Oshenerth. Nothing like it had ever soared through the seas of her own world.

On the backs of each ray rode a number of spralakers fantastically diverse in shape, size, and proportion. The common denominator was their demeanor; a focused fury that was shared and escalating. Armed with spears, knives, and their own integral chitinous armor, Irina didn't see how despite their numbers they could prove much of a threat out in the open ocean to the far more agile mersons and manyarms.

She quickly found out.

As always, it was on the sea floor where the spralakers would have an advantage, where their multiple legs could firmly grip rock and coral to assure them a solid, stable fighting platform. Countervailing merson and manyarm tactics required that they strike from above, where their greater maneuverability put them in command. That was how Jorosab and the others began the battle. They did not expect the presence of the rays to force any difference in tactics. Fish or rays, it was all the same. Except that it wasn't.

As expected the intercepting force dove low, heading for the bottom. But the rays did not disembark their scuttling passengers onto the reef. Instead, they formed into a series of circles underneath the expedition and commenced a rapid ascent. Whenever a merson or manyarm tried to swim out past the farthest edge of the swiftly rising formation, several rays broke clear to force the breakaway individual back.

Irina found herself hemmed in with the others as they discovered that they were being herded closer and closer to the looming mirrorsky. Meanwhile plenty of merson and manyarm arrows found their marks. Trailing dark blood, wounded rays fluttered aimlessly out of the rising circular formation or crashed into the reef below, dumping their frustrated, wailing crustacean passengers onto the coral and too far from the fighting to participate. But even those shafts that struck home did not always put a ray out of action. Their skin was incredibly tough. Many arrowpoints failed to penetrate.

Whenever a member of the expedition charged downward and attempted to break through the circle, they were immediately met by a barrage of spears or knives. These were usually but not always avoided. Merson spears and manyarm arrows were taking a terrible toll among the attackers, but the reduced numbers maintained their ascending circle and continued to press their adversaries skyward.

The strategy was clear. Force the members of the expedition steadily upward until they could ascend no farther and then engage them in the kind of close quarter hand-to-claw, hand-to-tentacle combat in which the hard-shelled spralakers excelled. It became a race to see if the expedition's archers could reduce the number of attackers to the point where their upward-pressing disc of mounted rays collapsed. And so before merson and manyarm hit, not the wall, but the sky.

Sting rays, golden rays, eagle rays—all were sizable, but by themselves not large enough to force an agile swimmer up against the mirrorsky. Only the mantas were big enough to do that. Only the so-called devil fish, with their thirty-foot wide winged bodies, could force a merson upward while shutting off every avenue of escape.

One fighter who tried to make a dash between two of the rising mantas was not fast enough. Caught in a crossfire of spears and knives flung by eager spralakers, she sustained first one, then several deep wounds. Finned legs slowing, arms crossed over her chest, she struggled to swim clear. Leaping off the end of one manta's wing, several spralakers caught her on the way down. No single, merciful killing thrust was forthcoming; clinging to her head and body, the pitiless crustaceans proceeded to hack her to pieces.

The rippling underside of the mirrorsky was now near enough for Irina to look over her shoulder and make out the blurry, distorted, but still recognizable orb of the sun riding high in a long unvisited sky. She could feel its heat on her shoulders and back. Around and below her the battle raged. Pierced by arrows and then by spears, more of the swirling, circling rays were sent spiraling downward. Below the intense fighting, it was raining spralakers. Poor swimmers at best, they kicked and flailed in futile attempts to remain high enough in the water column to continue to participate in the fight. Eager arriving scavengers began to pick them off, while those of the wounded who landed on the reef below were quickly singled out for consumption by marauding morays and hungry groupers.

So much activity this close to the surface should have drawn the attention of aerial predators, but apparently there were none. Irina found herself wondering if anything flew in the sky of Oshenerth or walked on its dry land.

A mad thrashing off to her right made her whirl. She recognized the isolated fighter immediately. Poylee had been cornered by a pair of spralaker-carrying mantas. With one of the winged monsters circling on either side of her she could not flee in any direction without running into waiting spralaker spears. If she tried to swim downward to regain maneuverable water, she would find herself caught in a potentially deadly crossfire. All she could do was strike out with her spear and keep fending off the giants and their hard-shelled riders. Meanwhile the mantas continued to close in, forcing her inexorably upward toward the mirrorsky.

Behind the cut-off skirmish a third manta could be seen approaching; slowly, but gathering speed. Instead of readying their weapons for attack, the spralakers clinging to its back were hunkering down and digging their feet and claws into the giant ray's tough epidermis. As the manta continued to accelerate, Irina sensed what was coming. She looked around for help. With bow-armed Sathi and Tythe flanking him, Oxothyr was occupied elsewhere. Chachel and Glint were wreaking havoc among a group of panicking eagle rays and their increasingly flustered riders. Riding the back of a bucking manta, Jorosab was ridding it of its hardshelled tenants with scything arcs of his long knife, like a sushi chef gone mad.

She looked around. Poylee's spine and shoulders were pressed right up against the mirrorsky. At least she couldn't be attacked from that direction. But the security was deceptive. One of the two circling mantas darted closer, forcing the young merson's back to actually break the surface. At the same time the wings of the approaching third manta thrust downward harder than ever. The spralakers riding its back and wings flattened themselves against their massive mount.

Unseen by Poylee, the second manta came up directly beneath her and forced her through the mirrorsky. As it did so, the spralakers on its back scuttled around to cling to its underside.

Kicking as hard as she could, Irina shot forward. Intercepting the surfaced manta, she struck out with the butt end of her spear. Catching the spralakers hanging from its belly by surprise, she knocked several off before they noted her presence. By then she was pushing herself hard, hard, out of the water as she pulled herself onto the manta's back.

For the first time in weeks she felt the sun on her skin. It seemed as if she had stuck her face into an oven. Then her outstretched left arm slammed into Poylee's side. The shock reverberated through her. Lying atop the surfaced manta, she inhaled several times. The bloat of air filling her lungs was an alien sensation, as if she had swallowed a helium-filled balloon. But unlike Poylee, who was clawing at her gills while flopping atop the manta's expansive back like a fish out of water, she did not gag.

Shoving forcefully, she pushed the choking Poylee off the surfaced manta and back into the water near its tail. As the two of them sank beneath the surface, the searing sun was eclipsed by a rapidly expanding shadow.

Having launched itself completely out of the water, the ton of airborne manta landed hard on the back of its brethren. The impact forced the second manta deeper down but it suffered no damage from the collision. Had Poylee been caught between the pair, however, she would have been smashed as completely as Glint crushed a clam for breakfast.

Holding the merson by an arm Irina continued to kick vigorously, sending both of them hurling downward. Behind them the water boiled as the no longer airborne manta flapped hard to slide off the back of its brother. The water around them was filled with irate, cursing spralakers, furious that the carefully planned attack had failed. All the muttering and activity finally drew the attention of other mersons and manyarms, who arrived and began to cleanse the immediate area.

Regaining control of herself, a hacking, coughing Poylee finally recovered enough strength to push Irina away from her. Throughout it all she had somehow managed to hold onto her spear.

"How did you …?" Her astonished query was interrupted by another fit of coughing as bubbles bursting from her mouth. It did not matter. Irina had anticipated the question.

"I saw what was happening, saw the third manta coming toward you and picking up speed. It looks like I can still breathe out of the water, at least a little."

"Demon." A recovering Poylee massaged her neck with her free hand.

"Changeling," a relieved Irina corrected her. "You *might* say thank you."

"I was getting to that." Poylee looked annoyed at having the omission pointed out. "If I hadn't been smashed, they would have held me above the mirrorsky until I drowned. I—thank you, Irina," she finally finished. "You did save my life."

Irina smiled. "You would've done the same for me."

"No I wouldn't." Turning and lowering her spear, the merson kicked hard to rejoin the battle.

Watching legs and hips, fins and webbing recede in the direction of the fighting, Irina found herself in mind of an old saying. "'Tis better to deal with an honest enemy than a lying friend." Like many old sayings, she was not sure she bought the premise. It was, however, one she apparently was going to have to live with. Scissor-kicking her legs and gripping her weapon, she headed off determinedly in Poylee's wake.

By now the members of the expeditionary force had killed, wounded, or driven off the remainder of the attackers. Surviving rays and spralakers scattered. Out of the corner of an eye Irina saw one big bull ray snapped up, spralaker riders and all, by a fifteen-foot tiger shark that had been circling in wait among the coral. The ray uttered a single gasp as ragged teeth clamped down over its head, while those spralakers not immediately crushed or swallowed abandoned their ride for the presumed safety of the colorful coral labyrinth below. None of the mersons or manyarms pursued. Without a mount to transport them it was unlikely any spralakers would survive the long trek back to their place of origin. Those voracious and efficient independent operators the sharks would see to that.

None of the latter tried to make a move on any of the several injured members of the small expeditionary force. Not with armed fighters prepared and ready to defend the wounded. Besides, there were ample easier pickings. The reef beneath where the midwater skirmish had taken place was littered with the corpses of dead or dying rays and spralakers.

◊

Despite the day's success in battle, when the travelers settled down for the night beneath a huge stone arch fringed with thousands of brilliantly hued soft corals, Irina found Oxothyr sunk in as pensive a mood as ever. Nearby, his famuli were busily preparing dinner by stripping the shells from a pile of scavenged mollusks. In her still new, still alien surroundings there were often times when she had to force herself to eat, however visually unappealing the food on offer might be. One of her favorites was raw fish seasoned with cuttlefish ink, which Glint was happy to provide. It helped that as a surface dweller she had several times enjoyed variants of both dishes.

"Why so somber, shaman? We won."

"What—oh, good evening, changeling." His arms drifting aimlessly around him, as if he had forgotten they were attached to his body, the mage sat on a bulbous upthrust of dark green mushroom coral. Occasionally he would reach down to pluck out of one of the crevices a hors d'oeuvre in the form of a too-curious blenny, but it was obvious his thoughts and concentration lay on matters other than food. "Yes, we won."

She settled down beside him, careful to take a seat on a much smoother, more rounded hump of brain coral. Somewhere overhead, the unseen sun was setting. Sharply angled sunlight piercing the perfectly transparent, unpolluted water was transformed into a shower of twinkling gold coins.

"Pardon me for saying so, but you don't act like we won."

A tentacle coiled in her direction, making the gesture that she now knew stood in for a cephalopodan smile. The shaman's body morphed from a deep taupe to a more cheery fuchsia, with blue stripes.

"Take no notice of it. I am by nature a brooder. The corollary to great responsibility is often a chronic moodiness. I wish it were otherwise. I like to laugh as much as the next. If it's amusement you want, I suggest you seek out the company of a cuttlefish. Of all the manyarms they are the most prone to comedy."

"It's not that," she told him. Exhibiting a rare playfulness, the tip of another tentacle curled around her right big toe and tugged gently. She pulled back. "I think I can tell the difference now between when you're worried and when you're just thinking."

One golden eye swiveled toward her. "Your perception increases beyond mere simple physical realities. Yes, I don't deny it. Much about today's encounter concerns me."

"You're afraid we'll be attacked again?" Idly, she poked a finger at the flaring, multi-colored gills of the Christmas tree worms with whom she was sharing the brain coral. As in her own, more familiar seas back home, the thumbnail-sized parasols contracted sharply back into their burrows as soon as her fingers drew too near. Unlike those with which she was familiar, each time one here did so, it left a tiny annelid swear word in its wake.

"That is not it," the shaman told her. "We should not have been confronted at all. Not here. Not so soon after Siriswirll. It implies that our intentions are known to, or at least suspected by, our enemies. Some of those who escaped today will render a report of the encounter. Inevitably, additional attempts will follow. Some may be less significant and less effective, but we are too few to cope with an attack on a truly large scale. Another encounter might not find so many of us surviving. Our strength lies in our ability to pass through the water between Siriswirll and Benthicalia quietly and unnoticed." He paused as a dutiful Sathi offered him an armload of shelled mollusks. Popping one into his mouth, he spoke as he swallowed.

"We must endeavor avoid future attacks."

"How do you propose we do that?" a new, high-pitched voice inquired.

Irina looked around. Chachel and Glint had come up behind her. Having asked the question, the manyarm was now engaged in munching on half a spralaker. It was not an orderly meal. Instead of removing the meat or shell, the cuttlefish had simply started in on one side of the body of his dead foe and was methodically eating his way across to the other.

Looking past her in the deepening twilight without excluding her from the conversation, Oxothyr directed his reply to the new arrivals. "We must go deeper."

Merson and manyarm eyed one another. Chachel turned warily back to the shaman. "How much deeper?"

"Deep enough so that our enemies will not suspect that we have done so." A long arm gestured into the gathering night. "Deep enough so that those who hunt us will not look for us. Down below we are few enough in number to pass unnoticed. Spralakers and mersons do not see well in dim light." His gaze shifted to the feeding cuttlefish. "But manyarms do. At depth, we will have the advantage."

Chachel was dubious. "The spralakers are not stupid. After today's fight they will put even more scouts in this area, and are likely to offer a reward for information concerning our whereabouts."

Oxothyr flashed vermilion understanding. "Even so, by descending below the level where they might expect to find us, we will greatly increase our chances of avoiding such unwanted attention."

Using a tentacle to remove a leg from which he had stripped all the meat and casting the length of empty shell aside, Glint offered his own opinion. "I think it's a clever move, commander of arms. Even if they know to look for us deeper down, they will have a harder time finding us." He gestured in the direction of the main camp. "There are those, however, who are afraid of the deep. Even some manyarms who can make their own light to see by."

Oxothyr was not dissuaded. "Cowards and children can go home. Swimming to Benthicalia was never alleged to be a picnic excursion over pretty reef and clean sand. I don't want anyone with me who cannot commit." His body had turned an angry reddish purple. "If need be, I'll go on alone."

Chachel kicked forward. "I am with you as always, shaman. I do not fear the deep, and I look forward to confounding our enemies."

"For my friend," Glint declared around a mouthful of white spralaker flesh, "that amounts to a speech. Me, I don't make speeches. I just like to see new places—even where it's too dark to see them."

Irina became aware everyone was looking in her direction, including the shaman's two famuli. She felt pressured, but it did not matter. She had little choice, and if asked would have said as much. Truth be told, she would have volunteered to continue on anyway. Having already been exposed to multiple wonders, she was always ready to appreciate one more. From the descriptions she had heard of Benthicalia, including many that were probably more fanciful than real, it certainly qualified.

"Most will come, I think." Oxothyr's anger faded to auburn. "Some because they are brave, some because they are foolhardy, some because they are afraid of appearing afraid, some because they have lost friends in battle." He eyed the drifting Irina. "Some may even come because they would be embarrassed to be overshadowed by a changeling."

"You see?" Lateral fins rippling, body flaring with flowing black stripes, Glint turned toward her. "Already you are more helpful than you know."

*Yes*, she thought bitterly. I'm an alien, a monster to frighten, intimidate, or embarrass. What wonderful talent. How heartening to be thought of as so useful.

So heartening that she did not go on to mention that ever since she was a little girl she had been afraid of the dark.

◊

When they finally stopped descending and leveled off there was hardly any light left at all. That the sun and the mirrorsky continued to exist somewhere high overhead Irina did not doubt. But they were no longer visible. The realm of sunlight had been left behind.

As her eyes adjusted to the new conditions, she was barely able to make out the dim outlines of the mersons around her. The same problem did not exist for the manyarms. By activating the photophores within their skin, all were able to generate their own light. Surrounded by internally illuminated shapes glowing a ghostly blue-green, she kept pace without fear of getting lost. Weeks of continuous swimming had strengthened her leg muscles and tightened those elsewhere.

For sheer outrageous display of self-generated illumination, none could match Oxothyr. Jetting along backwards in the manner of his kind, the shaman toyed with flashing an extraordinary variety of patterns. While his companions could only generate blue-green, blue, or a few limited variations of red light, the mage was able to produce an entire rainbow of colors. It was the first time Irina had ever seen him engage in anything akin to showing off. One evening (she assumed it was evening because they had stopped to sleep), she ventured to compliment him on the colorful displays.

"It's beautiful, Oxothyr. I wish I could do something like it. I've always admired cephalopodan bioluminescence. Before now it was always from a distance, or in pictures." She had to force herself to keep her vision from wandering out into the utter and complete blackness that enveloped the camp. "When night dives were offered, I always declined."

Resting comfortably nearby, the shaman turned an intense shade of cobalt blue. "Perhaps if you could generate your own light, like a manyarm, you would be less afraid of the Oshenerth night."

She looked away. "Maybe. I don't know. In any case, it doesn't matter. I'll have to settle for admiring your lights." Noticing the two famuli busy nearby, she added, "And Sathi and Tythe's too, of course."

In response, both stopped what they were doing to zip over to the changeling in their midst.

"Sweet visitor," Tythe whispered, "I would lend you my lights if I could."

"Try this." Halting close to her, Sathi promptly ejected several small bubbles of ink—the cephalopodan equivalent of a human blowing smoke rings. Jet black in daylight, at depth the liquid glowed a beautiful bright chartreuse. As the bubbles drifted around her head, a captivated Irina found herself encircled by liquid light. It was intense enough to illuminate her hands, arms, and torso. Had she been in possession of a book, she could have read by the organic radiance. As the bubbles began to fade she waved a hand through several, stirring the light like electric syrup.

"That was wonderful!" Reaching out, she let her right hand stroke the famulus from head to tail. The body-length squid performed a delighted roll.

"That *was* interesting," Oxothyr admitted from nearby, "and not a little flattering." He moved closer. "Try this, changeling Irina."

Chanting sonorously, Oxothyr expelled a flush of ink that was considerably greater in volume than the bubbles emitted by his assistant. So completely did it swaddle her in a bath of lambent colors that for a panicky moment she could neither see nor breathe. As she kicked and flailed at the smothering cloud of dazzling fluid it dissipated rapidly.

But—the enchanted shimmering light did not.

Looking first at her outstretched arms and then down at herself, she let out a little gasp. Beneath her skin small beads of blue-green luminescence now burned with a cold chemical light. The glow marched down her arms and legs, clung to the fins on her calves and the webbing between her fingers and toes. A more intense hue flared from the tips of each strand of her hair, as if her floating tresses had been transformed into a headful of blue-infused fiber optics. Red highlights flared from the tips of her fingers, ears, and locales concealed by her increasingly threadbare bathing suit.

Glint inspected her thoughtfully before finally pronouncing judgment. "Now this is the kind of magic I can appreciate! Irina-changeling, you've become beautiful. The mage has made you half-manyarm." He pivoted in the water. "Come with me. This is something that needs to be shared with my cousins."

Overcome by what she had become, Irina peered down at her ensorcelled bioluminescent self. "You really like it?"

"Take it from me," the cuttlefish assured her, "you will have the squid tying their arms in knots."

As they swam off to share Oxothyr's entertaining morsel of magicking with others of his kind and a seemingly dismissive Chachel left to take his rest, a figure that had been hovering in the darkness now came forward. Its expression was hard, its voice tart, its attitude demanding.

"Why did you do that for her?" Spear in hand, Poylee hovered at a close but respectful distance from the shaman.

"Because she asked." Arms coiled and rippled around the shaman's body.

"Well, I'm asking also." Holding her spear perpendicular to the rocky ground, which at this depth was largely devoid of coral, Poylee readied herself to receive a shower of light.

"There is no need." Backing away, Oxothyr began the process of squeezing himself into the fissure in the rocks he had chosen for his bed. Despite his size, having no bones allowed him to fit into a hole much smaller than seemed possible. "The inner glow that radiates from you already singles you out as special, Poylee, and lights up the area around you. Good-night." Folding his arms in front of him and changing their color and pattern to perfectly mimic the surrounding stone, the shaman effectively disappeared into his surroundings. Just like magic.

Poylee mulled pressing the matter, decided against it. More than a little conflicted, she swam slowly off to rejoin the other members of the party. She was not entirely sure what had just transpired, but the more she thought about it, the more she became convinced that she had just been rebuffed with a compliment.

# – XV –

rina suspected that her body's spectacular subcutaneous shimmering would not last, but while it did, she intended to fully enjoy it. Beyond Oxothyr's dexterous conscription of what she chose to think of as enchanted luciferase, her newfound glow extended to her spirit as well as her skin. Able now to see with reasonable clarity everything within her immediate vicinity, her fear of the near-darkness began to recede.

If there was a drawback to her altered state of individual luminosity, it was that it threatened to attract the attention not only of her fellow travelers but of numerous dark zone lifeforms. Though surrounded and watched over by the other members of the group, she remained wary. As a diver she had never been so deep. But she had seen pictures of what lived in the depths of her own seas. If similarities with Oshenerth held true, then out in the darkness nightmares dwelled.

Confirming both her suspicions and her fears, the following day one such horror approached to within arm's length. It had a bloated, skeletal body with nearly transparent skin stretched over thin bones. Filled with long, needle-like teeth, the jaws could open the full width of the body, allowing the fiendish predator to swallow prey even larger than as itself. A bright blue glowing lure dancing at the end of a worm-like appendage protruding from its skull. It halted close to Irina's face, surveyed this strange potential meal that was too large to fit into even its expansive mouth (for which the potential meal was most thankful), and then departed, dashing away with a speed that belied its stocky build. Its indifference was not surprising.

The monster was only a couple of inches long.

Though their appearance was stupendously fearsome, most of the ogres of the deep were small, like the inquisitive anglerfish she had just confronted. But not all were so harmless. She remained alert, monitoring her companions for any sign that something dangerous and larger than her hand might be in the vicinity. Despite the internal glow Oxothyr had bestowed on her she could still see only a short distance into the darkness.

The mersons did better. Somewhere out front, his path lit only by a few small bioluminescent eels fastened like bracelets around his wrists, ankles, and neck, Chachel was swimming point. The hunter was incredibly brave and must have nerves of steel, she thought. Or else he was just crazy, like so many claimed. Or maybe he just didn't care.

Where they paused one day for a midday meal, there was no greenery to be found. At this depth, in the absence of light, photosynthesis could not take place and plants could not grow. Deep-sea corals were primarily black and red. Sitting beneath an overhanging charcoal-gray branch coral as tall as a building, chewing and swallowing pieces of fresh fish and rubbery non-soluble strips of a particularly tasty beche-de-mer, she marveled at the untouched coral growth. Merson women adorned themselves with jewelry fashioned from such coral together with shells and found gemstones and thought little of it. Back home, a single such coral "tree" would be worth—she could not put a price on it.

In its natural state it was more beautiful to look at than if polished fragments of it had been hanging around her neck.

A streamlined shape materialized in front of her and she started slightly, wondering if she would ever get used to the velocities squid and cuttlefish regarded as normal. Sathi extended one of his two longer hunting arms toward her.

"Here," the famulus squeaked. "Master Oxothyr says you should swallow this."

Taking the tablet from the squid's tentacle, Irina frowned. The crude reddish disc was the size of a quarter. "I don't know if it's a bitter pill or not," she quipped, "but it's an awfully big one. Why should I take it? What's it for?"

Bioluminescent spots and slashes danced along the famulus' flanks. "The Master says it is to keep your insides from blowing up as we go deeper."

"Oh." She nodded slowly. "That sounds like a good reason. I'll do it."

The squid's body bobbed once in acknowledgement. Then he was gone in a blur of blue-green luminescence.

She studied the oversized pill. From Sathi's blunt description of the consequences that would result if she did not take it, it was clear that the tablet had to do with the increasing pressure she had been feeling as the expedition continued its descent. Evidently the mersons, like their companions the manyarms, had the ability to adjust to and cope with the greater pressures to be found at depth. Oxothyr's pill was therefore a preventative. Some sort of barometric prophylactic. She had no idea what the pill was made of or how the shaman had contrived it.

Her ignorance caused her no hesitation. By now she trusted Oxothyr completely. Even if she had not, she had no choice. Parting her lips, she shoved the pill into her mouth and sent it careening down her throat. Its diameter caused it to go down awkwardly.

Some of that was due to her body's instinctive modification of the swallowing reflex. She could hardly chase the pill with a glass of water. Despite not having had, in its former sense, a drink in weeks, she had yet to miss the feeling. In Oshenerth thirst was an all but forgotten sensation.

Not long after the midday meal and the resumption of their journey, she noticed that a dim light which had appeared in front of her had begun to grow stronger. Members of the expedition clustered closer to one another. Seeing Oxothyr in the middle of the gathering, she kicked harder to join him.

The intensifying glow came from the returning Chachel and Glint. She arrived just in time to hear their report. Chachel glanced in her direction but said nothing. For someone who vocally and at length evinced not the slightest interest in her, she had caught him looking at her on more than one occasion. The luminescent eel secured around his neck did nothing to inform his expression.

"Something coming this way," Glint was telling everyone. "It's odd. You can feel pressure as if from many individuals, and yet it is slight. Large, but not massive. And there's something else accompanying it."

"Spralakers?" one of the manyarm soldiers drifting nearby inquired anxiously.

"No." Chachel hovered in the glow cast by his friend. "Music."

◊

Unsurprisingly, in the dark and quiet of the deep they heard the approaching procession before they could see it. The harmony had a strange synchronization that reminded Irina of hundreds of differently tuned bells. Yet the actual sound was entirely new to her. More than anything else, it put her in mind of a multitude of distant electric harps. Only when the increasing blue-red glow in the distance began to resolve itself into individual shapes did a cautious Oxothyr venture an identification.

"A coelenterate chorus! I have heard of such, but have never seen one." Emulating his eagerness, his body turned bright yellow with small puce spots. "We must be careful."

"Why?" Reaching down, Irina nonchalantly pushed aside the tip of a coiling tentacle that was absently trying to loop itself around her left ankle.

"Because that which is rarely encountered is always worthy of caution," the shaman explained.

But as the deep-water chorus drew close enough so that individual shapes could be more precisely distinguished, and as the sight and sound took her breath away, she found that circumspection was the farthest thing from her mind. She was sure she had seen more beautiful sights underwater—but at the moment she could not think of one.

Jellyfish she had encountered before. Usually as individuals, occasionally in small groups, drifting in aimless glutinous indifference through waters both warm and chill. Sometimes they had been as quiescent as the dead, while on other occasions their pastel-tinged bells had throbbed like transparent round hearts as simple reflex action pushed them spasmodically through the water. Certainly she had never seen them dance.

Much less sing.

A cornucopia of light, sound, and movement, the gelatinous procession approached the travelers in a parade of individual glories. Some of the jellies had specks of impossibly intense crimson and gold running around the edges of their bodies as well as through them, like so many electrified rubies and citrines chasing one another in endless procession. Others sent waves of limpid blue spots running down their trailing tentacles, passionate streams of turquoise fire that dripped away into darkness like incandescent tears.

This flashing, coruscating carnival of bioluminescence was accompanied by a melodious ringing and chiming that put Irina in mind of a traveling Balinese temple procession. Not for nothing in Oshenerth were the bodies of such jellyfish called bells. They rang and tinkled and clanged in perfect mystic counterpoint to the viscous light show. It was as if all the bells in an orchestra's percussion section had suddenly come to life and decided to mate in an orgy of reverberation with several randy gamelans. She had never imagined, much less heard, anything quite like it.

Sliding in and out, through and among the hundreds of trailing photophore-flashing tentacles were several dozen arrow-like fish. Silver of side and tiny of eye, they generated a different but complimentary sound as they rubbed against the tentacles. They were, she realized in amazement, playing the lethal stinging strands like bows on strings.

Pulsing in time to the music they generated and strobing their internal lights in perfect visual counterpoint, the glutinous chorale was in no hurry to drift on by. Its dawdling progress was fine with Irina. Being a spectacle she might never encounter again, she was keen to savor it for as long as possible. Indeed, once in the vicinity of the captivated travelers the procession seemed to slow, as if its constituents' rhopalia, or sensory organs, perceived that their energetic visual and auditory efforts had found an admiring audience.

215

Irina realized that she could not turn away from so much splendor nor close her ears to the hypnotically seductive sounds. Hovering motionless in the dark water she stared and smiled at the nomadic parade, wishing that the presentation might never end. Barely aware of the mersons and manyarms around her, she noticed that though this was their world they were equally entranced by the phantasmagoric display. Even Oxothyr seemed spellbound. Very dimly, a part of her realized that there might be something wrong with this. But the notion evaporated almost as fast as it had formed in her mind.

So focused had become her attention and that of her companions, merson and manyarm alike, that they did not notice nor did it trouble them that the rhythmic, pulsating swarm of sight and sound had ceased moving along its original path and was now drifting toward them with imperceptible patience. Each and every member of the expedition had been seduced by beauty. Utterly entranced by what they were seeing and hearing, it occurred to no one that the procession of soft-bodied medusae might be as dangerous as they were striking.

Of them all, it was Chachel who had fought hardest against the dazzling paralysis. Characteristically morose, he was less subject to the effects of beauteous light and mesmerizing sound than his more ebullient companions. But even he was not immune. One especially glorious jelly shimmied and chimed before his eyes, its alluring array of bioluminescent lights strobing the same splendid pattern over and over again, over and over, over and over. Like the others, he found himself lost in a haze of numbing majesty. Overcome with uncharacteristic emotion and seeking to share it, he turned and embraced the nearest individual.

It happened to be Poylee. She did not hesitate to embrace him back.

At a distance, Irina noted the entwining. It meant nothing to her. Why should it, when she found herself wholly subsumed in the glistening ballet pirouetting before her? *Come closer*, the music and the lights and the motion seemed to be saying. *Partake of the joy and the wonder.* Share in the boundless sensation. Dimly aware that her feet and lower legs seemed to be moving of their own accord, she felt herself being drawn inexorably forward by a beauty she could barely fathom.

Then something was ripping at the bell of the medusa hovering just in front of her, shredding the fragile radiance. The repetitive pattern of bioluminescence the jelly was generating changed to one reflecting discontinuous alarm. She blinked, as if abruptly startled out of a dream. Peering down, she saw that a dozen potentially lethal tentacles dangled less than a foot from her body. Hastily, she backed away.

Looking around, she saw that one by one the other members of the expedition were slowly emerging from the stasis into which they had slipped. The coelenterate procession's wonderfully harmonious music was collapsing into harsh dissonance. Lights that had been flashing on and off in perfect synchronicity dissolved in bursts of distressed color. Instead of continuing to press their sting-immune silver bodies between and against hanging tentacles in order to generate melody, the numerous bow-fish had drawn themselves up against the bodies of their protectors. They huddled there against the underside of their chosen bells, seeking security.

Meanwhile the enraged Sathi and Tythe continued to rip into one medusa after another, tearing them apart with the suckers on their arms or shredding the frail bodies with their sharp beaks. Each time one was attacked and had its mesmerizing lights and music interrupted, another dazed merson or bewildered manyarm found full consciousness restored to them.

Fleeing at far greater velocity than they had shown themselves capable of attaining previously, the surviving jellyfish and their slender-bodied Piscean cohorts fled into the concealing darkness. Internal lights were turned off and all sound suppressed to cloak their escape.

As soon as they realized what had taken place, the recovering members of the expedition gathered around the two now exhausted famuli. Grateful merson hands stroked the squids' silvery sides while the tentacles of their fellow manyarms entwined with those of their jelly-coated saviors.

"How did you know what was happening?" a grateful Jorosab asked.

"Yes," wondered Glint. "Somehow you two were immune." The cuttlefish was pulsing an embarrassed orange. "I didn't even realize what was happening to me."

"None of us did." Having pushed a reluctant Poylee away from him, a plainly bemused Chachel was struggling to make sense of what had overcome them all. Irina was as curious as anyone. Unsurprisingly, it was Oxothyr who hazarded an explanation.

"In this place of darkness, the action of so many bright lights blinking in rhythmic sequence combined with suitably complimentary music had the effect of numbing one's perception. I myself was not aware of what was occurring." An arm gestured expansively. "There is not one of you here who is not adept with spear or knife, bow or axe. These are weapons of heft and solidity. They are far easier to parry than soothing sensations." He turned to his assistants. "Yet when all others were entranced you two were not affected. I am most anxious to know why."

One famulus looked at the other. It was left to Tythe to respond.

"I do not know, Master Oxothyr. I can only say that I did not feel myself influenced as you describe."

"Nor I," added Sathi. He seemed as mystified as his companion by their immunity to the medusas' mesmerizing music and dance.

Oxothyr pressed for enlightenment. "You did not find the lights dominating your thinking, the music anesthetizing your emotions?" The two smaller cephalopods were united in their response.

"I just heard ringing noises," insisted Sathi.

"I just saw some colored lights," declared Tythe.

Oxothyr pondered their replies for a moment before turning to his attentive audience. "I think I understand what happened. While exhibiting an admirable eagerness in their chores and a demonstrable willingness to learn, neither of my attendants has ever revealed anything that might be construed as exceptional curiosity. Or even, to be charitable, what might be called average curiosity. They are loyal, and efficient, and reasonably competent at carrying out those tasks that I choose to give them. Initiative is an unknown concept to them. If they suffer from any explicit affliction, it is a certain quality of overarching dullness." Reaching out, he put a tentacle around each of them. It was a gesture of gratitude, not intimacy.

"We need all of us to be thankful for their keen lack of imagination. They were not affected by the medusas' spellbinding music and captivating luminance because they were incapable of appreciating it."

As Oxothyr backed away, the rest of the expedition crowded around the two famuli to further express their gratitude. Irina was among them. It was instructive to see that even the best led and most carefully planned outing could suffer from an excess of intelligence. Come to think of it, she could remember more than one night out with her girlfriends that had ended badly when they had allowed themselves to be overcome by too much light, too much music, and too much physical attractiveness on the part of the opposite sex. On those occasions, however, salvation had not been a matter of abbreviated squid id, and had usually involved immersion in liquids of a kind other than salt water.

For their part, the two famuli soon sought surcease from the surfeit of gratitude, and were visibly relieved when the expedition resumed its journey in the wake of the near-fatal melodious interruption.

◊

Days later they had lost not only the last of the light but whatever residual heat filtered down from the surface. She ought to have been freezing, Irina knew. Instead, she was cool but comfortable. Despite wearing next to nothing, her merson companions also showed no signs of discomfort. As for the expedition's manyarms, they could remain comfortable throughout a significant range of temperatures.

"Why aren't we cold?" she asked Chachel, swimming parallel to his dimly lit form. "Don't your kind ever get cold?"

"Of course we do." Though he would have preferred to avoid casual conversation, now that she had swum up alongside and formally engaged him, he could hardly just swim away. The hunter could be curt, he could be abrupt, but outright rudeness did not make for pleasant journeying. In such a small group it behooved everyone to remain on at least minimally polite terms with as many traveling companions as possible. So instead of brushing her off, he offered what he hoped would be a brief yet adequate explanation.

"People—mersons—can tolerate cold quite well." He gestured downward. "Were we to go much deeper than this, we would indeed begin to suffer. But we are not so deep yet that the chill affects us seriously." Reaching out, he touched the center of her chest, just between a pair of Oxothyr's enchanted blue lights. Her instinctive recoil caused him to frown.

"I was just trying to make a point about pressure. Your changeling form has adapted to that also."

"Oh. Of course." She felt foolish. And perhaps also just a little disappointed. "I was going to ask about that, too."

"You have a proper body now. One that is comfortable in and suited to the realworld, as opposed to your previous ugly demon form." She did not argue his point, fully aware that any countervailing arguments she might offer would carry no weight here. "The temperature should not bother you unless it drops considerably more—which I do not think it will." He gestured down into the blackness below them. "Do you understand?"

"I think I …"

"Good!" Having discharged his obligation to be civil, he kicked hard and shot ahead, his personal lights fading into the distance.

The man would rather kill than converse, she told herself irritably. She'd met more convivial sharks. Not to mention octopods, squids, and one particularly ostentatious cuttlefish. Why should she care about his reactions, anyway? Because he happened to have been one of two who had saved her? The more she got to know Chachel, the more convinced she became that if not for Glint's presence on the same hunting excursion that had led to them finding her, the gruff merson would have left her to rot on the surface. He was as *boorish* a man as she had ever met.

No, not man, she reminded herself. Merson. They had even less in common than met the eye. Oxothyr was a better friend, Glint continually expressed more interest in her welfare. Then there was Poylee, who continued to treat her like some sort of otherworldly infection. Finding herself drawn closer to exotic cephalopods than to fellow bipeds suggested it was definitely time to press for a return to where she belonged.

Except that she could not find the way home without help and she could not plausibly pester Oxothyr into spending the time to facilitate the attempt. Not with a war going on. She caught herself. It was the first time she'd thought of what she had seen over the course of the past several weeks in terms of a war. The word had not been used by the mersons or by the manyarms. An oversight, she was certain. What else to call it when hostile species invaded your territory, destroyed innocent communities, and slaughtered the inhabitants? Did the mersons think by not using the word that they might somehow minimize the consequences? Surely these folk were not that foolish?

Everyone had spoken repeatedly of the abnormality, even Oxothyr. Had she landed, or rather sunk, into the first real war this world had ever experienced? Fighting was not unknown, as evinced by the enmity that existed between mersons and manyarms on one side and spralakers on the other. But perhaps such hostile encounters had previously been restricted to isolated, petty disputes. Rightly or wrongly, that was the impression she had received whenever such matters were discussed.

If that was the case, then what could have happened to change things? What was different that had caused skirmishing to blossom into full-scale hostilities?

*Me.*

No, that couldn't be. She had done nothing. Only arrive, and that not of her own free will. She could not possibly be responsible for the unprecedented upsurge in aggressive spralaker activity. The cause had to lie elsewhere. It had to.

She could not bear to think otherwise.

Despite making a strenuous effort to put the unsettling notion out of her mind, she was still thinking about it that evening (evening being a relative term at such sunless depths) when she began to take notice of a phenomenon as peculiar as it was welcome, and which related directly to the question she had posed earlier to Chachel. As she continued to slowly descend, along with the others she ought to have been getting colder. But for the last hour or so the surrounding water had been growing warmer. That made less than no sense. You didn't get more comfortable the deeper you went.

She heard the roaring before she could see the source. Faint at first, little more than a background hum, it rose gradually in volume to become a dirge, a bellow, and finally a sustained tectonic chant.

Swimming just a few feet above the gray, gently undulating sea floor she reached down to touch the ground. The rocky surface was unmistakably warm to the touch, and noticeably warmer than the surrounding dark water. In addition to the heat it was emitting, the rock was transmitting subtle vibrations. She lifted her gaze. Somewhere not far ahead, the Earth was howling. These increasingly intrusive geological incongruities did not appear to trouble her companions in the least. They showed no reaction to the rising temperature or noise.

Catching up to Glint, she swam alongside the manyarm hunter. Like his fellow cephalopods the cuttlefish was a free-swimming bundle of red and green lights, a tiny tentacled blimp who occasionally cut loose with a burst of blue-white light that gave him the appearance of an escaped advertisement for some otherworldly cinema.

"Black smokers ahead," he explained in reply to her question. "Phenomenal protrusions they are. Generating heat, and interesting smells, and supporting all manner of wondrous beings. I wish we had some on the reef: we could make more metal. But you find them only down deep."

Black smokers—what little she knew about them had been gleaned from sporadic encounters with relevant science articles. Volcanic vents spewing all manner of superheated gases and fluids from inside the Earth precipitated out exotic minerals that condensed in deep cold to water to form stalagmite-like towers. The creatures that dwelled in similar infernal conditions in her world were so bizarre as not to be believed. What might their counterparts here be like?

She soon found out.

Not knowing what to expect, she envisioned a dozen or so erupting chimneys. As revealed in the lights of the expedition, the reality was quite different.

She was unable to count the number of smokers. By the dozens, the thundering towers stretched off into the dark distance, sending an equal number of black plumes fuming impressively upward. It was the Devil's own calliope, belching superhot mineral-laden black smoke and water. While Chachel and Glint and the rest of the party continued toward them without pausing, she hesitated.

"We're not going *into* that hell, are we?" she asked Arrelouf , one of the group's two female merson soldiers.

"Into and through it, I would imagine." The glowing necklace around her neck casting her features in soft relief, she smiled thinly. "Are you afraid, changeling?"

Irina considered. "Yes. Yes, I'm afraid. Superheated sulphides and poisonous gases have that effect on me."

"I don't understand your wordings, but it's good to be afraid." With a quick scissor kick the other woman darted forward. "It keeps one from going to sleep at the wrong time."

Aware that by now most of the expeditionary force had passed her by, a resigned Irina hurried to rejoin them. The stentorian escaping-steam thrum of the smokers was frightening, but far less so than the prospect of being left behind in the black of the deep.

Clouds of phosphorescent blind shrimp swirled around the smokers, ribbons of living red and white that prospected the algae that in turn thrived on the rich deposits of minerals. Here in the complete absence of sunlight there was life abundant. Other bizarre creatures scrambled to make a living among the storms of shrimp, including a number of spralakers. But these were small, scattered, and few in number. Their pale white half-blind selves posed no threat to the travelers, though they invariably ran to hide when the group came into view, and hurled undersized curses at them once the mersons and manyarms were safely past.

"Be careful!"

Strong fingers wrapped around Irina's left arm and yanked her painfully in that direction. Looking around, she saw Poylee glaring back at her.

"I'll thank you not to grab me like that." Irina's tone was hard and flat.

"Fine. Next time I'll let you boil." With a couple of kicks, the merson moved away.

Boil? It took Irina a moment to spot the crevice she had nearly swam directly over. Little more than a crack in the earth, it had only just begun to precipitate out the accumulating mineral deposits that would one day lead to the formation of another tower. Cautiously extending an arm, she let her fingers flutter forward—only to hastily pull them back. The temperature of the narrow jet of water emerging from the unobtrusive vent was in the hundreds of degrees. Because the aperture was unobstructed and not laden with the usual dissolved dark minerals, she hadn't noticed it. Had she continued swimming in the same direction she would have passed right over and through it—and received a severe scalding.

As the expedition moved deeper into the forest of smokers, some of which towered hundreds of feet overhead, it took her several moments to find Poylee again.

"Why did you do that?" She searched the merson's face, seeking nonverbal explanation. "Why didn't you let me burn myself?" She lowered her voice. "I know you wouldn't object to that, even if I'm not sure why."

The other woman was silent for a moment. Then, "I don't want you to die. I don't even, really, want you to be disfigured. That's not who I am. I just wish, I want—I'd rather you just wouldn't *be*." For the second time in the space of a few minutes, she swam off into the darkness. Leaving Irina to follow more slowly and wonder why she should feel guilty for "being."

It wasn't long before a new noise rose above the constant, continuous rumble of the hydrothermal vents. The sound was familiar yet foreign. The nearer the group came to it the more recognizable it became. Yet Irina was still unable to identify it. There was an edge to the collective din that reminded her of something so commonplace that she was simultaneously intrigued and frustrated. Very shortly it revealed itself to the group. Awareness did not keep several of the mersons from smiling, while she found herself grinning from ear to ear.

The chattering was the communal laughter that emanated from a colony of twenty-foot long tube worms.

And why shouldn't worms laugh, she asked herself as she finned forward? Were she to find herself trapped by birth and circumstance in one place, unable ever to move and forever fastened to rocks that had coagulated from the sulphurous blood of Hell itself, would she not seek relief in the form of laughter? Crimson plumes protruding from long white tubes alternated sieve feeding with a collective cackling as the worms strained hydrogen sulphide, carbon dioxide, and oxygen from the surrounding water to feed the trapped internal bacteria that supplied them with nourishment. Waving slowly back and forth in the confused currents like thick pulpy reeds, the colony acknowledged the arrival of the travelers with a burst of sarcastic hilarity.

"Look at them, flesh from the surface!" commented one worm.

Bending forward in a perfect arc, another thrust its beak-like red plume in Irina's direction. "All those unnecessary protuberances. Not streamlined at all," it observed.

"Have to chase their food," chortled another. "All those pieces of body hanging off. Disgusting!"

Her companions might be used to such insults, but Irina was not. "You're criticizing me? You're a *worm*. A very big worm, to be sure, but still just a worm."

The one that had curved forward to examine her now straightened. "'Just' a worm? Are you so ignorant you know so little? Why, don't you realize where you'd be without worms?"

She ground her teeth. "No. Why don't you tell me where I'd be?"

Two of the bright red plumes faced one another. "Wormless!"

This time several members of the expeditionary force joined the tube worm colony in shared mirth. Aware that she'd been had, Irina wondered if the subcutaneous lighting Oxothyr had given her was strong enough to mask the flush she felt spreading over her cheeks. These giant deep-sea Riftia might be capable of complex speech, but their sense of humor was decidedly lowbrow.

She was gratified to see that Oxothyr had little patience for such juvenile jollity. "We must get to Benthicalia. It is a matter of the greatest importance." An arm gestured forward. "Landmarks hereabouts are scarce, as smokers tend to look much the same."

"Like us, I suppose," commented one of the worms sardonically.

"Contrary to what you might think, we are quite distinguishable from one another," insisted the first speaker's neighbor.

"How?" As soon as she asked, Irina wished she hadn't.

But the tube worm surprised her with a straightforward reply. "By our respective senses of humor, of course. Since we are all approximately the same size, shape, color, and asexual, status within our colonies is determined by one's ability to make the others laugh. Not as easy as you might think, since besides feeding it is our principal activity. I ask you, flesh-thing, what is more valuable, more welcome, and more gratifying than a new joke?"

"I see your point," she admitted, relieved not to have been made the butt of one again.

To emphasize the urgency of their situation, Oxothyr pointed with three arms. "I believe *this* direction to be the right one, but I would appreciate any correction you feel is necessary."

"Benthicalia," one of the worms murmured, swaying slowly from side to side as it spoke. "We have heard of it. There are worms there, too, and many smokers. Travelers this way are rare, but they do tell tales. We cannot visit our cousins, but others can visit for us." The red filter-head dipped close to the hovering octopus. "You are indeed set on the correct path, manyarm. Keep straight and you will come to Benthicalia in due course." Straightening, it concluded with easygoing solemnity. "We will not keep you long, but it would be very discourteous of you not to pay for this valuable information. We must do a trade."

Drifting over to Arrelouf, Irina could not contain her curiosity. "They have no buildings, no goods of any kind. At least, none that I can see. What could we possibly trade with them?"

Arrelouf eyed her as one would a child, then remembered that this changeling had little knowledge of the realworld.

"Why, jokes, of course."

Despite the darkness, the danger from the superheated venting taking place all around, the nauseating omnipresent stink of sulphur and other noxious materials being ejected from the ground, and her own uncertainty, the ensuing half hour that was spent among the field of giant tube worms was among the most relaxing, and certainly the most unexpectedly entertaining, she had yet experienced in the surrounds of Oshenerth.

# – XVI –

**A** little laughter lasts a long time in the way down deep, Irina discovered. A useful thing to recall whenever the small group of determined travelers found themselves crossing open plains. The scattered smoker forests became a welcome sight. Their oppressive roaring was offset by the presence of so much more life than was encountered elsewhere, and by the welcome heat the hydrothermal vents generated. One could grow accustomed to such a place, she decided. Everywhere around the pillar-like smokers a multitude of lifeforms were in constant motion, struggling for survival amid perpetual noise, darkness, and moisture. Not so very different from Seattle in January.

It was impossible to tell time. In the absence of sunlight night and day became meaningless, abstract terms. The travelers rested when a majority showed signs of fatigue and moved on when that same majority felt sufficiently refreshed. Food was taken communally. While they were capable of eating on the swim, it was safer to settle down in one place and alternate mealtimes. As Chachel tersely pointed out to her, two kinds of dangers haunted the deep: those you could see, and those that lurked just beyond the range of the lights the expedition generated. When they stopped to sleep, mealtime was another interlude that required the posting of guards—both around the group and above it.

She was beginning to think talk of such dangers exaggerated. For one thing, dark depths would find far fewer sharks on patrol. Though their other senses allowed them to hunt perfectly well in the absence of light, the sleek carnivores preferred to see their prey. While a big hungry seven-gill might pose a genuine menace, in her world at least, such species were more scavenger than predator. What else might lurk in the depths of Oshenerth just beyond her range of vision she did not know.

When an example finally did present itself, it was not at all what she expected. Doubtless because it was a creature that was completely outside her experience.

They had paused to rest among a cluster of the hissing, fuming, mineralized towers, careful not to drift too close to jets of superheated water that could boil a merson or manyarm alive, when the smoker serpent came coiling out of the darkness like a giant worm emerging from an obsidian apple. The deepwater predators Irina had seen so far had ranged from merson-size to tiny. The smoker serpent was huge.

As it coiled toward them, mersons ducked behind the hardened pillars of smokers, careful not to make contact with the hot rock itself. The manyarm members of the expedition obtruded their siphons and scattered in all directions, trailing bioluminescent tentacles like sprays of fireworks.

Clutching roughly at her, a hand pulled Irina back behind the crumbly black column of a dormant smoker. "Are your brains as feeble as the rest of you?" A grim-faced Chachel glared at her. "Hide, run, keep out of its way! Or would you rather be food?"

"I—I'm sorry." Abashed, she didn't look at him. "It's just that I've never seen anything like it and ..."

Gripping his spear tightly, he peered cautiously around the pillar. Stretching more than a hundred feet from snout to tail, its narrow body highlighted with luminescent spots flashing scarlet, the smoker serpent was not difficult to follow.

"I'm sure its insides are equally fascinating," Chachel whispered tightly, "yet I have no wish to view them personally. Stay here."

She complied without argument. Though she had already tested herself in battle against the spralakers at Siriswirll, this was a very different environment featuring a decidedly more imposing adversary, for all that there was only one of it.

Other than the radiant red bioluminescence that illuminated its flanks, the body of the smoker serpent was nearly transparent. A glass dragon, she thought. As it twisted and writhed among the stone towers, when available light was just right and strong enough she could clearly see its internal organs through the pigmentless flesh. Darker blood pulsed through veins of translucent tubing. She could also see light gleam from its foot-long upper and three-foot long lower fangs, each of which was as slender as a rapier and as sharp as a needle. Evolved to catch and hold oversized prey in a single bite, once impaled on those dreadful daggers even a large, powerful fish would be unable to escape.

Huge, perfectly round, and glowing a soft blue-green, the conspicuously convex eyes were as big around as truck tires and as vacant of intelligence as the forest of smoking columns they were presently scanning. This was no chary scavenger, she decided as she shrank back further behind the protective pillar. The red-limned serpent was vigorously stalking prey. At the moment, that meant her and her friends.

In the weeks gone by, she had seen many marvels. Here was one she would have been content to avoid, and wished would go away. Maybe the rapid, jerky movements of its would-be prey would frustrate it and cause it to go elsewhere, she told herself hopefully.

Then it looped with unexpected speed around one of the tallest smokers, struck like a snake, and caught one of Glint's counterparts in its trap-like jaws. Bayoneted on the outsized lower fangs, the unfortunate cuttlefish warrior screamed and went completely white. Even in the course of the clash at Siriswirll Irina had never heard such a scream. It sounded like that of a child mixed with the yowl of an injured cat.

From their hiding places near the scene of the attack, every merson in the group popped into view. They were joined by the rest of the manyarms who, bows and smaller spears at the ready, came rocketing in out of the darkness where they had sought refuge. One weapon after another struck the serpent's wildly undulating flanks, which leaked blood only slightly less dark than the water around it.

Enraged and hurt, the serpent lunged furiously at its multiple attackers. Swimming in to strike and then darting quickly away, mersons and manyarms worked together to decoy and evade the gaping, slashing mouth. The desperate semaphorings of the unfortunate cuttlefish still skewered on the teeth of the serpent's lower jaw grew increasingly more feeble.

Diving down on the creature from above, Chachel took careful aim and, approaching dangerously close, with all his strength thrust his spear straight down into the back of the serpent's skull. The thin bone was incredibly resistant and the spear point slid off to one side, missing the brain. But enough nerves were severed or damaged to send the monster into a paroxysm of fury. Black smokers collapsed as the spasming body smashed into their deceptively fragile sides. Hardened mineral deposits splintered and powdered, filling the otherwise perfectly clear water with coarse debris that made it difficult to see.

Kicking backward, waving both arms as she tried to clear the water in front of her, Irina sought to distance herself from the rapidly clouding chaos. It was as if a cave was suddenly coalescing around her, reducing her vision and threatening to clog her gills. She started to cough. Brushing frantically at her neck, she tried to keep the water she was breathing as clean as possible. Inhaling ancient volcanic grit would be as harmful to her new gills as it would have been to her old lungs.

Worst of all, in the thickening rain of ash and gravel she couldn't see what was going on around her. Unlimbering her own spear from the scabbard on her back, she prepared to defend herself against anything that might come at her from out of the gloom. She was not ashamed to admit later that when something reached out of the grainy murk to touch her right shoulder she screamed as loud as she could. It was the first time she had screamed underwater and she was surprised at how shrill it sounded in her own ears.

The appendage that had made contact belonged to a brightly glowing Glint.

"Calm yourself, Irina-changeling. It's over. The hunter proves himself yet again."

Around her the dark ocean fumed and boiled. "It doesn't feel like it's over," she responded. "Or look like it."

"There is no current here." The luminous cuttlefish moved up alongside her. "Though it looks to be the same consistency and weight, much of the material of which these pillars are formed is lighter than normal rock. The broken bits will take some time to settle to the ground. Come."

She followed but did not put away her weapon. Only when the twitching but expiring body of the smoker serpent came into view did she halfheartedly slide the spear back into the holder strapped to her back. As the rain of dark grit began to thin, she was able to see the rest of the monster's body. It lay stretched out between and among those smoking towers it had not smashed to bits in the course of its death throes. Chachel's spear, she noted, was still sticking out of the back of the creature's skull.

Sathi and another, larger squid were slowly and respectfully easing the dead body of the ill-fated female cuttlefish up off the pair of stilled fangs on which she had been impaled. The stockier cephalopod's corpse was dark now, the bright internal lights dimmed. Her ten arms hung limp, like a basket of dead eels.

Irina had witnessed cephalopodan funerals before, following the fighting at Siriswirll. Feeling even more the alien outsider than usual at such moments, she had kept her distance.

Though the dead soldier was half again as long as her, two-thirds of its length was made up of tentacles. These now hung loose and lifeless as the corpse was carried through the water by an octopus and squid. Only the glow from their internal lights enabled her to see the body. When the female had bled to death in the mouth of the smoker serpent, so had her bioluminescence. The usually compelling, complex cuttlefish eyes were as dark as the surrounding water.

Disposing of the body would have been a solemn enough occasion near the mirrorsky, where the ceremony would have been brightly lit by shafting sunlight. Here in the inky depths it was as if death pressed close all around. Irina could not have stood aside even had her presence gone unrequested. Far better to attend a funeral and be in the presence of others than to linger too long with total blackness clawing at one's back—and the back of one's mind.

Words of praise and remembrance were intoned. Both mersons and manyarms took turns speaking of the dead female's bravery, of her dedication to her extended family and her contributions to the social life of the Sandrift community. When Irina's turn came she spoke simply, raising her voice just enough to enable herself to be heard above the steady roar and rumble of the surrounding smokers.

"Huysalee fought so that I could live." Having scarcely made the acquaintance of the dead fighter, she had nothing more to add. But the looks on the faces of the attending mersons and the color changes that flashed through the bodies of the hovering manyarms indicated that she had done just fine.

It was then that she noticed Chachel was not present. Reluctantly, she swam over to where Poylee was hovering parallel to the ground and remarked on the hunter's absence.

Waving an arm at the all-encompassing darkness, it was impossible to tell if the merson was annoyed at Irina's presence, by her question, or was simply disgusted with Chachel.

"He's out there somewhere, scouting. He should be here. But I suppose someone has to keep watch, even at a time like this."

Irina looked around. It was pure reflex, since there was nothing to see in the darkness except her companions and the occasional burst of light from some phosphorescent algae or lifeform clinging to the smoking towers.

"By himself?"

Poylee rolled her eyes. "No, of course not. That ridiculous cuttlefish friend of his is with him. Chachel can carry light enough, but he still can't see as well in the dark as a manyarm." Her tone was reproving. "You should know that by now. Haven't you learned anything in all the time you've spent among us?"

Irina did know that, and she had learned much. One of the things she had learned was that there was no point in arguing with or getting into a fight with Poylee, whose inexplicable animosity gave no indication of subsiding. Having explained several times that there was nothing between her and the hunter Chachel and that she had no interest in him, she saw no point in repeating the disclaimers yet again. The eccentric notion that such a relationship existed had not merely found a place to fester in Poylee's mind, it had taken up permanent residence there.

When the last admiring words had been spoken, the expedition's manyarms gathered together on one side of the deceased cuttlefish.

Coming up behind or beneath them, the mersons took firm hold of their multi-limbed companions. This bracing support enabled the manyarms to unleash the full power of their propulsive siphons without blasting themselves in the opposite direction. The combined watery thrust sent the increasingly pale corpse tumbling off into the darkness, the dead Huysalee's arms spinning around her like a slow-motion pinwheel.

Only when she had passed completely from sight did the surviving manyarms abandon their formation and begin to gather up their belongings. The final send-off was unexpectedly poignant.

It was only later that she was able to catch up to Glint. Swimming easily alongside the softly glowing cuttlefish, she voiced an old concern that her Oshenerth surroundings had made new again.

"Tell me, Glint: what does your kind think happens to the essence of a person after they die?"

The cuttlefish cocked one eye at her as he jetted along. "That's easy. They get eaten."

"No, no," she corrected him, "I don't mean the body. I mean the soul, the spiritual part. Do manyarms believe in such a thing? My people do."

The luminous cephalopod did not answer immediately. When he finally did, it was clear he had given the matter more than his usual thought.

"I think such a belief may be a consequence of living in void. If there is nothing around you to hold reality together, nothing you can feel, I can see how such a belief might take hold. But here below the mirrorsky we are always in contact with actual matter." He gestured thoughtfully with a tentacle. "If there is such a thing as the essence of which you speak, I believe it would be touchable, or capable of being sensed—or eaten."

She still felt that Glint was not fully comprehending the concept she was trying to express. Probably Oxothyr would have a better grasp of the nature of the individual soul. Having heard what the cuttlefish had to say on the matter, however, she was not sure she wanted to discuss the notion with the shaman. She had always been comfortable with the belief that everyone had a soul and she did not want to take a chance on being argued out of it. Not in this cold, dark place where she felt that the belief was both necessary and reassuring.

It was an idealization she might have found difficult to sustain in a chillier, far distant corner of Oshenerth.

◊

Borne by two dozen spralakers of varying size and species and flanked by members of his personal armed retinue, Kulakak's palanquin advanced slowly through the forest. Reaching all the way from the rocky ground to the mirrorsky, thick strands of leafy green kelp towered two hundred feet and more above the procession. It was an unusually clear day and the light filtering down through the dark green made a magic of its own not even Sajjabax could have outdone.

The kelp forest lay just outside the capital city of Xayyac. Behind the entourage it sprawled across layers of terraced rock, obscuring the seams of gray basaltic stone. Often on such excursions Kulakak would look back at the vast metropolis of which he was supreme ruler. But not now. Not today.

All his thoughts were concentrated on determining how best to proceed now that the manyarm shaman who had been the difference in the battle for Siriswirll had been located. *Where* that troublesome sac-head had been discovered was something of a surprise in itself. If not for the extensive network of spralaker spies spread throughout nearly all of Oshenerth, the rival mage's whereabouts would have remained unknown.

Of course, the Great Lord's spies did not know for certain the intended destination of the esteemed manyarm and his fast-moving escort. Any attempt to find out would likely have resulted in such overly bold scouts ending up not on the mark but on a menu. But they had been able to observe, from a safe distance, the deep-water travelers' presence, mark their passing, and note the direction they had taken upon departure from the surviving town of Siriswirll. All the signs and inferences pointed to them heading for a logical destination.

Benthicalia.

He was not displeased by this assumption. In striking a single overwhelming blow he would at one swoop remove two of the greatest continuing threats to the Overturning: this meddling shaman *and* the most powerful city in the southwestern reefs. The depth at which Benthicalia lay was unusual for a merson-manyarm community, but it would not hinder the work of his soldiers. Most of them could fight as efficiently at depth as if their backs were in contact with the mirrorsky itself.

"Gubujul!"

Sporting an assortment of polished stones and trailing tendrils of glimmer-stained sea whip, the red-banded Paramount Advisor's appearance was even more outlandish than usual. No doubt if pressed as to the need for such an extravagant display he would reply that any excursion beyond the bounds of the royal court demanded an effort to awe the populace. As the Great Lord, Kulakak could have pointed out that he felt no such need. Instead, he said nothing. He understood well the importance of encouraging and rewarding those who served him. Those who under-performed their duties in spite of such magnanimous dispensations on his part could always be demoted to the level of a quick snack.

"The remnants of the force that destroyed Shakestone and nearly took Siriswirll have been combined with the Grand Legions of the Inflexible Palp," he informed his always attentive Advisor. "It is my plan to provision them better than any spralaker force has ever been equipped and send them south to reduce Benthicalia to rubble."

"Ah yes, that is where the party of the shadowy manyarm shaman was reported to be heading." Gubujul's multiple antennae gave a timorous flutter. "Benthicalia is said to be strongly defended, my Lord. There are walls there. Real walls, not like the crude obstructions our forces encountered at Siriswirll."

"Exactly. Taking such a city will shatter any semblance of defiance to our rule in the southern reefs," Kulakak pontificated. "Word of its destruction will spread like oil, smothering any thought of resistance. With Benthicalia subjugated, our waiting multitudes will be assured safe passage southward and have no difficulty in taking full control of that territory. All that richness, all that complex and colorful living space, shall be ours."

"And what of the present residents?" Gubujul knew the answer, but he never tired of hearing it declaimed from the Great

Lord's mouth. Kulakak had a way of making the inevitable sound twice delicious.

"Some will flee to the great southern plains and eventually starve there. Most, I am convinced, will be content, even relieved, to remain as our slaves. As for the finned folk, it will be between them and us as it has always been: some will fight against us, some will offer allegiance, and the rest will become fit for food or indifference." He sounded more than pleased. "Already there are those in the south who are smart enough to perceive which way the current is running and ally themselves with us."

Gubujul was dutifully impressed. "Yet again my Lord has drawn forth certainty from disaster."

Reaching down over the side of the palanquin, a heavy, powerful claw struck the gracile advisor hard enough to send him tumbling legs over antennae, but not quite hard enough to break anything.

"No talk of that! Not yet. The encounter at Siriswirll gave birth only to enlightenment; not to triumph, and not to defeat. It is true the retreat was badly managed, but many survived to fight again another day, and much was learned. Much that will be used to great effect against the fortifications of Benthicalia."

Staggering back to his feet, Gubujul used his long, slender forearms to clean and straighten his aching antennae. "Yes, my Lord. I am certain it shall be as you say. When do you leave to take command of the Legions of the Inflexible?"

From his divan atop the palanquin the Great Lord Kulakak peered down at the Paramount Advisor. "I? I am needed here, Gubujul. To supervise the war, to plan strategy for the Overturning, to organize the thousand and one details it demands. Also to deal with the venerable Sajjabax, his works and his madness: a task no one else can manage since all seem to lose control and purpose and courage when brought into his presence."

"I see, my Lord." Gubujul thought hard. "Then to whom will you give command of the operation?"

Silence ensued, saved for the click-clacking footfall of the Great Lord's multi-legged bearers and the submissive muttering of those spralakers, watching safely from a distance, who farmed and hunted in the forest.

Gubujul's red-banded white exoskeleton was comparatively impenetrable, but the workings of his mind were not.

"Oh no, my Lord—I couldn't!"

Stalked eyes bent sharply in the Paramount Advisor's direction. "I am sorry, Gubujul. I must have picked up some algae in my hearing organs. Did I hear you say you 'couldn't'?"

The shocked stenopus swallowed hard. "What I meant to say, my Lord, is that I am not worthy of such an honor. Your offer of it momentarily stunned me. I am flattered and overwhelmed. But as a counselor who has always been focused on matters of a non-military nature I would be remiss in my duties if I did not confess that, despite your confidence in me, it might be in the best interests of the spralaker people if another other than myself was put in charge of so important a martial venture."

Silence enveloped the royal palanquin. Then laughter boomed across the gently rolling ground, to disperse among the sky-sweeping green growths.

"That's one reason why I keep you around, Gubujul. You never fail to amuse me. As concerns movements in the field, the planning and executing of them will be the province of the Marshals of the Legions. Surely you did not think I expected *you* to devise actual strategy?"

"I was unsure, my Lord. Not that I lack self-assurance but ..."

"But you haven't ever carried out a raid on anything larger than the burrow of a female spralaker with whom you desired to mate. Rest assured, Paramount Advisor, that I know your limitations as well as your qualifications, and that I would no more put you in command of a real skirmish than I would ask you to fight a sardine."

"Ah," murmured Gubujul, feeling simultaneously much appreciated and duly snubbed.

Inclining his bulk over the side of the palanquin, the Great Lord leaned closer. "I must have someone in overall charge whom I can trust implicitly. Someone who I am confident will let the commanders in the field carry out their work without interference from some meddling bureaucrat who thinks he or she knows better. Someone who will act as my direct representative and be able at a word to settle arguments on my behalf. Someone who knows exactly what will happen to him if he fails in any respect to carry out my exact wishes." Leaning still closer, the Great Lord locked eyes with those of the Paramount Advisor.

"It appears that someone, Gubujul, is to be you."

The much smaller, slimmer spralaker nodded dolefully. "I would fain still decline the honor, my Lord."

Kulakak settled back onto his divan, and the palanquin and its bearers shuddered under his shifting weight. "Ever the modest and reticent servant, Gubujul. Especially when calculating the promise of potential reward against the consequences of possible failure. Such equivocating makes for an advisor who lives long, though not necessarily one of greatest value. Still, you are the best I have. You serve willingly and out of fear: a functional combination. Come back covered in the hair of mersons and the beaks of manyarms and I promise you will swim in glory. The Overturning goes on. As it must," he concluded pensively. "For all our sakes."

"Yes, my Lord." Further excuses, evasions, and verbal circum-locutions would only risk the Great Lord's wrath, Gubujul knew. Like it or not, he had just been appointed supreme spralaker commander in the South. While uncertainty was an accepted component of his daily struggle for existence, he believed that somehow he would be able to rise to this new challenge.

He knew also that if he did not, this would be his last opportunity to enjoy a walk in the forest.

# – XVII –

Irina had been enchanted by Sandrift, sobered by Shakestone, and impressed by Siriswirll. So it was not unreasonable for her to believe that she had some idea what to expect of Benthicalia.

She was as wrong as she was overwhelmed.

When her companions had called it a city, she had envisioned something like Siriswirll, only on a larger scale. She was simply not prepared for the sight that greeted her eyes as the group swam over a last rocky rise and the city came into view. Slammed them was more accurate, since during the preceding days of travel in near darkness they had become accustomed to a much more muted level of illumination.

Rising from the depths toward the unseen mirrorsky, Benthicalia spilled over the terraces of multiple ancient and now drowned shorelines. Every succeeding level (she counted more than two dozen) was crowded with fantastical structures each of which was more wondrous than the next, and all were ablaze with light.

"How …?"

Jetting easily alongside her, Oxothyr anticipated her query. "It is the light that fascinates. It is the light for which Benthicalia is famed. Look hard, changeling Irina, and you will be able to recognize, and to comprehend."

She strained to do just that, but still needed help from the manyarm to understand what she was seeing. What was immediately evident was that a great deal more magic was at work here than she had encountered previously anywhere else in Oshenerth.

Shining and flashing within transparent longitudinal and vertical containers, tens of thousands of light-emitting fish and other bioluminescent ocean dwellers bathed the city in pale blue and yellow light. From a distance the streets and spires looked, she thought, like a cluster of exploding stars. The variety of containers themselves were as fascinating as the photophoric lifeforms they kept in check. As the visitors began their final approach, she saw that the fabulous transparencies were fashioned neither of glass nor crystal. Instead, they were sundry species of giant tunicates that had been trained to let food in to feed their captive light-emitters as well as themselves, but not to let the smaller glowing creatures escape. Here was a city where lights were not manufactured, she mused, or purchased from a store, but rather where they were grown and nurtured.

From every level, rose towers of brightly colored deep-sea coral. Rose, or rather thrust, she corrected herself. In Benthicalia, as many towers grew sideways as upward, creating a latticework of coralline architecture bedecked with sculpture both living and dead. Benthicalian artisans had decorated numerous buildings with bas-reliefs depicting scenes from the city's history, its surroundings, and its daily life.

Each individual animal serving as home to thousands of anemone fish, the tentacles of gigantic anemones swayed back and forth in the mild currents that kept the city clean. Some of the brightly colored immobile creatures were the size of a city bus.

The lowest level of the metropolis was dominated by a great coral stadium. Examining the huge spherical structure, Irina inquired as to its function. Sporting events, Oxothyr informed her, and theater, and other entertainments and civic functions.

"Look to the center of the uppermost level of the city. That is where we will find the Tornal."

Rotating his body, the shaman pointed to a rocky promontory. Clinging like a live thing to the jutting shelf was a small limestone citadel composed of red and yellow fire coral that had been carefully cultivated to produce a fanciful hodgepodge of interconnected spires, spheres, and chambers. Though it served as a meeting place of considerable importance there was no sign of armament, no occupied guard stations. They were not necessary, since the coral of which the structure was composed was itself a more than adequate deterrent to unauthorized entry. Mere contact with fire coral would leave flesh burning and stinging for days. Extensive contact could result in paralysis, and even death.

A glance showed that while mersons, manyarms, and fish could enter the city from any angle, stone walls far higher and more permanent than anything she had seen before provided an insurmountable barrier to any marauding spralakers.

She indicated the Palace of the Tornal. "That's where we're going, then?"

The shaman turned an amused orange. "Even the bearers of important news do not simply float in on the Tornal."

"Not even you?" she ventured curiously.

"Not even I, changeling flatterer. We must make a formal request for a meeting and await approval. Only then can we present ourselves."

She hesitated. "Am I included in this?"

"We are all a part of it. That is as it should be. One never knows who may recall an item of significance that would otherwise be overlooked, or have something of consequence to contribute." He flashed gentle amusement. "Perhaps even a changeling still uncertain of herself and her place in the world. Experience has shown me that it is the highly knowledgeable and experienced who often overlook the obvious." Noting her misgiving, he added, "You will be fine, Irina-changeling. You have adapted well."

She blushed slightly at the compliment, wondering if the flush was visible at this depth. "I'm trying. Really hard."

"Trying is better than dying," he remarked impassively.

The city was no less astonishing up close than it had been when viewed from a distance. Criss-crossing channels cut through the rock and coral took the place of streets. Noticing dozens of reef fish moving freely among the resident mersons and manyarms, she wondered how they were able to survive so far beneath the mirrorsky. Once more it was left to Oxothyr to explain.

"A large field of black smokers fumes and boils off to the west," he told her as he gestured in that direction. "An elaborate system of sculpted coral conduits carries superheated water to the lowest level of the city. Useful minerals are removed there and the water then is allowed to percolate upwards through a network of smaller tubes. You will find the outlets scattered throughout the city across all levels. That is how creatures accustomed to warmer waters can be made comfortable here." Several arms gestured in unison.

"As you have already seen, life at this depth is less abundant than nearer the mirrorsky. For a city the size of Benthicalia to thrive here, food must be brought in from above. Minerals and other materials found or mined nearby are exchanged for food and other substances with the inhabitants of the shallows."

She considered. "If food is in such short supply, why do any of your kind or any mersons choose to live down here instead of higher up where it's warmer, brighter, and easier to find something to eat?"

Wise old eyes regarded her with what she decided (or maybe hoped) was something less than pity. "My young changeling, while food is life, there is more to life than food. Benthicalia is famed for its culture, as a place to stimulate and exchange ideas, and as a community that offers peace in a setting of great solitude. It is those from above who come here to find rest and rejuvenation; not the other way around. Have you no such communities in your own world?"

Irina could think of several, but since there was no point in naming them she merely nodded.

Oxothyr appeared satisfied. "In our time here you must try to avail yourself of such edifying enrichment. It is incumbent upon one fortunate enough to be able to visit Benthicalia to do more than simply stare at pretty lights and gawk at noteworthy buildings."

"Will there be time?" She found herself marveling at a cylindrical tower that sprouted branches like a baobab. Providing living quarters for numerous manyarms, each branch terminated in a red-hued globe filled with swimming deep-sea fish that all emitting the same steady vermilion glow.

Led by Chachel, the travelers rounded a corner and began to follow a sharply angled avenue up to the next level of the city. "Despite the urgency of the message we bring," Oxothyr told her, "I do not expect the Tornal to grant us an audience for at least a day or two. That will give you time to absorb at least a few wonders."

"You'll show me around?" she asked hopefully as she performed a relaxing barrel roll beside him.

"Certainly not. I have far more pressing matters to attend to. If you cannot make your own way around a city as civilized and welcoming as Benthicalia, then I fear that your future in the realworld will amount to very little." Letting forth a larger blast from his siphon he jetted on ahead, leaving her adrift in her own presumption.

Unlike in a terrestrial city, the structures that clung to the wide terraces on which Benthicalia was built were as easy to reach for residents and visitors alike as if they had been laid out on a flat mesa. Beneath the mirrorsky, up and down required no more effort to reach than did back and forward. Even more than in Sandrift and elsewhere, it was in Benthicalia that Irina truly came to appreciate the ease of access than came from free swimming as opposed to gravity-bound walking.

In the pleasant visitors' residence where they found accommodation, windows served the same function as doors. Though there was a view from every chamber, there were no decks or porches. There was no need for such when one could drift outside a room, hover, turn somersaults, and take in the expansive, twinkling view from any conceivable angle. One spoke of moving in and out rather than up and down.

Unlike her companions, she was assigned her own separate living space. Whether this was out of deference to her presumed changeling sensibilities or because no one wanted to be around her any longer than was necessary she did not know and did not care. After weeks of living in intimate proximity to crowds of travelers and fighters, she was glad of the solitude.

There was not much to do in the warren-like residence while she and everyone else waited for a response to Oxothyr's request for a meeting with the Tornal. Pale maroon with splotches of blue, the capsule-like chamber had been nurtured out of solid coral and then cultivated and hewn to add storage areas, a hygienic chamber whose facilities operated through the use of pressure differentials, and a small separate sleeping area dominated by enormous sponges that grew horizontally from the base of one wall. These provided as comfortable a sleeping platform as any she had yet encountered.

So much so, in fact, that she overslept. In the near total absence of daylight she only found out what had happened because she asked the time of a desk clerk. Juggling half a dozen thin inscribed tablets, the octopod flushed a polite pink as she provided not only the time but a brief explanation of how the inhabitants of the city managed to keep track of it in the absence of normal day and night.

"We keep time with fish," she explained to the inquisitive visitor in a tone that was not at all condescending.

"Fish?" Irina had a vision of a clock face with herring forming the numbers of the hours and a pair of mackerel serving as ticking hour and minute hands.

"They're on contract to the city." The clerk emphasized her words by gesturing conversationally with several tentacles that were not occupied in other tasks. "I think it's a school of amberjack who have the responsibility now. They migrate in a continuous vertical column. The ones at the top note the time according to the light and pass it down the line to the ones at the bottom. The last in line informs a city time worker who is responsible for seeing that the information is disseminated throughout the community. So despite the absence of natural light, we in Benthicalia always know what time it is."

"Ingenious," murmured an admiring Irina.

"Piscean," corrected the octopus amiably. "I would never wish to be a fish myself, but they do have other uses besides as food." She indicated a carved stone bowl resting on the coral counter. It was brimming with live mussels. "Snack?"

"Uh, no thanks. I don't think my teeth are up to it."

Several bands of commiserating blue ran through the length of the clerk's body. "You unfortunate mersons. Give me a beak over teeth any day."

As Irina explored the habitat, the other members of the Sandrift-Siriswirll group were nowhere to be found. Oxothyr's whereabouts she knew: the shaman was off conducting important business, foremost of which was striving to obtain the meeting with the Tornal. The others were doubtless relaxing according to their individual tastes, recuperating from the long and difficult journey from Siriswirll. The strange changeling had been left to her own devices. That no one felt it necessary to look after her was a back-handed compliment to how well she had adapted, but it left her wondering how to proceed.

Gathering her nerve, she decided to go exploring on her own. She could not really get lost. Benthicalia was a big city, yes, but it did not compare in size or complexity to those of her own world. If she ran out of light, she would know it was time to retrace her kicks.

Swimming through the streets and passageways, exploring and marveling at the metropolitan surroundings, it took her a moment to realize why the act of simply moving around was such a pleasure. There were no vehicles, no forms of mass transit here. They were not necessary in a place where an individual's own personal top speed was the benchmark for commuting. Some swimmers were, of course, faster than others. No merson could keep up with a manyarm, and many fish could out swim them. When you could as easily go over something as around it, distances shrank rapidly.

The city being divided into twenty-six levels instead of districts or boroughs, she amused herself by swimming from the fifteenth, where she and her companions had taken up residence, all the way up to the tenth. Evaluating each level along the way, she saw little difference between them. There were no pockets of poverty or great mansions. Wealth here was accounted in different ways than at home. Knowledge and skills still counted for much, but rewards took forms other than the crass accumulation of material things.

As the day wore on she could detect no lessening of or increase in activity. Sunk in and surrounded by darkness, the city functioned around the clock. She knew only that she was starting to get tired when she swam into an establishment from which music of a particular strain was emanating loudly.

Clearly very popular, the place was as crowded as any she had encountered. She moved freely within, staring wide-eyed at the lavishly decorated interior. Never had she seen so many colorful deep-sea colors. Hanging from the ceiling, the skeletons of black, red, and pink coral had been polished to a high sheen. Decked out in such natural jewels, the ceiling glistened like a magician's cave.

Along with piped-in warm water, mersons and manyarms circulated through the large artificial cavern. Many were chatting animatedly, others were eating, a few were dancing. What drinking took place involved downing sealed thin-skinned tubes of edible material that had been filled with various dark, flavored liquids. Here one did not have to look hard to discern someone who had imbibed too much of the wrong fluid. Since their mouths tended to open before they had finished swallowing, a visible haze hung around the heads and in front of their faces of the heaviest drinkers.

The establishment was home in equal numbers to mersons and manyarms, with a number of less intelligent but still interested fish finning cautiously among them. Seated atop a raised dais off to one side was the band whose music had first drawn her inside. Percussion was provided by (perhaps unsurprisingly) a large blue-ringed octopus each of whose eight arms held a stone hammer. Striking large shells of different sizes produced not only varying tones but also generated a different-colored pulse of light from the small bioluminescent lifeforms that inhabited each shell. When a shell cracked after receiving one too many blows, the octopod's assistant replaced it with another of the same size, much as guitar player might replace a snapped string. Nary a beat was missed.

A trio of yellow trumpetfish needed no extraneous instruments to supply a jazzy counterpoint, while an oversized pufferfish attended to what looked like some finely tuned cast-off plumbing. A cuttlefish smaller than Glint clutched several armfuls of empty bivalves whose halves she adeptly clicked like castanets. Among all the tootling and clacking and banging there was not a single stringed instrument. That one could be fashioned she had no doubt, but it was evident that any sound generated by such a device would not carry well underwater.

Drifting off to one side, she watched as a pair of squid dominated the area reserved for dancing. Their incredible ballet could not have been replicated by the most agile of mersons. Locking arms, propelled by their siphons, they shifted and swung in all directions while their bodies simultaneously changed colors in complimentary patterns. Other waltzing manyarms and tangoing mersons admiringly made space for them.

"Like to join them?"

The three mersons who had come up behind her were large, young, and manifestly male. Their attention was clearly fixated on her and not the action elsewhere in the establishment. Another time, another place, another world, she might have been flattered. Not here. Besides, in close proximity even to the friends she had made she still found the regular in-and-out pulsing of gill flaps anything but attractive. She eased away from them.

With a single powerful scissor kick, one swam around in front of her to block her way. Another hovered overhead. Gazing fixedly at her while floating upside-down with his face level with hers, he reached out and began to finger multiple strands of her drifting blonde tresses.

"Never seen hair this color. What kind of merson are you? Not from the city, that's plain. Are there others like you?"

"If possible two more of you," echoed one of his companions.

Twisting away, she flipped her hair out of the fondling fingers, her quick spin winding it around her head like a golden band. It would not stay like that for long, but at least for now it was out of reach.

"There's just one of me," she snapped, "and the one of me isn't interested in either of the three of you. Leave me alone."

"Cannot do that." Reaching out, the first speaker put a hand on her shoulder and drew it slowly downward. "I personally am too obsessed with the new. You are a very new, *silash*."

The last word was merson slang, uncivil and borderline vile. She looked around. No one had been attracted to the conversion, no one was interested in the confrontation. Apparently in a place like this you were on your own, be you merson, manyarm, or changeling. She realized now it had been foolish to go off by herself. This was not simple, rustic Sandrift or even its larger cousin Siriswirll. Merson culture was neither homogeneous nor inherently idyllic. Threats existed in this world that had nothing to do with sharks or spralakers.

She'd found herself caught in similar situations once or twice before. But both times the surroundings had been familiar, the testosterone-fueled tropes typical, and the means for extricating herself practiced and polished. Here everything was different, for all that certain aspects of life seemed universal even in another world and even under the water.

"I'm asking you nicely." She found herself swatting away hands in all directions. "To leave me alone. Or I'll yell for the police."

"Police?" Two of the self-confident nuisances exchanged a glance. "What are 'police'?"

"I think she means the civil guard," suggested the third member of the disagreeable trio. He moved a little closer. They were hemming her in now; from front, back, and above, reducing her room to maneuver, to get away. Blasting out so much percussion, the band made it difficult for her to make herself heard.

*Could* she make herself heard? How far would her cry for assistance travel underwater, swamped as it was likely to be by the wail of the band? Would anyone respond if they did hear her, and did anyone care? For all she knew of local culture, in Benthicalia this increasingly unpleasant confrontation was a common and accepted method through which representatives of one gender initiated contact with another. Certainly it was no less intrusive than the courtship rituals employed by certain species of dolphin in her own world.

She was no dolphin, and she wanted out.

In frustration as much as anger, she struck out at the nearest merson. Slowed by the intervening water, her slap barely grazed him. Worse, he appeared to take it as some kind of perverse invitation. Moving toward instead of away from her, he reached out to tickle the outer edge of her left gill flap. If it was supposed to send some kind of intimate sensual signal it failed miserably with Irina, reminding her as it did only of newfound opportunities for suffocation.

The merson behind her was intent on committing a gesture considerably more familiar though no less unwelcome when a horizontal blur slammed into him and knocked him prone in the water. Now some in the crowd did pause in their partying to turn and look, though no one seemed inclined to summon the aforementioned civil guard. Blinking at the abruptness of the intervention, Irina was too shaken to thank her rescuer.

Pivoting sharply in the water, having knocked insensible one of the trio who were vexing Irina, Poylee cocked both arms in front of her.

"I think I heard the changeling ask you nicely," she hissed.

The unconscious merson's cohorts barely glanced at the confrontational new arrival. They were too busy gaping at Irina. "A changeling!" echoed one. "That explains the strange hair."

"Yes." His companion nodded in the direction of their free-floating friend. "Welenhu has gone to sleep and left this intriguing creature for us to examine. We would be lax in our duty as friends if we were to retire without learning more." Putting his own hands out in front of him, he advanced on Poylee while his associate closed a new circle around the uncertain Irina.

Suddenly he was arching backwards. Having slid an arm around each side of the advancing merson's neck, his assailant clutched his own forearms with opposing hands. The result was a firm hold that forced tightly shut the gill flaps of Irina's tormentor. The merson thus restrained began to kick frantically. Locked together, the pair spun around and around in a series of increasingly desperate somersaults. Other patrons of the establishment backed up to give the fighters more room as the thoroughly blasé band segued smoothly into another, somewhat faster, selection.

As he slowly suffocated, the wild flailing and kicking of the merson who had been surprised from behind began to moderate. After he passed out but before he died, Chachel released the double-arm choke hold and swam to pull the last remaining assailant off an increasingly hard-pressed Poylee. Swimming to the first and still unconscious merson, Irina stood watch over him to make sure he didn't revive in time to rejoin the fray. Out of the corner of an eye she saw a nest of arms come into view: Glint had arrived.

Gesturing to where Chachel now had his hands full with the third and largest of the troublemakers, she snapped at the splendidly hued cephalopod. "Why don't you go help Chachel? Isn't he still your friend?"

The cuttlefish replied with considerable dignity. "I don't interfere in the mating rituals of mersons."

The male beside her was starting to revive. Extending a leg, she shoved a webbed foot against his left gill flap. His eyelids fluttered and he promptly passed out again.

"This isn't a mating ritual, you ghost of a calamari dinner! It's a fight! A brutal, kicking, scratching, head-butting fight!"

Unperturbed, the cuttlefish cocked one eye at her. "Where mersons are concerned, it is often impossible to tell where one begins and the other lets off." Extending themselves, several tentacles gestured. "Chachel fights sharks single-handedly and with only two arms. I am not concerned as to the eventual outcome of this encounter, nor should you be."

The fact remained that despite the manyarm's reassurances, she was concerned. Her anxiety level dropped when she saw Chachel spin his opponent into a wall. Coral was notoriously unyielding. Her apprehension eased still more as Chachel, holding onto the dazed merson with one hand, began pummeling him with the other. Blood from the unlucky merson's face began to flow into the surrounding water in tight little trickles, like threads of cuttlefish ink. At this depth and in the bioluminescent light, it appeared dark green instead of red.

Poylee finally managed to pull Chachel off the now comatose nuisance. The excitement over, those patrons who had stopped to watch now returned to their momentarily interrupted pursuits of eating, dancing, conversing, and listening to the music of the band, which had never paused in its playing. There was no sign of any representatives of the civil guard.

Benthicalia might be beautiful, and sophisticated, and the most advanced metropolis in this part of Oshenerth, Irina reflected, but it was not without blemishes of its own.

She swam over to where Poylee, irritated and stressed, was working to catch her breath. The merson appeared unharmed.

"Poylee, I don't know how to ...."

"Oh, shut up, changeling!" The female growled through clenched teeth. "Can't you do anything right? After all this time among us? You don't have the sense of a spasmed oyster!" Before Irina could say a word, the first of her two saviors was kicking hard for the exit.

Duly unsettled, she approached Chachel more cautiously. At least he let her talk long enough to express her gratitude before he initiated his own verbal pummeling. This was at once less irate and more forceful than Poylee's.

"From now on I suggest you don't go anywhere without the company of a *real* merson, or one of the manyarms in our group."

Did he ever blink, she wondered? Come to think of it, while the reflex gesture was common enough here, it was not necessary. A merson's eyes were always moist.

"You are a lot of trouble, changeling," he finished.

"I don't mean to be." She was not going to cry, she told herself. How could she, when her rising anger threatened to overcome her relief at having been rescued from an increasingly unpleasant set of circumstances. "I've been trying to see and learn as much about your world as possible. That's what I was doing out on my own. That's what I was doing here."

"Learning a thing is not much good if it's the last thing you learn. Watch where you stick your head, changeling, lest you shove it into a hole occupied by a drunken moray and end up withdrawing without it." He nodded to where the bodies of two of the unconscious mersons had drifted up against each other. "Or worse."

She was struck by a sudden thought. "How did you know where to find me? I didn't tell anyone where I was going. I couldn't have, since I didn't know myself."

Instead of replying, he just stared at her. The longer he held the gaze the more his expression seemed to soften. Or maybe, she thought inconclusively, it was just the effect of the shifting luminescence in the enclosed space and the distortions caused by the constant movement of water within the busy establishment.

In any case, he didn't answer. After a pause that seemed even longer than it was, he turned and swam away, picking a path through the churning crowd as easily and effortlessly as he would have through a school of skipjack. Unsurprisingly, Poylee was right behind him. Watching her trail close behind the hunter as he left the establishment, it struck Irina suddenly what kind of fish the young female reminded her of.

A remora.

"What are you smiling at? You were in an uncomfortable situation. You should not be smiling."

Her accuser was Glint. Responding to the stimulus of his present dynamic surroundings, he had strained his chromatophores to saturate his skin with intense orange color infused with sequencing purple bands, all lit by his own internally generated pale blue and red bioluminescence. It was a sight to supersede any human—or merson—make-up. Among cephalopods, cosmetics were not only intrinsic, they were a biological imperative.

She turned to face the leisurely writhing mass of colorful tentacles and the body to which they were attached. "Smiling? Was I smiling?"

"I think that you were." The cuttlefish drifted closer. "Though I suppose with changelings, as with mersons, a sensible person can never be sure. I heard your question." An arm gestured in the direction of the way out. "When Chachel found out that you had left to explore the city on your own, he became uneasy."

"Really?" She found herself staring at the exit Chachel and Poylee had taken.

"I think he was more irritated than troubled. Nevertheless, he opted to follow you to ensure your continued well-being. He thinks that you may in some way be connected to everything out of the ordinary that has happened since I saved you from drowning in the void."

"*You* saved me?" she responded.

"Ah, I was correct. That *is* a smile. Both of us saved you, of course. I float corrected."

She was thinking hard. "He followed me to look after me just because of that?"

"Of course." Glint sounded guileless. "Why else would he do so?"

*Why else indeed*, she thought to herself. "And Poylee?"

"The merson accompanied him for the same reason. Why else would *she* have done so?"

*I can't imagine.* This time Irina knew the cuttlefish would recognize her wider smile. Was he conversant enough with human/merson expression to also distinguish the real meaning behind it? If not, she saw no reason to point out that Poylee's principal goal in life was to stick as close to the hunter as mersonly possible, lest he ...

Lest he what? More useless, time-wasting speculation on a subject that did not interest her anyway.

"Are you feeling unwell, Irina-changeling? The look on your face is most peculiar."

"I'm fine." Maintaining an intentionally broad grin, she raised her voice so that her words resounded well above the pounding of the band. "I'm fine! And since I'm fine, there is much more of the city I'd like to see." She extended her right arm. "As everyone seems to be so 'worried' about me—Glint, would you do me the honor of being my escort for the remainder of our resting time?"

Extending outward from the sucker-filled body, a pair of strong hunting tentacles serpentined around her bare arm. "I would be pleased to do so, Irina, since I am not presently interested in making the acquaintance of a mate-worthy female of my own kind. It is not the right time of the month."

"How do you know? You can't see the moonlight down here."

"The moonli—oh, you mean the disc that breathes silver life into the mirrorsky. No, I cannot see it." Another arm gestured upward. "But we manyarms know when the time is right. The knowing of it is born into us. You might say," he added as his epidermis changed from orange to mauve, "that the why of it is a different kind of light that dwells within each of us."

If only, she mused as they departed the establishment in tandem, interpreting the motivations of other mersons was as easy for her as was the telling of time for a manyarm.

# - XVIII -

**S**queezed into the very back of the room, his arms curled tightly about him, Oxothyr lay staring and shivering at the single opening.

Though he was considerably bigger than the mersons who had accompanied him all the way from Sandrift, like his fellow manyarms he needed only a small space in which to reside. The absence of bones—irritating, pointy, restrictive things—allowed him and his kind to fit into spaces seemingly far too small for their bodies. In addition, if he so desired, he could through the application of a modest piece of manyarm magick make himself thin enough to pass through the eye of a needle. Or in the case of fellow shaman-sorcerers, through the needle of an eye.

There was no need. The residential burrow he had been given was deep, dark, quiet, and suitably oxygenated. He reposed there in silence, attended only by his own thoughts.

These days those were not the best of company. The coldness he was feeling came not from the surrounding water but from within. Something Was In Motion, and it gripped him like plague. The suckers on his arms contracted from the tension and for the most part he kept his siphon tucked well inside his body.

He believed that his falling internal temperature was somehow connected to the sudden and wholly atypical boldness of the spralakers. By what means, only the Deep Oracle might know. The Tornal *had* to grant him and his companions an audience. Only they were possessed of sufficient sensitivity to establish the Oracle's whereabouts.

He thought back over the singular events of the past weeks. The size of the spralaker forces that had invaded the southern reefs was unparalleled, as was their level of coordination and their tactics. Who was commanding them, and why? Prior to now, spralakers and mersons and manyarms had never engaged in anything more extensive than low-level skirmishes. The majority of clashes took place between individuals or small foraging parties. That the hardshells should now muster themselves in sufficient force to enable them to attack and destroy entire communities was extraordinary.

Outside forces were clearly at work. Did they somehow involve the surprising arrival of the changeling? Though he doubted it, he did not possess sufficient information to positively disavow a connection.

And what of that alien chill that continued to afflict him so deeply? Less sensitive to such subtle changes, the others did not feel it. But eventually they would, he feared. It had to be stopped, as the spralakers had to be stopped. And he must lead the way. Always he must lead the way.

He was tired, was Oxothyr. Tired of always having to provide surcease and solution. Tired of supplicants and complainers. Tired of constantly having to correct his famuli, who were presently mindlessly delighting in the glib pleasures of the city.

He could let the coming coldness take its course, could release the irksome mersons and common manyarms to deal with the spralakers as they saw fit. Why must he always be the one to give advice? Why must he be the one to whom everyone turned for resolution?

He knew the answer to that self-posed question himself. They turned to him for answers because he was the only one who had them.

He sighed, filling a portion of the unlit ceiling with bubbles. He was hungry. Crisis was never well met on an empty stomach. Arms, eyes, and internal organs he could sacrifice and still press on. But if ever he found his appetite waning, then he would know for certain he was in serious trouble. He started to ease his great bulk out of the impossibly small, narrow chamber.

Others were depending on him. Hundreds, thousands of others, from the villagers of Siriswirll to the nomads of the Halastweraa Pinnacles. Benthicalia itself was in danger. Only, none of them knew it yet. He wondered if the Tornal was aware. If so, he was likely to soon find out. He needed to.

Time was ticking away like a periwinkle caught in a current, never to be recovered.

He found Chachel relaxing, insofar as the hunter was capable of engaging in an act of repose, on a sponge lounge just outside the main dining area of the travelers' lodge where the visitors had taken up temporary abode. The merson was finishing the last of a flatfish that had been seared in hot water piped in from a nearby field of black smokers. The cooking process had imparted a slight mineral taste to the white flesh that actually enhanced its flavor.

"Satisfactory to your taste, hunter?"

Chachel reacted to the shaman's greeting. "Well enough. Different certainly from the food one gets at home. I am not sure I approve of this practice of 'cooking.' Will you eat?"

"In a little while. At the moment I am nourished by other things, most notably that one overriding subject which consumes the majority of my waking hours. And occasionally, I must admit, of some that are not of the waking."

"I'm sorry to hear that." Chachel downed the last of his fish, chewing methodically. "Myself, I never have any trouble sleeping."

"You sleep the sleep of the just." Disdaining a lounge while ignoring the lie, Oxothyr settled onto a pulpit fashioned of his own coiled arms.

"Hardly."

"I hear that you had to extricate the changeling from an unwieldy social situation."

The hunter nodded. "She may know much of the void, but here her ignorance never ceases to amaze." He shrugged. "I preserve her because of your interest in her, nothing else. Glint is looking after her." He licked sticky oil from his fingers.

"I appreciate your assistance. As I have ever since we left Sandrift. I fear I will be compelled to call upon it more than once in the days ahead."

Unexpectedly, Chachel showed actual curiosity. "What happens if this Tornal helps us to find your Deep Oracle, and it in turn knows the cause of this coldness that keeps bothering you as well as whatever's behind the spralakers' sudden brazenness?"

"That will depend, my proficient twin-limbed killer, on the nature of that explanation."

Chachel grunted. For once, he was displaying impatience and not impertinence. "I guess I can't expect you to share answers you don't have."

"When I know, all will know," Oxothyr promised him. He would have elaborated, if not for an unexpected interruption.

Even without its capacious stomach distended, the gulper eel was an odd looker. The several strands of deep-sea gems that had been attached to its rotund upper body sparkled in the light that illuminated the outside of nearby structures. With its enormous brown gut and tiny eyes it resembled an oversized internal parasite, though it was as efficient a hunter of small fish as any of its more physically attractive reef-dwelling namesakes. It was also excessively respectful. Hovering before manyarm and merson like a length of bloated, severed kelp, it bowed low before addressing them with deep-voiced formality.

"I bring the most remarkable news. I have been sent to inform you that at exactly midday tomorrow you have been granted an audience with the full Tornal. I hope you are aware of what an exceptional privilege has been bestowed upon you."

"Thanks," replied Chachel nonchalantly. The hunter was distinctly unimpressed.

Oxothyr was more forthcoming, and more tactful. "Please convey to the Tornal the gratitude of my companions and myself. Is the invitation restricted to me or may all attend? I know everyone would find it instructive and enlightening."

Its empty belly sac swaying from side to side in the slight current, the gulper peered back uncertainly out of tiny eyes that had little use for anything more than minimal light.

"I was not told to say that their attendance would be rejected."

Oxothyr looked pleased. "Then we will present ourselves at the designated time."

Eyeing the watching Chachel with a disdain arising from the knowledge that despite the merson's larger size the gulper could ingest him in one swallow, the herald turned and slithered off into the city. As soon as it was out of sight, the hunter turned back to the manyarmed mage.

"Do you really want everyone present for this, shaman?"

"It is everyone's life that is at stake," the octopus replied somberly. "Therefore everyone both deserves and needs to be present." He turned back to the hunter. "Will you do me the good of relaying to them the specifics of our invitation?"

"That I can do." Chachel turned to go, paused. "Oxothyr?"

The octopus regarded the merson archly. "What is it, two-arm?"

"Is it necessary for me to be present at this meeting? You know how I dislike being around many others in an enclosed space."

"You can command your nerves for this one occasion. Don't you realize the honor that is being conferred on us, on we simple visitors from a small village high up on the reef line? The Tornal keep to themselves and are not easily met. They do not agree to see just anybody."

"With all respect, shaman, like the few other honors that have been sent my way this too is one I would prefer to decline."

The mage spread all eight of his arms wide, increasing himself enormously in size and appearance. "Then if you won't come for the honor, you'll attend as an important fighting representative of the free swimmers of the Southern Reefs. I prefer those charged with the defense of everyone's homes and everyone's freedom to acquire information relevant to such security in person. And finally, if you won't come for the honor or for the knowledge, you'll come for me."

Not even Chachel the Hunter could ignore the shaman's subsequent cephalopodan glare. He proffered a resigned nod by way of response. "As you wish, shaman. Though I find your confidence in me to be grossly misplaced."

"No," Oxothyr replied brusquely. "It is you, Chachel, who finds confidence in yourself misplaced. One day I hope that doubt will disappear like blood in the water. Now go, and notify our companions. And when you find those two wastrels Sathi and Tythe, tell them to shut their beaks and high their tentacles back here. I have need of them."

They parted then: Chachel upward to the next level of the city where the majority of visitors from Sandrift and Siriswirll had gone to indulge themselves in its urbane delights, Oxothyr back to his borrowed burrow to collect his thoughts for the critical meeting tomorrow. They left nothing behind them but light.

One by one Chachel tracked down the members of the escort that had accompanied him and the shaman on the long journey from Siriswirll to inform them of the critical meeting that had been arranged for the morrow. Reactions to the news varied among mersons and manyarms without regard to species. Some evinced excitement, others curiosity, a few fear, and others indifference. They had volunteered to come along to see, to learn, and if necessary to fight. Conversation and conferences they were happy to leave to the shaman. But with Oxothyr decreeing that they participate, none dared declare that they would be otherwise than in attendance.

As always, Poylee was glad to greet Chachel and reluctant to see him go. Learning that he was moving fast in order to carry out the shaman's mandate, she knew she had no justification for trying to detain him. Though she wanted to, she did not try.

It was all so very unfair, she reflected as she eased back onto the outside lounge where she had been resting. She wanted nothing but Chachel, whereas the hunter wanted nothing, period. He was polite, even friendly in his limited and imperfect way, but no matter how hard she tried, no matter how subtle she strove to be in her entreaties and invitations and inadvertent little touches, he did not respond. She could school with any male in Sandrift. Instead, she had chosen to try to inveigle a loner, and a damaged one at that. Everyone knew the story of Chachel's life, of the death of his parents at the teeth of marauding sharks, and of his subsequent choice of a life of self-imposed isolation.

She could bring him out of that, she knew. Bring him to full flower and the richness of the life she sensed was locked deep within him. She could open him to the realworld as easily and effectively as a child could open a clam with a knife. If only he would let her. If only he would give her the chance.

Well, she would persist. Through indifference, and callousness, and even war with the spralakers. Eventually he would see her as she knew he could, and should. Eventually, she would break through the shell he had secreted around himself. Nothing and no one could stop her. She was not troubled by his apathy, she did not fear death at the claws of the spralakers, she was not worried about how much time it might take to make her dream a reality. Only one thing really concerned her.

The changeling.

With her long golden hair, her strange pale body, and her knowledge of another world, the changeling presented challenges Poylee feared she could not counter. Could not, because she knew nothing of them and could not understand them. How could she fight newness? Above all there was the one thing that left her truly apprehensive about the effect the changeling might have on her carefully nurtured relationship with the fearless and heroic hunter.

It was that the changeling did not appear to care about such matters at all.

◊

Midday following was as dark as the midday that had preceded it. Without doubt or question it would be equally as dark as the midday that would follow it, and all those that would follow them.

The mood, if not the surrounding illumination, was bright among the travelers who had come all the way from Sandrift and Siriswirll. There had been no need to clean themselves preparatory to the incipient meeting. Underwater, everyone and everything was always clean. Having journeyed light, they had little in the way of individual frills with which to adorn themselves. Of them all Poylee, unsurprisingly, made the most she could of the opportunity, without even knowing if this Tornal gathering would respond. Her strenuous if limited efforts in the service of personal beautification were intended, of course, as much for Chachel's edification as for that of some shadowy assemblage with which she was unfamiliar.

There was need of directions but not an escort. Chatting and murmuring among themselves and with Oxothyr setting the pace in the lead, the band of travel-hardened visitors made their way to the Palace of the Tornal. As they drew near, what had been excited conversation soon faded of its own accord. Oxothyr did not have to say a word.

When a manyarm catches its breath in amazement, it simply goes motionless in the water. When a merson does so, the gill flaps of males and females alike tend to open as wide their mouths. Such was the case with every one of the visitors, Irina included.

Constructed on a ledge that projected outward from the city's highest terrace, the Palace of the Tornal commanded a sweeping view over all of Benthicalia. As they swam slowly up to the main coralline arch that marked the entrance, the visitors could look out upon all twenty-five remaining levels of the great metropolis spread out below. Illuminated by tens of thousands of streaks and spots of blue and green, yellow and red bioluminescence, Benthicalia seen from above resembled the Milky Way viewed on a clear night from above the mirrorsky.

Following behind Oxothyr, Irina turned onto her back as she continued swimming. Gazing upward from this highest point of the city, the faintest of pale blue glows tickled her retinas, indicating that high, high above in the shallows it was now midday. Somewhere up there the sun slanted down through clear warm waters, eliminating the need for bioluminescence, phosphorescence, and all manner of internal biochemically-generated illumination. Her first weeks in Oshenerth had seen her pining for dry land. The most recent ones found her yearning for a glimpse of the sun. What else, she wondered, would she next be forced to miss, to give up, to surrender in order simply to survive here?

She pushed such thoughts and the clinging depression that accompanied them aside. Ahead lay a new wonder that, if it did not exactly compensate for the absence of daylight, was at least striking enough to distract her from looming melancholy.

Cultivated largely from muted yellow and dark red fire coral, the walls and spires of the palace were their own defense. In addition, anemones the size of trucks had been transplanted to the walls and roofs, the turrets and hollow living quarters, and nurtured until they had reached gargantuan size. A sting from a single tentacle of any one such stationary giant would be more than strong enough to kill a merson, spralaker, or any other uninvited intruder. The correspondingly larger than normal anemone fish who dwelled within the lethal arms were trained to raise the alarm in the event of an attack.

In addition to the anemones and the walls of fire coral, more nimble sentries were also present. Mersons armed with halberds tipped with razor-sharp mother-of-pearl flanked the main archway. Emblems of office fashioned from found gemstones set in beaten gold hung from their wrists and ankles and covered their shaved skulls. Chain mail armor that was ceremonial more than functional covered their torsos and lower bodies. Composed entirely of strung pearls that ranged in hue from gray-black to pure white, they glistened like platoons of fireflies in the light emitted by the bioluminescent growths that bedecked the walls.

Corridors high and wide flared off in multiple directions from a spherical entry hall that had need of neither floor nor ceiling. Drifting together in its center, the visitors waited until the most magnificently ornamented cuttlefish Irina had ever seen came jetting importantly toward them. In addition to the strobing luminescence it generated within its own body, it trailed streamers of colored pearls backward from its mantle while the edges of its gently rippling lateral fins had been lined with hundreds of tiny colored diamonds. Catching the surrounding bioluminescence, the gems sparkled with a hundred different colors. In sunlight near the surface, so wondrously bejeweled a manyarm would have thrown back too much light for a mere mortal to gaze upon directly.

"My name is Qespangl," he informed them. "The Tornal await your presence." Gold-flecked eyes of piercing black flicked rapidly over each of the visitors before coming to settle on Oxothyr. If the majordomo was impressed by the shaman's quiet charisma, he did not show it. "Keep your questions brief and to the point. The Tornal are alert and miss nothing, but they tire easily."

Awestruck by both the magnificent surroundings in which they found themselves and by the self-evident solemnity of the occasion, scarce but a few whispers passed among the travelers as they followed their glittering guide deeper into the palace complex. It was, a silent Irina reflected as she marveled at one dazzling artwork and architectural fillip after another, a long way from the simple coral homes and shops of distant Sandrift.

Eventually the corridor opened into an enormous bubble. Soaring arches of deep red fire coral supported huge curved panels of transparent, impossibly thin crystal. Such a structure would have been impossible to sustain on the surface, where gravity would have collapsed it as if it had been made of spun sugar. Underwater, filaments of quarried quartz served as supports in the absence of steel. Still, it seemed to an enthralled Irina that the pressure at Benthicalia's depth would crush so expansive and fragile an edifice.

"The assembly is held in place by something stronger than stone," Oxothyr explained in response to her question as they swam slowly forward.

"Something crystalline?" she speculated.

"Something charmed," he corrected her. "Not all magic is fleeting. Sometimes sortilege can be called upon to serve as superstructure." The tip of one tentacle curved around to touch his beak. "Quiet now."

They were approaching the Tornal. As they drew near, the august members of that esteemed company turned to face the recently arrived supplicants. Irina was startled to see that unlike her and her companions, the revered members did not swim or float but were compelled to sit upon a platform built up out of swirled and beaded gold. While each of them was a manyarm true and through to the core, as indisputably so as Oxothyr or Glint, Sathi or Tythe, the most sprightly of them could swim but feebly at best. Though not inherently infirm, each would have to be helped from place to place by more robust assistants.

It took Irina a moment to recognize the Tornal for what they were. The knowledge that enabled her to identify them came from university studies concluded long ago. She breathed in her astonishment softly, her gill flaps collapsing against the sides of her neck as she did so.

The Tornal was comprised of ten individuals in all, the total possibly representative of the number of arms boasted by cuttlefish and squid, though not by octopods or the more primitive nautiloids. The manyarms who formed the body of the Tornal differed not only from all those she had so far encountered in Oshenerth, but from those she knew from the seas of home as well, except in one respect.

Every one of the incredibly aged beings now confronting the visitors had an external shell.

*Ammonites*, she thought to herself. Living relics from a time that was ancient to both Oshenerth and to her world. Unlike modern manyarms they wore their huge, coiled, thick-shelled homes on their backs. Alternating with the five ammonites were five orthoceras: manyarms whose shells resembled those of an ammonite that had been stretched out straight as an arrow. In addition to their natural markings and patterns, each individual was decked out in jewels and bits of bright metal that had been set into recesses that had been engraved into their respective shells.

How old was the Tornal, she found herself wondering? A few hundred years? A few thousand? A million or more? She whispered her wonderment to an attentive Oxothyr.

"No one knows," he murmured in response. His arms were fully extended and coiled at the ends. "Not even the Tornal themselves. Their collective memories are so vast and comprehensive that the earliest of them have withered with the passage of time. Fortunately our request involves specifics of a far more contemporary nature."

Mindful of the shaman's earlier admonition to keep conversation to a minimum, Irina nodded but did not reply. Peering past the hovering octopod she espied Chachel and Glint. Both struck her as being as overwhelmed by their present surroundings as everyone else. She expected that of Glint, but this was the first time since she had made his acquaintance that she had ever seen Chachel the hunter truly impressed.

Laboriously pulling herself forward until her heavy shell and body rested near the front edge of the golden platform, the glittering ammonite nearest the center flourished her short, thick tentacles at the visitors and addressed them in a voice that reeked of eons—but not senility. As she spoke, the light in the remarkable and nearly transparent chamber brightened and the curving crystalline panels themselves took on a warm amber hue. The huge, coiled shell emitted a pallid blue light that strengthened and faded with the speaker's voice. It seemed that even the very words of the Tornal, an awed Tythe whispered to Sathi, were charged with prickles of enchantment.

As she regarded the line of glowing ancients arrayed before her, Irina found questions coalescing inside her like the rising bubbles in a newly opened bottle of champagne. Could they answer queries about the birth and evolution of life in her own world? What did they know of the connections between both worlds and their respective oceans? Between them, the primeval hard-shelled sages might hold the answers to questions that had teased and tormented researchers for centuries.

So powerful was the sudden lust for knowledge that she felt herself growing queasy as she contemplated the multitude of possibilities. Once Oxothyr had asked his question, would any of the rest of them be given the opportunity to pose some of their own? Having at last made the acquaintance of the Tornal, she could hardly imagine herself retiring from their august presence in submissive silence.

As events developed, not even Oxothyr would have the chance to voice the query that had driven him and his multi-species escort to fight their way all the way from the upper reefs down to deep Benthicalia.

Having emerged in front of the others, the shaman calmly and confidently introduced himself and his companions. He then began to lay out, in the simplest terms, their reason for coming to the city and requesting the present audience.

"Currents are changing, venerable ones. Incomprehensibilities speckle the calm waters of the reefs like a plankton bloom, blocking one's vision and confounding perception. Change is coming that I sense bodes not well. Possibly not for the deep, but certainly not for the reefs. I am myself as pregnant with questions and concerns regarding this matter as is a wrasse heavy with roe."

The ammonite who had trundled painstakingly forward eyed her fellow ancients on her left, then on her right. "We live not in the light of the reef and so do not share the unsettling sensations of which you speak, shaman."

"It is not clarification of my nightmare dreaming that I seek," Oxothyr explained respectfully, "but illumination of a different kind. All I and my companions would ask of you is that ..."

*"Revered teachers!"*

Every one of the visitors turned in the direction of the unexpected interruption, which was as loud as it was impassioned. Even the thus far silent members of the Tornal bestirred themselves to stare.

The disruption came from the cuttlefish majordomo who had escorted the travelers into the Tornal's presence. He did not look particularly wild-eyed, a dumbfounded Irina decided. At least, no more so than Glint or any other specimen of his kind. An abnormal trembling had taken hold of his exquisitely adorned fins. Most telling of all, his body had gone completely white—an unmistakable sign among cephalopodan folk of fear, terror, or the deepest possible anxiety.

The ammonite who was serving as Speaker for the Tornal responded placidly. "Verbal intimation of panic is insufficiently informative. Explain this intrusion." When the cuttlefish hesitated, eyeing the visitors, the old one added, "In this chamber there are no secrets from honest supplicants. Speak."

Plainly, the cuttlefish was struggling to control himself. "A group of commercial scavengers was scouring the valley to the east of the Halatanea Smokers. They returned as fast as they could in order to pass on the news."

One of the long, spear-shaped orthoceras spoke up, grumbling. "What news?"

Since it could not turn its head, the cuttlefish shifted its entire body to more squarely face the speaker. "Spralakers! Tens of thousands of them, armed and eager, coming this way from not one but two directions." As he spoke, the cuttlefish gestured wildly with all ten arms. Seen from the front, Irina thought, the agitated major domo looked like a nest of cobras on drugs.

"Two separate armies," the cuttlefish continued frantically. "One approaching the terraces from the southern plains, the other advancing along the middle shelf."

Edging together until their tentacles all but touched, the Tornal hurriedly caucused among themselves. They did not talk long.

"Alert those in charge of the city's defenses," commanded the ammonite speaker stridently. "Let those who would flee in the face of danger do so. All who remain will be expected to stay, stand, and fight!"

"This is an outrageous provocation," declared another ammonite, his short tentacles writhing in front of his face. "Outrageous, and futile."

"They will all perish." The orthocera beside him spoke knowingly. "The spralakers understand only how to fight among themselves. They do not know how to contest with an adversary who is organized and determined. What can they possibly be hoping to achieve in trying to attack Benthicalia?"

Before another member of the Tornal could comment, Oxothyr raised several arms to attract their attention. In order to do so he had to shove aside the pair of frantic famuli who tried their utmost to restrain him.

"I believe I may have an answer to that."

The Speaker-for-the-Tornal turned incredibly aged eyes on the octopod shaman from far Sandrift. "Any explanation for this apparent outbreak of mass spralaker lunacy would be most welcome."

"You may not think so after you have heard it." Oxothyr plunged on in spite of his assistants' obvious unease.

"I believe they may be looking for us."

# – XIX –

**G**ubujul had to admit that the trappings of power which attached to the nominal commander of a vast military force exceeded in allure even those that accrued to the position of Paramount Advisor to the Great Lord. In the absence of Kulakak himself, the ranks of dedicated and determined soldiers were left looking up to *him*. The senior officers of the two armies felt otherwise, seeing the Lord's hand-picked Advisor as inexperienced and untested. In the course of the long march southwest, however, Gubujul managed to win them over one by one. To some he promised favors of a personal nature, to others promotion, to still others an assurance that despite his position he would not interfere with their decisions on the field of battle.

"I know my abilities," he informed them, "and I know my limitations. I am here to give you support, not to obstruct your efforts. The last thing any of us want is to return home in failure. Better to die here, in glorious struggle on behalf of all our people!"

His words went down well. They ought to, he reflected. Having survived many years rising through the murderous, self-aggrandizing levels at court, they had been honed to perfection.

Though not in line for the throne—he could never defeat the prospective challengers in combat—his official position was so fraught with uncertainty that it was not actively sought. Living every day on the cusp of death, living or dying at the whim of the Great Lord, was not a way of life that appealed to many. Gubujul, in contrast, thrived on the pressure. Compared to dealing with the Great Lord's unpredictable moods, supervising a vast military campaign bordered on a vacation.

Regular communications reached him from the Second Army. The intent was to approach Benthicalia from two directions; from the flat, shelving plain at its base and from the deep reef above. A coordinated attack by the two spralaker armies would force the city's defenders to divide their forces. Gravity would aid his own troops as, once over the outer walls, they cast themselves upon the inner city like grains of sand stirred up by an earthquake. The tremors that would shake and finally destroy Benthicalia would come from the feet of his soldiers.

The senior officers were confident. Few of them had supported the previous limited incursions into the southern reefs, even though these had resulted in the destruction of the town known as Shakestone and the near taking of the much larger community called Siriswirll. The Marshals had always argued for an all-out onslaught in force. Now they felt they had been given the troops to do the job.

"The mersons and the manyarms are swifter and far more agile," Mud Marshal Cavaumaz had pointed out, "but we are individually strong, and we have the advantage of numbers. If we stick to our strengths we will surely win the day."

Certainly the First Army was an impressive force. Incorporating soldiers drawn from throughout the many species of spralaker who lived in the northern waters, they covered the reef lines and ridges with their bodies, advancing sideways in endless number. Legions of impressed or engaged eagle, bull, golden, and manta rays transported hundreds of fighters at a time across chasms too deep to scuttle or too wide to swim.

Though they brought supplies with them, both armies felt free to live off the sea bottom, scavenging as they marched. Entire reef systems were scoured of life as the two armies advancing in parallel consumed everything along their route down to the coral polyps themselves. Unallied fish, inadvertent invertebrates, slow-moving mollusks, innocent worms and panicked nudibranchs—all vanished into the thousands of voracious, ever-hungry maws of the two spralaker forces. Small villages unfortunate enough to lie in the path of either army simply vanished. Such pleasant encounters offered the tirelessly marching soldiers welcome diversion in the form of entertaining opportunities to pillage and murder. As for the fate of the residents of these unceremoniously obliterated communities, the usual taking of prisoners was superceded by the need for both armies to continuously replenish their respective larders.

For the one in charge, the long march to the southwest passed pleasantly. Never in any danger, Gubujul essentially had an entire army at his personal beck and call. The day eventually came, however, when the lights of Benthicalia could be discerned as a faint glow in the distance, and the time for relaxation and effortless if minor triumphs was at an end.

Crouching respectfully before him on the last ridge line facing Benthicalia was the trio of spralakers who comprised the First Army's strategic brain trust. Each had risen through the ranks to assume the exalted title of Mud Marshal of the Hardshelled. Two were crab-folk. Bejuryar was a smaller but no less fearless member of the same species as the Great Lord himself. Cavaumaz was a fiddler, whose great metal-inlaid right claw was ever poised to snip off a piece of any subordinate who disappointed him—or the head of a merson. Smallest but perhaps toughest of all was Taww, a squat lobster whose mastery of tactics had seen her overcome physical inadequacies that would have soon discouraged a lesser spralaker.

"Everything is in readiness, Paramount Advisor." In a sign of deference Bejuryar dipped his eyestalks forward. "We await only your command to begin the assault."

Gubujul wished for more light so as to render the jewels he was wearing suitably magnificent. He felt certain that their bioluminescent bezels were insufficient to adequately accentuate his carefully sculpted splendor.

"What word from Marshal Xorovic and the Second Army?"

"They are in position, Paramount Advisor." Cavaumaz gestured with his oversized right claw. The inner edges of the enormous pincer had been ground to battle-ready razor-sharpness, their gripping edges refined and filed down to killing points.

"Xorovic and I have worked together in the past, on traditional smaller raiding expeditions in the far north. We know each other and our mutual stratagems well, and will act as one."

Gubujul's multiple antennae bobbed and weaved as his much smaller front pincers opened and closed nervously. The magnitude of what he was about to unleash weighed heavily on him.

"I have complete confidence in you all. I will look on, and be available to give what advice and suggestion I can, but will otherwise stay out of your way."

Insignia gleaming in the reduced light, Marshall Taww scuttled slightly forward. "We will be relying on you, should the need necessitate, to introduce into the forthcoming clash those special weapons with which you alone have been furnished, Paramount Advisor."

Nodding, Gubujul glanced reflexively across the stone mount in the direction of his personal retinue. Squatting there among other attendants and servants, four stout spralakers surrounded an oval container that had been fashioned from the upper shells of a pair of captured and long-since consumed hawksbills. Polished to a high, dark brown sheen, the shimmering turtle-shell crate contained certain disturbing talismans the use of which the dread Sajjabax had charged to Gubujul's care and to Gubujul alone.

The Paramount Advisor quite understood the Marshal's concern. Knowing what sinister devices the box held and having been instructed in their use, Gubujul was as afraid for himself should he have to make use of them as he was for their intended targets. In fact, he was downright terrified of the glistening container's contents, though of course he dared not show it.

"Do not worry," he assured the diminutive Marshal with more bravado than he felt. "If and when the need for such intervention arises, I will be there to support you with a sampling of the supreme sortilege of which only the great shaman Sajjabax himself is master."

*If what lies within doesn't tear me to pieces first*, he concluded bleakly to himself.

◊

At first there was panic. It was to be expected. While remote villages and far-flung foraging parties working the most distant northerly reefs had historically been subject to occasional isolated attack by roving packs of enterprising spralakers, Benthicalia's size and strength had kept it from ever being assaulted. That reputation combined with the status enjoyed by the resident and revered Tornal had been sufficient to ensure the city's security for hundreds of years. Suddenly finding itself threatened by not one but two entire spralaker armies came as a shock that found its residents unprepared.

Order was restored quickly enough, however, as municipal authorities unlimbered long-dormant plans for the city's defense in the event of such an unlikely assault. A principal reason Benthicalia had never been attacked was simply because it *did* boast strong, if untested, defenses. When broken, the seals on long disused armories revealed mountains of weaponry. This was rapidly dispersed among an increasingly resolute citizenry. The giant deep-water anemones that thrived atop many buildings were alerted to their forthcoming duties via communication with the fish that lived among them.

Comprised of thousands of coral structures, the maze that was Benthicalia was turned into a death trap for any spralaker that might make it past the city's outer defenses. Even an aged manyarm, if well-armed, could prove nearly impossible to extract from a hole. Any merson could swim circles around an armed spralaker. Citizens invested with long-established rank were quickly assembled into a determined, mobile fighting force under the supervision of the professionals who were responsible for defending travelers and the general population from marauding sharks and other more conventional threats.

Befitting a community its size, Benthicalia rapidly put into the field two contingents of willing fighters each of which by itself was far larger than the force that had driven the invading hardshells from threatened Siriswirll. Confidence and determination soon replaced the panic that had greeted the initial reports of the spralaker incursion. Now under arms, citizens and soldiers alike prepared to defend their city, increasingly confident in their abilities and in the knowledge that in the collective wisdom of the Tornal they were supported by an accumulation of strategic skills that stretched a thousand years and more into Oshenerth's storied past.

Like a flat stone caught in a slow but strong current, the bemused contingent from Sandrift and Siriswirll found itself swept up in the frenzied preparations for the defense of the city. Drifting above the ancient, eroded outer wall of coral blocks that enclosed and protected the north side of the terraced metropolis from spralaker attack, the visitors from the upper reefs argued among themselves how they could best be of assistance in the forthcoming clash. As transients they constituted an independent entity that would be allowed to make its own decisions and operate according to its own rules. So long as their actions did not conflict with Tornal-transmitted tactics, they could participate in the forthcoming fight however they saw fit.

While there was little doubt among the visitors that they were obligated to take part in the great battle to come, there was at least one who was not afraid to dissent.

Floating in near darkness high above the city wall, his face visible only because of a necklace of semi-soft luminescent tunicates, Chachel peered into the dark distance and voiced his discontent.

"We helped to save Siriswirll and nearly got killed for our trouble. We've come all this way to Benthicalia so that Oxothyr could ask his question of the Tornal." Turning slightly in the water, he looked to his right. "If the danger that brought us here in the first place exceeds that threatened by this impending onslaught, shaman, shouldn't you ask your question and see us away from here before chaos erupts all around like the black smokers that surround the city?"

"I might have expected you to say something like that." Nearby, Jorosab growled his contempt. "I'm only surprised it took you this long. Of course, someone missing half a leg and a whole eye might be expected to be hesitant to go into battle against a fully-equipped army." When Chachel refused to be baited and simply ignored him, the muscular Sandrift soldier used his spear to gesture at the city behind them. "These people need our help."

Chachel gazed stonily at his colleague. "So does the shaman." His attention snapped back to Oxothyr.

*Everyone needs my help*, the elderly octopod mused tiredly. Individuals like the changeling. Towns like Siriswirll. Cities like Benthicalia. Perhaps all of Oshenerth. With every passing day he was increasingly aware of the burden that had been placed on him by his damnable perception. He would have been happy to be free of it. Yet he could no more ignore what he sensed than he could blind himself to the neediness of those depending on him.

*I should have mated*, he thought wearily. *I should have had offspring.* How he longed for the peaceful, scholarly confines of his secure, silent abode in the reef near Sandrift! For the time to study, to learn, to analyze. Instead of private revelation he found himself compelled to spend precious life-hours preserving public welfare. He was only able to rationalize his continuing efforts by reminding himself that if the lands of the reefs fell to the looming threat from the north, his cozy refuge would be overwhelmed as utterly as that of any simple villager or farmer. While not a deciding factor, it was nice when private needs inadvertently benefited the public good.

He could have simply fled. To the distant west, perhaps, and its mysterious but purportedly hospitable waters. He could have taken Sathi and Tythe with him and left the defiant Chachel and the confused changeling Irina and all the bewildered and panicky inhabitants of Sandrift and Siriswirll and Benthicalia and all the other towns and cities of the south to their own devices. But that, in its turn, would have given rise to another problem.

He would have been obliged thereafter to live with himself.

He became aware they were all staring at him, his two anxious famuli included. So many eyes, so many needs—merson as well as manyarm. Knowing they were expecting him to respond, he raised one arm.

"You are both correct. Jorosab is right when he declares that the people of Benthicalia deserve our support." Penetrating eyes shifted in the dim light. "Chachel is right when he says that we should stay focused on the greater danger. You ask me to resolve the conundrum. I need not do so because it is resolved for us."

Fittingly, both Chachel and Jorosab looked confused by the shaman's finding. So did Poylee, who had taken the opportunity to show her support for the hunter's position by moving closer to him. Not that it mattered to her what position he espoused.

Oxothyr proceeded to explain himself. "The two spralaker armies are almost within striking distance of the city. As at Shakestone, they will be intent on slaughter and plunder. To ensure that they maximize both, they will have sent out flanking patrols in every direction. Were we to try and leave now, even after having gained the Tornal's answer to my question, the chances of running into such a patrol would be very great. The hardshells are not likely to repeat the mistake they made at Siriswirll and allow the city's residents to put out a call for reinforcements."

Chachel remained defiant. "Our people have been hardened by travel and by battle. There is no spralaker patrol we could not defeat."

Oxothyr was as patient with his explanations as the hunter was keen with his objections. "I do not disagree with your assessment of our fighting ability. Any such success, though, would be conditional upon the length of time required to achieve it. A patrol encountered need only send out a single messenger to request assistance. If we could not defeat our adversaries speedily, we would run the very real risk of being set upon by hastily summoned spralaker reinforcements. Remember that we speak now of advancing *armies*. This is not Siriswirll."

As an ordinary (if marginal) citizen of Sandrift, Chachel could think of several additional objections to the shaman's reasoning. As a highly experienced hunter, he could not. Grudgingly, he conceded the octopod's point.

"Then we stay and fight!" Jorosab sounded vindicated.

"Only as long as we must," Oxothyr explained. "The instant I think we can obtain an answer from the Tornal as to the possible whereabouts of the Deep Oracle, we will leave—even if we have to fight our way out. As I said, both of your positions in this matter are valid."

He hoped his response had satisfied their contradictory concerns. More importantly, he had maintained peace within the group.

Drifting off to one side, Irina had looked on in silence while paying close attention to the debate. The surrounding intermittent light served to concentrate one's attention and senses wonderfully well. Though she thought she had grown used to the all-pervasive deep-sea gloom, she found herself having to glance down often at the reassuring bioluminescent radiance of the metropolis below. Many of the intense points of blue, green, and red light were in motion as Benthicalia's inhabitants scurried and swam to and fro to prepare the defense of the city. Viewing the fever of activity from above was akin to watching clusters of stars caught in a whirlpool.

The more she drifted in the pale organic luminosity and the more she thought about Chachel's objections over staying to aid in the defense of the city, the more she felt herself out of place. High up in the sun-kissed reefs where she was surrounded by gaudy sea life, where everywhere she looked there was a new life form, a new wonder, a new delight, it was easier to come to terms with her mysteriously altered existence. In contrast, and despite the undeniable attractions Benthicalia offered, down in the dark depths the alienness of her changed surroundings pressed in much closer, constricting her thoughts and challenging her perceptions.

She missed her former life. She missed her friends, ordinary everyday entertainment, familiar food, stress-free socializing. She missed going to work in the morning, even though it meant day after day of peering into other peoples' mouths. She missed knowing what was going on in *her* world even though there was more than enough happening in this one to occupy anyone's mind.

Missing all that, she wondered if she herself was missed.

Why couldn't she have been offered a choice? Why had fate and the sea decided to pick on her? What had she done to so offend Providence that it had caused her to be dragged down beneath the surface to dwell among touchy water-breathing humanoids and frequently inscrutable cephalopods?

Then she remembered that the alternative would probably have been drowning or death from starvation and exposure. Viewed in that light her present circumstances, an incipient war notwithstanding, seemed less of an imposition.

Oxothyr was pointing in her direction. Following the shaman's gestures, Chachel and Jorosab had also turned toward her. Drifting near the hunter, Poylee favored Irina with the usual half-loathing, half-bemused expression she reserved especially for the changeling from the void.

"What do you think, Irina?" the manyarm mage asked her.

The unexpected and unprecedented request for her opinion left her more than a little startled. "What? I'm not sure I ..."

"The shaman wants to know what you think we should do." Poylee interrupted impatiently, as though explaining to a child. "Not that I understand why he should care, but it seems that he does."

Irina considered. Maybe Oxothyr thought that because of her alien origins she might bring some unexpected insight to the quandary. Maybe he felt she could access information beyond their ken. Perhaps he hoped she might offer a solution neither he nor any of the rest of them could see. If so, the shaman was bound to find her response disappointing.

"I haven't got a clue," she finally declared. Though she was addressing herself to Oxothyr, all heard.

"That's just what I've been saying all along." Having delivered herself of that opinion Poylee inverted herself, her feet pointing surfaceward, and dove toward the city. Jorosab followed on her heels.

Chachel held back long enough to swim up to Irina. Unlike Poylee his expression was impossible to read, being as it was merely one of many variations of his entrenched stoicism.

"You really have no suggestions as to how we, as visitors to this place, should proceed?" Stolid though his tone was, he could not entirely keep his disappointment from showing.

She shook her head. "Despite what some people may choose to believe, I don't have any mystical powers, Chachel. To foresee, or predict, or anything else. If I did, do you think I'd have let myself lapse into the condition I was in when you and Glint found me?"

He nodded appreciatively. "At least you are honest. Most would try to boast, or at least to demur in hopes of elevating their standing in the eyes of their companions. I commend you on your candor." With that he turned and, replicating Poylee's dive and accompanied by Glint, headed back down toward the lights of the city.

She watched him depart, wondering as she did so why she might wish for him to compliment something more intimate and less esoteric than her integrity. The light touch of a tentacle broke her contemplation and made her turn.

All hypnotically weaving arms and pulsing bioluminescence, Oxothyr had come up behind her. Glowing green and lined with bright blue spots, Sathi and Tythe flanked the shaman like patrol boats escorting a cruiser.

"I did not mean for my question to make you uncomfortable, Irina-changeling." Uncoiling to its full length in front of her, another arm gestured downward. "As their experience to such phenomena as yourself is limited, so inevitably must be their responses."

"It's all right, shaman." She shrugged. "I'm getting used to it. I just wonder why they think I might be able to do something special when I couldn't prevent myself from nearly dying before I was brought to Sandrift."

"I don't think they *believe* you can do something," he replied softly. "I think it is their hope." Great round, black-gold eyes regarded her in the near-darkness. "As it is mine, for all that I know better."

"Such hopes are misplaced," she informed him without hesitation. "I'm only a person, like Poylee or like yourself." A slight smile creased her face as the two famuli giggled. "Well, maybe not exactly like yourself."

"But you are not like anyone else, Irina-changeling. You are only like you. As are we all." He sighed, expelling a flow of slightly warmer water and just the tiniest splotch of phosphorescent ink by way of punctuation. "Come. Time contracts, and as the spralaker armies draw near the open water even here becomes a less friendly venue for casual banter." He and the two famuli started downward, swimming backward with deliberate slowness so that she could keep up.

"The spralakers," she ventured as she joined them. "They don't really have a chance of conquering Benthicalia, do they?"

"We don't know their full strength," Oxothyr replied. "We do not know who leads them or what skills they might possess. In the realworld, everything is possible. Merely because one objects to tragedy does not mean it will not occur. Benthicalia's defenses appear strong, and its people have the leadership of the Tornal. No matter the spralaker numbers or capabilities, they will not find this city as easy to capture as an isolated bommie defended by a couple of manyarms and a few bewildered fish."

They were nearly back in the city when she thought to ask, "Do they fight on behalf of this singular coldness you've spoken of, Oxothyr? Is that what these unusual spralaker incursions are all about?"

"I wish I knew, Irina-changeling. It is one of many things I wish I knew." Oxothyr did not have a brow to furrow, but the highly flexible skin above his eyes crinkled. "I cannot say if there is a connection between this lesser peril and the greater one I continue to sense." He turned a vivid pink spotted with yellow. "Be so good as to allow me enough room in which to contemplate one apocalypse at a time, please."

"Yes," piped up Tythe. "Your presence and your constant questions crowd out important thoughts in the Master's mind!"

Sweeping outward, a tentacle whacked the squid between head and mantle, sending the much smaller cephalopod spinning through the water like a misguided torpedo. "I can manage my own intellectual luggage, thank you, famulus."

The squid's arms drooped low as he regained control and leveled out. "I apologize, Master. My concern was, as always, for your welfare."

"Your concern is recognized. Be conscious of your position, lest I tender it to another." Looking back at Irina, who was swimming downward beside him, he added almost casually, "Would you possibly be open to such an offer? If you remain among us you must one day pick a profession."

The bubbles that emerged from her throat carried her laughter upward. "I'm pretty good with all the standard dental tools, and I can spot problem areas almost as well as the several dentists I worked for, but I'm afraid I don't have any aptitude for magic."

"How," the eight-armed, slack-bodied shaman asked, cocking one vertically pupiled eye in her direction, "do you know— changeling?"

◊

Had she not already seen for herself what the spralakers were capable of, Irina would not have believed them able to pose a danger to a city as large and resourceful as Benthicalia. The best of the hardshells could swim but poorly, leaving them always at the mercy of attack from above. Most could only walk, and therefore only attack, sideways. Those crustaceans who could advance in a straightforward manner, such as the caridae and nephropidae, suffered from their own deficiencies. With the exception of Sajjabax's notably ferocious family, the majority of caridae were more like Gubujul—fragile and easily dispatched. In contrast, the powerful nephropidae tended to be slow-moving as well as slow-witted.

It was left to exceptional individuals such as Gubujul and his Marshals to promulgate strategy, and to the mid-level spralaker officers to maintain control over the surging mass of lesser-minded soldiers. Such troops were brave to the point of recklessness, but they needed constant guidance.

Irina knew nothing of the Paramount Advisor and his general staff as she hovered with her companions above the city's North Wall and gazed out at what appeared to be a lake of muttering fire. The light came from the emanations of the tens of thousands of bioluminescent salps, corals, fish, and other growths and creatures that the first spralaker army had suborned for its use. Stretching off into the distant dark, it was a sweeping glow that faded only with distance. In contrast, the hair-raising skitter-scratch that echoed across the intervening plain arose from the chattering of thousands of spralaker throats. Passing through water far more lucidly than it ever could through air, it was clearly audible throughout the city.

"There are an awful lot of them," she whispered worriedly. "More than at Siriswirll."

"Far more."

Hanging beside her, Chachel used one hand to make a minor adjustment to his prosthetic right leg even as the other gripped a spear tightly. Three other bone shafts, each equally as long and deadly as the one he held, were slung in a scabbard across his back. Nearby, Poylee clutched her own weapons while Glint brandished a pair of short, powerful bows. The cuttlefish bore four small arrow quivers; one each strapped to his dorsal side, the ventral, left and right. A few dozen cuttlefish and squid so armed could unleash hundreds of short bone or urchin shafts at once even while maneuvering nimbly through the water. No spralaker could match their agility or rate of firepower. On the other hand, an arrow had to hit just the right spot to best a hardshell's natural armor.

The spear Irina held loosely in her right hand and the short, curved bone sword strapped to her waist felt less foreign now after the battle at Siriswirll. Despite the newfound skill with which they had been employed, in close quarters she would still rely on the knife from her own world, with its titanium blade and composite handle.

Hopefully she would not be called upon to use any of them. Though Oxothyr and Jorosab had volunteered their group to the defense of the East Wall, their offer had been refused. As guests and non-residents, they were not obligated to participate in the defense of the city. It was enough that they were willing to contribute to the reserve forces.

She continued to gaze out at the seemingly endless flickering mass of blue and green light. "I asked Oxothyr, but what do you think, Chachel? Do you believe they can take the city?"

The hunter grunted. "The wall here is old but high and well-built. It is not a temporary defensive structure like the one that was put up by the citizens of Siriswirll." He paused. "But I have never seen or heard of so many spralakers in one place. And this that we are facing is only one of two such armies. The other, we have been told by our scouts, will likely be attacking the lower terraces. The city must therefore defend itself on two fronts, north and west, much like a hunter caught between circling sharks." Turning in the water, his features thrown into relief by the city light from behind and below, he met her gaze evenly.

"I honestly cannot speak to the eventual outcome, Irina. I don't know enough about formal military tactics. I know how to cope with a school of makos, or engage in formal duel with a billfish, but military matters of this scope are outside my experience." He gestured with his spear. "There is a difference between a hunter and a soldier."

"I'm neither one," she murmured softly. "My trade involves healing, not destroying."

Kicking once, he crossed the rest of the way to her. His voice lost some of its habitual hardness. "You did well at Siriswirll. I saw you thrust."

She looked over at him. "It wasn't as hard as I thought. I was fighting oversized prawns and crabs—spralakers—and not people. I don't know if I could kill a merson, for example." Suddenly uncomfortably aware of his proximity she glanced to one side, where Glint was looking on patiently and, uncharacteristically, in silence. "And I don't know if I can ever eat calamari again."

"What's 'calamari'?" the cuttlefish asked curiously.

"Not you," she was able to explain truthfully. "Right now I don't want to go there." She turned back to Chachel. "I'm helping Oxothyr because he's helping me."

The hunter nodded somberly, his chin almost touching hers. She was breathing faster. "Poor, honest changeling," he murmured gently. "Nothing more could be expected of you." Pivoting in the water, he backed off as he returned his attention to the looming spralaker horde. She swallowed. Something had just happened, and she wasn't sure what.

"They'll be coming soon," he announced in his familiar curt tone. "Don't forget—with the sidewalkers, aim your spear for the open mouth and your knife for the eyes. Watch always the sideways swing of the main claws."

"I—I'll remember," she assured him. She felt she had to say something else. Something more. Keeping her voice low, she added, "Whatever happens, Chachel, I want to thank you and Glint again for everything you've done for me. And no matter the outcome, I want you to know that I don't think—I don't think that you're a hostile, antisocial recluse."

He looked back at her. She thought he might have smiled, albeit briefly, but she could not be certain.

"Ah, Irina-changeling, that's where you're wrong."

Kicking forcefully, he moved farther away from her and toward Glint. Using every one of his ten arms, the cuttlefish had begun notching arrows simultaneously into both bows. Looking on, she considered Chachel's words in light of his actions, seeking contradiction. Seeking, and hoping for it.

Finding it, and possibly other revelations, would have to wait until later.

Uttered in unison by ten thousand inhuman throats, a great grating, nerve-tingling ululation had arisen in the north.

The spralakers were coming.

# – XX –

**T**here seemed no end to them.

Whether the marching masses ended at the limits of her vision or extended onward all the way to the distant reaches of the lower reefs Irina could not tell. Then the first lines of foe, all spears and knives and scimitar-like claws, were assailing the great outer wall of the city and reality overcame speculation.

Just as it had been at Siriswirll, the collective assault bore only passing resemblance to an attack on land. Projectiles shot or thrown through water were soon slowed by the medium that surrounded them, though short-range thrusts and heaves were sufficiently robust to frequently find their mark. Unlike a human army, the spralaker horde had no need of scaling ladders to ascend the wall. Powerful gripping legs allowed the weakest of them to commence the vertical ascent under their own power, their climbing abilities putting to shame the most accomplished human mountaineers.

Their ease of ascent was countered by defenders who could, essentially, fly. Swimming at high speed, troops of mersons and manyarms soared above the advancing hard-shelled host, diving upon them to attack with spears and arrows. Teams consisting of four mersons apiece carried nets each of which supported a single large, heavy rock. Dropped from a safe height, each massive stone could crush the protective shells of one or more spralakers below. With so many massed targets to choose from, the stone-droppers did not even have to aim.

Their inner lights dimmed, a squad of unseen, nearly blind spralakers succeeded in scaling the wall at the level of the seventeenth terrace. In the absence of illumination their intrusion passed unobserved until they were over the top and in among the city's noncombatants. There they murdered in darkness and with abandon until their presence was frantically noted and a troop from the community's reserve forces was sent to surround and exterminate them.

No such difficulties of discernment declared themselves on the main field of battle, where the presence of bioluminescence in abundance permitted defender and assailant alike to see each other clearly with an eye to mutual destruction. Used to yellowish light, Irina found the blue-green-lit chaos unsettling, though no more so than the casualties that were rapidly mounting into the hundreds on the spralaker side and the dozens on that of Benthicalia. Plucked from where they lay or drifted, the wounded were rushed to medical facilities deep within the city. Stopping bleeding under pressure and under water, she learned, required the application of carefully conserved organic materials and, in some cases, more than a little Tornal-taught magic. The result was that people died, but not in numbers that would otherwise have been the case.

The clash along several sections of wall generated light enough to illuminate the surrounding black water for hundreds of feet in every direction. Still, the line of battle was so long and deep that she could see only a portion of it, and nothing at all of the equally ferocious clash that was taking place at the same time between the defenders of the city's westernmost terrace and the spralaker Second Army. Though not privy to the reports that passed between the commanders of both locations, she gleaned enough from what little she overheard to know that the struggle transpiring to the west was every bit as hard-fought and extensive as the one taking place before her.

Lit by their own internally generated luminescence or that of the smaller creatures traveling upon them, galaxies of spralakers threw themselves at star clusters of defenders. The water above the advancing multitude of red and white and blue-tinged shell and claw was shot through with sprinting mersons and even faster manyarms. Occasionally descending to engage in hand-to-claw combat, mersons dodged around claws capable of pulling off limbs while manyarms relied on their greater agility and an occasional burst of disorienting fluorescent ink to protect themselves. Everywhere, water was suffused with blood.

It was disturbing to see that the spralakers had solved the problem of almost always having to attack while moving sideways. Riding atop their larger brethren like turrets atop tanks, smaller spralakers were able to turn and fire in any direction while their mounts maintained a steady sideways advance. This unsettling development represented yet another new and unexpected tactic on the part of the enemy.

"So much cooperation, so much preparation." Watching the battle from a portico of purple coral behind and above the city wall, his arms writhing with anxiety, Oxothyr scrutinized the continuing offensive with evident alarm. "Something has happened to alter their customary fighting technique. The spralaker spirit has been imbued not only with new fervor, but fresh ideas. That is what unsettles me."

"You still have no idea what's behind all these changes you see?" Irina stayed close to the shaman, feeing safer in the shelter of his waving tentacles than anywhere else.

"Only that every time I fixate on such things I feel afresh the coldness of which I have so often spoken. I think that if I could only reach through to the source, I would find the explanation I seek. Despite my most forceful efforts to that end it remains tantalizingly out of reach." His body turned a quietly amused pale orange. "When one has eight arms and something still remains out of reach, it is more disconcerting than you can imagine."

To change the subject and hopefully relieve the mage of his restless discomfort, she used her spear to point toward the raging battle. "So many of the spralakers generate no light of their own, yet these thousands appear well-equipped with illumination."

"As are mersons," the shaman reminded her. "Yet there are some spralakers who can produce their own illumination, as can many of my own kind." Reaching out with one cable-like arm, he eased her slightly forward. "There, to the northeast. The defense weakens. I see spralakers coming over the wall. Ready yourself."

Clutching her spear tighter, she looked where he was pointing. Having cleared the upper parapet of defenders, lines of white shell were scrabbling over the top of the stonework despite the death frenzied mersons and manyarms were raining down on them from above. Burbles and cackles of jubilation emanated from the triumphant spralakers.

They were in for a surprise.

The enemy's screeches of triumph proved premature. Hidden behind Benthicalia's outer wall was a second barrier. Lower than the one that fronted it, at first glance it seemed as if it surely would prove even easier for the invaders to surmount than the first. Unlike the outer wall, it was composed entirely of deep-water red and black coral. Polyps that had been grown, cajoled, and manipulated to create an obstacle that instead of being smooth-faced like the outer wall was riddled with points, projections, and protuberances. The resulting coral maze was deep enough, tortuous enough, and sufficiently convoluted to stop a line of tanks or paralyze a mathematician.

Surprised by the presence of the second barrier, the intruding spralakers immediately started to clamber up this unexpected inner fortification. Their efforts soon gave rise to growing confusion. Amalgamated arcs and upthrusts of sharp coral defied easy ascent. They scored and sometimes even punctured the shells that scraped against them. Surmounting the initial stone knots, one heavily armed adversary after another found themselves confronting a dip, or hollow, or series of sharp extrusions. Crack spralaker troops became lost or trapped within the impenetrable, unyielding maze. Unable to advance or retreat or even move sideways, they became easy targets for the boneless manyarms who could slip effortlessly through the very same gaps that had ensnared their brawny but blundering enemies.

The scenario was repeated along the length of the central terraces. Time and again, groups of spralakers would succeed in driving the defenders from the top of the outer wall, only to find themselves cornered when they attempted to penetrate the second and far more difficult inner fortifications.

Which was not to say that damage was not done and destruction not meted out by the attacking horde. Massive spralakers swinging clubs studded with needle-sharp sea urchin spines ripped apart manyarm and merson bodies alike. Smaller aggressors hurled bundles of razor clams, urchin spines, and nematocyst sachets from short slings, bringing down swooping defenders who in search of the easier kill dipped too close to the marching multitude.

When word of the existence of the previously unseen inner defensive wall finally reached the general staff of the spralaker First Army, it developed that Gubujul's experienced Mud Marshals had a countering tactic for it as well. Like so many of the stratagems that infused traditional hardshell warfare, it relied for success on the engagement of the slow but steady.

Big as buses, hulking multilegged representatives of the homaridae were brought forward. More heavily armored than any of their smaller cousins, they set to work with their huge front claws at chewing away sections of the outer wall. Once it was breached, they would not repeat the mistake of trying to climb over the inner coral labyrinth. They would simply, if slowly, chew their way through it as well, and into the unprotected city proper.

Seeing what was happening and quickly divining the intent, Benthicalia's defenders immediately launched a fresh succession of attacks from above. So heavily built were the coral-grinding homaridae that stones dropped from above simply glanced off their body armor. Meanwhile, the cream of the spralaker First Army did its best to keep the increasingly desperate merson and manyarm defenders from slowing the relentless, disciplined assault.

At the same time, swarms of much smaller spralakers, lesser cousins of Gubujul and his ilk, were sent scampering over sections of outer wall from which the defenders had been driven. Armed only with small knives, these thousands of prawns and other minor crustaceans were little threat to well-armed and trained merson and manyarm soldiers. But where their larger cousins found themselves slowed or trapped by the inner coral maze, these smaller invaders were able to negotiate the tubes and tunnels, hollows and cracks. By themselves they could not take the city—but they could occupy the attention of defenders whose skills were needed more urgently elsewhere, and sow panic and confusion through the community at large.

Several came swimming fitfully up toward Oxothyr and his companions. Sheathing her spear, Irina gripped her dive knife in one hand and the curved merson weapon she had been given in the other. These diminutive crustacean warriors were weak swimmers even by hardshell standards and she had no trouble dispatching dozens of them, as did Poylee and the others. Spralaker body parts were soon raining down on the section of inner city wall immediately below. A few mersons suffered superficial scratches in consequence of the massed attack while the swifter and more agile manyarms avoided injury altogether.

But while Irina and her friends were occupied in dealing with the widespread but ultimately feeble attack with all the gusto of a clutch of amateur ninja turned crazed sashimi chefs, they were therefore unable to assist elsewhere in the defense of the city. The widespread assault by thousands of lesser spralakers was not intended nor expected to conquer, but rather to divert, tie up, occupy, irritate, and otherwise buy time for the brute homaridae to complete their task of gnawing several routes through Benthicalia's inner as well as outer walls.

As soon as the swarm of lesser, poorly armed spralakers was sufficiently reduced in number, Irina and her friends were ordered to join in a group assault on the trio of homaridae who had breached the outer wall and had by now eaten a wide path halfway through the inner coral barrier. Weeks ago she would have been helpless to assist. Her legs would by now have been dead in the water. But day after day of swimming instead of walking had strengthened the muscles running from her hips to her feet to a degree where she could have competed seriously among the better swimmers back home. It was good that her endurance and speed had increased to the extent that they had. She was not competing for points now, or for gym club medals. Like her new-found friends, she was swimming for her life.

Soaring over the three mammoth homaridae, she joined her companions and dozens of reserve troops in launching spears, arrows, and rocks at the armored, bulldozing monsters below.

"Aim for the eyes!" she had been instructed, and she tried her best to do so. Meanwhile, she had to take care to keep out of range of the weapons wielded by the homaridae's escorts. A few of these armored bodyguards struggled to swim upward to confront the counterattack. Devoid of fins, they had to kick hard with their many legs to gain any height. While the best of their continuing attempts were invariably ineffective, Irina found herself admiring the effort that was put into them. Courage and determination were not the sole province of mersons and manyarms.

Though blinded by arrows shot from diving manyarms, one of the homaridae continued to grind resolutely forward until a succession of well-aimed stones eventually cracked the shell covering its head. Spears flung through the resulting fissures finally pierced its brain. It slowed, stopped, and was unceremoniously shoved aside by one of its still functioning brethren. A lucky arrow severed a vital nerve in a second monster, sending it running in wild circles to trample a number of its own followers. Able at last to concentrate all their efforts on the final surviving homaridae, the increasingly confident Benthicalian forces were preparing to put it permanently out of action and out of life when the spralakers launched a full-scale fresh offensive.

Chaos ensued.

Embracing a diversity of lethal jellyfish, the spralakers riding on an assortment of rays dove down on the wall's defenders from above. The deadly coelenterates the hardshell riders wrangled had been trained to fire and release their nematocysts on command. By surrendering their poison cells in this unnatural fashion they would eventually be left without the means to defend or feed themselves, like honeybees deprived of their stingers. This concerned their handlers not in the slightest.

Caught unawares by this new kind of symbiotic attack, soft-skinned mersons and manyarms were hard-pressed to dodge the tiny but lethal missiles. While the forcefully expressed nematocysts could not travel very far underwater, at close range they could be fatal.

Incapacitated by the stings a number of defenders went limp in the water, their muscles paralyzed by an assortment of jellyfish toxins. Those who did not succumb to the poison on the spot drifted downward, there to be set upon and gleefully pulled to pieces by the eager spralakers who awaited them.

Twisting and turning to avoid water that was now filled with thousands of tiny, deadly darts, Irina found herself joining her surviving companions in retreat. The ray-led attack force pursued them over the walls and into the city. There the spralaker riders proceeded to rain death onto the open corridors and pathways below. Their assault was only eventually offset when in their zeal to commit slaughter, some of them dove too low.

But while the spralakers could train domesticated jellyfish to fire their poisonous nematocysts, they were not the only creatures who commanded such weapons.

Long resident on the roofs and spires of Benthicalia, tenant anemones responded to the diving attacks by unleashing stinging cells of their own. Their paralyzed wings stilled, stunned rays spiraled downward toward the city streets. There they and their riders suffered the same fate as those mersons and manyarms caught outside the city walls. Residents swarmed over them, chopping the unfortunate rays into pieces while hunting down their scuttling spralaker riders as the latter frantically tried to conceal themselves in clefts and crevices in the surrounding buildings.

All along the city walls to the east and to the west the battle raged. The deep sea was filled with screams and shrieks, hisses and chittering as mersons and manyarms, spralakers and rays were laid low by a vast assortment of weapons and willpower. Once gained, neither side was willing to concede so much as a foot of territory. Neither backed away from confrontation despite frequent disparities in strength and numbers. All fighters exhibited the unique individual characteristics for which they were noted.

Along with increasing exhaustion Irina found herself yielding to a growing numbness. Had the struggle been taking place in the shallows where blood would show red instead of black she did not know if she could have continued. As it was, she had a hard enough time swimming through clouds of dark liquid whose composition she knew was thicker than water.

◊

Frustration at the faltering progress of the offensive induced Cavaumaz to position himself in the forward ranks of the attack. Even from a distance, Gubujul could see the great right claw of the Mud Marshal rising and falling above the fray as the fearless general officer sought to rally and reinvigorate the assault. The Paramount Advisor's attention was almost immediately diverted by the arrival of Bejuryar and Taww.

"How goes the latest offensive?" Fiddling restively with a strand of small pearls trailing from the base of one antenna, Gubujul tried to devote his attention equally to both of the general officers.

Taww's tone reflected her mood. "Not well, Paramount Advisor."

"Not at all as we hoped," added the bigger Bejuryar.

Discounting these off-putting assessments, Gubujul strove to appear assured. "Time and numbers are our allies. With them on our side we will eventually overcome and overwhelm."

"I'd rather have another ten battalions than all the time in the world," Taww countered curtly. "The city is strong, its fighters determined, and whoever is formulating defensive strategy most capable."

"What of our small-knife and ray swarms?" Gubujul asked tentatively.

"Effective in spots. Not sufficiently dominant to turn the tide. They have shown themselves able to penetrate and wreak temporary havoc, but not to triumph." Extending to their maximum length, Bejuryar's eyestalks inclined toward his titular, if not strategic, superior. "Should you be in possession of any devices seriously thaumaturgic, Paramount Advisor, now would be a most excellent time for their reveal."

"I don't know if ..." Gubujul stiffened. Not his spine, for he did not have one, but the muscles that ran along his shell. Here was his chance to shine. Now more than ever he would be compelled to live up to the lofty position that had been bestowed upon him, or fail in the trying.

"Come with me," he told the two senior officers briskly.

Well to the rear of the fighting, the stacked cylinders of tightly woven sea fan lay innocuous and untouched among the small mountain of stores that had accompanied the spralaker First Army all the way from the Northlands. Sentries not yet bored with their good fortune at having been assigned to relatively safe guard duty snapped to attention at the unannounced and unexpected arrival of the Paramount Advisor and the two Mud Marshals. Gubujul indicated the mound of six-foot long cylinders.

"There!"

Taww eyed the pile dubiously. "Your pardon, Paramount Advisor Gubujul, but—'there' what?"

All six of their superior's antennae were in motion. "You will see." *I hope*, he added quietly to himself.

The shaman Sajjabax's instructions had been very specific, and Gubujul had taken care to memorize them faithfully. Now was the moment to put both faith and memory to the test. His legs fluttering to drive him through the water, he approached the forefront of the collection of cylinders. Raising both long arms, he spread wide the pincers at each end and intoned as vigorously as he could in his lamentably high-pitched voice.

"*Seremus serivane! Columin fatalune,*" he declaimed forcefully in the old language of his cannibal spralaker ancestors. Turning, he clamped both claws shut, pointed them in the direction of Benthicalia, and commanded evocatively, "Seek and kill!"

A long moment transpired. Nothing happened. The always impatient Taww uttered something under her breath that, while incomprehensible, stank clearly of disgust. Attentive to the taxing work that lay ahead, a more phlegmatic Bejuryar started to turn away. If Gubujul could have perspired, he would have begun to do so.

"Wait." Eyes forward, claws clenched, Taww stopped and pointed. "What's happening there?"

The sealed end of one container had begun to bulge outward. Nearby, a second cylinder showed evidence of a comparable swelling. Within minutes every one of the stacked tubes was showing signs of similar internal pressure, as if something within was straining to emerge. Or be born.

Without sound or warning the first cylinder burst apart. That which had been contained within not so much by tight sea fan weave but by Sajjabax's spell exploded forth. A second cylinder ruptured, then two more.

With instinct born of long soldiering, both Marshals pulled eyes and limbs back into their bodies as the swarm of strange creatures shot past overhead. Panicked guards scrambled for cover. It was left to Gubujul, antennae waving gracefully, to stand tall and proud as the last of the apparitions sped off, heading south at incredible speed. He did so not because he was any braver than Taww or Bejuryar or the flustered sentries, but because he didn't know any better.

Emerging from where they had withdrawn into his shell, Bejuryar's eyestalks turned in the direction taken by the bevy of departed specters. So fast were they traveling that they had already passed from view.

"What—what *are* those things?"

Though Gubujul's forearms were too long to place on the hips he did not have, his satisfaction was nonetheless evident. "The great mystic Sajjabax made them. By crossing spears hewn from the toughest bone with the swiftest of fish, he has brought forth the Talspears." All eight of his legs kicking in unison, he started swimming back toward the mount of rock he had chosen for his point of dominion. "I regret only that there is not enough light for us to see clearly the devastation they are about to inflict on our enemies."

"I saw the creatures." Taww had to work hard to keep up with the Paramount Advisor. "They had no eyes that I could see. How will they know to tell friend from foe?"

Enjoying his moment of ascendancy, Gubujul glanced condescendingly over at the Mud Marshal. "That is a mark of the estimable Sajjabax's acumen. No Talspear, I was told, will harm anything that wears a shell or its skeleton on its outside. All spralakers have shells or exoskeletons. No mersons do, nor any manyarms save the lazy nautilus."

Walking sideways in parallel to the others, Bejuryar found himself marveling at the sagacity of the great and terrible Sajjabax. "This is a fearsome creation. With the wisdom of the wizard on our side, we may yet prevail utterly."

Flush with the triumph of the moment, Gubujul could only agree. "I for one have never doubted it."

◊

Having returned to the vicinity of the inner barrier, Irina was hovering just above the thrusting projections of the still unbreached coral maze when the initial wave of Talspears struck. It was Chachel, however, who first identified this latest attack as something radically different than anything that had preceded it and marking a new and frightening escalation of spralaker warfare.

Drifting beside the merson while holding onto her own weapon, Irina strained to see beyond the still largely intact outer wall. "Something's coming this way that I don't recognize, Chachel. I think," she squinted into the blue-green light, "it must be some kind of fish. More allies of the spralakers?"

"Not fish." Kicking once, Chachel moved slightly forward of the changeling. "Not like anything I've ever seen before."

"Nor I," added Glint from where he was floating just beneath his friend. "What kind of creatures can these be?"

"Unnatural ones. Manifestations of some foul magic." Though knowing little of sorcery himself, Chachel could recognize it when he saw it. His eyes widened. In all the time she had known him, Irina had never seen the hunter so unsettled. "Glint! Go and find Oxothyr and bring him here. Quickly! Tell him there is evil aswim only he can deal with." He waved an arm at the hovering cephalopod. "Go in haste!"

Spinning around, the cuttlefish vanished cityward in a flash of lingering bioluminescence and trailing tentacles.

Increasingly uneasy, Irina instinctively drifted closer to the bigger merson. "What is it, Chachel? If not some kind of fish, what do you see?"

"Not spralakers. Not manyarms, or fish, or anything else born of an honest egg. I see spears with tails and fins and tiny eyes, and they are moving faster than any possible forbearer." Legs scissoring, he arched his back and dove straight down toward the fortification of the inner wall.

Irina followed without having to be told.

# – XXI –

he Talspears struck the city's outer defenses with the force of a seaquake. Like attenuated torpedoes, they brushed aside parrying attempts by mersons and manyarms alike. Their great speed enabled them to not only run down but also pierce completely through the boneless bodies of vulnerable manyarms. Slaying a merson occasionally gave them pause when they encountered part of a skeleton. Such attacks forced the deadly creations to have to back up and work their way free of the clinging corpses they created.

Mayhem broke out all along the city's northern defenses as one defender after another fell to the streaking, stiletto-like destroyers. Killing them proved nearly impossible. Composed of solid bone except for their flexible tails and fins, the Talspears could not be injured by weapons made of similar material. They were too slender and moved too fast to be hit by otherwise accurate manyarm arrows. Unlike the chunkier, slow-moving spralakers on whose behalf they fought, stones cast in their direction or dropped from above were easily dodged. The Talspears were agile, fast, and lethal.

At great risk to themselves, a number of mersons and manyarms managed to grab hold of solitary Talspears. The friction created by their clinging bodies slowed the slayers and the added weight dragged some down to the walls themselves. There the struggling, pinioned Talspears could be pounded with rocks until their slender bodies cracked. When they did so, they leaked a viscous, reeking fluid that smelled like anything but blood. When one such successful kill occurred close to Irina, the stench of the fetid liquid put her mind of the worst examples of advanced oral necrosis.

Swooping and diving along the length of the inner and outer north walls, the Talspears picked off defenders like needles attacking an anthill. They were too fast and too lethal. Minding Chachel's counsel to stay close, Irina joined Poylee in guarding the hunter's back. Only his agility and his special ability to clot water allowed him to ward off a Talspear that came their way. Shunted aside by Chachel's talent, it streaked past, heading for the inner wall. Irina watched it go, then turned away. There would be others.

A shout from a familiar voice made her turn.

"Glint!" Whirling, she saw the familiar streamlined shape of the glowing cuttlefish heading tail-first toward her. Her heart lifted as she saw that Oxothyr was with him.

And the shaman was not alone.

Borne along by a host of mersons and manyarms, the entire Tornal accompanied the cuttlefish and the mage. A hopeful Irina recognized each ancient ammonite, every wizened orthocera. Clearly, Glint and Oxothyr had convinced the legendary overlords of Benthicalia that the situation was sufficiently dire to demand their personal attention. They would not have left the safety of the palace otherwise.

What could they do, she asked herself. Not only were they incredibly old, they were feeble and slow. Like the spralakers, their bodies were designed for bottom-living. The most active of them could barely elevate into the water column and then swim but fitfully. How could they possibly counter the lightning-fast attacks of the spralakers' malevolent latest weapon? She asked the question of Oxothyr as soon as he rejoined her and her companions. Unhappily, the shaman's response was less than encouraging.

"I wish I knew, Irina-changeling." The octopod's eyes were focused on a flat area on the top of the inner coral wall where, one by one, the Tornal were being gently placed by their solicitous attendants. "But this I do know. Watch, observe, and pay attention, for I am convinced what we are about to see is some of the true wet magic of the ancients."

But even the most efficacious magic takes time to make ready, and the stronger the sortilege, the more time is required for proper preparation. Becoming aware of the cluster of caucusing Tornal, half a dozen Talspears changed course and streaked toward them. Blood and bits of flesh trailed from their sleek flanks and sharp points.

Detecting their approach, several mersons and manyarms swam hard to intercept. Those who managed to do so found themselves mercilessly skewered, knocked aside, or simply avoided as the finned spears homed in on their chosen targets. Looking on from a distance, a wide-eyed Irina caught her breath.

As they took note of the incoming attack, one by one the Tornal's attendants scattered. Having no weapons of their own there was nothing they could do to protect the masters. Increasing its speed and leaving a trail of froth in its wake, the lead Talspear chose as its target the Speaker-to-the-Tornal herself, and struck home with mindless ferocity.

To promptly glance off, leaving behind nothing more damaging than a slight scrape on the Speaker's thick, coiled shell.

The other attacking Talspears' efforts at assassination fared no better. Conjured by Sajjabax, they had been imbued by him with the wherewithal to pierce the soft bodies of spralakers' traditional enemies. Mersons and manyarms were fast and agile, but unlike the spralakers they grew no protective shells.

But the members of the Tornal, ancient and supposedly primitive relatives of modern manyarms, did.

Again and again the determined Talspears swept around in tight circles to launch themselves at the virtually immobile Tornal—and again and again their well-aimed strikes merely slid off the solid shells of ammonite and orthocera. Preoccupied with mounting frustration, wholly single-minded, they ignored everything else. And so one by one they were brought down by the grim-faced mersons and active manyarms who had arrived to swarm them in ever greater numbers.

Elsewhere the fight against their fleet, deadly clones began to turn as alert mersons brought forth from the city tough, finely-woven fishing nets. The inherent speed of the Talspears was not enough to save them once they were entangled in one or more of the nets. Such mesh devices were useless against the spralakers, the smallest of whom could cut their way free with sharp, powerful claws. But against the otherwise deadly Talspears they proved extremely effective, since the living lances had no claws of their own or hands with which to wield net-slicing knives. One by one they were entangled, brought to a halt, and methodically smashed to pieces.

There remained the ongoing threat from the methodically grinding homaridae, who under the protection of swarms of shepherding spralaker soldiers continued to gnaw away at both the outer and inner city walls. Spreading themselves in a line along the top of the inner coral maze, the Tornal raised their tentacles and began to chant in unison. Their primordial sing-song resounded through the coral but did not reach very far.

"What are they singing?" From above, Irina looked on in fascination.

"I do not know." A tangle of luminescent arms hovering beside her, Oxothyr strove for comprehension. "I am acquainted with many spells and chants, but this I cannot identify. It is very old, I think. Some of the wordings I can grasp, but others are strangers to me."

Suddenly Irina found herself pointing. "Look! What's happening there?"

Oxothyr stared. "Odd. The silver light of the night sky far above us is not at its brightest, nor is it the right time of year."

She blinked in confusion. "The right time for what?"

"For the coral to give birth."

All along the length of the high, convoluted inner wall, the coral was spawning. Every kind, every variety, every size, shape, and color had begun to spew forth billows of eggs and milt, all of it ablaze with internal phosphorescence. Steered by the current-chanting of the Tornal, the clouds of luminescent procreation were carried not upward as usual toward the light of the unseen moon, but outward. North, toward the attacking spralaker army.

"I see," Irina murmured. "All those eggs and sperm will stick to the eyes of the enemy, and blind them."

"Yes," agreed Oxothyr, "and perhaps, just perhaps, something else. I think there is more to this than sticks to the eye, changeling."

Given impetus by the Tornal's droning mantra, the living clouds swept toward the outer wall. Those defenders who were unable to swim up and out of the way soon found their clothes and skin and bare flesh coated with hundreds of bits of the highly adhesive macrobiotic mass. Other than inciting some severe itching, the coral spawn caused mersons and manyarms no difficulty.

The reaction was very different when the enormous billowing mass drifted over the outer stone wall and began to settle like a malignant nebula atop the front lines of the besieging spralaker army.

A collective high-pitched shrieking wafted up to where Irina hovered close by the somber shaman. It was louder and more shrill than that which accompanied the typical howl of battle, as if routine death had been magnified by some new horror. Gazing into the dimly-lit distance she could make out where whole clusters of spralaker troops had begun to fray, break, and finally flee. The surviving wall-breaching homaridae they were supposed to defend also turned to try and escape, but like its protectors the tank-like, slow-moving monsters could not escape the smothering of the spreading coral spawn.

The living corals that comprised the inner wall of Benthicalia had fully absorbed the potent enchantment levied upon them by the Tornal. Their spawn had become more than sticky, their presence more than aggravating. Wet magic had transformed them. Now they sought more than simply to mate and attach themselves to a firm foundation.

The Tornal enchantment had turned them hungry.

Specifically, it had inculcated in each and every egg and sperm an appetite for calcium. An appetite whose satiation found most immediate satisfaction in the form the principal chemical component of spralaker shells. A couple of mersons who inadvertently inhaled some of the cloud lost a few teeth to this effect, but those were the only casualties suffered by the shell-less defenders. The mersons' bones were shielded from the voraciously enchanted coral spawn by their soft flesh, and the manyarms had even less to fear. Bending, Chachel made sure the place where his prosthetic half right leg met flesh was tightly sealed against intrusion.

A dense fog of luminous eggs and milt settled on the giant boring homaridae. Huge claws and legs began to scratch, then to strike, and finally to flail at their own body. Transformed spawn ate its way into the shell of every spralaker with whom it came in contact. All along the inner and outer wall the enemy onslaught began to falter as panic spread through the ranks. It is unreasonable to expect a soldier of any species to sustain courage when one's comrades are being devoured before their very eyes.

Those spralakers whose shells were only partially consumed found their soft inner bodies now exposed to the weapons of patrolling mersons and manyarms. Unaffected by the spawn as long as they kept their mouths closed, merson spearmen picked off rising numbers of the increasingly vulnerable enemy. Finding their targets devoid of natural armor, manyarm archers were able to loose their arrows to ever greater effect. The battle for Benthicalia threatened to become a rout fit to make the one at Siriswirll look like an orderly retreat.

From their position atop a stone spire of temporary dominion the trio of Mud Marshals and the Paramount Advisor could make out the spreading pandemonium. Increasingly ill at ease, they had to wait for a runner to arrive with an explanation.

"Spawning coral does not devour shell." Bejuryar was not panicked, but his indecisive tone reflected his sudden confusion. "Eggs and milt do not parasitize."

"There is great sorcery at work here!" Cavaumaz was more conclusive. He and Taww turned as one to the flustered Gubujul. "Our soldiers are brave, but they cannot fight theurgy. Weapon must counter weapon! Type must battle type." With his oversized right claw he pointed past the anxious stenopus toward the shadowy turtleshell box. "Talspears are of no use against small eating things in the millions. We need something vaster and more inclusive."

"I will see...." Turning, Gubujul kicked his way toward Sajjabax's enigmatic container. "There must be something!"

There had to be something, he told himself as the Marshals followed close behind, or they all might as well keep going in the direction he was presently swimming.

The key to the mysterious box swung from a braided chain looped around the Paramount Advisor's neck—or rather, that portion of his integrated body where a neck would have been if he'd had one. It had hung there ever since the Great Lord himself had slipped it over Gubujul's antennae prior to the army's departure from the northlands. Reaching up with a claw, he gripped the sliver of metal firmly between his pincers and pushed it into the lock on the box. The lock itself was an intricate and expensive mechanism, metal that had been forged in the heat of northern black smokers.

Within the lock, something shifted. It might also have cried out softly, though in the din and confusion of battle Gubujul could not be certain.

Removing the key, he let it fall down below his head. With both banded arms he lifted up the curved, polished shell that formed the upper half of the container. He could feel all three of his Marshals crowding close behind him. Their presence was real and physical, not imaginary and mental. Every time they moved, the small volume of water they displaced was sensed by his own body.

The interior of the box was dark. An impatient Taww held out a small, brightly glowing sea slug. The creature's blue-green light illuminated the shallow interior space. Gubujul caught his breath. For once, the constant weaving of his multiple antennae ceased. The box contained a shell.

That was all. A shell, nothing more. No crackling wands, no stoppered vials of olivine volcanic glass, no engraved and bejeweled boxes of precious potion. There was no tablet inscribed with awe-inspiring ciphers, no enchanted weapon gleaming in the dim light. Just a shell. Modest in size, mottled ivory in color, spiral in execution. It lay on a bed of soft salps, barely bestirred by the slight current, mocking those who gazed upon it.

Taww gave voice to what she as well as her colleagues were thinking. "Is this a joke, Paramount Advisor? Or a decoy? Are the true tools of potent necromancy sequestered elsewhere?"

Gubujul was nearly speechless. "I—I'm as shocked as you are. I don't know what to ..."

"It is the Great Lord's way of telling us we have only our own courage and weapons to reply upon," Bejuryar concluded gravely.

"That, or the shaman Sajjabax's sense of humor come to the fore." Cavaumaz sounded resigned. "That is the trouble when one relies upon a master of magic who is demonstrably mad."

Gubujul continued to stare at the shell. True, Sajjabax was quite insane. But while many qualities could be attributed to the court conjurer, the Paramount Advisor had never known humor to be among them. Therefore this cone-shaped shell in its elaborate box must represent something more than just a cavalier attempt at mordant farce. As the three Marshals squabbled among themselves, he reached into the box and picked the shell up in both sets of pincers.

It appeared to be a very ordinary shell, long since abandoned by whatever had once lived in it. Off-white with dark brown splotches, the spiral growth was half his body length. The tip had been broken off. No, wait—he looked closer. The pointed end had been deliberately and carefully sheared, not broken. Where had he seen something like this? At court, of course. Commands shouted through such carefully modified shells emerged enhanced. Experimentally, he brought the trimmed and polished end to his mouth and spoke into it.

It was fortunate the wider, open end of the shell was not pointed at the bickering Marshals, or he would have lost his entire general staff at the mention of a single careless word.

Amplified approximately one and a half million times beyond belief, the sonic blast that emerged from the shell blew a perfect hole in the nearby reef. A dozen unlucky soldiers who happened to be positioned there found themselves blown off the rocks and out of sight. Several less fortunate comrades had their shells and themselves smashed flat.

Lowering the spiral from his mouth, Gubujul eyed it in wonder. Having instantly ceased their bickering, the three Marshals were gaping at him in astonishment. Taww, unsurprisingly, was the first to regain her voice.

"Sound," she marveled. "It magnifies sound. Through what realm or reason or magic I cannot imagine." At the tips of her eyestalks, her slightly oval blue eyes seemed to brighten. "Magnifies it enough to shatter stone." Built as she was parallel to the ground, it was always a strain for her to look up at her colleagues. "Should it not be used to sound a greeting to our friends within the city that lies before us?"

Bejuryar moved to one side. Lowering his massive claw, Cavaumaz scuttled to the other. Stepping forward, Taww demonstrated her usual presumption by placing her right claw firmly against the flank of the far more gracile Gubujul.

"Speak now for all of us, Paramount Advisor. Speak for the First Army. Speak for the northlands entire. Speak for the Great Lord himself and speak for Sajjabax, the rightful and undisputed master of all that is the unknown." Raising her other claw, she gestured in the direction of distant Benthicalia. "Say a word to our adversaries."

Nodding, Gubujul raised the spiral shell in both long, red-banded arms, took aim as best he could with its perfectly round, gaping open end, and declaimed a commoner insult with as much force as he could muster.

What went into the small open end of the spiral shell was a terse curse. What emerged was—something greater.

Instead of dissipating, the Paramount Advisor's slur maintained its coherence even as it strengthened. A shaped charge of focused sound, it grew and grew as it propagated swiftly through the water. The echo of its passing over the milling troops of the First Army tossed unsecured bodies like gymnasts and sent others slamming into their neighbors. Weapons were knocked from claws and strong legs lost their grip on the uneven, rocky ground. Confusion and uncertainty reigned in force. All this was as nothing compared to what happened when the sonic charge struck the outer wall of the city.

Detonating against the stonework in an eruption of sound, the blast sent defenders flying in all directions. Legs and tentacles flailed furiously as their owners sought to regain their equilibrium in the water. Those who were defending directly on or immediately above the section of wall that was impacted were not only flung aside like strips of sea grass, they had each and every one been rendered totally deaf by the concussion.

When the first reports came back to Gubujul and his staff, there was general jubilation. "Curse again," Taww urged him, "and again and again, Paramount Advisor. And when you have tired of visiting insults upon our enemies, we will pass the shell among us and continue your excellent vocal labors!"

A second blast from the shell knocked down the section of outer wall beside the first. The third shattered the maze-work coral behind, producing the first unobstructed route into the city proper. When a crack squadron of merson fighters made a desperate attempt to swoop down on the promontory where Gubujul and his staff were perched, those who were not slain outright by the Paramount Advisor's lookouts were blown in pieces halfway to the mirrorsky by a short blast from the deadly trumpet.

Bejuryar pestered Gubujul for a chance to try out the accursed shell himself, while Cavaumaz was more restrained. The Paramount Advisor spurned both requests. He was having too much fun. For once he was the one dealing out destruction instead of simply passing along orders or facilitating the efforts of others. For once it was he and not the Great Lord who was the dispenser of the people's vengeance. As the shrewd Taww had suggested, he would keep blowing until he could rage no more. Only then would he turn the sorceral weapon over to his enthusiastic subordinates.

A feeling of power he had never felt before surged through him. With both long arms, he lifted the shell once more to his mouth.

◊

From above, a bewildered Irina had a clear view of the destruction. Something invisible had blown a hole in first the outer and then the inner walls that protected the city. Something invisible, and very loud. The first sonic clubbing had forced her to clap her hands to her ears. She winced again when it was repeated. Below, confusion had set in among the Tornal. This reverberant bludgeon of the spralakers was something the likes of which they had never encountered before.

Buoyed by the very visible consequences, the first detachments of spralaker soldiers had begun to surge toward the breach. As they started forward, a fourth aural charge slammed into the outer wall. The gap was widening rapidly. Soon it would be so expansive that no counterattack, no matter how substantial, would be sufficient to keep the enemy from spreading into the city. Something had to be done to counter the devastating and demoralizing noise, and soon.

Snapping his arms out behind him, Oxothyr warned Irina to stay where she was. With a blast from his siphon, the shaman sped down toward the coral ridge where the Tornal were debating what to do next.

In his absence, a curious Chachel swam up beside her. "What does the mage intend?"

"I've no idea. Maybe he just wants to hear what they're saying."

The hunter looked down to where a sizable section of the outer wall had been destroyed and the inner had already been breached. "Someone had better do more than talk or listen, or we will find ourselves having to abandon Benthicalia and fall back in the direction of Sandrift. The stories that will be told of this day will not be comforting ones."

A renewed burst of activity below caused her to point. "They're doing something, but what?"

The hunter shook his head. "I see some of the Tornal scattering in all directions, and their escort even more so. They must be giving the order to bring up reinforcements. Perhaps they are going to try and somehow plug the gaps in the walls."

She shook her head. "It won't do any good if they can't stop the source of that sound."

But she was wrong.

The call went out the length and breadth of Benthicalia. A call for the help of every citizen who was not actively participating in the defense of the walls. A call for them to respond to the request made by Oxothyr, passed along by the Tornal, and disseminated throughout the population. A call for …

Sponges.

There were thousands of them scattered throughout the city. Flaunting every color of the rainbow despite the light-absorbing depth, they were cultivated for everything from residential comfort to external decoration. Some were hand-sized, others huge. Irrespective of size, shape, and color, one by one they were ripped from their locations and brought forward as fast as possible to the site of the breach in the city's ramparts.

As armed mersons and manyarms provided cover, dozens and then hundreds of the uprooted sponges were jammed into the uneven gap. Under Oxothyr's direction, others were attached with organic adhesive all along the still-standing sections of outer north wall. But not before they had been sculpted into cones and cavities according to the shaman's specific instructions and pierced with thousands of tiny holes and slits.

A rising thunder caused Chachel to grab Irina around the waist and kick upward. "Here it comes again!" he shouted warningly. Shaking her head in disgust at the sight, Poylee joined them. Glint rose with ease. Though Irina could have ascended by herself, she made no move to dislodge the hunter's helpful arm.

Booming through the water, the next burst of destructive sound came screaming toward the city. This one was intended to crush a second section of inner wall. It burst upon the hastily erected hedge of perforated sponges—and vanished into silence. Watching and listening from above, Irina was put in mind of the cones and sound-absorbing tiles that lined a typical recording studio. Like them, Oxothyr's sponges had been modified to soak up noise.

The makeshift defense had done its job flawlessly. It continued to do so as blast after blast of crashing sound was cast at the city—no longer to damaging effect.

Even underwater, she mused, it appeared that physics could occasionally trump magic.

◊

Among Gubujul and his staff frustration rose as discharge after sonic discharge failed to make any further impact on the city walls.

"This is absurd, simply absurd!" Cavaumaz could not believe the reports they were receiving. "Sponges! How can commonplace sponges, which can be shredded by the smallest newborn, stand against something as powerful as the shaman Sajjabax's shaped sound?"

Bejuryar confessed himself equally baffled. "I could poke a hole in one with my eye, let alone a claw." He was staring in disbelief at the distant, still shining, inviolate expanse that was Benthicalia. "There is great magic at work here."

"Perhaps not magic." All of them, including a distraught Gubujul, looked down at Taww. "Perhaps something even stronger than magic."

"What could be stronger than the eminent Sajjabax's magic?" Bejuryar growled scornfully.

The squat lobster gazed up at her colleague. "Intelligence." Turning, she nodded in the direction of the city. "Put down the shell, Paramount Advisor. Though we know not how, it is plain that its power has been countered. What other mystic weaponry do you have at your disposal?"

Among these three general officers, at least, a downcast Gubujul was not ashamed to show his disappointment. "You saw for yourselves. There was only the spiral shell. The box is empty."

"Then we are come to rely on the oldest of spralaker tactics. One that promises the least glory. One that involves the simplest of stratagems. But one that in the past our people have demonstrated can work. It demands, most of all, that quality which our armies and our soldiers are so often sorely lacking."

Cavaumaz stared down at her. After a moment's thought, he found himself nodding slowly in agreement, his shell bobbing forward, his eyes turning back toward the distant city. When he spoke, it was in concert with Bejuryar. Their tone was one of resignation, but not defeat. Standing beside them, Gubujul found that much as he did not want to, he had no choice but to agree.

"Siege."

# – XXII –

Days passed, and weeks, but within Benthicalia time seemed to slow to an increasingly despondent crawl. The deep-water gardens cultivated within the city could not feed its population by themselves. Limited stockpiles that had never been intended to cope with such an emergency were steadily drawn down. The usual hunting expeditions had to be forgone, since sizable teams of hunters bearing large nets would draw too much hostile attention. Even smaller foraging parties were quickly intercepted by patrolling squadrons of ray-riding spralakers. Dispersing and swimming hard, their members were able to make it safely back to the city. But they invariably did so without being able to bring back any food.

Unable to break through the city's defenses, the two besieging spralaker armies had settled down to enforce a complete blockade. Nothing was allowed to get in or out. While the Tornal were able to exploit specific and fairly simple spells to turn otherwise inedible organic matter such as weavings, decorative sea fans, and scavenged spralaker shell into food, their efforts would ultimately only buy time. The spralaker strategy was plain enough. If they could not overrun the inhabitants of Benthicalia, they would starve them out.

It was not a glamorous way to win a battle. The victors would not be able to drape themselves in the intestines of the defeated.

But it would be a victory nonetheless. And having conquered the city, the spralaker armies would then be able to move freely south and west along the reef lines, annihilating every smaller and weaker community in their path. They had to be stopped at Benthicalia.

Regardless of whether his fighting limbs are supported by stiff bone or flexible muscle, whether his eyes point forward or to the side, even the bravest soldier cannot long carry on a struggle on an empty stomach.

And while the now sponge-clad walls of the city held high and strong, the interminable assaults and vexing sorties periodically mounted by the besieging spralakers took a steady toll on the defenders. Every merson lost to a lucky throw, each manyarm surprised from behind while out on patrol, was a soldier who could not be replaced. As the steady attrition continued among the ranks of defenders, the mood inside the city grew increasingly glum. Hammered from two directions by death and hunger, desperate citizens began to whisper hesitantly of abandoning the city and fleeing for their lives.

Even an outsider like Irina could see the foolishness inherent in such talk. If trained, heavily-armed foraging parties could not escape the attention of spralaker patrols, how could families laden down with offspring and household goods hope to do so? Such dismal scenarios were among the many that she and her new friends discussed as they hovered at the front of the audience chamber in the blue-green lit Palace of the Tornal.

Several members of that august assembly were unenthusiastically debating strategy among themselves. Off to one side Oxothyr was arguing loudly with a pair of ammonites and one ten-foot long orthocera. Though the details of their deliberations were easy to hear in the enclosed chamber, Irina found her thoughts drifting absently.

It had all been so fascinating, her mysterious transformation and the time spent here in Oshenerth. Throughout it all she had faced manifold dangers and had come face to face with a watery death on many occasions. But now that it seemed to be closing in on her with an inexorability she had not encountered previously, she found herself longing more than ever before for her former life. For the gentle caress of sunshine on bare skin. For the taste of familiar foods. For laughter and conversation that did not have to travel through the medium of liquid to reach her ears. For the simple feeling of being *dry*.

Something nudged her inappropriately and she whirled furiously. It was only Glint, come up behind her. The cuttlefish's bioluminescence trolled in waves of glowing maroon through his mantle.

"What—why did you do that?" Conscious that her hands had balled into fists, she relaxed the clenched fingers.

"Anger has a way of dispelling misery, however invalid-seeming the approach," the cuttlefish explained blithely. "What were you so intense about?"

She faltered. "I—I don't really remember. Something that had to do with dying."

"Oh, well then." The cuttlefish changed color to a subdued and soothing turquoise. "I suppose I should have let you simmer, like a black smoker that's been plugged."

"No." Her spirits did not exactly rise, but neither did they sink any further. "Thanks for trying to help, Glint." Pivoting in the water, she turned her attention back to Oxothyr and the deliberating Tornal. "Do you think they'll come up with anything?"

"You mean a way of raising the siege?" Hovering beside her, the cuttlefish repeatedly twisted his arms together; back and forth, back and forth, like a piece of steel cable continuously fraying and then rebraiding itself. "They'd better think of something, Irina-changeling." Unfolding from the muscular coil, one of his two longer hunting tentacles curled up and under to stroke his ventral side. "I'm *starving*. Eventually I'll shrink until only my head and arms are left."

"Then there'll still be enough left to complain with," she told him, making sure to add a grin to show that she was joking.

No such humor was evident among the Tornal. Already old and weary when the spralaker onslaught had begun, they were now almost too tired to debate. Their exhaustion conferred one benefit: they were increasingly disposed to listen to anything arising outside their immediate circle that smacked of a reasonable suggestion, whether it involved means magical or prosaic.

Unsurprisingly then, they were more than ready to pay attention to Oxothyr.

Irina readied herself for whatever the shaman was going to say when he broke away from the ammonites with whom he had been conversing and swam over to rejoin them. Beside her, Glint stiffened. They were quickly joined by Chachel, Poylee, Sathi, Tythe, and the stolid Jorosab. The mage eyed each of them in turn.

"We have come a long way together, my friends. We have suffered together, and triumphed together. Now we face a set of circumstances more daunting and desperate than any that have gone before. The city is collapsing in upon itself. Soon the siphons of its defenders will be incapable of expelling water and their arms too weak to fling spears. Before that happens we must act." With one arm, he gestured in the direction of the Tornal, who had ceased talking among themselves and were moving slowly to reform their familiar line.

"I have been given permission to try something. As outsiders, we are allowed somewhat more freedom of action than the city's inhabitants. The Tornal have charged them with sustaining the defense of the community to the last hand or tentacle. That is not surprising." Suckered arms traced cryptic patterns in the softly lit water. "We, however, swim under no such restrictions."

The shaman's words hinted at where he was leading. It was his unblinking stare, however, that revealed to Irina his intentions. These he soon confirmed with words. She felt a shiver pass through her that had nothing to do with the temperature of the surrounding water.

"At this particular time of year," he continued, "there exist some distance from here potential allies who could make a significant contribution to the defense of Benthicalia. Unfortunately, they have no interest in socializing. They prefer the solitary life, and tend to keep to themselves. Except in one certain place, at this particular time of the year. But if they could be persuaded, this one time, to lend assistance, I believe they would make all the difference."

"Who is so persuasive as you, esteemed shaman?" Jorosab exclaimed admiringly.

"At least one or two others, I hope. I cannot go. I must stay and do what I can do help defend the city. If these others of whom I speak agree to help, it will do no good if they arrive too late to find anything left worth preserving." His great glistening eyes roamed over his silent, attentive audience.

"Those most suited to this desperate work must be the swiftest of swimmers and most skilled at avoiding detection. There is no knowing how many spralaker patrols they will have to avoid in order to slip safely clear of the city and into the depths beyond. Since they cannot allow themselves to be slowed by an excess of supplies they must also be self-reliant and able to feed themselves with whatever they encounter as they travel. They must be used to journeying on their own." His scrutiny finally came to an end—facing Chachel and Glint. Irina was not surprised, for all that she wished it could have been otherwise.

The choice was easy enough, she knew. Inevitable, even. Who better to attempt a risky dash through spralaker lines than the pair of exceptional hunters? But asking them to be persuasive of others, let alone apparently apathetic potential allies? True, Glint could be amusing, and the cuttlefish could hold a conversation with anyone. But convincing? She wasn't so sure. As for Chachel, well, a penchant for the non-verbal and antisocial were not qualities one often associated with a skilled diplomat.

Since the notion had readily occurred to her it was not surprising Oxothyr had already thought of it.

"This is Oultm." As the shaman edged to one side, he revealed hovering behind him a much smaller octopus. Glowing pale pink spotted with azure, he was the same size as Glint. Small holes showed in the upper edges of his tentacles where jewelry had been removed. The octopod had stripped down for the journey to come.

The mage turned back to Chachel and Glint. "Keep him safe. He speaks many dialects and often intercedes for the Tornal with visiting travelers from afar. Now it is his turn to travel. The Tornal tell me that if he cannot convince these others to help, then there is no one in Benthicalia or all the southern reefs who can."

"A talker, eh?" Glint jetted over to the hovering envoy. "I'll try not to bore you."

"You already have," declared the diplomat primly, curling his arms close around him.

Another might have been offended. Not Glint. He simply swam a slow circle around the octopod, inspecting him from every angle. "No healed wounds. No missing suckers. Mantle unmarred by scars. Not a fighter, then."

"Only with words." Oultm pivoted to meet the cuttlefish's eyes. "Keep me alive and perhaps together we can do something to help my poor city."

"Sure." Glint jetted back to rejoin Chachel. "And if you fail, your presence will ease the burden of finding food on the way back."

"Let's not begin this treacherous trek in quarrel," Chachel admonished his streamlined companion.

Though flashing red, Glint seemed amenable. "As you wish. I can wait until later."

"Then it is settled." Spreading his arms wide, Oxothyr came forward to embrace all three of them at once. "The hunters will ensure the safety of our emissary, and he will endeavor to sway our potential allies. Be aware as you interact with them," he cautioned as he backed off, "that this time of year they are as likely to eat you as to engage in extended conversation."

"We'll try to keep our chat short then," Glint commented blithely.

There was little time to spend on words of encouragement and offerings of hope. Poylee proved more reluctant than anyone to take leave of the travelers, even offering to accompany them. Saving Chachel the trouble of making such a decision, Oxothyr firmly quashed the notion.

"Even three is two too many for such a desperate business," he explained. "The fewer in number who go out, the less likely they are to be detected."

Fighting to keep from sobbing, Poylee was unwilling to grant the logic of the octopod's argument. "Then why not send only two? Or just the lone envoy?"

Oxothyr could have declined to explain himself again and no one else would have questioned his judgment. But he was not that kind of shaman, to retreat behind an impenetrable aura of omnipotence. Though he had eight arms, he needed only three to tick off his reasons.

"First, a diplomat is not necessarily a fighter. In this case, obviously. Second, it would not be proper for Oultm to present himself without at least some kind of an escort. And lastly, it being critical that those whose assistance we seek be convinced that the well-being of all is at stake, it is vital that at least one merson go along to add the weight of his people's involvement to the argument."

The explanation was enough to subdue Poylee, if not to please her. She had to settle for embracing an unresponsive Chachel to such a degree that others had to pull her, albeit gently, away. As for Glint, the cuttlefish was farewelled with equal fervor by a female of his kind. And another. Then a few more. And then several more still. Looking on, a surprised Irina decided that she did not really know the cuttlefish any better than she did his merson cohort.

Reflecting the gravity of their mission, they were given a ritual send-off that was hopeful but restrained. One at a time, each member of the Tornal ceremonially entwined tentacles with Glint and Oultm, and tentacle to arm with Chachel. The two hunters were provided with the finest, sharpest weapons in the city's armory, including bone spears with costly metal tips. Preserved, odorless, high-energy food was supplied in special low-drag carryalls.

Their actual departure was quick. Leave-taking took place via a small opening at the base of an unprepossessing section of south wall. The spralakers would expect anyone trying to flee Benthicalia to swim first for the surface, and if that route was blocked, to then head in a direction opposite the two besieging armies. That was where the majority of outlying spralaker-ray squadrons could be expected to focus their efforts. The area most likely to go unpatrolled was the ground; the one part of the realworld where spralakers and not mersons or manyarms held sway.

The minimizing of light being critical to slipping past enemy sentries unobserved, Glint and Oultm reduced their personal bioluminescence to the least amount possible. Chachel buried the small but bright glow-globes he carried inside the tightly woven pack slung across his back.

Then, having made their final farewells, they embarked on the desperate journey.

◊

Once outside the city, in the absence of adequate illumination they had to feel their way across the rocky surface. Chachel let Glint lead the way, since the cuttlefish's sensitivity to changes in water pressure could detect obstacles more efficiently than the touch of merson fingers.

Despite the care they had taken with their departure, on two occasions they encountered spralaker patrols. Once while they were hugging the ground, but in time to extinguish their own weak lights and let the enemy pass by. The second time they were nearly caught off-guard by a quartet of bull rays transporting more than a dozen spralaker fighters. Instead of stopping, the anxious trio kept moving through the darkness. While the more acute vision of the two cephalopods allowed them to find their way forward, a silently grumbling Chachel was reduced to holding onto a couple of Glint's trailing tentacles so that he would not lose track of his companions.

They were three days out from Benthicalia before the hunters felt it was safe enough to return both internal and external lights to full strength. A nervous Oultm protested the decision, but in this instance he was overruled.

"You take care of the talk," Chachel told the smaller octopod firmly, "and Glint and I will take care of you."

The edgy envoy kept pivoting on his axis, peering into the surrounding dark water with unashamed unease. "I still think we're too close to the city to be advertising our presence so."

Glint flashed indifference. "Bring forth the light or proceed in darkness as you please, beak-walker. I prefer to make it easy to see my companion, and for him to see me. The deep is no place to lose track of one's friends."

"It's no place to boast of one's presence, either." Oultm gave a visible shudder. "There are dangers out here away from the city greater than those posed by marauding spralakers."

This time Chachel spoke up before the cuttlefish could reply. "Glint and I are hunters, emissary. We have spent many days and many trips by ourselves in places villagers would fear to swim. We know the currents and the darkness. They are old friends." He hefted the beautifully wrought spear held loosely in his webbed left hand. "Sharks are not the only ones who can hunt successfully at night."

Still dubious, Oultm dribbled out a short spurt of bubbles. "Well, that gifted country shaman of yours certainly seemed to have confidence in you. I suppose I can do no less."

"You always have a choice." Raising an arm, Glint pointed back through the blackness at the route they had already traversed. "Benthicalia lies several days swim in that direction. Good luck. We will make do without you."

Adjusting his siphon, Oultm shot closer to the cuttlefish. The two cephalopods continued swimming close and in parallel. "You think I am afraid."

"No." Glint let a ripple of red race along the length of his soft body. "I *know* you are afraid. I know this because I am afraid, and my limb- and eye-challenged friend Chachel is afraid. And if *we* are afraid, it would be all out of proportion normal if a puny sputtering babble-beak like yourself was not."

"Then we have something else in common." Verifying his credentials as a diplomat, Oultm allowed every one of the cuttlefish's insults to pass unnoticed.

"'Else'?" Had he possessed one, Glint would have arched an eyebrow.

"We all desire the salvation of Benthicalia, the great burden with which all of us have been charged."

For once Glint had no ready comeback. The trio swam on in silence.

Foraging proved less of a problem than Oxothyr had feared. The rocky plain and deep-sea corals were virtual larders, flush with edible mollusks of all kinds. There were slow-moving fish to be speared, soft growths for Chachel to chew (which his wholly carnivorous companions declined to sample), peculiar but tasty glowing lifeforms to be swallowed whole.

There were also innumerable small spralakers whose flesh would have been a welcome addition to their haphazard meals. Under normal conditions all three travelers would have feasted on the foul-mouthed but otherwise harmless hardshells. But despite the distance they had come from Benthicalia, there was no way of knowing how far the northerner's patrols ranged. The last thing any of the travelers wanted was for some shrieking small meal to alert their enemies. It was not as if they were lacking for nourishment.

Notwithstanding his lofty standing, Oultm proved himself a perfectly adequate scavenger. From time to time he would wander off by himself, only to return soon thereafter with something fleshy and edible. Glint was faster and Chachel stronger, and both of them had more experience. By pooling their efforts they had no need to dip into the stores they had brought with them from Benthicalia.

It was Glint who first spotted the approaching line of blue lights. Instantly on guard, Chachel gripped his spear a little tighter as he went vertical in the water to scrutinize the oncoming glow. Though the line of luminance wavered slightly from side to side, the lights of which it was composed stayed in single file.

"Not rays." He grunted uncertainly. "Phosphorescent salps? Or some other communal organism?" He looked around unhappily. Comprised of undulating sand and mud, the surrounding terrain offered little in the way of cover.

"Can't tell." Rising higher, Glint lifted a pair of tentacles. "Whatever it is, it's not putting out much of a scent."

Chachel had dropped so low that his feet were kicking up mud and miniscule particles of organic matter. Whatever was generating the light, it was going to pass directly over them.

"If I might …" Oultm began. They never had a chance to consider the diplomat's opinion, because within minutes it was raining spralakers. Dozens of them, the majority as big or bigger than Glint.

They came parachuting down off the sides and back of the biggest oarfish the hunters had ever seen. A good seventy feet in length, its body was remarkably flattened, forming a gigantic silvery, weaving ribbon. Narrow, wide open jaws sucked in whatever prey they encountered. Though just a fish, its great size made it as intimidating as any sea serpent—another denizen of the deep for which it was often mistaken in the seas of Irina's world.

The spralakers who had been clinging to its back and flanks had kept their own internal and claw-held lights turned off so as not to attract attention. This ploy had certainly deceived the trio of emissaries, who from below had been able to detect only the normal blue bioluminescence running along the oarfish's length.

The instant they identified the actual threat, the travelers scattered. All they had to do to evade the surprise attack was get up off the ground and into the water column where the weak-swimming hardshells could not follow. The only problem was that not all of the attacking spralakers let go of their oarfish transport. At least half remained attached. Their multiple legs allowed them to maintain a firm grip on the ribbon-like spine of their mount while still unlimbering their weapons.

The patrol's strategy was immediately apparent. Have the oarfish loop above the travelers. If Chachel or his companions made a break for shallower water, spear or shoot them as they came up. Defeating that tactic was simple: all the emissaries had to do was stay below the circling oarfish. But that allowed those spralakers who had already dropped from their weaving mount to attack the emissaries beside or below them. Close-quarter combat was soon joined.

Glint and Chachel swam into battle without saying a word. There was neither need nor reason for them to waste energy on unnecessary conversation. As veteran hunting partners, they had long ago been obliged to develop stratagems for mutual defense. These stood them in good stead now.

Spear aimed outward, Chachel held his place in the water column while Glint circled overhead, tentacles fully extended and both bows notched. Exhibiting acumen if not boldness, Oultm promptly assumed a stance tail to tail with the cuttlefish. Facing in opposite directions, the two cephalopods were positioned to cope with an attack from any direction, including from above. Rising as one, the three armed and wary travelers commenced a slow ascent from the sandy bottom.

But every time they looked, every time they shifted direction slightly, the way up to freedom was blocked by a silvery flash of spralaker-riding oarfish.

So intent was Chachel on finding a potential escape route that he nearly failed to notice the green and red spralaker that, legs churning furiously, came flying at him out of the darkness. By the time he could react to its leap, it was already inside the killing point of his spear. Each powerful claw held a curved blade high. By bringing both weapons down and toward one another at the same time, the hardshell warrior was perfectly capable of cutting off a merson's head.

Keeping a firm grip on his spear and using the point to ward off another spralaker who was cutting at his legs, Chachel used his free hand to pull his knife from its woven sheath. As the soaring soldier descended toward him, the hunter struck upward. The short, sharp blow was delivered swiftly.

Whether delivered by merson, manyarm, or spralaker, wide sweeping swings and hacks were of minimal efficacy when fighting underwater. The broader the stroke, the more the intervening water would slow it down and reduce its effectiveness. That was why, for example, no manyarm enveloped its quarry unless it had already been caught, and tentacles seeking prey always lashed out straight and never in a curve. It was why a long knife or short sword was efficient, but never a saber. To slay underwater one was best advised to stab, not slice.

The point of Chachel's well-honed bone blade went straight up into the softer underside of the leaping spralaker, passing through the chelae and into its brain. Severing the relevant nerves caused its claws to lock in striking position but no longer able to strike. Bringing both knees up to his chest, Chachel kicked his dead adversary off the blade even as he was searching for another hardshell to kill.

He didn't have to look far. The mêlée raged around him. Oultm and Glint both had their own short swords out, the spralakers having closed too tight to allow the cuttlefish to make any further use of his bows and arrows. Thus far all the dark blood swirling around the combatants belonged to the attackers. Chachel feared that if the fight continued for much longer that was likely to change. There were too many of the hardshells. Unless he and his companions could get farther off the sea floor and gain enough height to make full use of their superior mobility, the likelihood of them completing their mission, much less seeing Benthicalia or Sandrift again, was small. If only that damned oarfish ...!

"Glint!" he roared. "Cover me! I'm going up." Before the embattled cuttlefish could respond, Chachel was already kicking hard and ascending.

Anticipating that sooner or later their quarry must try to make a break for open water, spralaker riders were waiting for him.

Several dozen still clung to the back and sides of the huge oarfish. Illuminated by the lights they carried or had attached to their bodies as well as by those of the oarfish itself, they were easy to pick out in the dark water. Woven double-pouches holding hundreds of short throwing blades and curved knives were slung on either side of the willowy, flattened fish like elongated saddlebags. There was only one way to avoid the manifold riders and their lethal arsenal of weapons. There was only one possible angle of attack that would make it difficult for them to strike at him as Chachel came near.

Ignoring the added danger and taking a deep breath, Chachel swam directly for the head.

Luminous, convex blue eyes wider than his face gazed blankly back at him as, spear fully extended from his right arm, he came rocketing toward the front of the oarfish. Detecting the fast-closing non-hardshell swimmer, the spralaker riders took aim with their various blades as their monster mount snapped at him. The oarfish was not fast, but it was surprisingly quick for such a large predator. In addition to avoiding the mouthful of long, needle-like teeth that could swallow him whole, Chachel had to deal with the efforts of the spralakers on its back. Spinning its way through the water, one accurately-flung, palm-sized metal scythe just missed taking off his left foot.

Failing to skewer him on its furiously gnashing teeth, the enraged oarfish twisted sharply to its right. This whipped a section of its heavy body directly toward Chachel, allowing the spralakers on its back to let loose with a broadside of cutting edge weaponry at close range. Some of it he was able to dodge. Only skills honed from years of solitary hunting or later, in tandem with Glint, allowed him to deflect the oncoming spears, knives, arrows, and throwing blades. His own spear was a whirlwind in the water, a white blur the hunter manipulated with a skill that to his chattering, howling, and increasingly frustrated attackers seemed to border on the supernatural. They had no way of knowing that he was in fact manipulating the water as well.

Leaping from its perch near the tail of the oarfish as it snapped around to try and deal the maddeningly evasive merson a stunning blow, one spralaker flung itself straight at the hunter. Claws extended with every intention of ripping out the merson's gills, the hardshell flew straight at his face. Noting the attack at the last possible instant, Chachel strained his remaining calf muscle as he kicked sharply upward. Claws snapping, the weak-swimming spralaker passed just beneath him. Drawing his knees up toward his chest, the elusive hunter simultaneously thrust straight down with his principle weapon. Aided by the sudden density of water a murmuring Chachel put behind the spear butt, it went right through the spralaker's shell to pierce its brain. Flailing claws stilled as the multiple feathery legs ceased swimming.

Grabbing onto the body of the dead hardshell and using it as a shield, Chachel kicked as hard as he could toward the oarfish, which had curved back to make another pass at him. As the great fish drew near, its spralaker riders let loose with another fusillade of lethal weapons. All of them glanced off the dead spralaker's thick shell or stuck harmlessly into its lifeless body. When the oarfish opened its jaws wide to once again snap at the hunter, its teeth clamped down instead on the spralaker corpse.

The instant those narrow but deadly jaws closed on the body of the deceased hardshell, Chachel shot forward over the fringe-topped skull to plant the metal point of his spear in the center of the oarfish's head, directly above and between the eyes.

The giant serpentine shape convulsed. The spralakers riding on its spine and flanks forgot about the lone merson in their midst as they fought with all their strength to hang onto their mortally wounded mount. Water displaced by the spasming oarfish sent Chachel tumbling backward as helplessly as if he had been caught in an upcurrent. When he was finally able to regain his balance, the oarfish and its remaining riders were a pale blue blur receding into the darkness in the direction of distant Benthicalia.

Reaching over a shoulder toward the spear quiver strapped to his back, he found that he had one weapon left. He would have to take care not to waste it. Arching his back and pointing his feet toward the mirrorsky, he swam straight down to where a flurry of bioluminescence showed the location of the ongoing battle below.

He arrived just in time. Swirling about a common axis, Glint and Oultm had been unable to find an escape route leading upward. Spralakers could not swim fast enough to catch any cephalopod in the open water, not even the languorous nautilus, but they could stay afloat well enough to keep quarry trapped beneath them. Slamming into them from above, Chachel surprised the hovering hardshells from behind. Striking out with his spear and knife, he put several of them down before his return was even noticed. That enabled the two hard-pressed manyarms to finally climb to a level where their much greater maneuverability meant they no longer presented easily cornered targets to their assailants.

Seeing that their quarry had succeeded in safely rising clear of the sand and that the oarfish on which they relied for transport had unaccountably gone missing, the surviving spralaker soldiers decided that no mere trio of softbodies was worth the sacrifice of any more of their lives. Breaking off the engagement, the hardshell survivors went scurrying off in the direction Benthicalia and their vanished mount. Chachel followed for awhile, harrying the retreat from above, until he realized that neither of his companions was participating in the rout. The envoy Oultm he expected to hang back, but where was Glint? It wasn't like the cuttlefish not to share in a hard-won victory. Concerned, he spun about and returned to the scene of battle.

Above a dark sandy plain strewn with the corpses of dead spralakers whose bodies were already the subject of tentative nibbles from small scavengers he found the usually aloof Oultm attending solicitously to the cuttlefish. Something was not right. Coming closer, Chachel soon saw the source of the envoy's concern.

There was not a lot of blood, but it was clear that Glint had been hurt. The cuttlefish's eyes were half closed. Reflective of his pain, bands of white cascaded in waves down the length of his body from head to tail. Unexpectedly unsettled by a surge of emotion he had not experienced since his youth, Chachel swam close to his injured friend.

"How bad is it, Glint?"

Opening his eyes fully, the cuttlefish looked over at him. "I've felt better. The spralakers?"

Chachel jerked his head to his left, briefly glancing back over his shoulder. "Done. Finished. Gone. I don't know if their fish will survive. The rest will have to walk all the way back to Benthicalia."

"Would that we had the time to pick off each and every one of them from above. Ah well." One eye shifted to regard the unexpectedly attentive Oultm. "Critical undertakings do not allow time for such pleasurable diversions as revenge."

It was then Chachel noticed that his friend was missing an arm. He looked closer. Two. A merson suffering the loss of both arms would be condemned to a gradual, unpleasant death. Counting the absence of a third limb, Chachel swallowed.

Noticing the direction of his companion's gaze, Glint made an effort to suppress the tell-tale bands of white pain that were shooting through his body. "Not to grieve, my friend." Two tentacles longer than the rest flicked forward to just tap the tip of Chachel's nose. "Both my capturing arms are intact. As to the loss of the others, well, better an arm than an eye, of which I like you have only two. I can still hunt." A blush of pink flushed his mantle. "I may just tilt to the left a little while doing so, is all."

They stayed there awhile as Chachel tended to Glint's wounds. A concerned Oultm looked on. Only when the ends of the cuttlefish's amputated limbs had been treated with sticky salve and patched with nudibranch intestines did they prepare to resume their journey, moving to recover the supplies they had been forced to drop in the heat of battle.

Preoccupied with thoughts of his fellow manyarm's injuries as well as the challenging task that still lay before them, Oultm was picking his backpack off the sandy patch where it had come to rest when the badly wounded but by no means deceased spralaker that had been lying in wait in the sand in hopes of just such an opportunity jumped him from behind. The envoy never saw him. Engaged in recovering their own provisions, neither did Glint or Chachel. The emissary should have died right there, on the spot, his soft mantle torn apart by the spralaker's glistening curved blade.

Instead, it was the hardshell that went down. The two spears that pierced its shell just above and between its eyes were short, but no less lethal for their abbreviated length. Hearing the assassin's death cries, an alarmed Chachel and Glint rushed to the envoy's side. Arriving to see that he was not alone, they slowed. One of Oultm's saviors promptly pivoted in the water to face the two startled hunters.

"Oxothyr felt that any group attempting to escape Benthicalia that consisted of more than three individuals stood a good chance of drawing the attention of outriding spralaker patrols." The famulus Sathi looked at Glint. "Apparently three was enough to do so."

"I'm sorry we arrived too late to help in the fight." Flashing his own cheerful internal glow, a curious Tythe swam up to inspect the damage to Glint's arms. "Maybe the shaman can grow you some new ones."

Bobbing in the water, Sathi concurred. "Oxothyr is very good at making things grow."

Spreading his eight arms wide, Oultm turned red as he politely embraced first one squid and then the other. "You saved my life."

"We know," said Tythe matter-of-factly. "What matters is that this vital diplomatic mission will go on."

As he watched the diverse assortment of cephalopods—squid, octopus, and cuttlefish—converse via an enviable fusion of words and color changes, Chachel found himself having to deal with a jumble of emotions. There was no doubt that the mission had been saved only thanks to the timely arrival of the two famuli. On the other hand, he experienced a rush of resentment at the realization that the shaman must have thought from the beginning that the two hunters might need looking-after and additional help. That this had turned out to be true did nothing to mitigate Chachel's annoyance.

"Well, I'm glad you're here," he finally snapped as he swam off to pick up his pack. The quartet of manyarms watched him go.

"What's wrong with your friend?" a puzzled Sathi asked Glint.

The injured cuttlefish was already feeling better. Manyarms healed very fast. He flashed a shrug. "Who can say? If I ever come to truly understand mersons and what motivates them, then I'll be ready to proclaim myself master of all Oshenerth."

Nearby, Tythe indicated agreement. "I think it must be all those bones they have to carry around inside them. Must grate on the nerve endings."

"As do your interminable simpleton's explanations on everyone else." Rising slightly above the others, Sathi gazed in the direction of Benthicalia. "If the master was here he would say we are talking too much and moving too little. The spralakers who fled may encounter and inform others of their kind. If any return to this spot, we should not be here."

Acknowledging the wisdom of the famulus's observation, his fellow manyarms moved to gather up the rest of their own gear. As

Chachel chose not to explain his perplexing mood change, his tentacled companions left him to his brooding. His humor gradually improved, and very soon thereafter the unexpectedly enlarged group was once more swimming hard into the darkness, into the west, and into the unknown.

# – XXIII –

As one sunless day after another passed with no sign of relief and the tightening siege wore on relentlessly, the mood within the walls of Benthicalia did not turn altogether defeatist, but it most assuredly reflected an increasing sense of desperation. With Oxothyr consulting regularly with the Tornal, every non-traditional assault attempted by the spralakers was turned back. These intermittent defeats of the enemy's repeatedly ineffectual and sometimes supernatural efforts comprised the only good news for the city's residents, who increasingly had to do without the staples usually supplied through foraging or trade. The former had been rendered impossible by spralaker patrols, and the latter by the blockade that seemed to strengthen day by day. The city was in danger of being overcome not by frontal martial assaults, though these continued on a regular basis, but by slow strangulation.

Every day at the same time, Oxothyr would swim to the highest level of the city. There he would hover alone and for a long while, staring off into the south. Whenever he would espy a distant glow his tentacles would flex in anticipation and his mantle would turn a hopeful yellow. And every time, the outlying lights turned out to belong to a spralaker patrol, or other enemy forces maneuvering in the distance. Then he would sink back down, speaking to no one on the way, and sequester himself silently in the small residential burrow he had made his temporary home.

Irina felt sorry for him. Laboring under a tremendous and largely self-imposed sense of responsibility, the shaman was a prisoner of his own melancholy ruminations. Isolated by his own skills and abilities, he had no one to talk to, no one to confide in. Certainly not an otherworldly changeling. He could not even take pleasure in the usual emotional release to be gained by railing at his famuli, whom she finally learned had been sent off in secret to watch over the Tornal diplomat and his resilient but tiny escort.

It was while waiting in armed reserve as the spralakers mounted yet another in their series of interminable assaults on the north wall that a touch on her arm made her turn. It was Poylee. Despite displaying a recent slow-to-heal scar on her left cheek and another on the front of her right thigh, courtesy of slashing spralaker weapons that had both just missed their intended kill, the merson who had first taken Irina in was still beautiful. At the moment, though, her usual feistiness was absent and she appeared atypically subdued.

Expecting to endure the habitual chiding that would lay out in detail everything she was doing wrong, from the way she was holding her spear to her posture in the water, Irina was surprised by the merson's muted tone. It was unlike Poylee to approach her with anything other than criticism.

"Are you feeling all right, Irina?"

"What?" It took the pale blonde a moment to adjust the defenses that had gone up the instant she had spotted the other woman coming toward her.

In lieu of customary sarcasm, Poylee offered a smile that was almost shy. "I asked if you were doing well. How are your injuries?" She did not have to inquire if Irina had suffered any. Every defender of the wall had taken at least one hit.

"I'm okay." Irina stared back at the lithe female shape hovering before her. "Bruised, almost got knocked out during this morning's attack, but okay." She nodded in the direction of Poylee's leg. "Not as bad as you." Turning, she gestured in the direction of the current skirmish. "One thing I don't understand: with all this blood in the water, I'd think every shark in Oshenerth would be patrolling these battlefields."

Poylee's smile faded. "Be assured they are out there, in the distance, just beyond the fighting. You can bet your gill filters on that. But remember: sharks are food like any other fish. They are not especially wise, but they are ever cautious, attacking in strength only when the numbers are on their side and preferably when their intended prey is already sick or injured. Out in the dark they wait to pick off any stragglers who come their way." With the point of her spear she indicated the battlefield beyond the wall. "When this is finally over, it is they who will emerge victorious—no matter which side wins. It is their tribe that will thrive on the leftovers."

Irina nodded, paused a moment, then added, "How about you, Poylee? Are *you* all right? You seem different. I don't know— pleasant."

The merson turned away. "I—I'm sorry, Irina. I haven't been very nice to you recently, have I?"

"No," Irina agreed without hesitation. "You haven't. I know how much you think of Chachel, and I've tried to prove to you every way I know how that I'm not interested in him. All I'm interested in is finding a way back to my own world, my own life."

"I know, I know." Poylee turned back to the visitor. "I can't help myself about such things. If Chachel would show some interest …"

"I think he does," Irina said gently. "I've seen evidence of it."

"No," Poylee protested more vociferously, "*interest*. What you are seeing is tolerance. Kindness, at best." She inhaled deeply, her gill flaps flaring wide as she exhaled. "I don't suppose it matters any more. By now he must be dead. Him and that foolish cuttlefish who hunts beside him and gives him bad advice."

Cold water seemed to leak into Irina's heart, chilling her soul as well as her body. "You've heard something. You know something."

"No," Poylee murmured. The other female's reply left Irina more relieved than she would have thought possible. "It's just a feeling. I'm very sensitive to such things. Just a feeling, and the fact that he and Glint and that ridiculous envoy have been gone for so long." Her face came up and she looked straight at Irina. In the soft blue-green glow illuminating the city below, her eyes were pleading. "Oxothyr agrees, though he won't commit himself and outwardly, at least, refuses to give up hope. But I know it, Irina. I *know* it!"

"Nothing is known until it's proven." A single kick brought her close enough to put an arm around the downcast merson.

What was she doing mumbling profundities, Irina asked herself? Wasn't that Oxothyr's job? Who was she to be offering comfort at a time and in a place like this, where she was the most outside of outsiders? She knew next to nothing of this world. Maybe Poylee wasn't merely speculating. Maybe she really was "sensitive" to such things. In a world like Oshenerth, where octopod shamans and ancient ammonites repelled magic cast forth by murderous crab-folk, was it any greater leap of faith to believe that a water-breathing humanoid might be able to tell when someone she was emotionally close to had expired?

She found herself holding Poylee a little tighter. Some things, it seemed, transcended physical reality. The need for friends. The need to be comforted. When the time came, she wondered dejectedly, who would comfort her?

"The enemy has breached the Wall to the south of the Clarion bulwark!" Darting to and fro among the scattered ranks of the greatly reduced reserve force, a streaking squid flashed emergency alternating bands of white and black. "Everyone is to move there to try and staunch the incursion!" Shouting alarm and strobing mad colors like a light bar ripped from the top of a police car, the squid vanished into the thinned ranks of reservists gathered behind the two females. In response to his alarm, the armed mersons and manyarms began to swim off in the designated direction.

Letting her consoling arm drift free, a solemn Irina backed away from Poylee. "We'd better go. From the sound of it, they'll be needing every spear."

"Yes." Poylee collected herself, and Irina could see a little of the merson's momentarily dimmed spirit return. "Let's move."

"That's better." Irina offered an encouraging smile. "Nothing like killing a few spralakers to take your mind off depressing thoughts."

Poylee all but snarled. "No, you're wrong there. I need to kill a *lot* of spralakers!"

"One day," Irina told her as they swam south in parallel, "I'll have to tell you my aunt's recipe for cioppino...."

◊

Bejuryar could hardly contain his excitement when the courier delivered the report. He forced himself to steady the waving of his eyestalks as he hurried to share the news with his fellow Marshals and the amateurish but well-meaning Paramount Advisor who had been placed in command over them.

He found both Taww and Cavaumaz debating tactics over a meal of diced beche-de-mer. Rubbery tidbits halted halfway to mouths as he burst upon them.

"Stop what you are doing, my friends! Stop now!"

Sardonic as ever, Taww threw her colleague an arch look. "Stop planning the battle, or eating?"

So delighted was Bejuryar that the mockery barely registered. "Both!" He waved the sheet of flexible, flattened cartilage on which the essence of the report had been inscribed. "Thanks to the relentless effort and great sacrifice of our homaridae diggers, an entire section of the enemy's North Wall has collapsed."

Accepting the news thoughtfully, Gubujul was far from ready to make merry. "The outer wall?" he asked hesitantly. "Or the cursed inner?"

"As I said—both! The outer *and* that damnably frustrating interior maze. At last we have a clear path into the city."

Cautious and argumentative to the last, Taww piped up. "An excellent opportunity for the enemy to lay a trap, catching our forces in a gap such as you describe when they attempt to rush forward."

"I do not think so." Bejuryar oozed newly minted confidence. "According to the report I received, the breach is much wider than any we have managed thus far. Too wide to pin down our brave troops as they advance." Remembering protocol, he aimed both eyestalks at the Great Lord's personal representative, who thus far had not commented. "The decision is yours to make, Paramount Advisor. Should we attack now with all our strength and reserves?"

Confronted with the need to render a crucial decision, Gubujul naturally hesitated.

Cavaumaz took advantage of the Paramount Advisor's silence. "This may be our best opportunity to at long last break both the fighting strength and the will of the city's defenders. If the gap is indeed sufficiently expansive, they will only be able to attack and slow the advance of our entering force's flanks, near where their defensive wall remains standing. Our soldiers in the center should be able to press forward relatively unimpeded."

"And if we hesitate too long," Bejuryar pointed out, leaving Gubujul little room to equivocate, "they will have time and opportunity to rebuild the outer wall and regenerate the inner."

Still Gubujul was silent. Unable to proceed without his consent, his general staff waited impatiently for him to deliver a verdict. Seeing the Paramount Advisor sunk deep in thought, Taww was convinced he must be mulling over every aspect of the critical strategic determination that had to be made. She was wrong.

*Would only that I were back in court,* Gubujul was thinking anxiously, *being asked to deliver a decision on what style of preparation to apply to the Great Lord's evening meal.* Seeing the three Mud Marshals staring unblinkingly back at him he knew he could no more avoid the answer they impatiently awaited than he could the responsibility that he had accepted.

"If you think now is the moment of conviction, then what can I do but concur?" Unable to escape liability, he chose to seize the moment. It having been thrust upon him, he more or less had no choice anyway. Inclining all six antennae in the direction of the besieged city, he raised both long, slender, red-and-white arms, and opened his pincers wide.

*"Death to the mersons! Death to the manyarms! Victory or dismemberment!"*

◊

By the time Irina and Poylee arrived with the rest of the armed reserve in the vicinity of the devastated section of North Wall, the merson had recovered much if not all of her customary vigor. Clutching her spear, eyes aflame, the smaller female was now spoiling for a fight. Even the disheartening sight of the lengthy segment of shattered city defenses that came into view as they swam over the top of the last intervening building failed to dampen her revived spirit.

"Let them come!" she growled, bubbles spurting from between her clenched teeth as she restlessly swapped the spear back and forth, back and forth, from hand to hand. "I embrace the ecstasy of evisceration!"

Irina only half heard the remainder of her companion's bloodcurdling oaths. Her attention and her focus were on a peculiar glowing mass that seemed to be approaching the city from the northeast, streaking toward them at a height well above that of the howling spralaker horde that thronged the plain outside the walls. As she stared, it grew visibly in breadth and brightness. Had all the fighting and tension over the past stress-filled days taken such a toll that now she was seeing things? She quieted Poylee long enough to point out the oncoming phenomenon.

"More spralakers riding rays?" she asked.

"Has to be. An awful lot of them, too." Drifting alongside the changeling, Poylee strained to see into the distance. "No, wait. On second sight, I think not. The profiles are too attenuated." Her fingers tightened on the shaft of her spear. "This is something new."

Irina felt herself tensing. "Whatever it is, it's coming this way awfully fast."

"Too fast." Poylee's passion gave way to new pessimism.

The lights continued to race toward them. As they passed over the rearmost ranks of the spralaker First Army, a great crustaceanal cry arose from the mass of pushing, shoving fighters. Without slowing, the vaguely cylindrical smattering of lights came straight for the city, aiming not at the wide gap that had been made in the broken inner and outer walls but at the open water space above it. By now the luminous mass was close enough for the individuals that comprised it to be identified.

Irina found herself swimming frantically backward and down, away from this latest incursion. The lights came from attacking spralaker troops, all right.

But they were not riding rays.

However the spralaker invaders had managed to make allies of the huge school of great barracuda was a mystery others would have to unravel. Those who were present to witness it and increasingly to be slain by it had neither the time nor the skill to expend on hasty analysis. Two highly-trained spralakers rode each of the lightning-fast predators: one to steer and guide, the other to unleash arrows of bone and urchin from behind. Pilot and gunner, Irina thought involuntarily, employing the only references she could think of to describe the ghost crab riders who clung to the spines of the swift marauders.

For the first time since the two spralaker armies had laid siege to Benthicalia, mersons and manyarms alike found themselves outmaneuvered in the water column. The mersons were stronger than the barracuda but not nearly as fast. Their manyarm allies were as fast but not as agile. Dashing in and through the ranks of the startled defenders, the spralaker riders picked off merson and manyarm alike before they could even strike back. Arrows and short spears did the damage. Arrows and spears—and the great barracuda's terrible, terrible teeth.

A silver silhouette chevroned with black shot past Irina before she had a chance to fling a spear at it. Below her, Poylee thrust out sharply. Her blade cut only water. Looking back, the spralaker riding the rear of the barracuda that had just grazed the two women let loose an arrow whose momentum thankfully was sufficiently reduced by the intervening distance so that it only nicked Irina's left shoulder.

She looked down at herself in surprise. In all the battles in which she had participated, this was the first time she had been cut. Dazed, she gawked at the gash and the free-flowing fluid, black at this depth, that was leaking out. The sifting curlicues of her blood reminded her of Arabic calligraphy.

Something slammed hard into her right side. Blinking in shock, she found Poylee gazing angrily back at her.

"Are you going to rise whitebelly up like a dead fish or are you going to *fight*?"

"I—sorry, Poylee." There was nothing wrong with her right arm, Irina realized. "You strike. I'll cover you."

The merson's responsive nod was curt but approving. Soon the two of them were joined by half a dozen other defenders, a mix of mersons and manyarms. As minutes passed, Irina found herself agonizing less and less over what she had come to realize was little more than a surface wound.

In addition to the weapons wielded by their riders, each barracuda carried slung beneath its missile-like body a narrow, cylindrical tube of hollow bone. These slender, capped containers had been carefully treated to give them an impermeable lining commensurate with Sajjabax's special instructions and incantations. As the school of predators dispersed across the city, their riders began to unstopper the tubes. Whenever a barracuda dipped head-down, some of the contents spilled out.

Spilled. Looking on from a distance, Irina had not expected that. She could see the thick, cohesive fluid, heavier than water, catch the blue-green light as it trickled and coiled downward in dozens of sinuous semi-transparent streams. Only when the first drops touched upon a structure and she could see the consequences did the truly invidious nature of the spralaker assault strike home.

"Poylee! Tell the others. Tell everyone: don't get near the liquid the barracuda are spreading!"

Though waiting attentively for the next spralaker ground assault, the fighters around her were sufficiently alarmed by her tone and conviction to turn in her direction.

"Why not?" Poylee wondered. "If it's only liquid …"

"It's not just 'liquid.'" With the point of her spear Irina indicated the place where she had seen the syrupy fluid make contact. "It's *acid*!"

Sure enough, where the diving barracuda had spilled the partial contents of its slender container a hole had been eaten right through the roof of the affected building. Irina feared that if she swam over to the cavity and looked in, she would be able to see the powerful unidentified acid continuing to eat its way all the way through to bedrock.

She found herself wondering: if the spralakers had possessed such a weapon all along, why had they not used it instead of the lumbering and far more vulnerable homaridae to try and take down one or more sections of the inner wall? A possible explanation struck her: their supply of the corrosive solution must be limited. They had held it and its special barracuda delivery system in reserve for a time when it could be unleashed to inflict maximum damage on the city—and maximum psychological damage to its stressed inhabitants.

There was a horrible logic to it. She could imagine how the city's non-fighters must be reacting to this new and unexpected means of assault. Thinking themselves safe, children and the elderly would now flee in mindless terror as the supposedly solid structures of their community literally dissolved around them. The resulting confusion and panic would find them inadvertently interfering with the city's hard-pressed defensive efforts—and in fleeing and exposing themselves, they would present the easiest targets of all to the waiting spralakers, who as she had already seen drew no distinction between fighters and non-combatants.

It was happening before her eyes, as more and more of the blurringly fast barracuda spread the contents of their containers across the length and breadth of the city. The crowns of elegant spires were reduced to lumps of melted calcium carbonate while expansive holes appeared in the roofs and walls of prominent public and private buildings. Even the graceful filigreed Palace of the Tornal was not spared from the attentions of the acid. The water resounded to the battle cries of triumphant spralakers, the challenges of still-defiant mersons, the gallant hisses of manyarms, and the screams of fear and alarm as panic began to spread like a virus throughout the metropolis.

What of the city's other battlefront, she suddenly found herself thinking? If another squadron of the seemingly unstoppable barracuda had also attacked from the deep west, then all might be lost. It struck her abruptly that she might well die here, far away from not only her own world but from the sun. Doomed to sink to the bottom of an alien ocean, there to decompose and become food for mindless scavengers.

Well, if that was to be her fate, at least she would not die alone. Poylee was on her right, flashing eyes alert, lethal spear aimed outward. The spralaker riders were coming so fast and from so many directions now that there was no need to seek out a place where the enemy was present. They were everywhere. Gripping her own weapon, her shoulder throbbing where she had been cut, Irina prepared to sell her life dearly.

Stationed above Benthicalia's nearly silent south wall, a pair of bow-armed cuttlefish could both see and hear the spreading breakdown of the city's defenses. Though they longed to swim to their companions' aid, they had been explicitly charged with defending this so far unassailed side of Benthicalia lest the ever-devious spralakers seek to open a new front to the south. So preoccupied were they with the raucous, mounting chaos inside the city that they nearly forgot to run the occasional check on the section of intact wall they were supposed to be guarding.

When they finally did turn and take notice of the astounding emergence from the far south, it was almost upon them.

The two stunned cephalopods gazed outward in awe. The lights coming toward them out of the darkness were brighter than anything either of them had ever seen. Well, that was not technically true. They were not as bright as the hot yellowness that illuminated the shallows beneath the mirrorsky. They were not as intense. To be entirely honest, they only did just qualify as breathtaking.

Both guards tilted their bodies back, back, their tails eventually pointing toward the ground as they gazed upward at the thousands upon thousands of discs and streaks and splotches of blue and green and red bioluminescence passing directly above them. Thousands that shone from barely one or two hundred bodies.

Drinking in the awe-inspiring sight, the smaller of the two cuttlefish found herself at a loss for words. Her cohort was struck almost as speechless, but finally did manage to blurt out a few words of greeting, as forcefully as he could.

*"Welcome to Benthicalia—cousins!"*

# – XXIV –

**H**aving already released their containers of acid, a trio of barracuda riders had trapped Irina and her companions against the side of one of the city's tallest coral towers. As the swift silver slayers and their pale riders drew closer and closer, tightening the circle around the increasingly disheartened and fatigued defenders, out of the corner of an eye Irina saw another group of swimmers approaching from the vicinity of the Tornal's palace. That holy of holies itself was threatening to succumb beneath a steady, withering assault; not only from the barracuda-riding ghost crabs but from the first columns of spralaker ground troops who had begun to pour into the city through the broad gap that had been made in the North Wall.

The small band that was hurrying toward her now was not comprised of spralakers or their allies, however. While she recognized none of the other fighters, there was no mistaking the bulky cephalopodan figure in the middle.

"Oxothyr!"

Hearing Irina's joyful shout, Poylee took her attention off a circling barracuda long enough to join in the changeling's excitement. Recognizing the shaman from Sandrift, she let out an elated cry of her own. The relief he was bringing with him might only be temporary, but it was most welcome.

Rushing in upon the circling barracuda from behind, Oxothyr and his followers managed to wound one and scatter the others. However fleeting, it was a victory of sorts, though the fighters surrounding Irina barely had strength enough left to taunt the retreating enemy with a few defiant shouts of their own.

"Thanks for coming, Oxothyr." Irina regretted she did not possess sufficient armature to greet the mage appropriately, in the manner of his own kind.

"I could see you were in serious trouble." A familiar S-shaped iris rotated toward her as a pair of arms gestured back the way he had come. "There was little more I could do at the palace in any case." Another tentacle slipped around her shoulders, and a fourth around Poylee's. "I am glad to find you both still alive, with all limbs intact."

"More or less." Irina pointed out the cut on her arm, then nodded forward. Doubtless awaiting reinforcements, two of the barracuda who had attacked the small group continued to patrol back and forth in front of the cluster of exhausted defenders. Their spectral hardshell riders held their short bows loaded and ready, waiting for an opportunity to strike.

"I am prepared to die." Hovering beside Irina, scarred and weary, Poylee looked resigned.

"Do not be in such a hurry to give up your life, which has enriched and irritated so many others in equal measure." Raising his voice, Oxothyr addressed the surviving defenders who had gathered around him. "All of you, hold your positions and stay alert!" Turning in the water, he looked back across the ravaged but still radiant city. "Something terrible is coming out of the south. I *feel* it."

Open-mouthed and open-gilled, Irina stared fixedly at the inscrutable shaman. "I'm sorry, Oxothyr, but if that was meant to be encouraging, it wasn't."

His body turning an unexpected pale blue striped with jade, the wizened octopod turned back to her. "I suppose I should explain further. This time, little changeling, the something terrible is on *our* side."

Spears aimed outward, remaining bows drawn taut, the small band of mersons and manyarms waited. The pair of barracuda and their spectral riders continued to sweep back and forth in front of them to prevent any escape. Ominously, they were soon joined by two more. Setting aside the shaman's perplexing assurance, Irina steeled herself for a final fight, expecting the quartet of barracuda and riders to charge at any moment.

And then, just like that and without warning, the four argent assassins and their deadly riders turned tail and shot away, disappearing at high speed in the direction of the despoiled North Wall. In their wake they left a small knot of stunned mersons and manyarms. Even well after it was clear that they had fled, neither Irina nor Poylee lowered their weapons.

"What ...?" Irina started to say.

Her question was interrupted by a new disturbance. Something was roiling the water. Looking around, she saw that every one of her fellow defenders was also struggling to maintain their position. Something was seriously perturbing the sea around them. Whatever it was, to displace so much volume at once she knew it had to be massive.

They were.

She saw the lights first. So strong was the approaching phosphorescence that whole sections of city around her were thrown into increased relief. Struggling against the disturbance and mindful of Oxothyr's pledge, she fought her way around the tower and against the push of moving water to see what was coming.

Squid. But not just—squid.

The force of oncoming manyarms were electric with their own bioluminescence. And riding the one in the lead was none other than the master of merson moroseness, the phlegmatic yet ever defiant Chachel. Stretched out flat, his legs trailing behind him, he clung with both hands to the leading edge of his mount's right fin. Beside him, a manyarm of modest size hung on with all ten—no, seven—of its tentacles. On the other side a small but determined octopod rode proud, for all that he was facing backward. All that kept them from being swept off the fins to which they were clinging was a cone of calmness: a small but very useful bit of water magic that had been called forth by the merson hunter.

The tail fin from which their bodies fluttered like flags was bigger than they were.

The water displaced by their collective mass shivered the towers of Benthicalia as nearly two hundred giant and colossal squid came thundering into the city. Spreading out, they began to pick off would-be pillagers; sometimes singly, often in whole groups. Giant squid with bodies more than twenty feet long snatched up spralakers and crushed them in powerful hunting tentacles extending another eighty feet in length. Desperate barracuda and their frantic ghost crab riders were plucked from the water as if they were standing still. Not as long but more massive, with enormous glowing eyes greater in diameter than a merson was tall, colossal squid weighing many tons crunched their way through the terrified invaders, ripping them apart with telephone-pole thick arms whose suckers were lined with brutal, curving hooks.

Rallying to the enormous swarm, the city's surviving defenders let out a collective bellow of defiance as they counterattacked. Driven from pathways and walls, rooms and acid-eaten buildings, panicked spralakers fled toward the open plains of the north and the depths to the west.

In Benthicalia, it began to snow.

At first taken completely aback, Irina finally managed to catch several of the drifting flakes in her hands. It was not snow, of course, but rather bits and pieces of shell. Spralaker shell.

Her reverie was interrupted by the chirupping arrival of two cephalopods considerably smaller than the leviathans who were driving the invading spralaker armies from the city and its surrounds.

"Good thing you sent us to look after the others, Master." Floating before Oxothyr, Sathi was letting his arms do additional talking.

"Yes, they never would have made it without our intervention," piped up a cheery Tythe from alongside his colleague.

"The thing was—well enough done," Oxothyr conceded by way of grudging compliment.

Irina expected him to say much more, but that was not the shaman's way. But if his words belied what he was feeling, the chromatophores in his skin did not. He turned a bright, congratulatory mauve as he shifted his position slightly to face the emissary Oultm.

"It is plain that I do not have to press you, noble one, for the details of your diplomacy, as the success of your efforts is self-evident."

Fluttering his eight arms just enough to position himself in front of the two famuli, Oultm the envoy halted before the shaman. For all that he was significantly smaller, the emissary managed to appear no less impressive.

"As had been surmised, the task did not prove to be an easy one, esteemed mage. Normally of a gruff and solitary disposition, the great ones of our kind had gathered, as they do in one place only once a year, exclusively to mate. Needless to say they did not take kindly to our presence, to our persistence, or to our entreaties."

"They talked of making us food!" Tythe blurted indignantly.

"Yes, quite," murmured Oultm, dismissing the interruption. "Yet by dint of perseverance and, need I add, the execution of great skill ..."

"Nearly got *us* executed," Sathi muttered from behind him.

"... I was able to convince them that the danger of which you spoke, venerable Oxothyr, would ultimately expand to embrace and overwhelm even them, in all their solitude and strength. Better for all, for them as well as for their smaller relations and their ancient friends the mersons, to begin to confront that danger here, at Benthicalia."

Arms drifting petal-like about his person, Oxothyr gazed thoughtfully at the diplomat. "But the danger of which I spoke involves a malevolence as yet unidentified, and may have nothing at all specifically to do with rampaging spralakers and their noxious ilk. That is why we need to consult the Deep Oracle."

The envoy shrugged orange. "Yes, well, I left that bit out, you see. In diplomacy as in other endeavors, avoidance is not a lie."

He would have said more, much more. After all, even the lowliest diplomat delights in the opportunity to elaborate on a triumph. But Oultm did not have the opportunity, as he soon found himself swarmed by jubilant mersons and elated manyarms anxious to offer their personal congratulations.

Beyond this and the many other pockets of joy that were springing up among those who realized that the city was saved, outside Benthicalia's walls a slaughter had commenced on a scale not witnessed in Oshenerth since primeval times. What little she could see of it from her present high location left Irina appalled. Despite the depredations they had inflicted, she found herself feeling almost sorry for the fleeing spralakers.

Able to do little enough against free-swimming mersons and normal-sized manyarms, the besieging hardshell armies had no counter for the two species of gigantic squid. In their defense, neither would most any other creature in the sea. Tentacles like steel cables swept the ground clean of whole platoons of soldiers. Beaks powerful enough to bite through iron crushed the shells of the largest invaders. Tooth-lined suckers ripped fleeing fighters inside out, paving the battlefield with internal organs that had been pulled from their protective shells. From a distance the bobbing, weaving bioluminescent lights of the giant and colossal squid gave the battlefield the look of a nocturnal airport gone berserk.

The shrieks of the hundreds of dying were no less terrible for not being human.

◊

Defeat came to the spralaker First Army on the cusp of its greatest victory. One moment its multitude, led by the acid-deploying barracuda and ghost crab strike force, had begun to swarm into and take the city. The next, all found themselves overwhelmed by prodigious horrors from the deep.

To Gubujul's credit, though no master of battlefield tactics himself, he was quick to descry the catastrophe in the making. As soon as he saw the gargantuan manyarms descend upon and begin to wreak unstoppable havoc on his troops, he gave the order to flee and disperse. He did not wait for confirmation from his Mud Marshals. The critical avoidance of complete annihilation could not wait on an afternoon of respectful discourse. Nor did he hesitate to apply this universal ruling to himself. Gathering his personal staff around him and commandeering a squadron of crack reserve troops, he set off on a northeast heading at the maximum speed that could be made. He would deal with any recriminations and second-guessing later. Were he not to keep himself alive, he reasoned, he would not be able to participate in any such post-conflict discussions.

Certainly the logic of his flight was unassailable.

Bejuryar received word while he was trying to withdraw to join up with the Paramount Advisor and his unit. As he was retreating from the vicinity of the North Wall, the plain around him was suddenly thrown into bright relief. Along with the troops accompanying him he found his eyestalks tilting back as he looked upward.

Something was descending toward them. Back home in the northlands on certain especially clear nights, when the mirrorsky was at its most tranquil and transparent, he had witnessed a similar phenomenon. Ripples in the mirrorsky shattered the night light into a thousand shimmering points of radiance. It was a sight that delighted the eyes and pleased the hearts of all who were privileged to observe it.

Here at depth the resemblance to that grand vision now found itself echoed. Echoed, and transmogrified into a tangled, writhing horror that was soon ripping the legs and claws off screaming soldiers all around him. Scuttling to find a way clear, shoving and pushing his way through ranks of terrified troops, the Mud Marshal sought to escape the hook-lined arms that reached and tore and eviscerated. Turning wildly, he caught a brief glimpse of a glowing blue-green eye that was bigger around than his shell was broad.

Then something angry and irresistible yanked his eyestalks out of his body, purging him of both vision and consciousness.

Though smaller than many of the fighters who were fleeing all around her, Taww dug her short but strong legs into a small thumb of rock that protruded from the plain and tried to rally them. Her efforts were futile. No shouted words, no furious commands, no orders no matter how forcefully delivered could stem the rout. Discipline within the First Army of the Northlands had imploded completely. It had become every hardshell for themselves.

Occasionally and in desperation she would thrust the long, curved knife gripped in her left claw at random into the fleeing rabble. Such warning thrusts did nothing to slow the retreat or stem the panic.

"Cowards!" she screeched. "Abandoners of eggs, deserters of burrows! Fugitives and renegades! Stand and fight! Are the claws of the First Army now good for nothing but the scraping of algae from rocks?"

A surge of displaced water nearly knocked her off the mound, but she held tight to the top of the small finger of rock. Dropping down in front of her was an enormous tangle of arms lined with razor-edged suckers. Several of the tentacles were already engaged in the gruesome task of separating spralaker soldiers from their limbs. One arm lunged toward her. Springing to one side and out into the water column, she deflected the strike with her knife. The massive questing appendage slid past.

It was so unjust, she reflected as she found herself floating free, to suffer this loss at the very moment of victory. Bringing the monsters of manyarm kind into the fray was unfair. So of course was the use of magic, the employment of which by the Great Lord's Paramount Advisor had been a key component of spralaker strategy. One invidious turn deserved another, she supposed. Continuing to parry and block the coiling tentacle that searched for her, she did not see the even more massive hunting arm that came curling around behind. Probably it was just as well.

It cracked her like an egg.

Of the three Mud Marshals who constituted the First Army's general staff, only Cavaumaz escaped to join up with Gubujul's force. Seriously reduced in strength, remnants of both the First and Second armies gradually gathered around their surviving leaders in straggling northeastward toward home. Each exhausted soldier had left many comrades and fellow fighters behind, usually in bits and pieces. The battlefields to the north and west of still unconquered Benthicalia were littered with the limbs and shells of the dismembered.

Only when they were many days march out from the defiant city did the Mud Marshal find the strength of spirit to speak to the Paramount Advisor.

"What will you do when we get home?" Looking nervously back over his shell, Cavaumaz added, "Assuming the monsters do not pursue and we succeed in safely reaching the northlands."

"Do?" Skittering along on slender, fragile, but still intact legs, Gubujul turned a doleful eye on the tactician. "I will beg for my life, of course. As will you and any other survivor of rank. I would expect we will all end up as part of a ceremonial meal in the palace."

One long, red-banded arm gestured in Cavaumaz's direction. "I will be honored by being a component of the main course. I fear you will have to be satisfied with being relegated to the rank of appetizer."

Cavaumaz did not look flattered. "You think it will be as bad as that?"

"As *bad?*" Bubbles burst from the Paramount Advisor's mouth as he failed to contain his laughter. "Why, that is my most optimistic assessment of our prospects, respected Marshal! More likely and much worse, we will be kept alive for the amusement of those who charged us with the success of this unfortunate enterprise." Like the bulk of the two spralaker armies, the laughter soon died. "But even that, I fear, is still not the worst option."

Though loath to hear the answer, a distraught Cavaumaz still found himself asking the inescapable question. "What might that be, Paramount Advisor?"

The stenopus turned to look more sharply at him. "At the Great Lord's discretion, we will be given to Sajjabax. I would far, far rather be consigned to the tender mercies of the kitchen or the torture chamber than to the exquisite ingenuity of the mad mage."

Cavaumaz swallowed hard. "Perhaps it lies within the demented wizard's province to prove merciful?"

"Yes," murmured Gubujul. "I am as confident of that as I am that when word of our final disposition is received, I will be sure to take steps to kill myself in as painless and expedient a manner as possible. You might consider preparing your own demise. One option would be to offer yourself up to the beaks of the manyarms before chancing the benevolence of the black-shining Sajjabax."

Cavaumaz was silent for awhile, still sneaking furtive glances back the way they had come. "We had no chance against them, did we?"

Gubujul gestured wearily. "Just one more day and we would have overrun the city, dealt with its inhabitants, and ensconced ourselves so thoroughly in its maze of passageways and buildings that not even the greatest and most powerful of the manyarms could have rooted us out. One more day." For the first time, he joined the Marshal in looking back in the direction of the distant city.

"Though diplomacy and protocol are more my métier, I have discovered that war is much like the currents that surge through all of Oshenerth. Never take anything about them for granted, for on a moment's notice they can sweep you up and carry you away, smash you against the rocks, or spin you into the center of a maelstrom from which you may not be strong enough to extricate yourself. Nothing about a strong current is predictable or certain."

"The judgment of the Great Lord ...," Cavaumaz began plaintively.

"No." Gubujul lengthened his stride slightly to take advantage of the slight following current. "That much, at least, *is* certain. Unless ..."

Though he knew his chances of surviving the fallout from the rout at Benthicalia lay somewhere on the downside of nil, the Paramount Advisor found himself beginning to plan, and to scheme. It was not in his nature to go quietly into the Empty Water.

An aide, all fluttering arms and quivering palps, intruded on his meditating. "Your pardon, Paramount Advisor, but we should increase our efforts to depart from this place."

"Why?" Cavaumaz had enough strength left for contempt. "The battle for Benthicalia is over. We have lost. There is no need now for haste. Only for recrimination."

The smaller crustacean inclined his body forward as a sign of respect, but a hint of defiance crept into his tone. Defiance, and dread. "Your pardon, my lord, but there is. The sharks who have been waiting Outside are now coming to seek the reward for their patience." One claw, trembling visibly, pointed out into the darkness. The darkness that was closing in inexorably around the ragged lines of exhausted, retreating troops. Wounded, bleeding troops.

"There are thousands of them, my lord."

◊

Though it was a long way indeed from battered Benthicalia to the great volcanic palace of the northlands, the illustrious and all-conquering Lord Kulakak did not have to wait for a herald to bring official word of the total defeat of his armies. All that was necessary was for him to confront the tightly restrained figure of Sajjabax where the mage was held captive in his alcove.

"Things are not going well," the wizard informed his master. "I sense panic and alarm, terror and dread." There was almost a hint of amusement in the mage's sepulchral voice. "It would seem that Benthicalia is not to become the summer residence you so ardently desired."

"Nor yours, remember," a quietly raging Kulakak growled. His great claws clenched and opened, clenched and opened. He longed for a shell to crush, an eye to put out, but none were at hand. Obtaining them was not difficult, but would take at least a moment or two, and would mean terminating his dialogue with the mage. Ordering up a sacrificial outlet for his fury would have to wait until later.

"It's the fault of that wretched, worthless advisor of mine. I should never have put him in overall command. I should have opted for ability over trust."

"Everything I perceive tells me that this setback is not the fault of the cunning and loyal Gubujul." Striking out with both main claws, Sajjabax attempted to kill the Great Lord. Though deep in thought Kulakak was not so preoccupied, however, as to let himself drift within range of the mage's murderous arms. The lethal cavitation unleashed by Sajjabax's double blow dissipated through the water long before the heat and pressure generated could do little more than tickle the Great Lord's shell. The conversation continued as if the blatant attempt at murder had not taken place.

"If the catastrophe is not the responsibility of the Paramount Advisor, then what?" Kulakak was as determined to know the reason for defeat as he would have been for the victory that was evidently not to be. "The First and Second armies of the northlands were strong, their leaders brave, the general staff of both suitably determined and experienced. What happened to bring about so complete a humiliation?"

"All is not transparent." Since he had no eyelids, it was never possible to tell what the enchanter Sajjabax was actually looking at. "In the confusion of defeat, there is contusion of perception. It clouds my vision. But one thing I do see clearly." On their stalks, his singular eyes inclined slightly forward and down.

"There is another magician."

That got the Great Lord's attention. "The mersons and the manyarms have a wizard of their own?"

"Not a true mage, I think." Unusually, Sajjabax was showing signs of strain. "A shaman. A simple rural practitioner of tricks and dispenser of potions. I cannot clearly divine the extent of his participation, but there is no doubt he is in someway connected to the disaster. There are others as well. Because of their great age I dismissed them as irrelevant. It is now become clear that while very old indeed, they are not wholly senile, and that at least some of their powers are retained. And," he paused, clearly struggling with the effort to see beyond the chamber, "there is something else. Something more. Or possibly something less. I cannot tell. Not— yet."

Kulakak's tone was grim. "Go on."

"I think it is, I believe it may be, some sort of—changeling. Its full involvement in the affairs of Oshenerth I cannot clearly glimpse. A strange creature, at once female and strong, if oddly conflicted. Weak-seeming, and yet ..." He went silent.

"And yet?" the Great Lord prompted him.

But the mage had gone quiescent, overcome once more by the madness that ebbed and flowed within him like a tide, revealing sometimes coherence and most of the time a hushed incomprehensibility. Frustrated, Kulakak turned and scuttled slowly away.

What now? he asked himself. What to do now that the intended cleansing of the southern reefs had been brought to a sudden and ignominious standstill? In the stillness of the palace and the shutdown of Sajjabax he found that he yearned for Gubujul's counsel. Had the Paramount Advisor escaped the calamity? What should be done with him if he returned to the capital? Kulakak knew that he needed the smaller spralaker's advice as never before. He also knew that upon setting eyes on the advisor he would be hard-pressed to keep from dismembering him one joint at a time.

He shrugged it off. Revenge was for the weak-minded, for those who could not control their emotions. For those who could not see the greater picture. And that picture showed him, as it had for some time now, that the south must somehow be conquered. Must be taken for the greater glory not only of Kulakak but for all spralakers.

Because if they did not vanquish the mersons and manyarms who controlled the southern reefs and take it for themselves, he and his kind were most surely doomed to a slow, lingering, and inevitable death.

◊

Only the outside of the Palace of the Tornal had been damaged. The intricately decorated interior, with its fluctuating bioluminescent lights and fluted silicate embellishments and gleaming reflective surfaces, was still intact.

So, it seemed, were the Tornal themselves. Looking on as they lumbered or dragged themselves laboriously out into the audience chamber, Irina counted carefully and could find none absent.

The ammonite who served as Speaker trundled slightly out front of the others, pulling herself along with her strong tentacles. Her coiled shell glistened with recent attention. Speeches would have to be given. Celebrations were anticipated. Congratulations had to be extended. The Tornal were not looking forward to it.

But first another obligation need be discharged.

The Speaker entwined tentacles with Oxothyr. "To your intervention we owe our continued existence."

The shaman dismissed the compliment. "It was your diplomat who persuaded the great deep ones to come to the salvation of the city."

"And it was the escort provided by the village of Sandrift that enabled Oultm to carry out his mission," declared a beautifully striped orthocera from nearby.

At the mention of their home, those mersons and manyarms in attendance let out a soft, concerted bubbling, the underwater equivalent of a collective sigh. Irina could only envy them. It appeared they would have a home to return to, one likely to be safe from any immediate future depredations by spralakers of any kind. Not only could she not return to her home, she did not even know where it was. Pushing the depressing thought aside, she tried to concentrate on the ceremony at hand. The Speaker for the Tornal was coming to the point that had brought Irina and her newfound friends to Benthicalia in the first place.

"What would you claim as reward?" the ammonite burbled. "Insofar as we have it; food, medium of exchange, supplies of any sort, they are yours for the asking. If it's a parade you wish, or acclamation of another kind, it will be done. Should you require …"

Sensing that the recitation of offerings could go on for quite some time, Oxothyr twisted a pair of arms in a certain fashion and made so bold as to cut the speaker off.

"We require only that for which we originally chose to visit your wondrous city, venerable speaker. The answer to a question that will hopefully allow us to seek the answer to a question. The information that, if you recall, I was on the verge of requesting from you when word first came of the spralaker offensive."

Bemused, the Speaker eyed her companions. "As with food, acclaim, or anything else that is to be found in our community, if we have this knowledge then it is yours for the asking."

Oxothyr turned a rich shade of indigo marked with bright yellow spots. The effect was striking. Looking on, Glint knew he could never have equaled it.

"We need to find the Deep Oracle, and have not the faintest notion of where to begin searching."

A murmur rose from the assembled Tornal. Listening intently, Irina felt she could make out no hint of dismay. They were simply debating the matter among themselves. The buzz of communication, she decided, bode well for the eventual response. It was not long in coming.

"We have discussed your request," the Speaker announced, "compared knowledge, and processed remembrances. By all accounts and based on what is known at present, the Deep Oracle should be keeping to itself somewhere in the vicinity of the Pinnacle of Clariondes."

A ripple ran through Oxothyr's entire mantle. "I know the place. I have never been there, but I recall more or less where it is. Thank you, masters of arcane seeking. That is all we needed to know." Pivoting in the water, he turned to leave and to take his friends and escort with him. Halting in the midst of the attentive gathering of fighters from Sandrift and Siriswirll, he paused to look back.

"If it would not be too much to ask, we *could* use some replenishing of our supplies. From here to the Pinnacle of Clariondes is a fair distance."

"A very fair distance," agreed another of the aged orthoceras.

"Considerably more than a fair distance," commented a weathered ammonite sagely.

With a fluttering of her multiple arms, the Speaker indicated that she concurred with these opinions. "If there is anything more we can do …"

"Everything's well enough done," declared a curt voice from behind and apart from the group of visitors. Irina did not have to turn to identify the owner of the voice that had rudely interrupted. Chachel continued. "We're finished here. Let's get moving." Without waiting for comment or response and accompanied by an equally fast-moving Glint, he turned and swam for the outer hallway.

"He is *so* impolite!" affirmed Poylee admiringly as she kicked hard to try and catch up to the hard-swimming hunter and his manyarm companion.

"And tactless," added Sathi from where he and Tythe flanked the patiently retiring Oxothyr.

"Brave, courageous—and utterly devoid of discretion," agreed the other famulus readily.

Irina considered joining Poylee but decided against it. Though she was an excellent swimmer whose magically augmented hands, feet, and legs had increased her speed remarkably, even on her best day she doubted she could keep pace with the irascible female merson. Instead, she found herself drifting closer to the more sedately leave-taking shaman and his supercilious famuli.

"So, Oxothyr, just how far away from Sandrift is this Deep Oracle we're looking for?"

A black S-shaped pupil focused on her. "It matters not how far the Pinnacle of Clariondes lies from Sandrift, but how far it is from here. We are not returning to our homes."

She was taken aback. "But I thought surely we would return, if only for a little while, so the fighters from there and from Siriswirll could spend some time with their friends and families before having to set out again."

"Time is the one thing we do not have, Irina-changeling. The spralakers have been beaten here at Benthicalia. Where and when they may strike next remains a treacherous unknown."

She considered that. "You think they'll attack the city again?"

"Perhaps, or having been vanquished here they may choose to concentrate their efforts elsewhere along the reefs. It does not matter. The spralakers are a sideshow."

Irina thought of the thousands on both sides who had just died or been maimed both within and outside the walls of Benthicalia. "Sideshow" was not a description she would have used to depict what she had just seen and experienced. Spreading her arms wide, she took in their immediate surroundings and by implication the rest of the city beyond.

"If this was nothing but a sideshow, then what do you consider a *real* danger?"

"That which comes this way and that I cannot discern. That which in order to identify we must seek the insight of the Oracle." His gaze rose past her, to focus on something beyond her ken. "That which chills me in the dark and to which I can as yet assign neither description, meaning, or name." A kindly arm snaked reassuringly around her.

"But come now. This is all new to you, and you must not fear the new but rather embrace it. The more you open yourself to the realworld, the more you will be infused with its meaning and beauty."

"I'm trying," she told him as they swam along together. "I'm really trying. Because I know," she choked slightly, "I know I might never get home again, and that I might have to spend the rest of my life here." She took a deep breath and forced a smile. "It's a good thing I like the water."

"How could one not like the water?" Tythe wondered from nearby. "The water *is* the world, and the world is water."

"Not entirely." Oxothyr corrected his famulus gently. "There is also the void."

Showing his opinion of that, Tythe went black all over and let out a snort of ink.

"We cannot expend the time to return to Sandrift or Siriswirll," the shaman explained as they left the audience chamber behind, "because the Deep Oracle does not long remain in any one place. It moves around. The Tornal's best guess is that it is presently to be found somewhere near the Pinnacle of Clariondes. I do not know about your world, but Oshenerth is a very big place. Linger here or anywhere else too long to recuperate and celebrate and we might lose forever our one opportunity to seek out the Oracle's counsel. Without it," he concluded, "I do not feel that I can identify the true nature of the greater menace that threatens us all. And if I cannot identify it, then I most surely cannot foresee a way to counter it."

She was silent for a long while, until they emerged from the palace back out into the crazy quilt of passageways that threaded the city from its uppermost level to the twenty-sixth one far below.

"It's that bad?" she finally ventured softly.

"I fear so. The very order of existence is in danger of being upturned. We must seek to right it."

A new thought struck her. "Why us? Why you? Why not the Tornal, or others better placed or more powerful or more experienced?"

"Because," he explained to her as one would to an infant, "we do not know if anyone else, anywhere, has perceived it, and as I just informed you, we do not have the time to seek, ask, and look around to learn if anyone else has. We must proceed as if we are the only ones to have acquired this painful information. Those who acquire knowledge," he finished, "are condemned to act upon it."

That seemed to satisfy her. Or at least, she asked no more questions. Not that day, or the next, or on up to the time they finally took their leave of Benthicalia.

It was just as well that she did not, Oxothyr mused. Had she pressed further, he would have been compelled by various self-imposed oaths and promises to answer her to the best of his ability, even when he believed that to do so might not be in her best interest.

After all, how could he explain to her that despite her lack of abilities relevant to the present desperate situation he felt she was somehow destined to play a critical role in the hopeful resolution of the forthcoming crisis?

# IF YOU LIKED

If you liked *Oshenerth*, you might also enjoy:

## *Gamearth*
Kevin J. Anderson

## *Mythology 101*
Jody Lynn Nye

## *The Worker Prince*
Bryan Thomas Schmidt

# ABOUT THE AUTHOR

Alan Dean Foster is the author of 125 books, hundreds of pieces of short fiction, essays, columns reviews, the occasional op-ed for the NY Times, and the story for the first Star Trek movie. Having visited more than 100 countries, he is still bemused by the human condition. He lives with his wife JoAnn and numerous dogs, cats, coyotes, hawks, and a resident family of bobcats in Prescott, Arizona.

# OTHER WORDFIRE PRESS TITLES

Our list of other WordFire Press authors and titles is always growing. To find out more and to see our selection of titles, visit us at:

wordfirepress.com

Made in the USA
Lexington, KY
15 June 2017